Queens KT-221-761

A collection of bestselling novels by
the world's leading romance writers

**Two novels from international
bestselling author**

PAULA
MARSHALL

PRAISE FOR PAULA MARSHALL:

"*Miss Jesmond's Heir* is a delightfully romantic tale
of lost heirs and love triumphant."
—*Romantic Times* on *Miss Jesmond's Heir*

"*Miss Jesmond's Heir* has everything a Regency fan
could want. It has a well-drawn picture of country
society with a plethora of interesting secondary
characters. It has mystery and intrigue. It has a
charming romance between an unusual hero and
heroine." —*The Romance Reader*

"*The Wolfe's Mate* has a whole lot going for it. It offers
a faithful re-creation of Regency society and life. It has
an interesting mystery… This is a very good Regency
romance." —*The Romance Reader*

"*My Lady Disdain* has a nice take on one of my favourite
plots – the forced marriage – and has good characters.
A most acceptable Regency romance."
—*The Romance Reader*

100 Reasons to Celebrate

We invite you to join us in celebrating
Mills & Boon's centenary. Gerald Mills and
Charles Boon founded Mills & Boon Limited
in 1908 and opened offices in London's Covent
Garden. Since then, Mills & Boon has become
a hallmark for romantic fiction, recognised
around the world.

We're proud of our 100 years of publishing
excellence, which wouldn't have been achieved
without the loyalty and enthusiasm of our
authors and readers.

Thank you!

Each month throughout the year there will
be something new and exciting to mark the
centenary, so watch for your favourite authors,
captivating new stories, special limited
edition collections…and more!

PAULA MARSHALL

Rogues and Rakes

Containing

**The Beckoning Dream
& The Lost Princess**

*M&B™ and M&B™ with the Rose Device
are trademarks of the publisher.
Harlequin Mills & Boon Limited, Eton House,
18-24 Paradise Road,
Richmond, Surrey TW9 1SR*

Rogues and Rakes © by Harlequin Books S.A. 2008

The Beckoning Dream and *The Lost Princess* were
first published in Great Britain by Harlequin Mills & Boon
Limited in separate, single volumes.

The Beckoning Dream © Paula Marshall 1997
The Lost Princess © Paula Marshall 1996

ISBN: 978 0 263 86677 3

025-0608

*Printed and bound in Spain
by Litografia Rosés S.A., Barcelona*

The Beckoning Dream

PAULA MARSHALL

The
Queens of Romance
Collection

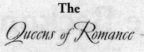

Much-loved author Paula Marshall has written over forty-five Historical romances for Mills & Boon and she has always been a very versatile author, with her novels spanning from the 15th century to the 1920s, and everything in between. She draws on historical fact to feed her imagination, and emotional truths to shape her characters, and her talent for vivid story-telling has awarded her a loyal and global readership.

This collection showcases two classic Paula Marshall titles, *The Lost Princess* and *The Beckoning Dream*.

The Lost Princess sees Paula's characters trail across Italy in 1460. It is a richly evocative story with drama, danger, excitement and, of course, romance. Whereas the restoration novel *The Beckoning Dream* is dedicated to the memory of Aphra Behn. A wit, poet, dramatist, novelist and secret agent, Aphra Behn lived the life of a free woman in the mid-seventeenth century, which was no mean achievement.

Paula Marshall was born in Leicester and grew up in Nottingham. Her father, a mathematician who as a result of being gassed in the first World War never really recovered his health, introduced her to a great many things. He taught her chess, cards, painting, and had her reading Dickens and Thackeray by the age of ten! Her great loves at school were History, English and Art; she found it difficult to decide whether she wanted to become the world's greatest novelist or the world's greatest painter!

After school she started work as a research librarian, working for her Library Examinations after work. She spent many happy days among old works and papers and remembers with affection working with the Byron collection at Newstead Abbey. This reading stood her in good stead when she began writing Regency romances – she had actually handled Byron's letters and possessions.

While working in the reference library Paula met her future husband. Also a librarian, he returned to complete his fellowship after he was demobbed from the RAF. They were studying the same texts and decided to work together. The result was that he got his fellowship – while she got *him*! Paula began a secondary career writing and lecturing on local history.

Paula has three children and when the third started school she returned to work, beginning a new career as a part-time lecturer in English and General Studies. After four years of teaching, she enrolled in the Open University and spent the next four years earning a First Class Honours BA in History.

Paula gets great pleasure from writing Mills & Boon® Historical romances where she can use her wide historical knowledge. She has lectured on everything in English history from the Civil War onwards, as well as US and Russian history, 1760-1980, and the psychology of war and revolution. Paula and her husband have spent their holidays travelling the world from the Arctic Circle, Scandinavia and Russia, around Europe to the USA and New Zealand. She finds that nearly everything she writes for Mills & Boon draws on this wealth of knowledge.

Author's Note to the Reader

This novel, like all of mine, is firmly based on fact, and is dedicated to the memory of Aphra Behn, wit, poet, dramatist, novelist and secret agent, who lived the life of a free woman in the mid-seventeenth century—no mean achievement. It has taken three hundred years for her reputation to be revived and her many talents to be properly appreciated.

One of her greatest achievements as an agent in Holland was to warn the British Government in 1667 that the Dutch Navy was about to launch a major attack on the naval bases of Sheerness and Chatham on the River Medway. Her warning was ignored, as she recorded in her autobiography, and for three hundred years her biographers and critics mocked her for having claimed that, had the Government heeded her report, a major disaster for the British Navy would have been avoided.

Three hundred years later, Aphra's claim was vindicated when her letter, giving details of the proposed attack, was discovered in the State Papers. In the same way, her right to be seen as the mother of the English novel and as the writer of a number of witty and actable plays was also derided until the Sixties of the present century when her work was looked at with fresh eyes.

Prologue

"True love is a beckoning dream." Old saying

Two men from the court of King Charles II at Whitehall sat on the side of the stage of the Duke of York's Theatre in the early spring of 1667. One of them was short and plump and was wearing a monstrous black-curled wig. The other was tall and muscular; his wig was blond, and his hooded eyes were blue. Both of them were magnificently dressed and were wearing half-masks so that it was impossible to detect their true identity.

They were watching a play called *The Braggart, or, Lackwit in Love,* which had just reached the scene where, as the script had it, the following ensued:

> *Enter to LACKWIT, BELINDA BELLAMOUR, disguised as a youth, one LUCIUS.*
> LACKWIT *Ho, there, sirrah! Art thou Mistress Belinda Bellamour's boy?*
> BELINDA *Nay, sir.*
> LACKWIT *How "Nay, sir"? What answer is that?*

Art thou not but just come from her quarters?
*BELINDA Aye, sir, but nay, sir. Aye, sir, I have
come from her quarters. Nay, sir, I am not her
boy—my mother was of quite a different kidney!
So, aye, sir, nay, sir!*
*LACKWIT Insolent child! (Makes to strike her
with his cane.)*
*BELINDA (Twisting away.) What is the world
coming to when a man may be beaten for speaking
the truth!*
*LACKWIT Man! Man! Thy mother's milk is still
on thy lips!*
BELINDA Aye, sir—but it is not Belinda's!

By now the audience—which was in on the joke of
Belinda's sex—was roaring its approval as Belinda defied Lackwit by jumping about the stage to dodge his
cane, showing a fine pair of legs as she did so.

Master Blond Wig drawled at his dark friend, "Now
that she has chosen to show them, her legs are better
than her breasts—and they, when visible, were sub-
lime. A new star for the stage."

He took in the pleasing sight that the actress playing
Belinda presented to the world in boy's clothes;
lustrous raven hair, deep violet eyes, a kissable mouth
and a body to stiffen a man's desire simply by looking
at it!

"Aye," agreed Black Wig, who was also appreci-
ating Belinda. "And a new playwright, too. The bills
proclaim that he is one Will Wagstaffe."

"Will Wagstaffe!" Blond Wig began to laugh.
"You jest, Hal."

"Nay, Stair, for that is what the playbill saith. And the doxy who affects the boy is none other than Mistress Cleone Dubois, who made a hit, a very hit, as Clarinda in *Love's Last Jest* by that same Wagstaffe whilst thou were out of town."

"Did she so? I do not believe in Will Wagstaffe, and nor should you," exclaimed Blond Wig. "But I have a mind to play a jest of my own."

The action of the play had come close to them whilst they spoke, as Belinda and Lackwit sparred. Blond Wig picked a fruit from the basket that the orange girl had left before them, and threw it straight at Belinda, whom nothing daunted, either as Belinda playing a boy on the stage or in her true nature when not an actress. On seeing the orange coming, she caught it neatly and flung it back at Blond Wig as hard as she could.

He retaliated by rolling it across the stage towards her as though it were a bowling ball. Mr Betterton, the doyen of all Restoration actors, who was playing Lackwit, jumped dexterously over it, so that it arrived at Belinda's feet.

She bent down, picked it up, and examined it before beginning to peel and eat it, segment by segment, exclaiming as she did so, "Why, Sir Lackwit, I do believe that the fruit thou hast refused is better than the wit. For that is dry, and this orange is juicy. I shall tell my Mistress Belinda that whilst you may have pith and self-importance, you lack the true Olympian oil which the Gods bestow on their favourites.

"But for the orange peel, this," and she threw the shards of the peel straight at Blond Wig, who was on his feet applauding her improvisation, as were the rest of the audience.

"The doxy is wittier than the man who writes her lines," exclaimed Blond Wig after bowing to the audience, who applauded him as heartily as they had rewarded Belinda. "And if you and the audience cannot see the jest in a man who writes plays calling himself Will Wagstaffe why, then, you and they are duller than I thought."

"Enough of this," whispered Betterton to Cleone as they grappled together in a mock and comic wrestling match. "Improvisation is well enough, and one of Rochester's Merry Gang interfering with the action on stage may have to be endured, but you need not encourage him."

"Need I not? But the audience, who is our master, approved."

"Aye so, but we risk every fool in town wanting to be part of the play." He turned himself back into Lackwit again in order to declaim in the direction of the pit, *"Why, I vow thou art as soft as a very girl, Master Lucius. You need some lessons in hardening thyself."*

"Dost think that thou are the man to give me them, Sir Lackwit?"

The pit roared again. Some of the bolder members threw pennies on to the stage at Belinda's feet. Blond Wig had produced a fan and waved it languidly in her direction.

"I vow and declare, Hal," he whispered to Black Wig, "Master Wagstaffe is as bawdily witty as his master, the other Will."

"And what Will is that, Stair?"

"Why, Shakespeare, man. Will Shakespeare. He who wags the staff. Is all the world as thick as a London fog in winter, these days?"

Black Wig couldn't think of a witty answer to that. He might be Henry Bennett, m'lord Arlington, King Charles II's Secretary of State who ruled England, but his wit was long term, carefully thought out, unlike that of his friend Blond Wig, otherwise Sir Alastair Cameron. Stair Cameron was known for his cutting tongue as well as his reputation for courage and contempt for everything and everybody. He was also known for his success with women.

And now, if Lord Arlington knew his man, his latest female target would be the pretty doxy on the stage who was back in skirts again, teasing and tempting Lackwit—as well as every red-blooded man in the audience. Her charms were such that she might even attract the attention of the King himself.

The pretty doxy on the stage was well aware that Blond Wig was making a dead set at her, as the saying went. At the end of the first Act, he bought a posy from a flower girl and tossed it to her as she left the stage.

She tossed it back at him.

In the second Act, he kissed his hand to her whenever the action on stage brought her near him.

Halfway through the third Act, Belinda pretended to woo Lackwit, and to allow him to woo her, her true lover, Giovanni Amoroso, being concealed behind a hedge to enjoy the fun. At the point when Lackwit had worked himself into a lather of desire, Blond Wig drew off one of his perfumed gloves and slung that in Belinda's direction at the very climax of her scene with Lackwit.

"Why, what have we here?" she extemporised, holding up the glove. "What hath Dan Cupid sent me as a love token?" She sniffed at it. "Fie upon him, it hath a vile stink. He may have it back."

And she slung it back at Blond Wig, who rose and bowed to her.

M'lord Arlington applauded him vigorously, whispering to his friend as he did so, "The wench will serve us well, will she not? Old Gower hath the right of it again. A pretty wit and a quick one. As quick as thine, Stair, I do declare."

"But shallow, like all women's wit, I dare swear. But I agree, she will do as well as another—and better than some. And mayhap she will tell me who Will Wagstaffe is, and where I may find the fellow."

"Hipped on Wagstaffe, Stair?"

"Aye, hipped on any pretty wit—particularly one of whom I do not know."

"Make the doxy thine, friend Stair, and she will tell thee all. Look, Lackwit hath learned that he truly lacks wit, and that Amoroso and Belinda are about to sing their love duet to signify that the play is over, and that he was cuckolded before he even wed his Mistress and made her wife!"

The play was, indeed, ending. Belinda was reciting the Epilogue, a poem in which she averred that she had followed the beckoning dream which led towards true love, and might now marry Amoroso.

"Truly a dream, that," Stair whispered to Arlington. "But not the kind one of which the lady speaks. I can think of no nightmare more troubling than that which ends in marriage.''

The Epilogue over, Mistress Dubois, Betterton, and the pretty boy who played Amoroso linked hands and were bowing to the audience, which was on its feet again, applauding the actors. Blond Wig was shouting huzzahs at Belinda, who refused to look at him.

''To the devil with him,'' hissed Belinda, or rather Mistress Cleone Dubois, to Betterton. ''He tried to ruin all my best scenes. Another courtier come to entertain himself by destroying us.''

''He got no change from you, Cleone, my pretty dear. On the contrary, your quick wits had them laughing at him as much as you.''

''And who the devil is he? I know his friend, Sir Hal Bennett, late made Lord Arlington, but not the human gadfly in the blond wig.''

Betterton smiled and bowed, his head almost touching his knees before he led the company offstage, before saying, ''Sir Alastair, known as Stair Cameron, Baronet. Rochester's friend—everybody's friend, aye, and enemy, too, gossip hath it. Avoid him like the plague that hath just left us. He would be no friend of thine, Cleone—or of any woman's. Mark me this, he will be in the Green Room this evening, to pursue you further.''

''May God forbid,'' Cleone shuddered. She trusted no man, least of all those who infested Charles's court. ''I want naught of him.''

But he wasn't in the Green Room. Sam Pepys was there, and Lord Arlington, who bowed at Cleone and said in a butter-melting voice, ''My felicitations, Mistress Dubois. You have grown since I last saw thee at Sir Thomas Gower's when you were Mistress Wood. A very child, were you not?''

He tittered a little behind a fine white handkerchief edged with lace. ''You look about you, mistress. Is it my friend you seek?''

The violet eyes were hard upon him. ''Nay, m'lord. Unless it is to teach him manners—if indeed it were possible to teach him anything.''

Sam Pepys, standing by them, gave a jolly guffaw. ''Come, come, mistress, you are too harsh. Stair Cameron is a right good fellow.''

Cleone rounded on him, shaking her fan in his direction, Belinda's fan. She knew who Sam Pepys was. The Secretary to the Navy, a womaniser and a gossip— but there was no harm in him.

''Fie upon you, too, sir. What, I wonder, would you say, if Stair Cameron entered your office and upset the contents of your inkpot on your newly written letter to your master, the King, ruining it? Would you think the destruction of your work a jolly jest to be applauded? For such were the offences he committed against me!''

Lord Arlington clapped his hands together, and even Sam himself joined in the joke. ''Why, madam,'' m'lord offered, ''you are as spirited a lady as you were a lass. I should introduce you to Sir Stair. How the fur and the feathers would fly, for I vow that in spirit you are well matched.''

Cleone stared at him, nothing daunted by his name or his position, something that pleased the man before her mightily. Oh, he had plans for Mistress Wood, also named Mistress Dubois, great plans. And now he could go to Sir Thomas Gower, his spymaster supreme, to tell him that Cleone Dubois was a lass of spirit who would serve them well.

What she said next had him laughing again behind his lace-gloved hand. "For," smiled Cleone, "it would please me greatly never to see Sir Stair Cameron again, either on stage, or off it. Unless it were to hand him such a *congé* from a woman as he has never received before. But enough of him. To talk of him wearies me. What thought you of the play, m'lord?"

Graciously, m'lord Arlington told the lady that he had enjoyed it, his smooth face even smoother than usual.

And all the time he was laughing to himself as he thought of the delightful possibility that the spirited lady and her tormentor might soon meet again—and wondered which of them would come off the best, as the fur and the feathers would inevitably fly like the orange, the posy and the perfumed glove!

Chapter One

1667

"Who the devil can that be at this hour, Catherine?"

Rob Wood had just carved himself a large chunk of cold bacon for his breakfast to go with the buttered slice of bread that his sister, whom he always insisted on calling by her true name, had cut for him.

He had no sooner transferred the bacon to his pewter plate than a vile hammering had begun on the door of their small house in Cob's Lane, London, not far from the Inns of Court where Rob was studying to be a lawyer. Or was supposed to be studying.

Rob was as idle as his sister was diligent. The only hard work he did was to write pamphlets attacking the rule of King Charles II and praising that of the late usurper and regicide, Cromwell. This was a particularly foolish act since England was at present at war with the Netherlanders—fighting them in order to prevent them from seizing the major share of the world's trade. Opposition to the king was thus bound to be seen as treason.

Catherine, who was busy buttering a slice of loaf for herself, said crossly, "Answer the door, Rob. Don't stand there yammering. It's probably Jem Hollins come to clean our chimneys."

Grumbling, Rob rose to do as he was bid. Although he was living entirely on his sister's earnings in the theatre, he resented that fact rather than being grateful for it. Their father, once a rich country gentleman, had supported Cromwell in the late Civil War. Charles II's Restoration had seen his estates confiscated; he had died penniless, leaving his two children to make their own way in the world.

Rob thought of himself as a dispossessed Crown Prince and behaved accordingly.

He never reached the door. Tired of trying to attract their attention, the Woods' importunate visitors ceased their knocking abruptly.

Shouting "Ho, there, take heed and attend to us," they knocked down the house door with iron-tipped staves of wood, before rushing in, seizing Rob and throwing him to the floor.

A third man, carrying a large piece of parchment importantly before him, put one foot on the struggling Rob, whilst a fourth placed himself between Catherine and her brother in case she tried to come to his assistance.

"By what authority—?" she began, using all the power of her stage voice to try to overawe them.

"By the authority vested in me by his most noble majesty, King Charles II, I hereby arrest Robert Wood for the crime of high treason, and detain his sister Catherine Wood, also known as Cleone Dubois, actress and whore, for questioning as to his activities."

"My sister's no whore," shouted Rob as he was hauled to his feet, his hands pinioned behind his back, "and I know of no law which says that a man may not speak or write freely of his opinions—unless you have just invented one."

If only Rob would learn to keep silent when challenged he would not find life so difficult, mourned Catherine as the leading tipstaff struck her brother across the mouth, bellowing, "That should silence your lying tongue, you treacherous rogue."

He and two of his fellows began to drag Rob outside. The fourth seized Catherine roughly by the arm with one hand, while running the other across her breasts.

Hissing at him, "No need of that, I have no desire either to have you fondle me, or to escape," Catherine brought her high-heeled shoe down hard on his instep. The tipstaff let out a shrill cry before striking her across the face with such force that she was thrown against the wall.

"Had I the time, you insolent bonaroba, you whore, I'd serve you as a man should serve a whore—later, perhaps," he roared at her as she tried to recover her balance.

And who am I to criticise poor Rob for not keeping his tongue under guard when I can't keep mine shut, either? Catherine thought as she walked painfully into the street. Outside a small crowd had gathered to watch the two Woods dragged away. She looked around her; where are they taking us? To prison? To Newgate? Or to the Tower of London itself?

She was destined for none of them, it seemed. She and Rob were half-walked, half-dragged to the nearest wharf on the Thames where two wherries were waiting. Rob was shoved into one, and she into the other.

The last she saw of him was his wherry making for the Tower, whilst she was rowed off in the opposite direction. To the Palace of Whitehall, no less, the King's home in London, and consequently, the seat of government. Catherine's mounting curiosity almost overcame her fear for herself, even as she worried over poor Rob's ultimate fate.

No time for that, though. She was bustled along Whitehall's gravelled walks towards one of the many buildings that made up the Palace precincts. The tip-staffs waved their staves, doors were opened for them, and presently, after traversing a number of long corridors, they came to a pair of double doors, on whose panels the tipstaffs knocked more subserviently than they had done in Cob's Lane.

Beyond the doors was a largish room, one wall of which consisted almost entirely of latticed windows looking out on a garden. A number of finely dressed gentlemen were standing about, but they left the room even as Catherine entered it.

At the opposite end from the doors was a long table, where a man whom she immediately recognised sat in state. Behind him, covering the whole wall, hung a huge tapestry showing the Greeks pouring out of the Wooden Horse to capture and destroy Troy.

Catherine had no time to admire wall hangings. She was too busy staring at Sir Thomas Gower. Sir Thomas had taken her father, Rob and herself into his household for a short time after King Charles's Restoration had made them homeless. He had been as kind to her father as his position as a powerful Royalist had permitted him to be.

Why had she been brought here? She was soon to find out.

"Come here, Mistress Wood," Sir Thomas bade her, and then, "Bring the lady a chair, she seems distressed. Place it before me. Sit, sit," he commanded her as she walked slowly forward, rubbing her arm, bruised where the tipstaff had seized it.

Now that she was near to Sir Thomas, Catherine could plainly tell that he had aged since she had last seen him. His face was lined with over sixty years of life, but he still possessed the calm gravity that had been so different from her father's impotent rage at what had happened to his pleasant life.

She could also see that level with herself, and in front of Sir Thomas's grand oak table on which books, ledgers and parchments stood at one end, was an arm-chair in which a man lounged. A man who was staring at her, not with Sir Thomas's kind and paternal stare, but hungrily, almost ferally, his blue eyes cruel.

Bewildered, but still retaining the steady calm for which her fellow actors admired her, Catherine returned Sir Thomas's grave look. She must not show her fear, but must keep her head so that Rob might not lose his, and pray that there might be a way out of the dire situation in which he had placed them.

"My dear Catherine," said Sir Thomas, kindness it-self, "I fear that your condition—or perhaps I should say, your brother's condition—is a sad one. Treason!" He shook his grey head helplessly. "An ugly word, my dear. Nevertheless, God willing, we might find a way through the wood for you.''

What wood was he speaking of? The good old man, Catherine thought dazedly, was being so tactful that she hardly knew what he was saying. The lounging fellow on her right, whose eyes were still so hard on her that she could feel them when she could no longer see them, grunted ''Ahem' in a meaningful tone—although his meaning escaped Catherine!

But apparently not Sir Thomas, for he threw a sideways glance at his unmannerly aide, and said smoothly. ''Ah, yes, Mistress Wood. I must be plain. We are not engaged in one of Master Wagstaffe's comedies, are we?''

''No, indeed,'' agreed Catherine.

''Whoever Master Wagstaffe is,'' drawled the lounging man. ''Another mystery.''

''No matter.'' Sir Thomas was a little brisk. ''I put it to you, Mistress Wood, that you do not share your brother's Republican views.''

''I doubt—'' and now Catherine was dry ''—that he shares them himself. Rob is a weathercock. An attack of the megrims and he is all for the late usurper. If the weather is fine, and there is good food on the table, then it is 'God save King Charles II'.''

Sir Thomas was suave. ''All the more reprehensible of him, then, mistress, to put his life in jeopardy by writing treason. You, I understand, are a good and loyal subject of the King?''

Since his question seemed to invite the answer ''Yes'', Catherine gave it to him.

''Oh, excellent,'' smiled Sir Thomas. ''So you would

be willing to do the state some service. You speak Dutch, mistress, do you not? Your late mother being a Netherlander, as I remember.''

This seemed neither here nor there, and its relevance to poor Rob seemed questionable, but doubtless there was some point to this that escaped her. The lounging man was fidgeting again.

Sir Thomas gave him a benevolent stare. ''Patience, Tom Trenchard, patience. We are almost at the heart of the matter.''

''Oh, excellent,'' drawled Tom Trenchard, mocking Sir Thomas's earlier remark. ''I had thought that we were trapped in the outworks for ever.''

This time Catherine favoured him with a close examination, particularly since Sir Thomas was allowing him more freedom than was usually given to an underling. The principal thing about him was that he was big, much bigger than any of the men in Betterton's company.

His shoulders were broad, his hands large, and he appeared to be at least six feet in height. His hair, his own, was of a burning red gold—more gold than red. It was neither long like the wigs of the King's courtiers, nor cropped short like one of Cromwell's Roundheads, but somewhere in between. It was neither straight nor curly, but again, was also somewhere in between, waving slightly.

His clothes were rough and serviceable. His shirt had been washed until it was yellow, and the weary lace at his throat and wrists was darned. His boots were the best thing about him, but even they were not those of a court gallant. Neither was his harsh and craggy face.

She already knew that he was mannerless, and he gave off the ineffable aura of all the soldiers whom she had ever met, being wild, but contained. Or almost contained. He saw her looking at him, and nodded thoughtfully. "You will know me again, mistress, I see."

"Do I need to?" Catherine countered, and then to Sir Thomas, "Forgive me, sir, for allowing my attention to stray," for she knew that the great ones of this world required all attention to be on them, and not on such lowly creatures as she judged herself and the lounging man to be.

He forgave her immediately. "Nay, mistress, you do well to inspect Master Trenchard. You will have much to do with him. As you have not denied either your loyalty, or your knowledge of Dutch, I am putting it to you, mistress, that you might oblige us by accompanying him to the Netherlands, there to use your skills as a linguist and as an actress. You will join him in an enterprise to persuade one William Grahame, who has done the state some service in the past, to bring off one final coup on our behalf.

"William Grahame has indicated to us that he is in a position to give us information about the disposition of the Dutch army and their fleet. He has also said that he will only do so to an emissary of my office who will meet him in the Low Countries at a place of his choosing. Once he has passed this information to us, and not before, your final task will be to bring him safely home to England again. He is weary of living abroad."

He beamed at her as he finished speaking. Tom Trenchard grunted, mannerless again, "And so we reach the point—at long last."

"Tom's grasp of diplomacy is poor, I fear," explained Sir Thomas needlessly. Catherine had already gathered that. She was already gathering something else, something which might help Rob, even before Sir Thomas mentally ticked off his next point.

"You must also understand, mistress, that success in this delicate matter—if you agree to undertake it—would prove most beneficial when the case of Master Robert Wood comes to trial—*if* it comes to trial, that is. The likelihood is that, with your kind co-operation, it will not."

"And if I refuse?" returned Catherine.

"Why then, alas, Master Robert Wood will pay the price for his folly on the headsman's block on Tower Hill."

"And if I accept, but fail, what then?" asked Catherine.

"Why then, you all fail. Master Tom Trenchard, Mistress Catherine Wood and Master Robert Wood. Such may—or may not be—God's will. Only He proposes and disposes."

"Although Sir Thomas Gower makes a good fist of imitating Him," drawled Tom Trenchard. "Particularly since it will not be his head on the plate handed to King Herod, whatever happens."

So there it was. The price of Rob's freedom was that she undertake a dangerous enterprise—and succeed in it.

"I have agreed with Master Betterton—" Catherine began, but Sir Thomas did not allow her to finish.

"Nay, mistress. I understand that Master Wagstaffe's

masterpiece has its last showing tonight—at which you
will, of course, be present to play Belinda.

"Moreover, Master Betterton would not, if asked by
those who have the power to do so, refuse to release
you for as long as is necessary. Particularly on the understanding that, when you return, you shall be the heroine of Master Wagstaffe's proposed new play—*The
Braggart Returns, or, Lackwit Married.* I look forward
to seeing it."

This time the look Sir Thomas gave her was that of
a fellow conspirator in a plot that had nothing to do
with his bully, Trenchard, or with William Grahame in
the Netherlands. Unwillingly, Catherine nodded.

"To save Rob, I will agree to your demands." She
had been left with no choice, for Sir Thomas had not
one hold over her but two. The greater, of course, was
his use of Rob to blackmail her. The lesser was his
knowledge of who Will Wagstaffe really was.

And it was also most likely sadly true that the only
reason why the authorities—or rather Sir Thomas
Gower—had ordered poor Rob to be arrested was to
compel her to be their agent and their interpreter.

"That is most wise of you, Mistress Wood. Your
loyalty to King Charles II does you great credit."

To which Catherine made no answer, for she could
not say, Be damned to King Charles II, I do but agree
to save Rob's neck. Tom Trenchard saw her mutinous
expression and read it correctly.

"What, silent, mistress?" he drawled. "No grand
pronouncements of your devotion to your King?"

"Quiet—but for the moment. And I have nothing to

say to *you*. Tell me, Sir Thomas, in what capacity will I accompany Master Trenchard here?''

''Why, as his wife, who fortunately speaks Dutch— and French. You are an actress, mistress. Playing the wife should present you with no difficulties.''

''Playing the husband will offer me none,'' interjected Tom meaningfully.

''And *that* is what I fear,'' returned Catherine robustly. ''I will not play the whore in order to play the wife. You understand me, sir, I am sure.''

''I concede that you have a ready tongue and have made a witty answer,'' drawled Tom. ''And I can only reply alas, yes, I understand you! Which may not be witty, but has the merit of being truthful.''

''Come now,'' ordered Sir Thomas, ''you are to be comrades, as well as loving husband and wife. Moreover, once in the Low Countries you are both to be noisily agreed in supporting the Republicans who wish to replace the King with a Cromwellian successor. Master Trenchard will claim to be a member of that family which followed the late Oliver so faithfully.

''And you, being half-Dutch, will acknowledge the Grand Pensionary, John De Witt, to be your man, not King Charles's nephew, the powerless Stadtholder.'' He paused.

''As a dutiful wife,'' remarked Catherine demurely, ''I shall be only too happy to echo the opinions of my husband.''

Tom Trenchard's chuckle was a rich one. ''Well said, mistress. I shall remind of you that—frequently.''

Sir Thomas smiled benevolently on the pair of them. ''I shall inform you both of the details of your journey.

You will travel by packet boat to Ostend and from thence to Antwerp in Flanders where you may hope to find Grahame—if he has not already made for Amsterdam, where I gather he has a reliable informer.

"You will, of course, follow him to Amsterdam, if necessary. You will send your despatches—in code— to my agent here, James Halsall, the King's Cupbearer. He will pass them on to me.

"You will pose as merchants buying goods who are sympathetic towards those unregenerate Republicans who still hold fast against our gracious King. To bend William Grahame to our will is your main aim—because like all such creatures he plays a double game. Why, last year he sold all the Stadtholder's agents in England to us, and now word hath it that the Stadtholder hath rewarded him with a pension—doubtless for selling *our* agents to *him*.

"Natheless, he is too valuable for us to carp at his dubious morals, and if gold and a pardon for his past sins brings him home to us with all his information— then so be it, whether there be blood on his hands, or no."

Sir Thomas was, for once, Catherine guessed, dropping his pretence of being a benevolent uncle, and doing so deliberately in order to impress on her the serious nature of her mission. She heard Tom Trenchard clapping his hands and laughing at Sir Thomas's unwonted cynicism.

She turned to stare at him. He was now slouched down in his chair, his feral eyes alight, one large hand slapping his coarse brown breeches above his spotless boots. The thought of spending much time in the Netherlands alone with him was enough to eat away at her normal self-control.

"It seems that only a trifle is needed to amuse you, Master Trenchard. I hope that you take heed of what I told you. I go to Holland as your supposed wife, not as your true whore. Remember that!"

"So long as you do, mistress, so long as you do."

The insolent swine was leering at her. He might not, by his dress, be one of King Charles's courtiers, but he certainly shared their morals. It did not help that Sir Thomas's smile remained pasted to his face as he informed her that she was to pack her bag immediately, and be ready to leave as soon as Tom Trenchard called on her.

"Which will not be until after your last performance tonight. And then you will do as Tom bids you—so far as this mission is concerned, that is."

Catherine ignored the possible *double entendre* in Sir Thomas's last statement. Instead, looking steadily at him, she made one last statement of her own.

"I may depend upon thee, Sir Thomas, that should I succeed, then my brother's safety is assured."

"My word upon it, mistress. And I have never broke it yet."

"Bent it a little, perhaps," added Tom Trenchard, disobligingly, viciously dotting Sir Thomas's i's for him, as appeared to be his habit.

Catherine, after giving him one scathing look, ignored him. She thought again that he was quite the most ill-favoured man she had ever seen, with his high forehead, strong nose, grim mouth and determined jaw. Only the piercing blue of his eyes redeemed him.

She addressed Sir Thomas. "I may leave, now? After the commotion your tipstaffs made, my neighbours doubtless think that I, like my brother, am lodged in the Tower. I should be happy to disoblige them."

"Indeed, mistress. I shall give orders that your brother be treated tenderly during his stay in the Tower, my word on it."

And that, thought Catherine, is as much, if not more, than I might have hoped. She gave Sir Thomas a giant curtsy as he waved her away. "Tell one of the footmen who guard the door to see thee home again, mistress," being his final words to her.

She had gone. Tom Trenchard rose to his feet, and drawled familiarly at Sir Thomas, "Exactly as I prophesied after I toyed with her at the play. The doxy has a ready wit and a brave spirit. I hope to enjoy both."

He laughed again when the wall hanging behind Sir Thomas shivered as Black Wig, otherwise Hal Bennet, m'lord Arlington, emerged from his hiding place where he had overheard every word of Catherine's interrogation.

"The wench will do, will she not?" said m'lord. "She may have been the fish at the end of your line, Thomas, but you had to play her carefully lest she landed back in the river again. I observe that you did not directly inform her that she is to use her female arts on Grahame to persuade him to turn coat yet once more—he being a noted womaniser. That may be done by Master Trenchard in Flanders or Holland—wheresoever you may find him!"

He swung on Tom Trenchard, otherwise Sir Stair Cameron, who was now pouring himself a goblet of wine from a jug on a side-table. "She knew thee not, Stair, I trust?"

"What, in this Alsatian get-up?" mocked Stair, referring to the London district where the City's criminals congregated. "I doubt me whether she could have recognised the King himself if he were dressed in these woundy hand-me-downs."

"Well suited for your errand in the Netherlands, Stair. None there would take you for the King's friend, rather the King's prisoner."

"Or the friend of m'lord Arlington who turned the Seigneur de Buat away from the Grand Pensionary and towards the Peace party—which cost Buat his head," riposted Stair.

Arlington's reply to his friend was a dry one. "His fault, Stair. He was careless, and handed the Pensionary a letter from me, not meant for the Pensionary's eyes. Do you take care, man. No careless heroics—nor careful ones, either."

Stair Cameron bowed low, sweeping the floor with his plumed hat that had been sitting by his feet.

"An old soldier heeds thee, m'lord. My only worry is the lady. She may, once she knows what her part in this is, take against Grahame and refuse to enchant him. Furthermore, playing the heroine at the Duke of York's Theatre is no great matter, and coolness shown on the boards might not mean coolness on life's stage when one's head might be loose on one's shoulders. We shall see."

Arlington dropped his jocular mode and flung an arm around his friend's shoulders. "If aught goes amiss, Stair, and the heavens begin to fall on thee, then abandon all, and come home. Abandon Grahame to the Netherlanders if you have cause to suspect his honesty. Let the wolves have the wolf—we owe him nothing.''

''And the lady?''

Arlington looked at Sir Thomas Gower, who shrugged his shoulders. ''Deal with her as common sense suggests. She is there not only to seduce Grahame, but to help you with your supposed insufficient Dutch and to give an air of truth to your claim to be a one-time solder turned merchant. You will both claim to have Republican leanings and in consequence are happy to spend some time in God's own Republic—which is the way in which the Netherlanders speak of Holland.''

Stair toasted Arlington with an upraised goblet. ''Well said, friend, and I swear to you that I shall try to persuade the Hollanders that I am God's own soldier—however unlikely that is in truth.''

Arlington ended the session with a clap of laughter. ''The age of miracles is back on earth, Stair, if thou and God may be mentioned in the same breath. Forget that—and come home safely with Grahame and the lady in thy pocket. Great shall be thy reward—on earth, if not in heaven.''

Stair Cameron bowed low again. ''Oh, I beg leave to doubt that, Hal. From what I know of our revered King Charles and his empty Treasury, I shall have to wait for heaven. What I do I do for you, and our friendship. Let that be enough.''

Sir Thomas Gower, who had poured a drink for himself and Arlington, had the final word. ''Long live friendship, then. A toast to that, and to the King's Majesty.''

Chapter Two

Catherine Wood, posing as Mistress Tom Trenchard, hung over the packet boat's side, vomiting her heart up. A spring crossing from London to Ostend was frequently unpleasant, and this one was no exception.

Nothing seemed to have gone right since the afternoon on which Tom Trenchard had called at her door to escort her to the docks. His appearance was as fly-by-night as it had been forty-eight hours before in Sir Thomas Gower's office. Behind him stood an equally ill-dressed manservant who had been pulling a little wagon on which Tom's two battered trunks rested.

The day was cold and a light drizzle had begun to fall. Tom was sporting a much darned cloak about his shoulders: it suitably matched his shabby lace. He leaned a familiar shoulder on the door post, grinning down at her from his great height.

"Well, mistress, do you intend to keep me standing in the rain forever? A true wife would invite her husband in."

"I am not your true wife, sir," Catherine riposted coldly, "but natheless you may come in." As Tom removed his hat in order to enter, she added, "Do you intend your man to remain outside growing wet whilst his master enjoys the fireside indoors? He may sit with my serving maid in the kitchen."

Tom was nothing put out. "Ah, a kind wife, I see, who considers the welfare of her husband's servants, as well as her husband. Do as the mistress bids, Geordie."

Geordie doffed a much-creased hat whose broad brim drooped to his shoulders. "And the trunks, Mistress Trenchard, may they come in, too?" He was so ill-shaven that it was difficult to tell whether he was as poorly favoured as his master.

Catherine nodded assent and followed Tom in. He was already seated before the hearth, and was pulling off his beautiful boots.

"You have made yourself at home, I see." Catherine could not help being acid. He was here on sufferance, solely because she was being blackmailed into doing something which she had no wish to do, in order to save her silly brother's life, and Tom was already behaving like the master of the house.

He must learn—and learn soon—that he could take no liberties with her. Alas, his next words simply went to prove that he had every intention of doing so. "Look you, Mistress Wood, or rather, Mistress Trenchard, from this moment on you are my wife, and what is a wife's is her husband's for him to do as he pleases with. If you are to pass as my wife without attracting comment, then I suggest that you remember that. A tankard of ale would not come amiss, *wife*."

Oh, it was plain that the next few weeks—pray God

that they were not months—were going to be difficult
ones, if the start of this misbegotten venture was a sample of her future! Unwillingly, Catherine bobbed a
mocking curtsy at him in a broad parody of a stage
serving maid before bustling into the kitchen to do as
she was bid. She could hear him laughing as she stage-
exited right, as it were.

Once in the kitchen, she found that Geordie had
made himself at home also, and was not only drinking
her good ale, but was eating a large slice from a fresh-
made loaf, liberally spread with new-churned butter. At
least *he* showed a little gratitude, pulling a greasy forelock and offering her a bobbing bow.

The whole effect was spoiled a little by his bulging
cheeks and eyes as he stuffed more bread into his
mouth. Plainly Master Tom Trenchard did not feed his
servant well.

Tom accepted the ale she handed him as his due—
waving her to a seat by her own fireside as though the
house were already his. From what pigsty had he grad-
uated to arrive at King Charles's court? If he were from
the court, that was. His rank and standing seemed dubious to say the least.

By his clothes he was virtually penniless, some sort
of hireling, called in to serve the nation's spymaster—
for that was surely Sir Thomas Gower's office. Yet Sir
Thomas had treated him almost as an equal, and he had
not hesitated to mock at Sir Thomas. Sir Thomas had
said that they would pose as merchants. He seemed an
unlikely merchant.

So, was he a gentleman down on his luck? And what
matter if he were not? These days gentlemen were as

nastily rapacious where women were concerned as their supposed inferiors, and at Whitehall the courtiers, led by such debauchees as m'lord Rochester, were the nastiest of all. No woman was safe with them. It would be as well to remember that.

"You are very quiet, wife? What ails you? A silent woman is a *lusus naturae*—almost against nature."

"I mislike sentences which assume that all women are the same woman. Men would not care to be told that because some men are dissolute rakes, then all must be so."

"Oh, wittily spoken—good enough for Master Wagstaffe, I vow. Tell me, my dear wife, does reciting the well-found words of learned playwrights result in your own lines in real life becoming as witty as theirs?"

Catherine widened her eyes. "La, sir, your intelligence quite overthrows me! Let me try to enlighten you. Am I, then, to suppose that Sir Thomas Gower and Lord Arlington's wisdom must transfer itself to you when you frequent their company?

"I see little sign of that; on the contrary, you maintain your usual coarse mode of speech. From this I deduce that my wit is therefore my own, and not the consequence of mixing with the geniuses who frequent the Duke's Theatre, be they actors or scribblers."

Tom was laughing as she finished, and before she could stop him he had put a large arm around her waist and hefted her on to his knee. "Shrew!" he hissed affably into her ear. "It is a good thing that you are not my true wife or you might earn a lesson in civility. As it is, let this serve."

He tipped her backwards and began to kiss her without so much as a by your leave, just like the rapacious gentlemen whose conduct she had just been silently lamenting. First he saluted each cheek, and then her mouth became his target.

The devil of it was that she would have expected him to be fierce and brutal in such forced loving, but no such thing. His mouth was as soft and gentle as a man's could be, stroking and teasing, rather than assaulting her, so that her treacherous body began to respond to him!

Fortunately, just when Catherine's senses were beginning to betray her, he loosed her a little to free his right hand, and her common sense immediately reasserted itself. Wrestling away from him, she broke free—to slide from his lap to the ground, and found herself facing his man Geordie, who wandered in still chewing as though he had not eaten for a week.

"I gave you no leave to do that, sir," she told him severely.

"Oho, that were quick work, master," Geordie announced, spewing crumbs around him, "not that one expects slow work when an actress is your doxy."

Catherine picked herself up from the floor and slapped the face, not of her unwanted would-be lover, but of his servant.

"Fie and for shame," she cried, "after I have warmed and fed you. I gave him no leave to kiss me, nor you to call me doxy."

"Bonaroba, rather," suggested Tom from behind her, using Alsatian slang to describe a whore.

Enraged, Catherine swung round and boxed his ears,

too. "We might as well start as we mean to go on," she announced. "I will not allow liberties *to* my person at your hands, nor liberties *about* my person from his tongue. You, sir, are a hedge captain, and your servant is naught but a cullion who needs to acquire a wash as well as manners."

Tom was openly laughing at her defiance. "Well, I at least am clean," he told her smugly. And, yes, that at least was true as she had discovered when trapped on his knee. His clothes might be shabby but his body smelled of yellow soap and lemon mixed.

"Oh, you are impossible, both of you," she raged. "Like master, like man. How am I to endure this ill-begotten enterprise in such unwanted company?"

"By accepting that, for the duration of it, we are man and wife, and Geordie is our only servant." Tom's tone was suddenly grave.

"I may not take my woman with me, then?"

"Indeed, not. The fewer who know anything of us, the better."

"But Geordie—" and Catherine's voice rose dangerously "—is to be relied on?"

"Very much so. We have been to the wars together, and he has twice saved my life."

To her look of disbelief at the mere idea of such a scarecrow saving anything, Geordie offered a brief nod. "True enough, mistress. Only fair to say that he saved mine more times than that."

"I trust him," said Tom belligerently, "and so must you. Your life may depend on it."

"Oh, in this ridiculous brouhaha everyone's life depends on someone else," declaimed Catherine bitterly.

"Mine on you, yours on me, and both of us on Geordie, and poor Rob's life depends on all three of us. It's better than a play. No, worse than a play, for no play would be so improbable."

"You're the actress, so you should know," was Tom's response to that. "In real life, my dear, everyone *does* depend on everyone else. 'Tis but the condition of fallen man."

Fear, impotence and anger, all finely mixed together, drove Catherine on. Her tongue turned nasty.

"Oh, we have turned preacher now, have we? Not surprising since we are to pass as canting Republicans. Canst thou whine a psalm through thy nose, preacher Tom? Or is that a trick to learn on the way to Antwerp? Pray learn it quickly so that you may leave a poor girl's virtue untouched as a good preacher should."

To her own surprise Catherine found herself half-laughing as she finished, and Tom's powerful face was also glowing with mirth. Geordie was watching them both with his rat-trap mouth turned down.

"Loose tongue," he muttered, "may loosen heads on shoulders, master. Because you have allowed your tongue to wag in the past and paid no forfeit for it, doth not mean that you may escape punishment for ever."

"There," exclaimed Catherine triumphantly, "even your servant can teach you common sense."

"Oh, is that what he is muttering at us? Come, mistress, we must have a council of war, but only when you have sent your serving maid to market to buy our supper for us."

This shocked Catherine a little. "You intend to stay here tonight?"

"Aye, mistress. The packet doth not sail until early tomorrow. We must be up at dawn and away."

What can't be cured, must be endured, would obviously have to be her motto, was Catherine's last despairing thought as she turned away from him. But he had not finished with her yet.

"Your baggage is packed, mistress?" he asked her commandingly. "You have an assortment of clothing both plain and fancy and are ready to leave?"

She had the satisfaction of assuring him that she was more than ready—at least so far as her luggage was concerned.

"And there is yet another thing, mistress. No good follower of the late Lord Protector would be saddled with a wife called Cleone—a heathen name, indeed. Your true name is Catherine, and so you shall be known. Or would you prefer Kate?"

More to annoy him for the orders he was throwing at her than for any other reason, Cleone replied tartly, "Catherine will do. As old Will Shakespeare said, 'A rose by any other name would smell as sweet,' so what shall it profit that I am called Cleone or Catherine: they both begin with a C."

Tom bowed as gracefully as any court cavalier. "Catherine it shall be. And I am Tom, always uttered with due humility as befits a good wife."

He gave her his white smile again and, for the first time, Catherine saw that it quite transformed his face. Not only were his teeth good, but the relaxing of his harsh features showed her the boy he must once have been.

Nay, Catherine, she told herself sternly, you are not to soften towards a hired bully who plainly sees you as his prey. To do so is to deliver yourself into his hands.

Surprisingly he made no demur when, later, after they had supped, she showed him into Rob's bedroom. She had thought that he might take advantage of her, try to pretend that she was his wife and must do a wife's duty. Instead, he had flung down the small pack he had carried upstairs, given her another of his slightly mocking bows and told her to try to get a good night's sleep.

"For, madam wife, we have several hard days ahead of us, and I would wish that you arrive before Grahame as fresh as a daisy in spring—or the violets that your eyes resemble."

"Fair words butter no parsnips with me, Master Trenchard," Catherine told him tartly.

Only for him to say, blue eyes mirthful, "Tom, dear wife, always Tom. Most wives would be happy to receive such a compliment from a husband to whom they have been married for the last five years."

"Ah, but as a Puritan and a preacher such fair words would lie ill upon thy tongue."

"Oh, a man may be a Puritan and a preacher, but he is still allowed to love his wife, lest the world end. Go forth and multiply, the Lord hath said, and how shall we do that if there be not love?"

"And the Devil can quote Scripture to achieve his

own ends," Catherine replied smartly. "Goodnight, dear husband, and sleep well."

"I would sleep better if I did not sleep alone," Tom informed the door soulfully as it closed behind her—and chuckled as she banged it.

And now, after boarding the packet without further incident, or much talk, and enduring a morning that began fair, but ended in storm and a high wind, Catherine found herself in the throes of seasickness. More than ever she wished that Rob had had the wisdom not to put his treasonous thoughts on paper.

A hand on her shoulder as she straightened up had her whirling around. It was Tom's. He was not being seasick, no, indeed, not he. Far from it—he looked disgustingly healthy, rosy even. Behind him lurked Geordie, looking green; a violent lurch of the ship brought him to the rail to join her in her offerings to the sea.

"Below with the pair of you," ordered Tom, laughter in his voice. "You will be better below decks."

"Not I, master," and, "Not I," echoed Catherine, but Tom was having none of it.

"Do as I bid you," he ordered Geordie, and as Catherine reached a temporary halt in her heavings he swept her up, to set her down only when they reached the companionway into the hold.

Below decks was truly nasty, as Catherine had expected, smelling of tar and worse things, but the boat's heavings did seem less distressing. Tom, having laid her down on what he called a bunk, brought over to her a large tin basin. Sitting beside her, he said, still vilely cheerful, "Use that if you feel sick again."

"I am over the worst, I think," Catherine told him, hoping that she was, but a moment later a huge wave sent the boat sliding sideways, which had her stomach heaving again. With a tenderness that surprised her, Tom held her head steady in order to help her, and when her paroxysms at last ended, he laid her gently down and pulled a dirty sheet over her.

How shaming to behave in such an abandoned manner before him! Not that he seemed to mind. On the contrary, having removed the basin, he came back again with it empty, carrying a damp cloth with which he gently wiped her sweating face.

This seemed to help, and he must have thought so, too, for he said in a kinder voice than he had ever used to her before, "This time, I think, the worst *is* over. Do you feel able to sit up yet?"

Speech seemed beyond Catherine, so she nodded, and struggled into a sitting position. From nowhere Tom produced a pillow with which he propped up her aching head.

"Geordie!" he bellowed at that gentlemen, who had been engaged in heaving his heart up into a bucket, but now seemed a little recovered. "Bring me my pack, if you can walk, that is."

Geordie appeared to take the "if" as an insult. "Course I can walk. I ain't been ill."

This patent lie amused Catherine, and she gave a weak laugh. Tom looked at her with approval as the staggering Geordie handed him his pack. He opened it, and produced a small pewter plate, two limes and a knife.

Catherine watched him, fascinated, as he cut the first

lime in half, handing one half to her, and the other to Geordie.

Geordie began to suck his, and Catherine, after a nod from Tom, followed suit, her mouth puckering as the acid liquid reached her tongue.

"Good," Tom told them both, "that should make you feel better!" He cut the second lime in half, and began to suck it vigorously also. "And now, some schnapps." His useful pack gave up a small tin cup, and first Catherine, then Geordie and finally himself, offered what he called, "a libation to the Gods of the sea, only down our throats and not over the side!"

Like the lime, the strong liquor seemed to settle, rather than distress, Catherine's stomach. She began to feel, as she told Tom, the drink talking a little, "more like herself".

He put a friendly arm around her which she felt too weak to reject—and then he gave her his final present, a disgusting object which he called a ship's biscuit.

"Eat that, and you will be quite recovered."

Her head spinning from the combined causes of an empty stomach brought about by seasickness, followed by a large draught of the strongest liquor she had ever drunk, Catherine managed to force it down. Her poor white face bore testimony to her revulsion as she did so.

Her reward was "Good girl!" and a tightening of Tom's arm. Her gratitude to him was expressed by her leaning against his strong warm body for further comfort. This resulted in a soft kiss on her cheek before Tom laid her down again, covering her with the sheet that had slipped its moorings during his ministrations.

"Try to sleep," he told her. "I am going on deck to stretch my legs a little." He beckoned at his man. "You, too, Geordie."

"Growing soft, are we, master?" growled Geordie at Tom as they reached the deck. The storm had lifted and the sea had grown calm again whilst they were below decks. "The schnapps did its work right well and the doxy would not have objected to a little—well, you know what!"

Tom's expression was an enigmatic one. "Oh, Geordie, Geordie—" he sighed "—you would never make a good chess player. At the moment I need her trust more than anything else in the world. Later—when it is gained—might be a different thing, a very different thing!"

Oh, blessed sleep "that knits up the ravell'd sleave of care", as old Will Shakespeare had it, thought Catherine drowsily as she awoke to feel refreshed. She was not alone. Tom Trenchard was seated on a bench, watching her, a tankard in his hand.

He lifted it to toast her. "You are with us again, dear wife, after sleeping the day away. Your colour has returned, I see." He drank briefly from the tankard, his brilliant blue eyes watching her over its rim before he handed it to her.

"Drink wife. We shall be in Ostend shortly, and there we may find shelter."

"Oh, blessed dry land," sighed Catherine, taking a long draught of ale. "I shall never wish to go to sea again."

"You were unlucky," Tom told her, "to find your-self in such a storm on your first voyage."

"And was it luck that you were not overset like poor Geordie and me?"

"Oh, I am never seasick," grinned Tom. "I have good sea legs. It is but one of my many talents," he added boastfully.

Catherine laughed and, easing herself out of the bunk, handed the tankard back to him. It was odd not to be sparring with him. She decided to prick the bub-ble of his conceit a little.

"Why, dear husband, I vow that you would well match the play wherein I late acted. *The Braggart* by name—*or Lackwit in Love*. Which title best befits you, do you think?"

Tom met her teasing look and answered her in kind. "Why, Master Will Wagstaffe may write a play taking me as hero, calling it *St George, or, England's Sav-iour*—and, if you do but behave yourself, you shall be the heroine. A new Belinda, no less."

Something in his tone alerted her. "You saw me play Belinda, then? At the Duke's Theatre?"

"Indeed, mistress, I had that honour. And a fine boy you made. I ne'er saw a better pair of legs—not even on a female rope dancer—and that is a splendid com-pliment, is it not?"

The look in Tom's eyes set Catherine blushing. He was stripping her of her clothing in his mind, no doubt of it. She swung away from him lest she destroy the new camaraderie that had sprung up between them since he had succoured her in the storm.

After all, they were to live together for some time,

although how long or short that might be Catherine did not know, and t'were better that they did not wrangle all the time.

By good fortune, to save them both, Geordie came down the companionway, his long face glummer than ever.

"Bad news, master, I fear."

"And when did you ever bring me good?" Tom exclaimed. "'Tis your favourite occupation! Spit it out, man. We had best all be glum together."

"Nothing less than that we may not dock at Ostend. There are rumours that the plague may be back, and the packet's master has decided that we must risk all and go on to a harbour near Antwerp."

"And that is bad news?" Tom taunted him, brows raised.

"Aye, for those of us who do not like the sea."

"Antwerp or Ostend, it is no great matter. I have enough schnapps left to make both you and my dear wife drunk and insensible for the rest of the sea trip should the storms begin again. Tell me, wife, will that do?"

For answer Catherine made him a grand stage curtsy, saying, "I know my duty, husband, to you and to our gracious King, and if I must be rendered unconscious to perform it, I shall be so with a good grace."

Tom rewarded her with a smacking kiss on the lips as she straightened up. "You hear that, Geordie? I shall expect no less from you."

"Oh, aye, master. But don't expect any pretty speeches from me."

"Certes, no. The next one will be the first! Back to your bunk, wife, to rest. So far, so good."

He was being so amazingly hearty that he made Catherine feel quite faint—and he was apparently having the same effect on Geordie, who sat grumblingly down on the dirty floor, complaining, "It's as well that some on us are happy."

Tom came over to sit on Catherine's bunk. "And that shall be our epitaph, or, as you stage folk say, our epilogue. Will Wagstaffe himself could not write a better, nor his predecessor, Stratford Will. Rest now, wife."

So she did, her mouth still treacherously tingling from his last kiss. Oh, he knew all the tricks of seduction did Master Tom Trenchard, and she must never forget that.

Chapter Three

Oh, the devil was in it that Hal Arlington had decided that William Grahame could best be snared by the wiles of a pretty woman so that, instead of carrying out this mission on his own, Stair was saddled with an actress who carped at his every word. And *her* every word was devoted to denying him her bed, which would have been the only thing that made having to drag Catherine around the Low Countries worthwhile!

The pox was on it that he had ever volunteered to try to turn Grahame at all! One last such junket, the very last, he had told Arlington and Sir Thomas, having at first refused to oblige them.

''I am seven years away from being a mercenary soldier for anyone to hire. If anyone deserves a quiet life, it is I. I have served my King both before his Restoration and after—as you well know.''

''The Dutch War goes badly—as you equally well know, Stair, and yours are the special talents we need.''

In a sense that had pained him, for were not those talents the ones that he had needed to survive in the penury which exile from England had forced upon him during the late usurper Cromwell's rule? Cunning, lying, cheating and killing, yes, killing, for that was the soldier's trade. Leading men in hopeless causes that he had won against all the odds, by using those same talents.

He thought that he had done with it, that he was now free to live a civilised life in peace. Not simply enjoying its ease, but also the pretty women to whom he need make no commitment, as well as music, the playhouse, books and the blessed quiet of his country estates, both in England and Scotland, when he was no longer at Court. Estates most fortunately restored to him when Charles II had come into his own again.

God knew, he no longer needed the money in order to survive. If he did this thing, he would do it for nothing, which, of course, Gower and Arlington also knew and was partly why they had asked him to be their agent in the Netherlands. As usual, the King's Treasury was empty, and not needing to pay him would be a bonus.

So, he had agreed. Only to discover that they had also decided that he needed a woman to pose as his wife, and a pretty woman at that, skilled in seductive arts, for Grahame had a reputation for being weak where women were concerned.

"As a bird is caught by lime, so will he be caught by a pair of fine eyes," Sir Thomas had said. "And we know the very doxy who will turn the trick for us."

In consequence, he had found himself in his own proper person at the Duke's Theatre, in company with Hal Arlington, trying to test the nerve of the young actress whom Sir Thomas knew that he could black-mail through her indiscreet and foolish brother.

And nerve she had, no doubt of it, by the way in which she had refused to let his unsettling jests with oranges, posies and gloves disturb her. She had also displayed a pretty wit, which she was now constantly exercising at his expense—except when she was sea-sick, that was.

Sir Stair Cameron, to be known in the Netherlands only as Tom Trenchard—Trenchard being his mother's name, and Tom his own second Christian name—was leaning disconsolate over the packet's side as it neared land, musing on his fate.

He lifted his face to feel the rain on it. Blessed, cleansing rain. By God, when this is over, he vowed, I shall refuse to engage in such tricks ever again, but now I must go below and help my disobliging doxy to ready herself to be on dry land again.

Tom did not reflect—for he never allowed the pos-sibility of failure to trouble him—that having to take a young, untried woman with him might put his mission in hazard, even cause it to fail. He had made such a point to Gower and Bennet but they had dismissed it. And so, perforce, had he to do the same.

All the same, the idea was there, very like a worm that secretly eats away at the foundations of a seem-ingly secure house until at last it falls.

He shrugged his broad shoulders. No more mewling and puking over what was past and could not be changed, he told himself, no looking backwards, either. Forwards, ever forwards, was the motto his father had adopted on being made a baronet, and he would try to live up to it, as had always been his habit.

The day was growing late, and it was likely that they would not dock until the morning. Once on shore they would travel to Antwerp where they might, please God, find Grahame and finish the business almost before it was begun.

Time to go below to wake his supposed wife from her schnapps-induced sleep.

"Aye, that will do very well, mistress, very well, indeed," announced Tom Trenchard approvingly. Catherine had dressed herself in a neat gown of the deepest rose. Its neckline was low and boat-shaped, but was modestly hidden by a high-necked jacket of padded pale mauve satin, trimmed with narrow bands of white fur, which reached the knee and was fastened with tiny bows of fine gold braid.

Round her slender neck was a small pearl necklace, and her hair, instead of being arranged in the wild confusion of curls popular at King Charles's court, was modestly strained back into a large knot, leaving a fringe to soften her high forehead.

This had the effect of enhancing rather than diminishing the delicate purity of her face and profile.

For his part, Tom had also changed out of his rough and serviceable clothing. Although he was not pretending to be a bluff and conventional Dutch burgher, he looked less of a wild mercenary captain and more of a man who was able to conduct himself properly out of an army camp as well as in it.

He was wearing jacket and breeches of well-worn,

but not threadbare, black velvet, trimmed with silver. His shirt was white, not a dirty cream, and he sported a white linen collar edged with lace that, if not rich, was at least respectable. His boots, as usual, were splendid. He had also shaved himself carefully so he looked less like the wild man of the woods, which Catherine had privately nicknamed him.

His hair was, for the first time since she had met him, carefully brushed and fell in deep red-gold waves to just below his ears. He carried a large steeple-crowned black hat with a pewter buckle holding its thin silver band.

The whole effect was impressive. No, he was not handsome, far from it, but he had a presence. The French had a saying, Catherine knew, that a woman of striking, but not beautiful looks, was *jolie laide,* which meant an ugly woman who was pretty or attractive in an unusual way. It could, she grudgingly admitted, be applied to Tom, who was better than handsome.

It did not mean that she liked him the more, simply that his brute strength attracted her more than the languor of the pretty gentlemen of King Charles's court did. She had held them off when they had tried to tumble her into bed, and so she would hold off Tom. She would be no man's whore, as she had told Sir Thomas Gower.

"Deep in thought?" offered Tom, who seemed to be a bit of a mind reader. "What interests you so much…wife…that you have just left me in spirit, if not in body?"

She would not be flustered. "Nothing, except that

this morning, for the first time, I feel dry land firm beneath my feet again.''

Forty-eight hours ago they had docked at a wharf on the coast well outside Antwerp itself, which by the Peace of Westphalia was closed to shipping. Antwerp was not Dutch territory, being situated in Flanders, territory still under the heel of the Austrian Empire, and it was always known as the Austrian Netherlands. Being so near to Holland, it would be a useful place to work from—if one were careful.

Once safely on land again, Catherine had found the ground heaving beneath her feet as though she were still on the packet. It had needed Tom's strong arms to steady her.

Today, however was a different matter. The inn at which they were staying was clean after a fashion that Catherine had never seen before. Its black-and-white tiled floors were spotless. A serving maid swept and washed them several times a day. The linen on her bed was not only white, but smelled sweet, as did the bed hangings. It was a far cry from the inns in which she had slept on the occasions when the players took to the roads in England.

The furniture in the inn was spare, but had been polished until it shone, as did the copper, pewter and silver dishes that adorned the table and sideboards. In the main inn parlour there was a mirror on one wall, and on the other hung a tapestry showing Jupiter turning himself into a swan in order to seduce Helen of Troy's mother, Leda.

Few private houses in London boasted such trappings as this inn in Antwerp. Tom had told her that everywhere in the Low Countries might such wealth and such cleanliness be found—''We are pigs, by comparison, living in stys,'' he had ended.

And now they were to visit the man whom Tom hoped would be their go-between with Grahame, one Amos Shooter, who might know where he was to be found. Early that morning, Tom had visited the address of the house that Sir Thomas Gower had given him as that of Grahame's lodgings, but had been told that no one named William Grahame had ever lived there!

''Not true, of course,'' Tom had said to her and Geordie, who was also tricked out like a maypole—his expression. ''But this business is a woundy chancy game.''

Game! He called it a game! Catherine was beginning to think of it as a nightmare.

''Now for my second man. One I think that I might—just—trust.''

''Thought you trusted no one, master,'' sniffed Geordie.

Tom ignored him. ''We must look well-found,'' he had ordered her. ''Not as though we are beggars come to cadge money from a rich friend. Do not overdo matters, though. That would be equally suspicious. Do you not have a small linen cap that you might wear, mistress? Bare heads are for unmarried women.''

Catherine shook her head. ''A pity, that,'' he sighed. ''Well, a good husband would be sure to buy his modest wife one, so we shall go to market tomorrow. Too late to go today!''

So, here they were, knocking at the stout oak door of a respectable red-brick mansion in Antwerp, not far from the market place, which was lined with medieval guild houses. It was opened by a fat, red-cheeked serving maid who bustled them through into a large room at the rear of the house, which opened on to a courtyard lined with flowers in terracotta tubs.

"Amos has done well, I see," Tom whispered in Catherine's ear as they followed the maid, for the house was even cleaner and better appointed than their inn. "I had heard that he had married wealth, but had not realised how much wealth. Ah, Amos, my old friend, we meet again," he said as Amos, a man as large as Tom, came to meet them.

Amos's welcome was warmer than Tom's. He threw his arms around him and embraced him lustily. His wife, a pretty woman, plump and rosy, greeted Catherine much more sedately.

Embraces over, Amos held Tom at arm's length, saying, "Old friend, you are larger than ever, and the world has treated you well enough, I see. And this is your wife? I thought you vowed that you'd never marry, Tom. Not after the beautiful Clarinda deceived you so!"

"Aye, Amos, but 'tis not only a woman's prerogative to change one's mind. This is my wife, Catherine, and yes, I thrive—a little. But not like you," and he gave Amos a poke in his fair round belly. "You carried not that when we were comrades in arms together, nor were you so finely housed and clothed!"

"Oh, but that was long ago. I am quite reformed these days. I am a respectable merchant now—and it is all Isabelle's doing." He threw his arms around his blushing wife and gave her a loving kiss.

So, the beautiful Clarinda—whoever she might be—deceived him, did she? thought Catherine. She must have been a brave lass to manage that! But she ignored this interesting news for the time being, concentrating instead on talking of polite nothings in French to Isabelle.

Polite nothings, indeed, seemed to be the order of the day. Amos bade Isabelle see that food and wine were served to their unexpected guests, and then began a loud discussion of long-gone battles and skirmishes with Tom, as well as memories of comrades long dead.

Tom had volunteered to her earlier that the greatest virtue a successful agent needed was patience. It was, perhaps, just as well that Catherine had learned it in a hard school, for at first Tom talked of everything but anything connected with their mission. It was very pleasant, though, to sit and laze in this well-appointed room, drinking wine and eating what in Scotland were called bannocks, well buttered.

Was Tom lazing as he laughed and talked and drank the good red wine? Or was he picking up hints and notions from his idle gossip with his friend? Catherine could not be sure. Names were flying between him and Amos. Tom had told her earlier, before they had left the inn, that Amos had no true convictions and had always signed up with the side that paid him the most. "Republican or Royalist, Turk or Christian—all were the same to him."

"And you?" she had asked him. "Were you like Amos?"

"Oh," he had told her, giving her the white smile

that transformed his face, "you shall tell me your opinion of that when this venture is successfully over."

He was as slippery as an eel—which in this kind of an enterprise was almost certainly an advantage. Seeing him now, one booted leg extended, wine glass in hand, one might have thought that the only care he had in the world was to gossip with an old friend, chance met.

"And William Grahame," Tom said at last. "What of him? I had heard that he had set up his household in Antwerp these days."

Was it her imagination or did something in Amos Shooter's bland, amiable face change? Did it harden a little so that something of the severe mercenary soldier that he had once been peeped through his genial merchant's mask? If so, the expression was so fleeting that it was gone almost before Catherine had seen it. He was laughing again.

"William Grahame, Tom? I had not thought that you knew him. Not your sort of fellow."

"True. I know him not. But I was told that he might be a useful man to make a friend of."

"No doubt, no doubt. He lodges but a mile away from here. He wanders, I am told, from town to town. About his business. Whatever that might be."

Did Amos Shooter truly not know aught of Grahame but his possible resting place? Both Tom and Catherine were asking themselves the same question, and getting the same answer. He did, but for whatever reason he was not admitting that he did.

Tom took a deep draught of wine—and changed the subject. The rest of the afternoon passed without incident. Mistress Shooter showed Catherine around the courtyard, and then took her through a little gate into a garden where herbs and vegetables grew, and, in summer, fruit on a sheltered wall.

Before they returned indoors, she said in her fractured English that she had learned from Amos, "Your husband should not trust this man Grahame overmuch. I tell you for your own good."

"Why?" asked Catherine, trying to look innocent, and succeeding. After all, she did not need to be a great actress for it to appear that she knew nothing—for that was true.

Isabelle Shooter shook her head at her. "I cannot tell you. I should not have said what I did. But you seem to be a good girl, even if your husband is perhaps not quite the jolly man he pretends to be."

Like Amos, then, thought Catherine cynically. But I would never have called Tom jolly. But, of course, he had been a jolly man this afternoon.

She said no more—for to know when to be silent is as great a gift, if not greater, than the ability to talk well, her Dutch mother had once said—which had the result that, when they returned to the big living room, Isabelle was holding her affectionately by the hand. She said to Tom as they left, "You have a pretty little wife, sir. Take care of her, I beg you."

"Now what brought that on?" Tom asked her once they were on their way back to the inn, Geordie walking behind them. He had spent a happy few hours in the servants' quarters, and was rather the worse for drinking a great quantity of the local light and gassy beer, although he was still able to walk.

"What?" Catherine asked, although she knew perfectly well what he meant.

"Amos's pretty wife holding you so lovingly by the hand?"

"She thought that I was an innocent, and needed protection. She told me that you were not to trust William Grahame overmuch."

"Did she, indeed? Believe me, I have no intention of trusting him at all—or Amos, either. And...?"

"There is no and... She said nothing more. Other than that you seemed a jolly man, but she did not think that you were. That you were pretending to be."

Tom stopped walking, with the result that the overset Geordie, his head drooping, walked into him and earned himself a few curses from Tom, before he answered her.

"Did she so? A wise lady, then. Which begs the question, that being so, if she were wise, why did she wed Amos?"

Catherine shrugged her shoulders. "Why does one marry anyone? For a hundred reasons—or none at all. And did the jolly Amos tell you where William Grahame might be found?"

"That he did. But he did not warn me, as his wife warned you. I fear that he may think me as devious as he is and that therefore I do not need warning. That bluff manner of his is not the true man."

"So I thought. But you and I are not the true man or the true woman either. So we are all quits—except, perhaps, for Isabelle."

Tom gave a great shout of laughter, which had the

heads of the few passers-by turning to look at them, and Geordie absent-mindedly walking into him again.

"I can see I must watch my words, wife. You would make Will Wagstaffe a good secretary—the kind who embroiders his master's words. There are many such around Whitehall. Why not in the playhouse?" He turned to throw a second set of oaths at Geordie for treading on his heels.

"Why not, indeed? And do not curse poor Geordie, for I swear that you probably drank more than he did."

"Ah, but I hold it so much better. Remind me to teach you the trick of it."

"I thank you, husband, but no. No man would wish a toping wife."

"Well said, and now we are home again. We must begin our campaign by deciding on what to say and do when we at last meet the elusive Master Grahame. Battles are won by those whose planning is good, and lost by those who do not plan at all. Remember that."

"As a useful hint to employ in the kitchen? My soldiers must be carrots and cabbages, all arranged properly in rows."

Bantering thus, they reached their rooms, where Tom called for more drink, and some food to stay them for the morrow.

Well, thought Catherine later that night as he staggered to the bed that he had made no attempt to share with her, sharing the unfortunate Geordie's instead, one thing was sure. Whatever Tom Trenchard might, or might not be, life with him was certainly never dull.

Nor did it so prove the next day. This time Catherine was told to dress more modestly, in an old grey gown,

with a large shawl. On the way to the address that
Amos had given them as that of William Grahame's,
Tom brought her a white linen matron's cap, elegant
with its small wings, and its lace frill that framed her
face prettily even if it hid the dark glory of her hair.

Tom was soberly dressed too, in a brown leather
jacket, coarse canvas breeches, his frayed cream shirt,
and, of course, his beautiful boots. They were always
constant! As was his black, steeple-crowned hat with
its battered feather.

Geordie, their ghost, followed them. Since arriving
in the Low Countries, he was wearing something that
passed as a livery: a shabby blue jacket and breeches,
grey woollen stockings and heavy, pewter-buckled
shoes. He carried a large staff with a silver knob on
the top. His sallow face was glummer than ever. One
wondered why he served Tom at all since he seemed
to take so little pleasure in the doing.

Tom had talked seriously to Catherine before they
left. "Hal Arlington told me that Grahame has a weakness for pretty women. Now you are a pretty woman,
but a married one, so if you are to attract him—and
distract him—you must do so modestly. Killing looks
from swiftly downcast eyes. A glance of admiration
should he say something witty. Later, when you know
him better, then you may go further."

Catherine threw him a furious look. For the last few
days she had been spending her time worrying over
Tom seducing her, and all the time she had been
brought along to try to seduce Grahame!

"And, pray, how far is that 'further' to be? Are you

here to play pimp to my strumpet? For if so, I tell you plainly that you may be in love with your role, but I am certainly not about to play the part which you and your two masters have assigned to me.''

''No need for that,'' Tom told her swiftly. ''You are to tease him only. Draw him on. Nothing more.''

Distaste showed on Catherine's face and rang in her voice. ''And that is almost worse than going the whole way! To lure a poor devil on with hopes that you are never going to satisfy is more indecent than being an honest whore.''

''Your choice,'' grinned Tom. ''If you prefer being the honest whore…''

''Oh—'' Catherine stamped her foot ''—if I were not between a rock and a hard place so that Rob's life depends on my complicity, I should take ship for England straightaway.''

''Well said, wife. I like a woman who knows the way of the world—so few do.''

''Oh…'' Catherine let out a long breath. He was impossible, but there was no point in telling him so. So she didn't.

After that, when he bought her the cap, she was minded not to thank him, but the expression on his hard face was so winning when he gave it to her, that she did so—even if a little ungraciously.

Grahame's house turned out to be a small one-storied wooden building on the outskirts of the city, surrounded by vegetable gardens with a dirt road running through them. A boy was poling along a small flat boat loaded with cabbages on the small canal that ran parallel with the road.

"Not lodgings, I think," Tom said thoughtfully as they left the road and walked up the path to the house through a neglected garden. "Something rented." He looked around him. "It's deathly quiet."

He shivered. "Too quiet. I would have thought a man of Grahame's persuasion would prefer to be lost in a crowded city than isolated here. Safer so."

It was the first time, but not the last, that Catherine was to hear him say something which had an immediate bearing on what was about to happen—and of which he could not have known.

For, as they reached the door but before they could knock on it they heard, coming from inside, the noise of a violent commotion, and male voices shouting.

"What the devil!" exclaimed Tom—and pushed at the door, which was not locked and opened immediately. He strode in, Geordie behind him, pushing Catherine on one side, and telling her not to follow them but to wait outside.

An order that she immediately disobeyed.

Chapter Four

Catherine found herself in a large room in which two, no three, men were struggling together. Tom was standing to one side, doubtless trying to decide which of them was the one he had come to meet—and must try to rescue.

It suddenly became plain that one of the men was losing an unequal fight with the two others and therefore was almost certainly William Grahame. Tom seized Geordie's staff and brought its metal tip hard down on the head of the man who now had Grahame by the throat.

He fell to the ground, unconscious. Tom then tossed his staff back to Geordie, and drew from inside his coat a long dagger. On seeing Tom coming at him with the dagger, Geordie behind him, the fellow of the unconscious man loosened his hold on Grahame and threw him bodily at Tom with such force that Tom lost his balance and collapsed across a settle, Grahame on top of him.

Having done so, the would-be assassin ran through the open door at the far end of the room, Geordie in pursuit, for Tom was busy disengaging himself from Grahame who was gasping his thanks at him.

"For," he said feelingly, "had you, whoever you are, not arrived in such a timely fashion, I was dead meat. I give you my thanks."

"My pleasure," said Tom. "And you, sir, must be William Grahame, whom I have come to speak with. Who is this—" and he prodded the man on the floor who was now stirring and groaning "—that with his fellow he sought so desperately to kill you?"

"Why, as to that, I know not," replied Grahame, who was visibly distressed by what had just passed. There were bruises on his face and throat and he had some difficulty in speaking. "Only that the two of them broke in through the door there and set about me." He pointed at the one through which his assailant and Geordie had disappeared.

For some reason Catherine—who had been standing back staring at the action, which was far more exciting and dangerous than that in any play in which she had acted—did not believe him. She wondered whether Tom also thought that Grahame might not be telling the truth.

Tom had sheathed his dagger again inside his coat, was hauling the groaning man to his feet and throwing him down on the settle, since he appeared to have difficulty in standing.

"Come, *mijnheer*," Tom began in broken Dutch, for he was of the opinion that these might be assassins sent by the Grand Pensionary, John de Witt, to dispose of a double agent whom he might now consider dangerous, "who sent you here to kill Master Grahame—and why?"

The man shook his head and seemed not to understand what Tom was saying. Grahame began to interrogate him, but Tom stopped him, saying, "Do not distress yourself, sir. My wife speaks good Dutch. Mine is poor and he may not understand what I was asking him. Wife?"

Catherine stepped forward, just as Geordie reappeared, looking glummer than ever.

"My apologies, Master, but I lost him. There is a small wood beyond the gardens where the path forks and I must have taken the wrong track..."

"No matter." Tom was brief. "Our friend here will soon tell us all. Begin, wife."

Catherine questioned their captive in Dutch and then in French, being proficient in both. He understood not them, nor English either—or so his shaking head and uncomprehending face appeared to say.

Tom lost patience. He surveyed the man silently for some minutes. He was anonymous in both face and dress, being like a score such as one might see in the street. At last he leaned forward to pull the man upright.

"Wife," he said, not turning his head towards Catherine, "do you go into the garden and not return until I call for you. I would fain question this piece of scum more severely and I would not have you present. Go!" he ordered her fiercely as she hesitated.

Nothing for it but to leave with Geordie, for Tom bade him to go with her and, "to look after the mistress with a little more care than you chased yon assassin!"

Catherine never quite knew what followed next for her back was towards Tom, Grahame and the would-be assassin when, just as she reached the door, she heard a shot behind her.

Shocked, she swung round to see Tom facing the assassin who was sinking to the floor, blood gushing from his mouth. Behind him stood Grahame, his face grim, a pistol in his hand.

"Now, why the devil did you do that?" enquired Tom of Grahame.

"To save you, of course," returned Grahame hardily. "See, he had drawn a dagger on you, it is on the floor near his hand. I had a pistol in my belt that I was not able to use against my assailants, their attack being so sudden, and I used it to save you, as you had saved me."

Tom's expression was deadly, thought Catherine, shivering a little, and he did not seem at all grateful to Master Grahame for saving his life.

"No," he said, his voice so cold and severe that Catherine scarcely knew it, "I was in no danger from this poor fool, despite his dagger. And now that you have slain him so incontinently, we can know no more of who paid him to slay *you*."

Grahame's expression was a sad one, but his voice was patient. "Forgive me. I had no time to think. I saw you being attacked, and acted accordingly."

Tom stood silent before giving a short laugh. "No, you must forgive me. You thought I was in danger and you acted promptly. For that I must thank you. You were not to know that I have been for many years a mercenary soldier who would not easily have fallen victim to such an amateur creature as this. After all, he and his accomplice were making heavy weather of killing a solitary man, unable to use his weaponry.''

Well, Catherine thought, a trifle indignant on Grahame's behalf, at last Tom had thanked Grahame, even if his thanks were belated.

Grahame inclined his head. ''We are quits, I think,'' he said, smiling. ''And now you must tell me who you are, and why you have sought me out here. And, most of all, who told you where to find me. I had thought this place unknown to all my enemies, and most of my friends.

''Then, in a few short minutes, there arrive both enemies and friends, for I take you, your wife and your servant to be my friends. Indeed, if you arrived as strangers, your actions have made you my friends.''

He smiled at them, before announcing, ''Wine,'' and going over to a *buffet*—the Low Countries word for a sideboard—where stood a decanter and several goblets of fine glass, a little at odds with the rough style of the house and the furnishings of the rooms in it. ''We must drink a toast to our survival.'' He had needed to step over the assassin's corpse to get there. Catherine felt quite faint at the casual way in which all three men were treating his death.

She was not surprised when Tom shook his head, saying, ''Wine later. First we must decide what to do with him,'' and he pointed at the body. ''If I am wrong in supposing that you do not wish to inform the authorities of what has passed this day, forgive me. If I am right, however, the evidence needs to be disposed of.''

Grahame continued to pour wine as though discussing murderous attacks and the hiding of dead bodies was an ordinary, everyday matter.

"There are enough canals about here, to hide a dozen such as he. Depend upon it, no one will seek to know what happened here today. The odds are on it that his companion will not return to confess his failure. These were but poor hirelings sent to dispose of me. It was their bad luck that you arrived."

And ours that we did, thought Catherine to whom a glass of wine seemed a most desirable thing. I have had a real baptism of fire today. If I had ever imagined that this enterprise was not a risky one, this episode has proved exactly how risky it is! I feel quite faint, but will not confess it.

She looked away from the dead man, and saw Tom gazing at her enquiringly. She gave him a small wry smile to try to tell him that, whilst she was shocked, she was not about to disgrace herself—or him—by doing anything so stupid as faint.

Pleased—and relieved—by her stoicism, Tom handed her his glass. "Drink up," he bade her. "It will make you feel better."

She made no demur, but drank down the good Rhenish wine, and listened to Tom and Grahame discussing what to do with the corpse.

"Your man may help me to carry this poor fool to the shed in the garden. He may lie until darkness falls when the canal shall be his resting place—for the time being, that is," said Grahame, his manner almost cheerful.

Geordie pulled a long face, but did as he was told.

Tom said nothing, but he was thinking a great deal. No stranger to violence himself, he found that Grahame's equanimity in the face of violent death—and a violent death which he had needlessly inflicted—was telling him something of the man quite other from what Gower and Arlington had believed of him in London.

This was no puling scholar who simply paid for the information which he painstakingly—almost safely—gathered and used to sell to either the Dutch or the English government, according to whichever would pay him the most at the time. He had killed before, and would doubtless kill again.

No, Grahame was a very dangerous man and not to be trusted. And who, exactly, was trying to kill him? And why? These questions ran through Tom's head, as he took the empty wine glass from Catherine and re-filled it for himself. Other thoughts were troubling him.

Were Gower and Arlington playing a double game with him and Catherine? Had they employed the assassins who had tried to kill Grahame—and so nearly succeeded? And had he and Catherine been sent as a blind so that they might disclaim responsibility if Grahame were found murdered? Their argument being that they would scarcely waste time sending emissaries to deal with a man they intended to kill.

Or was the Grand Pensionary responsible? Was it not possible that he, like Gower and Arlington, might have tired of Grahame's devious games, and decided to do away with him?

Worse still, were he and Catherine being manoeuvred by Gower and Arlington into a situation where they might be accused of killing Grahame? The possibilities were

endless; instead of cursing poor Catherine's presence, as
he had been doing, might he not be better employed asking himself why he had been so foolish as to agree to
this dubious venture at all!

"So, sir," Grahame said, handing Tom his glass of
Rhenish and seating him in a large chair opposite to
him, Geordie having been left in the garden to keep
watch at the back of the house. "Pray tell me who you
are, and why I am honoured by your presence," and
he lifted his glass to Tom, almost fawning on him.

Oh, the greasy swine! Tom had difficulty in not
laughing out loud at such a seductive attempt to charm.
There was something odd about Grahame, but exactly
what the oddness consisted of Tom did not yet know.

"My name is Thomas, Tom, Trenchard. I am a
member of that family, noted as a supporter of the late
Lord Protector. Colonel Ned Trenchard, now a soldier
for the Hapsburgs and the Empire, is a distant cousin.
I met him once in Nurnberg, when I was still a mere
lad."

Now that, at least was true, for Tom mixed truth with
lies to achieve a greater truth—as all such conspirators
do, and if pushed could describe Ned Trenchard accurately, aye, and others who were opposed to King
Charles as well.

"Indeed, indeed, Master Tom Trenchard. And what
does this cousin of Ned Trenchard come to me for? On
whose behalf? Not on his cousin's, I dare swear."

"No, indeed. On the contrary, for although my in-
clination lies towards the late Cromwell's cause, I do
not wish to see my country brought low by a foreign
power, even to bring down King Charles. That were to

leave us helpless before any European state which might wish to conquer us. And knowing my mind on this, I am sent by my masters in London to offer you what they believe you most dearly wish…''

Tom paused, and waited for Grahame to answer.

''And that wish is? Tell me, Master Trenchard, since you have just claimed to know my mind, what my mind is.''

Oh, a devil! A most cunning devil! He and Tom were a good pair, were they not? This was Catherine's immediate reaction to this conversation between two men, neither of whom could be trusted to tell the truth. She waited for Tom's answer.

It was his turn to raise his glass to Grahame before speaking. ''Why, Master Grahame, I believe that you have a great mind to return to the land of your birth, but that you do not wish to meet the headsman's axe shortly after arriving there!

''That being so, I am to inform you that a pardon awaits you if you give my masters, through me, not only what you know of the dispositions of the Dutch Army and Navy, but also what you have learned of the arrangements of the French forces. You see, I am being frank with you,'' Tom ended, trying to look as sincere as a man being insincere could.

''Oh, I do like a frank man,'' exclaimed Grahame, ''frankness not being much of a commodity on any exchange these days! You will, I know, be well aware that I may not be equally frank back. For it is my head that will roll if I accept this offer at face value. Pray forgive me for speaking the language of commerce, but we are in the Low Countries where commerce reigns, and commerce is what we are engaged in, is it not? Yes, I must have time to think.''

"I am authorised to give you time," Tom told him, "but not a great deal of it." Which last, at least, was truthful.

He had not expected, nor had Gower or Arlington, that Grahame would fall on his neck, and agree to come home immediately—hence their insistence that Catherine accompany him to act as bait.

Grahame's next words were unexpected. "Your wife speaks Dutch well, and French also, not always accomplishments which English women possess. How so?"

Truth would serve again, Tom thought, and Catherine should tell it. "My wife must answer you, Master Grahame, if she be so willing.''

So this was to be her baptism into the devious business of spying. She must not falter—nor did she, saying eagerly, "Indeed, husband. My father was married to a Dutch lady of good birth who spoke both Dutch and French well, and insisted that I learned to speak both languages well. And Latin, too, for she thought that girls as well as boys should have the education that the Dutch gave them, which the English do not.''

She ended by rising and dropping Grahame a neat curtsy.

"Convenient," was all that Grahame had to say to that. Tom did not inform him that Catherine was an actress—for that was no business of his, and he was pleased that her answer had been short and sweet with nothing volunteered that had not been asked for. She was now sitting down again, head bent, looking both submissive and wifely.

A strange warm feeling swept over Tom. It was not a feeling he had ever experienced before. He had no time to analyse this new sensation further, for he had more pressing matters on which to ponder.

He had probably gone as far as he could in this first meeting. He had laid Gower and Arlington's proposition before Grahame, and whether, if he returned to the English fold, they would hold to their promises to him, he did not know. It was not his business, but it was Grahame's. And if Grahame were as wily as Tom thought he was, it was likely that he would take a deal of time before making up his mind.

So far as Tom was concerned, there were other questions that needed an answer. Item: Why was Grahame living alone in the country without servants or helpers? Item: What was his connection with Amos Shooter, that Shooter should know the whereabouts of a double agent who was obviously in hiding?

All this whilst watching Grahame watch him as they drank their wine. Silences, Tom thought, often told one as much as words. Grahame ended this one by pouring Tom more wine, saying as he did so, "And who, may I ask—for perhaps I may not—told you where to find me?"

Again the truth was best. "Oh, you may ask, no secret there. None but my old friend and late companion in arms, Amos Shooter, now a fat burgher with a rich and pretty wife."

"He does not need to run back to England, then," was Grahame's dry comment. He looked across to where Catherine sat, silent and demure. "And *your* pretty wife. Why have you brought her along?"

Tom had a quick answer for him. "She has no family with whom she might stay, and I did not care to leave her alone. A woman alone is a target for the unscrupulous. My mission is surely not a dangerous one for me, and I would be happier with her by my side."

He came out with this in the dieaway tone of a man still in love with his wife, but who was well aware that others found her attractive.

"I would speak with you further, Master Trenchard, upon your position. Know that I am heartily sick of being an exile, and I have thought long on the matter. I am not yet completely at the point where I accept that the King's cause is the just and proper one, but my mind inclines that way."

Grahame was looking away from Tom as he said this, as though he were half-ashamed to say it. Tom took the bait offered. "I shall be most ready to entertain you at the inn where we are lodged, and where we may arrange to speak privately. Unless you prefer to meet me here."

Grahame flapped a wary hand. "No, no. Not here, nor at the inn, neither. Safer that you hire a coach and that you pick me up on the main highway at the point where the road leading to my house turns off. Thus we may speak in peace with none to overhear us."

"Except the coachman," Tom could not help saying.

"We shall speak in English. In any case, I shall not stay long here, but must find a safer place now that my enemies have tracked me down. Bring the coach to the spot of which I have spoken at noon tomorrow, and we will take matters further."

That appeared to be that. Grahame would say nothing further, but spoke largely and vaguely of having met the Grand Pensionary, and of one Benjamin Tite, who he said, pretended to be a merchant inclined to the English, but who was selling details about the British Fleet to the Dutch. Tom had never heard of Benjamin Tite, but did not tell Grahame so.

It was time to go. Time to leave Grahame to wonder how much Tom Trenchard and his masters knew of his double-dealing, and whether Tom Trenchard's pretty wife was a player in this new game that London had inaugurated. Tom swallowed his wine, and put down his glass, silently admiring its costly beauty, which was a little at odds with the shabby dwelling where Grahame had gone to ground.

To hide from whom? Why, everybody, of course, Tom thought, watching Grahame's deference to Catherine as she rose to put on her shawl. Geordie was summoned from the garden, and they made ready for the long walk back to the centre of Antwerp.

"At least," Tom said to Catherine, as they tramped steadily back to what was to be regarded as home, "we shall have the doubtful pleasure of riding in a coach tomorrow, for which I am sure Master Grahame expects us to pay."

Catherine had something to ask him. Something which had been troubling her as she had listened to him and Grahame tip-toe around one another.

"Sir—" she began, only to be interrupted.

Tom stopped, looked down at her, took her chin familiarly in his hand, tipped her face up towards his, and said, "Tom, husband, or Master Trenchard, if you please, Mistress Trenchard. To call me 'sir' sounds as though you are my servant, not my wife.''

To her astonishment, the touch of his big hand was doing strange things to Catherine. Oh, men had touched her in the past, and some, trying to overcome her resistance to their blandishments, more familiarly than this. She had always slapped their hand away, but no one's touch had affected her so strongly as Tom's did, here, in an Antwerp street.

She wanted to put her hand over his, so that the tingling pleasure that had invaded her whole body would not stop. Looking up at him, she saw, for the first time, his face clear and plain. Since their first meeting she had always avoided looking straight at him—something she was sure that he must have noticed, although he had never spoken of it.

But now she registered every detail of him. She saw the red-gold stubble on his chin, which had grown since his close shave early that morning. She saw the laughter lines around his eyes, and his eyes' amazing blue, clear and shining. Their whites, too were clear, with the faintest pale blue tinge, not bloodshot through debauchery, like many of those of the hangers-on around Charles II's court.

She saw also the power of his face, which seemed to cancel out its harshness and give him a strange handsomeness of his own. That transformation was something that she had seen before, but never so plainly as now.

It seemed to depend on the strong jut of his nose, the strength of his jaw and chin, and on his mouth, long and slightly curling so that his errant sense of humour—which she was so strongly resisting since it made her vulnerable to him—was plainly visible.

For a moment it gave him the appearance of a man of power, and she must never forget that he was not that, but was simply a penniless adventurer using her for his own ends—and she had no idea what they were.

"Master Trenchard, then—" she said at last, but before she could go on he interrupted her again.

"I had supposed that I might be Tom. I had even dared to suppose that *dear* Tom might be offered me, but, alas, the Gods are not kind, I see."

He released her chin as he spoke—and his spell was broken. He was ordinary Tom Trenchard again, not someone who appeared to be infinitely more powerful.

But the memory of how she had felt and what she had seen remained with Catherine even after their walk was over and they were back at the inn. Meantime, she finished her sentence.

"Now that I have met Master Grahame, I see why you are right to mistrust him, and Amos Shooter also. For if Shooter is an honest man, the simple merchant he pretends to be, how does he come to know of Grahame's secret hiding place?"

She hesitated, picking her words carefully before going on, "There is another thing. Why did Grahame kill the man who was attacking you? Were you really in danger? You seemed to think that you were not. And if you were not, why should Grahame needlessly kill a man who could give him useful information on the enemy who had hired him? Surely it was in Grahame's interest *not* to kill him?"

"Well argued, wife. I can see that you are going to

be a useful aide-de-camp, for that was the most suspicious thing that Grahame did during our time with him. The only reasonable inference is that he did not want me to know who his enemy was. And for the life of me I cannot think why Grahame should think that important enough to kill him. If you can think of a reason, pray tell me.''

He was testing her, Catherine was sure, for she was also sure that Tom had already thought of a reason—perhaps more than one.

"I suppose that it might reveal that he was not only spying on us for the Dutch, and on the Dutch for us, but that he might also be involved with the Spanish or the French.''

If Geordie had been travelling behind them as he had done on the way, Tom's sudden stop would have had Geordie almost tripping him up again. As it was, Geordie was walking ahead of them on the way back, his staff importantly raised as though she and Tom were substantial citizens instead of a pair of fly-by-nights, so Tom went unscathed.

It was she who was scathed, for Tom bent down and gave her a smacking kiss on the lips, bellowing "Well done, wife,'' when he lifted his head again. "My thoughts entirely, but I had not reckoned that you were such a fly customer as to read Grahame so quickly. I suppose all those confounded plays you have acted in, with double-dealing going on around the stage, have alerted you to the ways of the world.''

Tom's kiss had an even more powerful effect on Catherine than his hand on her chin. She felt quite faint. And where had all that come from? He had kissed her lightly when they had first met in London without it having had such an overpowering effect on her. What had changed?

It must have been the kind way he had treated her when she had been seasick. Yes, that was it, no doubt of it. She became aware that Tom was saying urgently, "Wife! Wife! Where have you gone?" and was passing a hand before her face. "Is aught wrong?"

Now why the devil was she suddenly dumbstruck and moon wandering in the middle of the day? "No, there's nothing wrong," she said, a trifle crossly. "I was possibly overcome by the compliment you paid me. Most unlike you!"

"That's better," he told her approvingly. "I would think that there was something wrong with *you* if you did not try to bite me. Now, since you have worked out why Grahame killed that poor wretch, perhaps you might like to try to tell me why Grahame was being so cautious with us. After all, we are only here because it was he who sent word to London, and yet he is behaving as though we took the initiative and are pursuing him."

"But we are pursuing him, are we not?" This seemed so plain to Catherine that she thought that it was scarce worth saying. "After all, he has the whip hand, has he not? It is he who has information to sell, and he who can dictate his terms to us. The reverse is not true. It is no loss to him if we retire emptyhanded."

Better and better, thought Tom as they turned into the road where their inn was situated. I have brought along a clever doxy—one who echoes my thoughts entirely. If I had feared, as I did, that I would have to spend my time explaining matters to her, I was wrong.

He looked down at her as she trotted by his side. The only trouble is that it would be dangerous if I allowed myself to feel anything for her—for my principal spur of action must be my mission—and not my companion on it.

All the same, he could not dismiss the supposed Mistress Catherine Trenchard from his thoughts—nor did he particularly wish to. Would she be as bold and adventurous in bed?

Time might tell.

Chapter Five

"How now, wife? What thought you of your first day in action?"

Catherine and Tom had eaten their supper in the upstairs parlour from which their bedroom led. Geordie had shared it with them, but had then been allowed to retire to the taproom downstairs—on condition that he did not get drunk.

Tom—a tankard of ale in his hand—was lounging before a fire in the great hearth for it was a cold day for early May. His unbooted legs were stretched out before him, he had wrenched off the linen cravat that had encircled his neck, and loosened the strings of his shirt. He appeared to be as unbuttoned and easy as a man might be. Violent death and the conspiracy in which they were both involved seemed far away.

His question caught Catherine both unawares and uneasy. It was the first time that she had found herself alone with him. Until now Geordie had been their constant companion, and she was a little worried as to what his dismissal might mean.

"I was somewhat surprised," she said slowly, "at

what an ordinary man William Grahame appeared to be. Had I met him in the street, I would not have thought that he was a violent man engaged in villainous doings. For sure, a man such as Grahame must be a villain.''

"Dear wife and dear actress," mocked Tom. "You have grown too used to the stage where a man announces himself to be a villain from the moment in which his script says enter. He sidles, he leers, he speaks with exaggeration. Now, were Grahame to behave like that as he goes about his treacherous business he would be immediately identified for what he is. Your true villain hides his colours, he does not flaunt them. He is anonymous, overlooked, lost in the crowd.''

"And does that mean that you are not a villain, Tom Trenchard? For you are not lost in the crowd, and no one would overlook you!''

"True, dear wife. But then, I am a villain of a different kind from Grahame. No one expects subtlety from me. I am openness itself. I am your true, simple-minded and honest villain.'' He was laughing as he finished speaking.

Your true, simple-minded honest villain! Well, at least he knew that he was. But was that a blind? To pretend that you were something of a fool might be the trick of a clever man. And, for sure, Tom Trenchard was not simple-minded, even though he might claim to be.

"Yes, wife," he continued, "you have been deceived by such as Will Wagstaffe, your newest playwright. And tell me, since he, too, is a deceiver, have you any notion of who he might be, and what his true name is?''

Catherine dropped her eyes and looked at her hands, neatly folded in the blue wool of her modest gown. She was silent for so long that Tom twitted her on it.

''Come, is the matter so secret that you may not answer me?''

''Why speak you thus of Master Wagstaffe? Why suppose him to be, as you say, a deceiver?''

''If your true honest villain has one thing, it is a nose. And my nose tells me that Wagstaffe is a false name. Come, mistress, tell me, have you not heard of Will Shakespeare, the very original Wagstaffe himself!''

Catherine began to laugh, as much at the comic face Tom was pulling as at what he was saying. ''Of course I have. But it still might be an honest name? Why suppose otherwise?''

''I think, mistress, that someone is playing a joke, laughing at us behind his hand. For the jests in *The Braggart, or, Lackwit in Love* are those of a man who likes to laugh at what others do not know. So, have you met him, this Wagstaffe? Or know of those who have met him?''

Catherine wondered why he was being so persistent over a matter of such little import. Here they were, dealing in life and death—for if William Grahame was fit to be a target for illwishers, so were they—and all that Tom Trenchard was worrying about was the true name of a hack playwright!

She told him so.

It troubled him not at all. For he laughed again, and

said, "Now, I wonder why you will not answer a simple question with a simple answer. Have you met him, mistress? Yeah, or nay?"

"Nay, then, I have met no such he," Catherine replied, her eyes down, busy looking at her restless hands that she could not command to stay still.

"And you have met those who have met him? Yea or nay?"

"Yea. Or rather, I know that Betterton hath met him. But Betterton doth not talk much, and he has said nothing of Wagstaffe. Only that he values his privacy."

"Bravo, mistress, the truth at last. And why I had to wrench it from you, like pulling teeth, defeats me."

"I respect a man who wishes his privacy to be respected. But you, I take it, as an honest villain, respect nothing."

Tom rose and bowed low to her, pulling off an imaginary hat and sweeping it along the ground. Catherine began to laugh; she could not help it. He was parodying a player pretending to be a gallant. When he straightened up, it was to see her laughing face.

Instead of staying upright, he dropped to his knees before her. "What would Master Wagstaffe have his honest villain say now?" he whispered before taking her face in his hands. "Come, mistress, this comedy has gone on long enough. Let's to bed, and pleasure the night away."

His hands were at her bosom, and his mouth met hers, to stifle any protest, she supposed. Or was it that he thought that no protest would be forthcoming? In any case Catherine found it difficult to pull her own mouth away, for it was a treacherous thing, which wanted to be kissed by him whether she willed it or no.

Oh, but this must stop—for who knew where it might end? Perhaps in the bed of which he had spoken! So she pushed him and his invading hands and mouth away, saying, "Fie on you, sir. I thought that I had made it plain back in London that we were only to pretend to be man and wife, and would not carry the pretence into bed."

"And fie on you, mistress, for assuming a virtue though you have it not, as the first Will once wrote. All the world knows that the virtue of actresses is but a cracked thing, a pot long broken."

"Not so with this actress," cried Catherine, jumping to her feet and making her way to the door. "Try to touch me so again and I'll return to London by the next boat, and leave our mission unaccomplished."

Tom was no whit daunted. Like the true and honest villain he claimed to be, he stood back to laugh at her, no whit deterred.

"What, mistress, would you run away and condemn your brother to the hangman? Go to, thou wouldst not do that!" He was speaking the language of the playhouse in the playactor's high stage voice, mocking her and it. But he was not attempting to try her virtue again.

Instead, "You are a pearl among women if you have remained unspotted, and since I have never met such a pearl, nor do I believe in one, why then, it is Tom Trenchard who is unlucky enough to be unable to please you. No matter, mistress, propinquity they say is a great thing, and I am a patient man. You may go to your bed alone—tonight.''

''As I do always,'' Catherine came out with proudly. It had been hard work keeping her virginity in the cruel world of the theatre. It was true that most actresses sold themselves in order to live, their pay being poor, but she had another string to her bow of which she was determined that Master Tom Trenchard should know nothing.

It was true that in some strange way he was attracting her more and more—but was not that simple lust speaking? Lust of which all the sages and poets had written again and again. True love might exist, but it was a rare commodity, hard to find—though it beckoned often—and certainly she would not find it in the arms of a scheming mercenary captain who scarcely ever spoke the truth—if he knew what the truth was, which was doubtful.

But if she were honest something in him called to her and for the life of her Catherine did not know what that something was. Perhaps she feared to look for an answer because she was afraid of what it might be, and of what it might tell her about herself!

She had often dreamed of a lover, someone whom she could admire and trust, and the kind creature whom she had always conjured up bore no resemblance at all to Tom Trenchard. Quite the contrary. Tom symbolised everything that she detested about the gallants who infested London and the court since Charles II's Restoration.

Loose, untrustworthy, selfish and ready to sacrifice anyone else to gain a moment's pleasure. Lackwits all, so far as she was concerned, fit only to be tricked as they went their merry way. Their master at King Charles's court, m'lord the Earl of Rochester, even called his followers The Merry Gang—and they pursued virtuous and unvirtuous women alike.

Well, Tom Trenchard would not gain any such pleasure with Mistress Catherine Wood, known also as Cleone Dubois, and now Catherine Trenchard. It was enough to make a poor girl dizzy to have such a multitude of names—only one of which was truly hers—and that being the only one she never used!

Which, I suppose, makes me as big a liar as he is. But I am only one through necessity! And even as she thought this a little voice in her head said, But what if it is necessity which drives him on, too? What then?

Catherine took this somewhat unwelcome thought to bed with her. She had no notion of what thoughts Master Tom Trenchard took to bed with him—if any.

It was raining in the morning. The sky was grey, and as they ate breakfast Tom said cheerfully, ''It is as well that our meeting today is to be by coach. We need not venture into the open. The coachman will drive his carriage into the inn yard, to save us from walking to it in the rain. Or so the innkeeper says. He thinks that we are off on a pleasure jaunt.''

Could the innkeeper really believe that we are rich enough to spend our time doing any such thing? thought Catherine. Perhaps he could. Tom was looking a little magnificent this morning; he was in his black velvet again. As he had bidden her the night before, she matched him in one of her best gowns, violet with silver trimmings. Geordie, to his disgust she later found, was to be left behind, unbeautified.

"You may guard our rooms," Tom told him privately. "Not that there is anything either incriminating or valuable in them, but it would be useful to know whether anyone thought that there might be."

He received a sullen nod of the head, but Tom knew that despite his surly manner Geordie was as faithful a friend and servant as a man could have. Someone who was prepared to guard his master's secrets and carry out his orders, complainingly, it was true, but always obediently.

And so he told Catherine as their coach rolled towards their assignation with Grahame. Not that he had secrets, but that Geordie was a good and faithful servant—"nay friend," he added quickly. "And you may trust him too. You may not be my true wife, but Geordie will treat you as though you were."

Some time later Catherine was to have occasion to remember these words and act upon them—to her own consequent advantage. But on that grey morning she received them lightly, and thought little of them. Geordie was Geordie, Tom Trenchard's surly servant, and that was that.

The coach reached the meeting place where the road to William Grahame's home diverged, but he was not there. Tom ordered the coachman to stop a moment. To admire the view, he said. Which, seeing that there was no view worth speaking of, must have sounded a little odd. Doubtless the coachman was used to the vagaries of the notoriously mad English, for he said nothing.

Tom and Catherine alighted, "To stretch our legs," Tom said. The rain had stopped so they walked a little way down the road, loudly admiring the unadmirable canal. They had gone about two hundred yards when they saw Grahame running towards them.

He was carrying a small pack, and his face was white and strained. Fortunately they were out of sight of the coach and its driver, the road having taken a sharp turn to the left.

"Thank God you're here," he gasped at them. "Someone sent another assassin after me—I should have gone with you yester afternoon. Fortunately I was ready for him, I sat up all night, and he came just before dawn. I was delayed by having to dispose of him. You have a coach with you?"

"Beyond the bend," Tom said, waving his arm in that direction.

Catherine found that she had an unseemly desire to laugh—and worse, to laugh without restraint. For she had a sudden grim vision of the small canal growing full with all the bodies that Grahame was throwing in it, and for some odd reason this seemed droll. Tom later told her that shock, combined with the macabre, frequently had such an effect. Hysteria, the old Greeks called it, he said, and it seemed a strange thing for him to know.

Grahame refused to slacken his pace and she could only keep up with the two men by running—something her heavily skirted gown made difficult.

"At last," said Grahame breathlessly, when they were in the coach again. "Drive me back to Antwerp if you would. In the crowded city we shall not be conspicuous—as we are here.''

''I would have thought,'' said Tom Trenchard, that true, simple-minded, honest rogue, ''that Antwerp would have been a safer bolt-hole than the one where we met you yesterday.''

''I had reason to believe that I was safer there, for I thought that none knew of the house—but I was wrong. Some traitor has informed on me, and now I must try to hide myself again.''

He said nothing more for a time, but sat there mumchance, although the meeting had supposedly been arranged for him to have a private word with them.

As they reached the outskirts of the City Tom asked him gently, ''Have you had any further thoughts, Master Grahame, on those matters which we spoke of yesterday?''

''Indeed and indeed. There is, in fact, little for us to discuss. I have decided that I shall say no more until I have the King's pardon in my hand, here in the Low Countries. I am not minded to risk my life by passing on information to you without any such guarantee. I have no wish to find myself facing the gallows, or the headsman's axe, the moment I reach England.''

This came out in a surly, grumbling voice, as though he had been taking lessons from Geordie. It was plain to both Tom and Catherine that two attempts at his life had rendered Grahame not only fearful, but non-amenable.

''I can think of nothing further,'' Grahame complained, ''until I find a safe haven in Antwerp itself.

You will bid the coachman drive me to the main square. From there I have a safe house to go to—the address of which I shall reveal to no one—and from thence I will send you a message when I am ready to speak to you again.''

''No more than that?'' asked Tom.

''Not until you have sent word to England by the next boat, asking for a letter containing a written promise of a pardon. Only after that letter arrives shall we talk again. I do not expect the pardon itself to arrive immediately, you understand, I know that such matters take time.''

''And how do I contact you?'' asked Tom. Things had not gone as well as he had hoped, but in such enterprises as these, they rarely did.

Grahame smiled. ''Can you not guess, man? Speak to Amos Shooter. He will act as our go-between. You may trust him.''

''Trust Amos Shooter!'' exclaimed Tom when they had set Grahame down in the main square, and had paid and dismissed their coach. ''After meeting him again, I had as lief trust the devil. But as he is all we have, then trust him we must. But not much.''

He, too, fell silent until they were safely back in their parlour at the inn where Geordie had a cold meal waiting for them.

''Prepare to work, wife,'' Tom said through a mouthful of good Dutch ham. ''I want you to write a letter to London in the code we were given before we set out, informing them of Grahame's demands. I know you write a better hand than I do.''

He had discovered this on the previous day when

they had been practising the use of the code. Catherine's script was clear and clerkly, Tom's was ornate, flowing and hard to read.

"You shall be my secretary," he told her. "I shall devise strategy. Between us we must bring this awkward dog to heel."

Enciphering the letter, not the actual writing of it, took some time. Tom had told her what to say, and after that left her to it, going downstairs to join Geordie in the taproom.

Painstaking as always, Catherine reread the letter before adding her codename at its end. It was Oenone, the name of the nymph with whom Paris of Troy had fallen in love on Mount Ida before the three goddesses had made him choose between them.

He had given Venus the golden apple as the loveliest of the three, and she had rewarded him with the most beautiful woman on earth, Helen, the wife of the Greek King Menelaus. Paris had carried her off and as a result the Trojan War had been fought, Paris had been killed, and Troy had fallen.

Some jester back in London had chosen their names, for Tom had been given that of Menelaus, the deserted husband. Well, thought Catherine, they could scarcely have called him Paris, for Paris had been as beautiful as a god, which Tom Trenchard was not.

She thought that it would be some time before he returned so when she had finished the letter, she went over to her small trunk and fetched from it several sheets of paper and began to write on them.

She laughed to herself a little at Tom's surprise if

he were to read what she was so busily putting down on paper.

For Catherine had not lied when she had told Tom that she had not met the man, Will Wagstaffe, who had recently taken the London stage by storm and whose next play, *The Braggart, or, Lackwit Married,* had been commissioned by Betterton and was eagerly awaited. None but Betterton knew that Will Wagstaffe was no man, but the young actress who had played the heroine Belinda in *The Braggart, or, Lackwit in Love.*

When Catherine had handed the manuscript of her first play, *Love's Last Jest,* to Betterton, she had told him that she had been given it by a friend who wished him to read it, for she feared that if Betterton knew that she, a mere woman, had written a play, he would not have taken it seriously.

He had been fulsome in his praise of it, but had told her that at least two scenes needed to be rewritten to suit the talents of the actors whom he thought might play in them. "I shall have to meet Mr Wagstaffe to discuss the matter with him," he had ended. "I take it that Wagstaffe is not his real name."

"No, indeed," Catherine had said uneasily. She hardly knew how to tell him the truth, but needs must, she could not falter now.

"Wagstaffe is not a man," she blurted out at him. "Oh, Mr Betterton, pray forgive me, but 'tis I who wrote *Love's Last Jest,* and none other."

At first he had not believed her. But she had finally convinced him, and as she had originally thought, he was unhappy about the fact that a woman had written it. "Will the public come to see it?" he asked her. "We cannot afford a failure."

It was Catherine who had solved the problem for him. Much though she wanted to be acknowledged as the play's author, she knew that there was little chance of Betterton, or Tom Killigrew, the manager of the Duke's Theatre, putting the play on if they knew that she had written it.

"Need you," she suggested, "advertise it as by a woman at all? Wagstaffe was the name I gave myself, and Wagstaffe it may stay. You can tell Killigrew that that is not the author's real name, but that he is a recluse who wishes to have nothing to do with its staging, and desires no public acknowledgement as the play's author. You and I can work together to make any necessary alterations when it first goes into rehearsal."

"A splendid notion," said Betterton approvingly, "for your play is too good to lose. You, having been on the boards yourself, obviously know what will come well over the footlights. Will Wagstaffe shall take the credit, whilst you take the money."

And so it was. And it was strange that no one but Tom Trenchard had thought the name odd, although Catherine had, as he surmised, christened herself so in jest to get Betterton to read the play—and was then compelled to go on with the jest once it had been successful.

"The trouble is," Betterton had told her frankly, "that this play is so down to earth about the relationships between men and women, that it would ruin your reputation if it came to be known that you had written it. And you cannot want that. No, no, you must be Mrs Wilhelmina Wagstaffe only to me!''

The very last thing which Catherine wanted was that prying Tom Trenchard should discover who Will Wagstaffe really was. For he would be sure to think, as Betterton had suggested, that only a whore could have written it.

It was a pity that Wagstaffe's name had intrigued him so much. He had obviously seen the jest contained in the name, and not for the first time Catherine was surprised, not only by the depth of his knowledge, but also by his intuitive grasp. It was interesting, to say the least, how much that he did or said was at odds with his description of himself as a simple-minded rogue.

Given all this, it was really unsafe for her to be writing it in Antwerp at all, but the devil of it was that all the exciting things which had happened to her were spurring her on to write. New scenes, new jokes and new denouements were pouring into her brain so rapidly that she could scarce write quickly enough.

Sighing—for she thought that she heard Tom's footsteps on the stairs—Catherine stuffed her papers into the writing case inside her trunk and sat down demurely at the table. When Tom arrived, Geordie following, she was reading the letter which she had apparently just completed to make sure that it was correct.

"So, Mistress, you have finished this woundy business for me?''

"Aye, as a good wife should,'' Catherine told him sweetly—and caught Geordie's approving nod. Here was a woman who knew her place!

Tom read it over swiftly, scarcely mouthing the words aloud as he read—a trick that also betrayed to Catherine that she could not trust a word he said of himself. Few men but scholars could read anything without reading it aloud.

"Very fine," he told her. "Plain and simple. That may go as it stands. I shall ride this very night to the nearest harbour where an English packet leaves for home, for time is something that we have little of.

"Geordie shall stay with you as protection. You may let slip to our landlady that I am off on a business mission. As a good Lowlander, that will please her and prove that we are people of substance."

For no reason at all, for surely there was no danger here, Catherine was afraid for him. "How long will you be gone?"

Tom read her aright. "Never fear, sweeting. I shall be safe enough. I am not Grahame, who has never been to the wars." He was buckling on his rapier as he spoke, and picking up the horse pistol that Geordie had loaded for him.

"I have supped well, which is the first rule for a soldier on campaign. If by some mischance I do not return within two days, then you and Geordie must continue our mission without me, and pray that I may at last return here better late than never. I have left Geordie enough money to keep you both from starving. Follow Grahame, do not lose him, and use Amos Shooter—which may prove a little hard without me. You see, I trust you, sweeting. Here is my farewell to you."

Before Catherine could stop him he was enveloping

her in a bear hug, and was well and truly kissing her goodbye.

"Miss me a little, sweetheart," he told her, "and do you look after her for me, Geordie," and with these final words he was gone.

The room was strangely empty without him. And quiet, too. In the short time that they had been together, Catherine had grown accustomed to him; to his mockery as well as his rare tenderness and—confess it, Catherine!—to the feeling of safety that his mere presence gave her.

Geordie said, breaking the unaccustomed silence, "Do not fret, mistress. He will be back. It would be a rare man who could kill my master. He's a match for any three of 'em."

His earthy comfort set Catherine laughing, a tearful laugh. "Oh, Geordie, I wish that you could have gone with him. I would have felt happier so."

He shook his head, "Not on, mistress. My master would never have left you alone, not him. Oh, he trusts you, as he trusts me, but he would not leave a lone woman here among the wolves who would have murdered Grahame... No, no," and he shook his head again until Catherine thought that it would fall off his shoulders.

And so to bed, alone as usual. But it was strange not to think of him there, in the next room, with Geordie, and whether she trusted him, or no, Catherine was beginning to find that her world without Tom Trenchard in it was a quieter, but also a lonelier, sadder place.

Chapter Six

"Mistress Trenchard, is it not?"

To while away the second morning of Tom's absence, Catherine had gone shopping in Antwerp's vast market place, larger and busier than any she had visited before. Even though Antwerp might no longer be the richest port in Europe and one of its wealthiest cities, it was still a bustling and thriving place.

Not only was it famous as a centre where diamonds were cut, bought and sold, but it did a brisk trade with other European countries. Catherine had just been admiring some fine Brussels lace—far too expensive for her to buy—when Isabelle Shooter, a footman in attendance, came up to her.

"Indeed I am," Catherine replied. "We have the pleasure of meeting again."

Mrs Shooter—or should it be Madame? Catherine was not quite sure—looked around her. "Your husband is not with you, I see."

Some explanation seemed to be called for. Catherine offered it. "No, he is away on business, and I expect his return this evening. Meantime, his man, Geordie, guards me as you see.''

Isabelle Shooter quite saw. Geordie was staring glumly at her, his usual expression, but not one that she expected to find on a servant's face. Her own man stood by, his face coldly impassive—as a good servant's should be.

I really ought to know Geordie's surname, Catherine thought, not that Isabelle Shooter needs to be aware of it, but I should.

Isabelle was speaking again. ''My husband was saying only this morning that he would like you and Captain Trenchard to sup with us one evening. He would like to reminisce about old times when they were very young men together. I was on my way to the inn where you lodge when, by good fortune, I caught sight of you.

''Amos suggested that tomorrow evening would be a good time—he has a friend whom he would like Captain Trenchard to meet. You could send word by your man in the morning as to whether that would be convenient or no.''

Captain Trenchard, was he? What next? There seemed to be no doubt that Tom had been a soldier—as he had claimed. But what else had he been? Catherine was sure that he had been something else. This spying business appeared to be catching, for now she was practising it on him—and hoping that he would not practise it on her.

''Certainly, madame. I am sure that Tom, my husband, would be as pleased as I am to sup with you.''

''Excellent, Mrs Trenchard, then that is settled,'' and she gave Catherine her kind smile. ''Now I understand

that this is your first visit to Antwerp and, if you so
wish, it would give me great pleasure to show you
some of its fairest sights. We are near to our cathedral,
Notre Dame, which is not only the largest church in
Flanders, but has the tallest spire. Even better, inside it
are paintings by Peter Paul Rubens, which no one who
visits Antwerp should miss seeing.''

''That would give me great pleasure,'' said Catherine truthfully. ''It is most kind of you to offer.''

''Not all, my dear,'' and chatting agreeably, Isabelle
Shooter was as good as her word. Catherine spent a
happy hour forgetting about spies and plotting, and
whether Tom was safe or not.

It was as they were walking away from the cathedral
that Isabelle Shooter said something that set Catherine
thinking.

''Amos has given me some letters to post to his family in England, and I must not enjoy myself with you
so much that I forget to call at the office and see them
on their way.''

''There is a regular service to England, then, despite
the war?'' Catherine asked as casually as she could.

''Indeed, and since trade is our country's life blood
a good postal service is essential. If you are to be here
for some time, you may wish to use it to correspond
with your family in England. I will show you where to
go.''

Whilst Catherine was busy thanking Isabelle for her
continuing kindnesses, she was also busy remembering
that Tom had told her and Geordie that in order to send
their letter to England he would need to leave Antwerp
to find a packet boat which would deliver it! Either he

was ignorant that an efficient postal service existed, or he had been lying to her, and was engaged in some secret activity whilst almost certainly leaving his letter at the post office before he did so.

Given what she knew of him, Catherine was sure that he had been lying. The moment she and Isabelle had parted among exclamations of mutual friendship and gratitude, she turned on Geordie.

"Exactly what has your master been doing for the last two days, Geordie?" she asked him, her voice dangerous.

Geordie showed her his most defeated countenance. "Sending your letter on its way," he mumbled. "What else?"

"What else, indeed! You heard what Mrs Shooter said. That there is a good postal service between Antwerp and England. And since our letter was enciphered, there is no reason why we should not use it."

Geordie shrugged his shoulders. "He *said* that he was taking the letter to post elsewhere—that's all I know." He spoiled this a little by remarking ungraciously, "He don't tell me everything. That he don't. Only to look after you."

Catherine gave up. For the time being, at least. When Tom arrived back in Antwerp, *if* he arrived back, that was, she would ask him what games he was playing with them.

Her opportunity to do so came sooner than she had expected. On her return to the inn she found Tom seated in their small parlour, pulling off his boots.

"Oh, you're back," she said coldly, well aware that she sounded ungracious, and unwelcoming.

"And a very good day to you too, wife," Tom returned cheerfully. He was always cheerful, damn him, thought Catherine crossly. "And did you have a hard time of it, husband? Shall I send for a tankard of ale for you, my dear husband?" he added, tossing his second boot into the corner where Geordie retrieved it and began to polish it lovingly.

"Did you have a hard time of it, my dear husband?" Catherine echoed sardonically. "Travelling miles to deliver a letter which you could have safely posted in Antwerp? Or so Isabelle Shooter tells me. Where exactly were you? And what were you doing that you needed to lie to me?"

Tom was too busy tying the broad ribbons of his shoes to answer her immediately. At last he said, "Suppose I tell you that I did travel some distance to post the letter, would you believe me?"

"No!" Catherine's expression was mutinous.

"Then I shan't. And you are right not to believe me. It's a curst business that Isabelle Shooter chose to put a finger in the pie and enlighten you."

"She didn't do it deliberately. It only came out in passing."

"And now you are hectoring me *in passing,* I suppose."

Tom rose and walked over to where Catherine was standing, head high. Behind her Geordie was watching them both, a half-smile on his usually hangdog face.

"Suppose something had happened to you while you were away? How were Geordie and I to help you if we had no notion of where you were? Unless you had told Geordie what you were up to, that is."

"Nowt said to me, mistress," grumbled Geordie, admiring his handiwork on Tom's boots. "As I told you earlier."

"True enough," said Tom. "And know this, wife and servant. I had good reason to go on a dangerous errand without telling you. Mainly because what neither of you don't know you can't blab about—either in light conversation, or in answer to the questions of a torturer to save yourself further pain. Let that be enough—for that is all I shall tell you."

There was suddenly nothing light or cheerful about him. The unleashed power that Catherine had once or twice scented in him was fully in evidence. There was no gainsaying or arguing with him in this mood, that was plain.

"Yes, wife." He was very near to her now, his voice light and mocking again. "Nothing to say? Strange that, you are usually full of words."

Why should tears prick behind her eyes? Why should Geordie look so downcast?

"Yes, I *do* have something to say. By chance I met Isabelle Shooter in the square. She told me that she was bringing us an invitation to sup with them tomorrow evening. She said that Amos was inviting an old friend of yours so that you might speak of days gone by. I accepted on your behalf. Was I right to do so?"

He bent down to give her a gentle kiss on her nose, the kind of careless caress with which a man rewards an obedient wife.

"Very right. I wonder of whom Amos speaks? I shall discover tomorrow night perhaps. Did she say aught else?"

"Nothing of import. She showed me the cathedral and Rubens's paintings. Afterwards we drank tea at a stall not far away—and that is all."

"Quite enough," he told her, kissing her lightly again. "Geordie," he said over his shoulder to his servant, "if you clean my boots much more, you will wear them away.

"If you are hanging about because you harbour fears that I may beat the mistress for scorning me, then dismiss them. She is a clever lady, and sees far too much—which in this Godforsaken venture is an advantage, not a disadvantage. Be off with you, and arrange for our supper to be sent up before the hour is out."

So Geordie had appointed himself his supposed wife's protector—even from her supposed husband. This amused Tom Trenchard not a little. But it saddened him also. The devil of it was that he had had to deceive them both—but with the best of intentions.

Like Geordie, he shrugged his shoulders. Surely he was running mad to care what his supposed wife, the actress and doxy, Cleone Dubois, and his servant, Geordie Charlton, thought about his actions—which were no business of theirs, since he, and he alone, was the master agent whom Gower had sent to do the business of the State.

Both Tom and Catherine dressed themselves in the very finest garment that they had brought with them to Antwerp in order to visit Amos and Isabelle Shorter on the following evening.

There was a kind of armed truce between them. Tom had spent the day God knows where. He had gone out shortly after breakfast—without Geordie—and he did not return until the late afternoon—a little the worse for wear. He had plainly been drinking, but was by no means drunk.

Before he had left the inn that morning, Tom had ordered Geordie to keep watch over Catherine whilst he was gone. "Since you have appointed yourself my wife's knight, then knight you must be," he had said. "She is not to go anywhere without you, and you are to guard her at all times, even in the inn."

Geordie had made no reply so Tom added sternly, "You hear me, man?"

"Aye, master. I hear you. Your voice ain't a soft un."

So his supposed wife was making his usually taciturn servant mutinous, was she? No matter.

Tom was going to meet a man whose name he had been given by yet another agent during his two days' absence. It was that of one Giles Newman, who was a former crony, and now an enemy, of Colonel Bampfylde, the leader of a small army of Puritans in exile in the Netherlands who were busy plotting to start a revolution in England. Newman knew of Grahame's involvement through his informant, a deserter from Bampfylde's army.

It was probably a fruitless errand, and whilst Grahame might yet fall victim to Catherine's charms, his informant had also told him that Newman was a dour man, a woman-hater, since his wife had deserted him to become the mistress of a member of Charles II's court.

He was to be found most days at a tavern called The

Princess of Cleves where he had a room. Whether he was disaffected enough to give away both the secrets of the Dutch Navy and of Grahame, his informant did not know, "But no harm in trying, eh?"

The Princess of Cleves proved to be a small tavern in a dirty back alley, and was a notable exception to the general cleanliness of the taverns in Antwerp. It was more like one in St Giles back in London where the bully boys of Alsatia hung out, was Tom's verdict on it.

He looked pretty shabby himself, having left behind his good boots and his fine clothes. He had rammed a dirty-grey-felt steeple hat over a ratty-looking black wig which concealed his betraying red-gold hair. No one looked askance at him when he walked into the smoke-filled parlour, where games of chess and draughts were in full swing, since he looked like every seedy adventurer who was already there.

He asked the pot-bellied landlord whether Giles Newman was in his room—no one in the parlour seemed to answer to the description he had been given.

"Aye. Upstairs, first door on the right," drawled the landlord round his clay pipe.

Upstairs was reached by a crude, open-stepped wooden stairway that led to a long landing from which several doors opened. Tom rapped on Newman's, but no one answered. He rapped again. Still nothing—and he could hear no signs of life coming from inside.

The landlord might be mistaken, but Tom thought not. He pushed at the door—which opened. He found himself in a dark room, pitifully furnished, which stank vilely of tobacco. There was a small table in the centre of it on which a clay pipe rested, gently smoking. One wall contained a bunk bed, its curtains shut.

There was no sign of Giles Newman other than a pair of battered boots standing against the door and a shabby black cloak hanging above them. Tom hesitated a moment before pulling out the long dagger that he always carried with him, concealed by his dirty buff jacket.

Holding it at the ready, he walked over to the bed and flung its curtains back to find there, lying on his back, a man, horribly dead. He had been strangled, a useful method for a murderer who wanted to make sure that his victim could not cry for help. By all seeming the man was Newman, and his murderer was not long gone, for his body was still warm.

And now Tom was in a quandary. To go downstairs to tell the landlord what he had found was to invite both suspicion and investigation—neither of which a secret agent of the British crown wished to incur. To disappear through the dirty window on the opposite wall—which was wide open—and not to reappear in the tap room below was also to invite suspicion when Newman's body was found.

On balance, the second option seemed safer. But before he left he might as well take the opportunity to search Newman's room in case it contained anything that would give him some clue as to who had murdered him, or to his recent activities.

Tom looked carefully around him. A pack, half-full, had been thrown down on a chair beside the bed. A small book, and a pair of worn gloves, had spilled from it on to the floor.

He picked up the book and leafed through it. It was a collection of prayers and homilies. Newman's name had been written on the fly-leaf in a cramped hand. Whether or no he had used it to pray was doubtful. What he *had* used it for, however, was quite plain.

Certain letters had been ringed and others had been written below them. This told him that Newman had been corresponding with someone—who?—and this was the code that they had been using. The other man, or men, would possess a copy of the same book, similarly marked.

It was the work of a moment to slip it into the pocket of his buff jacket. Who knew how useful it might be in the future? From such small discoveries might a great secret be unravelled. Otherwise, though, the room was empty of anything but the sad and soiled bric-a-brac of Newman's lonely and wasted life.

He was considering what to do next when he heard the sound of footsteps outside. Someone was mounting the stairs and walking along the landing! It would not do to be found alone with a man brutally murdered. There was nowhere secret to hide, so Tom flattened himself against the wall by the door so that if anyone opened it he could leap upon them, and stun them before they knew that he was there.

He heard a man cursing loudly, and a door banging…followed by silence. Whoever had come upstairs had done so in order to go to their own room, not to find out what Tom Trenchard—or Giles Newman— was up to. He let his breath out in a great whoosh, and considered what to do next. Common sense told him to get as far away as possible from The Princess of Cleves as soon as he could.

He looked out of the window, which he judged to be just large enough for him to escape by. It was doubtless the means by which the murderer had entered to do his fell work.

Below it was a lean-to shed, whose roof was not more than ten feet above the ground. No one appeared to be about—other than a goat tethered in the corner of a small yard-cum-garden of a kind often found in the Low Countries. Beyond the garden was a narrow unpaved lane that ran behind the tavern and the adjoining houses.

Tom thought for a moment. It would be to his advantage if it were some time before Newman's body was found. Well, he could easily arrange that.

He walked over to the bed, threw Newman's body over his shoulder, and carried it to the open window. After that, as gently as he could, he manoeuvred Newman through it and allowed him to slide slowly down the sloping lean-to roof before he fell to the ground. With a bit of luck the ignorant yokels in the inn might assume he had fallen out of the window and killed himself in a drunken stupor.

All this Tom accomplished with a minimum of noise before he wriggled with some difficulty through the open window. From thence he slid down the roof, before jumping to the ground—just avoiding Newman's body.

He recovered himself, and walked away as coolly as he could, meeting no one either in the narrow lane at the back of the inn, or in the larger one to which it led.

When Newman's body was ultimately found, the landlord would be bound to remember the man who had asked for him—and who had never reappeared. Tom knew that there had been nothing distinctive about him, and fortunately the landlord had seemed half-asleep and quite indifferent to what was going on about him, as had been most of his customers.

He could only hope that the luck that had been with him so far in Antwerp would hold. In any case, it was likely that the death of such a man as Newman, down to his last groat, would not be considered worth an enquiry by the authorities. Good riddance to bad rubbish was probably their motto where such as he were concerned!

To allay any suspicions as to his own activities he carried on walking until he reached a more respectable tavern, The White Horse, where he called attention to himself by appearing to drink more than he actually did. Most of his ale went to water one of the large pot plants that adorned the inn. He also started a noisy quarrel, which he picked with a man against whom he played chess.

He had played to lose—but loudly complained when he did so. His presence there was sure to be remembered. Quietened down at last by the landlord and his recent opponent, he finally staggered out, reeling round the corner, only walking steadily when he was out of sight of the inn before returning to Geordie, Catherine, and something resembling normality before preparing to visit Amos.

Chapter Seven

"This is better than a slice of bread and hard cheese before a campfire on a cold night, eh, Tom?"

Amos Shooter raised a glassful of his best red wine high in order to toast Tom, Catherine, and the guest to whom he had wished to introduce Tom—who had turned out to be William Grahame. This evening Grahame was no longer the shabby man whom Catherine had first met. He was splendid in dark blue velvet and a collar of Brussels lace. His signet ring was a showy one: altogether he looked as rich a merchant as Amos himself.

The Shooters' dining room was truly a haven of comfort and wealth. The *buffet,* loaded with silver plate, was of richly carved oak, as was the massive dining table and its matching chairs. A tapestry, showing the *Judgment of Paris,* hung on one wall. Opposite to it was a painting of a young woman in a blue gown playing the virginals. When Catherine had admired it, Isabelle Shooter had told her that it was by a little-known Dutch painter, Jan Vermeer.

A convex mirror, framed elaborately in gold, and

supported by two gilt cherubs, adorned the third wall and reflected the company, turning them into caricatures of themselves. Catherine had never seen its like before.

On the fourth wall brocade hangings of the deepest blue, embroidered with silver fleurs-de-lis, hid a large lattice window. The dining room's black-and-white tiled floor stretched from it into the corridor outside. A Persian rug had been thrown down before the empty hearth beneath the mirror. Everything in the room and the house spoke of wealth and taste.

Isabelle had inherited the house from her father, but most of the furnishings had been acquired since her marriage to Amos. Earlier, flown a little with wine, he had twitted Tom about his apparent lack of success in life, and Tom had shrugged his shoulders sadly.

"We are not all winners like you, Amos," he had said, lying in his teeth. "But I have survived exile and am now reasonably content with my modest station. And after all, I have my greatest treasure with me, my dear wife Catherine."

"And Geordie, your faithful servant," Catherine could not help saying. "Do not forget Geordie!"

"Nay, I'd never do that—as Amos knows. Through poverty and modest affluence Geordie has always been faithful to me. Remember Geordie liberating a fowl for us, Amos, when we were besieging that town the Turks took in Macedonia—I forget its name."

"And a damned skinny thing it was, too—saving your presence, ladies," Amos had bellowed. "But better than starving, eh, Tom?"

It was then that he had reminisced about their difficult life together on campaign, and Tom had answered him in kind. Grahame smiled benignly at them as they spoke of battle, hardship, and death.

Neither he nor Tom were drinking heavily, leaving that to Amos, who quietened down a little when a great dish of oysters, new bread and butter, and sundry sliced lemons, accompanied by a small ewer of a spicy sauce, had been brought in, as well as a flagon of white wine and several large cheeses. The business of eating became more important than the business of talking.

Catherine had never seen such food nor such magnificence on a table before. In the middle of the snowy white damask cloth stood a centrepiece of gilded silver, consisting of two cherubs holding up a great dish on which reclined a pair of lovers in classical dress. ''Venus and Adonis,'' Isabelle told Catherine. ''It is a neat conceit, is it not?''

Neat, indeed! If we sold it it would keep Tom and me for years, was Catherine's inward thought—and then she blushed at herself. Tom and me! Whatever was she doing? She was going on as though they were really married, and not pretending to be so in order to find out what Amos Shooter and William Grahame were up to.

She was also troubled by Tom's behaviour—again as though she were his wife. Something was wrong with him, and had been wrong ever since he had returned to the inn smelling of drink and tobacco. He was oddly distrait, as though he were thinking of something else whilst he laughed and talked so easily over the supper table. With a sense of shock, Catherine realised that she only knew this because she had come to understand him so well.

I am turning into a female Geordie, was her amused response to this discovery. She caught Tom's eye on her, and gave him a dazzling smile. This seemed, for once, to overset him, for he looked away before squeezing lemon juice on to his oyster and swallowing it.

The oyster despatched, he spoke directly to Amos and Grahame. He thought that for once being straightforward might pay more than being devious. "Did either of you ever meet Giles Newman? He was one of those who joined Bampfylde's small army. A little bird told me that they had a falling out. I seem to remember that he was with us when we fought the Turks."

This was true. Tom had spent some time since finding Newman's body trying to puzzle out where he had met him before. It was only when he had idly mentioned Macedonia to Amos that he had remembered the man who had served with them there so briefly.

"That canting Puritan," snorted Amos through a mouthful of bread and cheese before Grahame could speak. He had long since demolished his share of the oysters. "Glad to see the back of him. Odd fellow. He had a little prayer book he used to read from. Always asked God to give us victory before we engaged in even the mildest skirmish.

"I could never imagine why he wasn't back in England, sharing in his kind's victory. Haven't thought of him for years. Certainly haven't seen him since then."

He cut himself another large chunk of cheese before

asking Grahame, ''Did you ever meet him? Once seen, never forgotten,'' and he gave a noisy laugh.

''Heard of him,'' offered Grahame, accepting more wine from the manservant who was unobtrusively waiting at table. ''Never met him—or if I ever did I don't recall him. Many like him, you know.''

Tom, who was watching Grahame and Shooter, too, in case either of them betrayed that they knew more about his affairs than they ought, wondered cynically whether one of the two men sitting opposite to him was Newman's murderer—or had hired his murderer. He also wondered how Amos had come to know Grahame.

Why he had been invited to meet Grahame was a simpler question to answer. Grahame almost certainly wished to speak to him and Catherine privately on neutral ground.

And so it proved, for once the topic of Giles Newman was over and then the meal, Amos helped his wife out of her chair, announcing jovially, ''I believe that Master Grahame and our two other guests have business to do together, and would be happy to engage in it in the privacy of our home. That being so, we shall leave them to talk for a little before we serve coffee in the parlour overlooking the garden.''

''A tactful man, our host,'' Grahame remarked once they were alone.

''Not always,'' Tom replied drily. ''But he has supplied a convenient opportunity for you to speak further with me on the matter we raised with you the other day.''

''True,'' said Grahame, ''for it would be wiser for

you not to be seen visiting me, nor me visiting you. There are curious eyes everywhere—as I'm sure you know.''

Tom had no time for further havering. ''So?'' he asked, raising his brows.

''So, *I* am curious. Have you yet written to your masters back in London, concerning the pardon of which we spoke?''

Tom looked meaningfully at Catherine, giving her, as the actors said, her cue, which she promptly accepted.

''Certainly, Master Grahame. On the very evening of the day on which we met you, I enciphered a letter to London containing your demands, and my husband saw that it was posted immediately.''

''Good, very good. I see that you have a useful wife, Captain Trenchard.''

''Master Trenchard or Tom, I am no longer a captain in any army,'' Tom returned. ''We shall speak with you when we receive a reply from London. And yes, my wife is useful—and loving! She is particularly adept at translating coded messages.''

This last, suitably cryptic, remark, Catherine assumed, was meant for her, not Grahame. She rewarded both men with her sweetest—and falsest—actress's smile.

Grahame responded to it. ''I will only say this to you, that the information I have relates to the plans of the Dutch Navy, and is of the greatest importance.''

Tom nodded thoughtfully on hearing this. Catherine, watching him, was suddenly seeing a different man.

She was beginning to wonder how many sides there were to Tom Trenchard.

"Moreover," Grahame added—Catherine thought that he was enjoying dangling bait before them—"I have other, most pertinent information regarding other great matters of state. But these must await my pardon."

Catherine took a hand in the game. Smiling her sweet smile again, she asked softly, "And there is nothing that will make you reconsider that decision, Master Grahame? For would not London look more favourably on you were you to send them such vital information without demanding an immediate return for so doing?"

Grahame rose and came over to where she sat to take her hand and kiss it. "Oh, you are a clever lady, are you not, Mistress Trenchard!" He paused before adding significantly, "I can think of some inducements that might persuade me..."

To his astonishment, Tom, who fully understood what Grahame was asking of Catherine, was filled with as much jealous rage as would have been appropriate were she actually his wife! A most inapt response, since beforehand he, Gower and Arlington had all agreed that to tempt Grahame with Catherine would be the ploy he would use in case he proved intransigent.

What had changed was that then he did not know her, and now he did. For the first time in his adventurous life he had come to respect a woman, not merely for her looks and the charm of her sex, but for the intelligence and courage which she also possessed, and was constantly displaying. It took him all his strength of will not to say something cutting both the Grahame—and to his supposed wife.

For Catherine, playing the game that she and Tom had previously agreed on, was still allowing him to hold her hand and was saying softly, "Oh, Master Grahame, something may be arranged, you may be sure of that."

Tom spoke at last in a cold voice. "I beg you to do as my wife asks, and reconsider."

Grahame bowed. "I note what you say, sir. And now we must adjourn in order to drink the Shooters' excellent coffee, a new and rare experience. They live well—as tonight's entertainment has proved."

It was plain that he intended to say no more. Nothing further of any great import was said by any of the company. Isabelle Shooter produced a guitar and sang to them, Catherine joining in at her bidding. The men listened and applauded. It was not, indeed, until they were walking home, Geordie behind them—he had been entertained in the kitchen—that anything serious was said at all, and that by Tom.

"Did you have to hold that scaly traitor's hand so lovingly?" he almost snarled at Catherine.

He was jealous! He must be. By the light of the moon Catherine looked up at him and his hard face was thunderous. He looked like a very Jove about to cast down a lightning bolt to destroy his enemies!

"Why, husband," she replied gaily and naughtily, for it was her turn to twit him, and she did not intend to miss the chance he had offered her, "I was but doing the bidding of you and those who sent me here. Charm William Grahame, you all said, if it be necessary. And since it seemed necessary, this poor girl did your bidding. And, having done so, I have earned from you, not praise, but blame. You leave me all at sea.''

She spread her hands out, and assumed an expression of charming bewilderment, looking both innocent and bewitching.

Yes, bewitching, thought Tom Trenchard savagely. But he must never forget that she was an actress, used to deceit. For was not all acting a deceit? The actor assumed courage, pity, despair, and innocence. And it was all a sham. How the devil was he to know, when dealing with such a Circe, whether she was innocent or not?

He told her so. Oh, thought Catherine gleefully. It is I who have him on the end of a string now, and not him me. Can it be that he is beginning to feel—oh, so inconveniently—a little of what I am beginning to feel for him?

For if he were jealous, what did that tell her about his feelings for her? A man could not be jealous of a woman whom he regarded as a mere tool, a sprat to catch a mackerel, as the saying had it. A mackerel called William Grahame!

Well, Master Tom Trenchard need not trouble himself overmuch, for the so-called Mistress Catherine Trenchard had not the slightest intention of getting into bed with William Grahame—or with any other man.

Keeping Tom Trenchard out of it, though, was quite another matter, Catherine was to find. His foul mood continued all the way back to their inn and was still there when they reached the parlour. He cast his hat down on one chair after sending Geordie away, before flinging himself into another and looking steadily at her.

"You seemed to take great pleasure in beginning to seduce Grahame—wife!"

"I was neither taking pleasure in seducing him, nor am I your wife," Catherine said evenly, removing her cap. An action that resulted in her hair falling about her shoulders. A glorious sight that did nothing to improve Tom's temper. He could only think how much Grahame would enjoy seeing it.

What Catherine was enjoying was that for once she was possessing power over Tom. At the same time the knowledge of his jealousy was doing strange things to her. Besides the desire to bait him a little, another stronger desire was growing.

She wanted to comfort him, to take his hand and stroke it, saying, "Nay, dearest heart, it was not his hand I wished to hold, but yours. Not he whom I wished to kiss, but you. Kiss me, Tom! Be comforted"—for her whole body yearned to comfort him.

Maudlin! She was growing maudlin, just like the girl in the play that she was writing who was equally besotted with a man whom Catherine had not yet decided was worthy of her.

But what had worth to do with love—or lust? For this must be lust, must it not? These internal quiverings at the mere sight of him, this desire to touch and hold him—to be touched and held by him—could only be lust. Was this splendid savage truly the one, the only one, whom Catherine Wood could love?

Tom rose and strode towards her. "What now, sweeting? Shall we practise together what you have offered Grahame? It would not do for your arts to be a little backward through lack of use.''

His voice was gentle, not angry, and the arms he slipped around her were gentle, too. And his kiss…Catherine drowned in it—again. Until she remembered the insult that he had offered her before the kiss. Her arts, indeed! They were of quite a different order from those of which he had accused her. He might rather have referred to *his* arts, for he was never the same with her twice together.

Now he was being gentle where before he had been rough: as gentle as he had been when he had been succouring her on the packet. Which was the true man? The one who had almost assaulted her the other evening—or the one who had been kindness itself when she had been seasick—and was being kind now?

''No, don't fear me, sweeting,'' he told her softly, his hand rising to stroke the lips which he had just kissed. ''I shall not hurt you—quite the contrary. Let us make the sweetest music of all together. I know that you are drawn to me, your bright eyes and your soft mouth tell me so—so why refuse me? Let us love the night away.''

Oh, the devil was in him, for he knew so well how to tempt a poor girl! This poor girl was almost ready to fall before him. How could she say to him, ''If I were not virgin I would gladly lie with you. But I am and wish to remain so. I have sworn my vows both to God and to Diana, and I will not break them.'' What did the other Will say? ''To thine own self be true, thou canst not then be false to any man.''

''No,'' she told him, and was proud of how steady

her voice was. "I will not lie with you. I am no whore, no matter that you think all actresses must be fallen women. I will tempt Grahame for you, but I shall not lie with him—how ever often you may ask me to do so."

His arms were around her again, and he was lifting her up. "Your pretty refusals only tempt me the more," he whispered to her. He was holding her as though she were a child and he kissed her as one might kiss a child as he carried her towards their bedroom. "If you wish me to woo you slowly and patiently so that you may regard your surrender as no surrender, then I will do as you wish."

Catherine had been so surprised by the speed with which he had scooped her up that at first she made no resistance, but as he kicked the bedroom door open, she began to struggle. "Let me down, you big bully. I vow you are worse than any Mohawk."

As she might have expected, this reference to the gangs of bully boys who roamed London's streets by night did not daunt him. He simply laughed at her. "If you think that, then you don't know Mohawks very well. Any self-respecting Mohawk would have pleasured you twice on the floor by now."

"And any self-respecting man would not take me against my will at all," she raged at him, beating on his broad chest with her fists.

"Hush, woman, and enjoy yourself," Tom said, throwing her on to the bed before bending over her and beginning to kiss her again, butterfly kisses, his hands behind his back, as though to emphasise that what he was doing was not against her will however much she cried out and protested.

Oh, she was nearly lost, for he knew the truth of her, damn him. Knew that, whatever she said, she desired him as much as he desired her. She also discovered another truth—an unwelcome one. In the past it had always been easy for her to keep her virginity for she had never truly been tempted before. No man's attraction for her had ever been powerful enough to breach her defences.

Whether or not she would have surrendered to him on the spot, without so much as an attempt to resist him, Catherine was never to know. "No," she whispered, half-heartedly. "No," trying to pull his hands away as Tom clambered on the bed to lie beside her and began to untie the laces of her bodice.

Even as he did so there was a noise of a door opening in the room outside, and of Geordie's voice, "Master?" he was calling plaintively, "Master?"

Tom's oath was ground out between his teeth as he rolled away from Catherine, and consigned Geordie to the lowest pit of Hell. Only the urgency in his servant's voice had the power to move him at all. Catherine, dazed, prostrate on the bed, could only regard Geordie as her unlikely saviour. She sat up slowly as Tom walked through the door to confront Geordie, who was looking even more hangdog than usual.

"Now what the devil is all this about, man?" he demanded. "And your explanation had better be a good one or I shall strangle you with your own guts."

This last came out in a half-comic, half-threatening growl that had Geordie cringing away from him.

"Be very sure, master, that I would not interrupt you at your…work, but that the reason is urgent. There is a sort of constable downstairs demanding to speak to you immediately, and threatening us all with arrest if you don't agree to see him at once."

"A constable? At this hour? What kind of constable?"

"A captain, a sort of soldier," Geordie whined. "How the devil should I know what these foreigners call themselves? I only know that he had a pair of dirty great pikemen with him, and I was like to be scared out of my wits."

"Difficult that," said Tom unkindly, "since you don't appear to possess any. Do you go downstairs, and tell him to come up at once."

"Too late, master," Geordie announced miserably, "for he is already here."

Pushing by him as he spoke came an important-looking fellow, wearing a steel bonnet and a steel cuirass over some sort of uniform. Two pikemen followed him. He was carrying a paper in his hand.

He looked from Tom to Catherine, who had advanced to stand beside him, before bellowing importantly, "If you are Thomas Trenchard, then my master, the chief magistrate, would have words with you on a matter of some urgency. You and your wife will accompany me to the Town Hall immediately."

Chapter Eight

Yawning behind his hand, the chief magistrate, one of the local representatives of the Austrian Empire, rose from his seat at a long table to greet them.

"Exceeding gracious of you to accede to my request so late into the night, Master Trenchard—and your good wife, too."

He spoke as though they had had any choice in the matter, thought Catherine sardonically, storing up all she saw and heard for future use in a play when she got back to London. If she ever did get back to London, that was!

The Town Hall was a splendid place, decorated with old arms and armour, recovered from Antwerp's long-ago sack. The tapestries on the wall were new and portrayed various episodes from the Bible: Abraham and Isaac, Joseph being sold into Egypt and the Judgement of Solomon—all in the richest of colours.

Despite his effusive greeting the magistrate, a still handsome and impressive man in his late fifties, made no attempt to offer them a chair but kept them standing whilst he sat and talked idly to them, asking how long they had been in Antwerp, from whence had they come, had they journeyed outside the city walls, and what was their business?

"I was a soldier, sir," replied Tom smoothly, telling the tale which he, Gower and Arlington had agreed on back in London. "My father left me a small competence and I have set up as a merchant in London, hoping to make a living out of importing luxuries from the Austrian Netherlands and Holland."

The magistrate steepled his hands together and remarked, as smooth as Tom, "Ah, that accounts for your visits to Amos Shooter, does it not?"

So they had been watched—as Tom was certain they would be. Had they trailed him on his visit to Giles Newman? Doubtless he had not long to wait to find out. He inclined his head and nodded, "Indeed. But I cannot believe that you have hailed me here in order to speak on matters of business."

This was, Catherine thought amusedly, the polite way of saying, "Hurry up and tell us exactly why we are here. We waste time otherwise." The magistrate was by no means put out.

"These are dangerous times," he said. "The French are at our borders, the English fight the Dutch. Naturally when foreigners arrive in our city we like to keep an eye on them and on their activities—and when a foreigner is found dead in our city we like to know how he came by his end—and why."

He paused. "I should be grateful for your help, sir."

This was cat-and-mouse tactics with a vengeance. It was difficult to know whether they were being threatened or not. Catherine, who not long ago had been fighting for her honour, now began to wonder whether she was fighting for her life. Tom seemed not a whit put out. He was as large and cheerful as ever.

"Whatever small thing we can do," he offered, smiling, "my wife and I will do it. Though I can guarantee that if a man was murdered, she for one did not do it. She faints at the sight of blood—and all violence distresses her."

Do I? Well, there's a thing about myself that I never knew—but a highly convenient one. I must remember to swoon if I am anywhere near a Flemish official when blood is about! With one clever stroke Tom has exempted me from all suspicion if the man was stabbed or cut down.

Catherine pulled out her kerchief and wiped her face with it as though the very idea of anything untoward distressed her.

"Interesting," said the magistrate with a frown. "I commiserate with you, Mistress Trenchard."

Why interesting? Was Tom's unspoken response. He had deliberately spoken of the murderer as being stabbed because he knew that Newman had been strangled. He hoped that, if it were Newman whom they were being questioned about, the magistrate would be likely to think him innocent of any knowledge of Newman's death if he got the mode of his dying wrong.

Catherine dropped a curtsy, and gave the magistrate a sweet smile, meant to disarm him. The magistrate smiled back before saying, "I wish to show Master Trenchard something, and now that he has told me of your aversion to violent death, I will spare you the sight."

He turned to Tom. "Come, sir. You will not object to doing me a small favour, I am sure. Your good wife will not be harmed during our absence. Blaise," he shouted to the footman who stood unobtrusively before a small door between the tapestries, "fetch Mistress Trenchard a glass of water. She looks a little faint. You, sir. This way."

The captain and the two pikemen behind them, a man carrying a branched candlestick before them, the magistrate walked Tom out of the main doorway, down a long panelled corridor to some stone steps that led down into the bowels of the building. He chatted agreeably all the way along the stone-floored passage that led to a heavy oak door.

He stood back to allow the captain to throw the door open. Before them was a large windowless room, lit only by a crude brass candelabra that stood by a long table which was covered by a grimy sheet. The magistrate led Tom to the table, threw back the sheet to reveal a very dead body, and said, looking sternly at him, "Do you know this man, Master Trenchard?"

Tom knew the man. It was Giles Newman. He decided to be exactly as truthful as he dared to be. "Yes. I knew him slightly. I last saw him in Macedonia when we were fighting the Turks. He left long before the campaign was over—sent on a mission to Vienna, it was said. Since then, nothing."

"Look well on him, Master Trenchard," said the magistrate, still holding the sheet back. "You came to speak with him, did you not? That is why you are in Antwerp, is it not?"

Tom said, and this at least was the truth. "No, sir. I

had no notion that Newman was resident in Antwerp, and my visit was, as I have said, solely concerned with trade.'' Which was what he had told Amos when they had talked privately together in the absence of the women.

"You may ask Amos Shooter, if you need confirmation of what I have told you,'' he added.

"Oh, I will, Master Trenchard, be assured of that.''

"I don't understand,'' said Tom slowly, "why you should connect me with Newman, a man I have not seen for many years.''

The magistrate threw the sheet back over the body and pulled a grimy piece of yellowed paper from his pocket. "This was discovered on Newman's body. Nothing of any value, and little in the way of private possessions was found in his room. This is the only thing which connects him with anyone else.''

Tom took the paper and read what was on it. Written there was the name Tom Trenchard—and nothing more. He shrugged his shoulders and handed the paper back to the magistrate. "I have no notion at all as to why he should have my name in his possession. Or of how he came to his death.''

"Oh, no, you know exactly how he came to his death,'' smiled the magistrate, watching him keenly. "You must have plainly seen when I showed you his body that he had been strangled. Did you strangle him, Master Trenchard?'' and he looked pointedly at Tom's large hands.

Tom spread those same hands, and shrugged his shoulders again. "No, indeed, I did not. My visit to

Antwerp, as I have already told you, is a peaceful one. I can shed no light on this poor fellow's murder.''

The magistrate had said nothing of where Newman had been found, nor of a stranger visiting the inn where he had lodged. Best, Tom thought, to say as little as possible himself, and let his interrogator lead the conversation. Were he in such a position in England, he would have used his superior rank and his considerable powers of mockery to unsettle the man before him. Here, however, in a foreign country, such a course of action would not be wise.

He could, however, ask a question that an innocent man might expect to put to someone who was questioning him so keenly.

"May I ask where his body was found?"

"Perhaps, Master Trenchard, you could tell me?"

Tom shook his head and smiled. "I was not lying when I said that I had not seen Giles Newman for many years. I regret that I cannot help you further."

"Or will not."

Tom shook his head again. "Cannot. You may question my wife on the matter—so long as you do not distress her."

"Oh, I will, Master Trenchard, I will, but not yet. You are sure that you have not spoken to Giles Newman today? At the inn where he lodged they said that a stranger called to see him, went to his room and did not return. Disappeared, in fact. Were you that stranger, Master Trenchard?"

Tom decided that bewilderment was the best defence. "Indeed not, sir. As I said, I have not seen Newman since Macedonia." He decided that his best defence was to be bold, to behave as though he had nothing to hide. "You have a description of this stranger?"

"Only that he was a large man, shabbily dressed. You are a large man, Master Trenchard, are you not?"

Tom looked down at his fine clothes. "There are many large men in Antwerp, sir, and many are shabbily dressed. Now I may be large but I am not shabby—as you see."

The magistrate smiled. "I see that you are dressed finely now, Master Trenchard—but were you this afternoon? Let us leave that for the present. I should now like to question your wife."

Well, it was a piece of luck, Tom thought, that the landlord of The Princess of Cleves had been half asleep and had been unable to give any details of the chance-come stranger that the magistrate could use.

What did worry him a little was the thought of an unprepared Catherine being quizzed by such a persistent and cunning inquisitor. But there was no help for it. He dared not protest. To do so would be suspicious. He followed the magistrate and his cohorts back to the courtroom.

The attendant who had brought Catherine a goblet of water, also handed her to a chair, for which she thanked him gratefully. The day had been a long one and she was tired. Had the magistrate deliberately ordered them to be brought before him at such a late hour in the hope that if they were tired they might be unintentionally indiscreet or careless when questioned?

If he had, then it behoved her to be careful. For she

knew of two dead men, not one, and both had been killed by William Grahame and thrown into the nearby canal. The best thing for her to do was to pose as a weak woman, easily overset. Which, she conceded glumly, was at the moment no pose at all. She had seldom felt weaker. On the other hand, this was more grist for the playwright's mill, and no mistake.

She wondered where Geordie had been taken and what he might be saying. For he had been led away from them by two burly lackeys as soon as they had arrived. At least he now had something real to complain about. And what were they doing to Tom—and where was he?

Catherine had rarely felt such relief from worry as she did when he walked back through the door by which he had left. His expression told her nothing, for it was as coolly cheerful as it always was.

"Good. Excellent," intoned the magistrate. "You have seen Mistress Trenchard to a chair, Blaise. Just as well, for I have some questions to ask her, and I would wish her to be comfortable when I do so. Your husband has asked me to treat you gently, my dear, and so I will. Answer me freely and truthfully and all shall be well."

"Yes, sir. I have nothing to hide." *Except that I am growing to be as big a liar as Tom.* She folded her hands in her lap and tried to keep them from trembling. She looked away from Tom so that the magistrate should not suspect that he was coaching her in any way.

Afterwards, she was to think how useful her stage training had been in this difficult new life into which

Rob's folly had precipitated her. She tried to pretend that she was on the stage, and that it was Master Betterton who was confronting her, a false smile on his lips. She was sure that the magistrate's smile was false.

"What brings you to Antwerp, Mistress Trenchard?"

That was an easy question to answer. "I am accompanying my husband to help him in his business venture. We are not rich and so I act as his secretary and clerk."

"Useful as well as beautiful, I see. And this dead man, Giles Newman, whom your husband once knew. Did you ever meet him?"

Catherine lifted her hands and clasped them before her. "No, indeed. We have met few in Antwerp so far. We supped this evening with Amos Shooter."

"Yes, we know that, Mistress Trenchard. And this man Newman, do you know how he died?"

How useful to be able to tell the truth, to say earnestly, "I have no notion, but I suppose that he was stabbed—from what was implied earlier."

"Would it surprise you to know that he was strangled, and his body thrown into a back alley from his bedroom window at the inn where he lodged?"

Catherine's reply was genuine and heartfelt—her actress's skills were not needed. "Oh, the poor man! Who could have done such a thing?"

"Who indeed? Your husband, perhaps?"

Catherine widened her eyes to their fullest extent. "Oh, no, for I would have known. He tells me everything, you see."

The magistrate shook his head. Every word the

woman before him uttered rang true. He had one eye on her husband and his expression never changed. It was one of husbandly pride.

What the magistrate could not know was that Tom was watching a consummate actress at work. His admiration of Catherine's quivering lips, her faltering voice, her expression of wide-eyed innocence, grew with each sentence she uttered. Nothing she said gave away the truth, that she, like him, was an agent of the British Crown.

He could see that, despite himself, the magistrate was gradually falling under her spell.

"Suppose I told you that Newman was trying to contact an agent of your government and was looking to sell information to him about the Dutch fleet. We know that your government has agents in the Low Countries. What we don't know is whether you and your husband are spies, or for whom you spy, and whether your husband killed Newman rather than pay him for his services—or because your masters ordered him to."

Catherine put her hands before her mouth, and then took them away to murmur faintly, "Oh, no. You cannot believe that of my husband and me. We are but simple merchants. Besides, why should you trouble whether or not such terrible things go on? You are neither English nor Dutch."

"That is so, but murder is murder, Mistress Trenchard, and we do not wish our neighbours and allies, the Dutch, to believe that we are aiding their enemies. Moreover, I think it possible that you may not be aware of all your husband's activities since you reached Antwerp. We know that on your first day here you walked into the country. May I ask why?''

A simple question again, requiring a simple answer. ''To see the countryside, of course—so different from our own.''

''You were not making a rendezvous with a possible informer, then?''

Catherine put on an expression of extreme and innocent puzzlement. ''Why, no. As my husband told you, we are here on business. There would be no one in the countryside with whom we might do business.''

Oh, you clever girl, thought Tom gleefully. Those quick wits, which I last saw demonstrated on the stage of the Duke's Theatre, are working now—to our advantage. He wondered what the magistrate was making of her.

It was difficult to tell. He changed tack a little, saying, his voice still mild, ''And this man, Giles Newman. Your husband has never spoken of him? You seemed to say that you had never met, or heard of him.''

Tom waited anxiously for Catherine's answer. If she lied and said that she had never heard his name, and if the magistrate's informant was Amos Shooter—for there was an informant, Tom was sure—then all her seeming innocence would go for nothing. For Shooter would be sure to have reported that Tom had spoken of Newman before his wife and the other guests at the supper party.

Catherine's brow was furrowed. She said slowly, ''I am not certain,'' and then, as though recalling something slight and scarcely heard, she murmured, ''Oh, yes. I remember now. He asked Amos Shooter at supper this evening if he had known Master Newman. It seemed that they were soldiers together, against the heathen. It was said in passing when they were gossiping of old times and old friends.''

She smiled at the magistrate as though she were relieved at being able to help him.

As a piece of acting it was masterly. Tom wanted to applaud. Catherine's answers were seamless—leaving little opportunity for further questioning. At each move on the magistrate's part, she had countered by using her pawn to attack his Queen.

''And that is all?'' he asked.

Catherine nodded. ''Yes. I am sorry that I cannot be more helpful, sir.''

Tom closed his eyes. This was either a master stroke—or a gross mistake. On balance it was probably the former—offering the image of a woman cocooned in naïve innocence. The magistrate gave a great sigh—and turned his attention to Tom again.

''One last question. Where were you this afternoon, Master Trenchard? With your wife—looking for bargains? Or were you looking for Master Newman?''

''Neither, sir. I wished entertainment and I visited an inn which seemed to provide it. It was not far from where we lodge. The White Horse it was called.''

He was being straightforward and bluff where Catherine had been straightforward and delicate. Both responses were designed to give an appearance of absolute truth.

''You could prove that, Master Trenchard?''

For the first time Tom hung back, as if he disliked having to answer.

"Alas, yes. I fear the landlord will remember me. I drank overmuch and made a fool of myself with one of the other drinkers over a game of chess. He had to call us to order." He paused, and offered the company a shamefaced smile. "I was not proud of my behaviour and consequently did not tell my wife of it, though I think she knew that I was a trifle unhappy—but could not guess the reason. Was not that so, wife?" he appealed to her.

So he had noticed that she was aware that something was wrong. How little he missed of what was happening about him! She would have to be careful in future not to betray her innermost feelings to him. For the moment it was enough for her to smile and blush prettily—and confirm what Tom had said.

It was over. The magistrate steepled his hands again and regarded them thoughtfully: the pretty, helpless-looking woman and the strong-faced man with the air of the soldier still about him. He had seen many such. Why did he not believe them? The evidence he had before him was flimsy and he could not detain them on it. They would both bear watching, that was for sure.

He rose to his feet again, and called the captain over to speak to him privately, his eyes on the woman, not the man, to see whether she did anything to betray fear or uneasiness.

She did not. She was smoothing her gown down and playing with the linen bands at her wrists as though she had not a care in the world. Presently she glanced at her husband and smiled at him. Not once had she shown any signs of the distress of which her husband had spoken. She was either a consummate actress—or a total innocent—and he had no notion which.

The captain departed. The magistrate sat down again, saying nothing, his hands performing their favourite trick. Tom looked from him to Catherine and back again. He was almost ready to speak when the captain reappeared, Geordie in tow. He abandoned him before the table and spoke briefly and rapidly to the magistrate in an undertone.

The magistrate waved a hand at Tom. "A word with you, Master Trenchard. We have spoken to your servant here, and he has confirmed what you have told us."

"The truth," Geordie wailed at them all. "I told 'em the truth, master. What the devil else could I do, even if I'd been tortured with hot pincers?"

The glance which the magistrate threw at him was one of a man compelled to look at some creature far beneath his notice.

"Be quiet, fellow. No one has harmed you. You, your master and mistress, are free to leave. But I warn you all that you will be watched. Should I have reason to believe that you are other than you claim to be, you will be brought before me again—and dealt with. Antwerp is not a city which takes kindly to the presence of spies and assassins. That is all."

"Not all, too much—" growled Geordie rudely.

To be silenced by Tom, who said sharply, "Behave yourself, Geordie. None of us has been badly treated.

We must respect the right of the governors of this city to see that its peace is kept.''

The bow he gave to the magistrate before he turned to offer his arm to Catherine saying, ''Come, wife, let's to bed,'' was a low one. It was imperative that they did not rage and storm loudly about their innocence.

He was both pleased and relieved that Catherine had chosen to act with bewildered simplicity—which must have made a much more favourable impression than behaving like a wounded virago. What was it that the Bard had said? ''The lady doth protest too much, methinks.''

Nevertheless, her hand on his arm was trembling, and he knew what an effort it must have been for her to remain cool and steady beneath the cannonade of questions directed at her.

It would have been difficult if she had been prepared for such an ordeal, but for her to go straight from their jousting in the bedroom to a court of inquisition must have imposed a strain on her under which many women might have buckled. Even her training as an actress had scarcely prepared her for this night's ordeal.

''That's my brave girl,'' he told her once they were safely away and walking back to the inn, Geordie behind them keeping up a constant litany of complaint. He, too, had played his part manfully—but he had done so before and would do so again.

But this night had been Catherine's baptism of fire, and she had acquitted herself brilliantly.

Catherine found sleep long in coming. She replayed the scene with the magistrate over and over again, trying to remember whether she had said anything incriminating, anything that the magistrate might remember and so call her back to question her again.

Tom made her drink a glass of wine and eat some bread and cheese before she retired to bed. He had put an arm around her, hugged her, kissed her on the cheek, and said only, "Thank you." There had been nothing overtly salacious about the hug or the kiss. They had merely been part of his thanks.

His last words had been, "We must talk in the morning when we are rested. Not now."

The worst thing was the feeling that they had been watched—and were being watched. If, up to now, Catherine had felt that she was simply playing a game, had not taken their mission seriously, what had passed at the Town Hall had proved exactly how serious it was. She was deep in a conspiracy that might prove fatal to all three of them if anything went wrong.

Worse, she now had three dead men to worry about, not two. If murder could be accounted straightforward, then the deaths of those who had been thrown in the canal could be described as such. Grahame had killed them because they were trying to kill him. But who was Newman? And why had he been killed? Tom had been out all that day—not simply during the afternoon. Had he killed him? And if so, why? Could she imagine him capable of strangling a man?

This was the thought which she struggled with. For, in truth, he *had* been disturbed when he had returned that evening. Was it possible that what had disturbed him was that he had killed Newman?

Everything went round and round in her tired brain

exactly like a caged squirrel bounding round and round
in its wheel. To imagine Tom as a solider was one
thing: as a cold-blooded murderer was quite another.

She was still tired when morning, and breakfast,
came. Tom seemed as disgustingly hearty and cheerful
as ever, Geordie as glum. But then, they were used to
this double life; she was not. Tom had ordered coffee
and made her drink two cups of it. She was not sure
that she liked it. It was too dear a luxury for her and
Rob to buy.

Tom told her that it was an acquired taste. "It stiff-
ens the sinews, drives away fear and the more you
drink of it, wife, the more you will like it. I have drunk
a great deal of it in London's coffee houses."

"Where decent women may not go," Catherine
grumbled, as disconsolate as Geordie for once. "And
coffee is a luxury that I cannot afford."

"Then you must drink as much of it as possible
while we are in the Low Countries, and when it has
made you bright and lively again we must speak of
what passed last night and decide on our future plans."

Yes, disgustingly cheerful was the only way to describe him, but he was right. Either the good food or
the two cups of coffee did the trick, because she felt
much livelier when breakfast was over and she was
sitting before the hearth, opposite to Tom, each of them
in a big leather-padded chair.

To her amusement, he began by imitating the magistrate, steepling his hands together and leaning his elbows on his knees. He adopted the same dry voice,
too, to ask her, "What do you consider the most im-

portant things we learned from the questioning to which we were subjected last night? At least two possibilities must be considered: neither of them pleasant. Can you guess what they are? You may take your time in answering me.''

Catherine's laughter was as much for his clever mimicry as its difference from his usual forthright and robust manner. She checked herself and tried to answer him seriously. To do so meant that she needed to think carefully. It might be useful to imagine that it was part of the plot in a play that she was writing.

''Well, wife?'' said Tom after several long moments of silence. Catherine thought with some annoyance that the happy smile pasted on his face was a superior one. Well, if it was there because he was expecting her to say something foolish, she would remove it.

''So far as I can see,'' she said slowly, ''we must assume that the authorities in Antwerp know why we are here—even though they may not be able to prove it. Which means that either they were waiting for us when we arrived in Antwerp, which raises the possibility that we were betrayed before we left England, and before we even began our mission—or...'' and she paused.

''Good, very good, wife.'' Tom's superior smile had disappeared. Yes, she was clever, this doxy Gower had foisted on him, and he would do well to listen to her. He always named her doxy to himself because he was refusing to admit that she was beginning to touch his heart, his mind and his senses. ''Go on. I am agog to learn what comes after 'or'.''

''Or we were betrayed soon after we arrived by

someone whom we met—or who was watching not us, but Amos Shooter or William Grahame. I do not know which of these suppositions I like the least. All of them are unsettling.''

Tom nodded his approval. "Exactly my thinking. And consider this. If Newman's body was found only late this afternoon how was it that they were able to find us so quickly? There may be no either/or, dear wife and Geordie, for we may be part of a double betrayal.''

He considered the time had arrived for him to be truthful. Not perfectly truthful, of course, for he had his necessary secrets.

"I must confess to you both my own secret doings. My journey the other day was to meet an informant whose name I was given before we left London. He, in turn, gave me Giles Newman's name, and his lodging, and I visited him this afternoon.''

He stopped in order to watch Catherine carefully. After all, for all he knew, she might be a traitor sent to keep watch over him—and ensure that he failed. It was not likely, but a wise man guarded his back at all times.

So far in his adventurous life, Tom had been good at guarding his back.

Catherine said and did nothing suspicious. Her glorious eyes were fixed on his, her lips were parted: she was all attention. Tom continued, "When I reached The Princess of Cleves, I found him dead in his room. Strangled. It was I who pitched him out of the window to delay discovery of his death. I also came away with this, the only thing of interest in his room," and he produced the prayer book, which he handed to Catherine.

She leafed through it in some puzzlement until she came to the passage with the ringed letters. She looked up at Tom.

"A code?" was all she said.

He nodded agreement. "Yes, proving that he was an agent, but for whom or what, we have no knowledge. We have too many fingers in the pie to know which hand they came from.

"Consider, all those with whom we have been associating could be working for any one or more of the following: the English, the Dutch, the French or the Austrians. To say nothing of the Spanish or the Cromwellian sympathisers and their so-called Republican Army. Pick any one or more of your choice."

What interested Catherine almost as much as this was that Tom had not only kept his involvement with Newman from Geordie and herself, but had confronted the magistrate with an aspect nearly as innocent as her own, giving nothing away. Her busy mind ran through more possibilities. She decided to provoke him, for now she could not trust him at all, and she wished to discover whether provocation might not spill some more truth from him.

"There is one person, or possibility, you did not mention," she said coolly, smiling at him.

He was genuinely puzzled. "I thought that I had covered everything. What have I missed?"

"Why, who but you, Tom Trenchard, adventurer, who might possibly be an agent for no one but himself!"

Before Tom, struck dumb by this sudden accusation, so cheerfully made, could answer, Geordie let out a cackle of laughter.

''Oh, aye, she has you there, master. A hit, a hit. A pity females cannot fence. She has given you the true *coup de Jarnac* without knowing what it is.'' And he bent double, laughing and cackling like a mad hen, as Tom rudely told him.

''Damn you, Geordie, you of all people know full well that I am no traitor.''

''Aye but does she? And you play your cards damnably close to your chest, master, and no mistake.''

Seething inside at the impudence of his two dependants, Tom came out with, ''And that is why I so often win. What are you grinning at, wife?'' he roared at Catherine, who was laughing at the commotion that her pointed remark had provoked.

''Everything. Nothing. Will someone please tell me what a *coup de Jarnac* is?'' Her face as she asked this was a picture of innocent, inquiring mischief.

For a moment Tom looked as though he were about to explode like the frog in the fable, Catherine thought irreverently. And then he began to laugh, his head flung back, before he bent down to scoop her up and dance her around the room before depositing her back in her chair.

''A trick. The *coup de Jarnac* is a trick in fencing when one man attacks the other, not in the expected manner, straightforwardly, but severs his hamstring, injuring him so that he cannot walk, or fight.''

''I see,'' cried Catherine breathlessly. And she did, for had she not done the equivalent of that to Tom in questioning him so sharply, so suddenly? Geordie had put his finger on the heart of the matter.

Geordie was watching them benevolently, head on one side. "Have no fear, mistress," he told her kindly. "You may trust the master. Oh, not as to detail, but as to the Grand Plan."

"Well, thank you, Geordie, for nothing," riposted Tom, giving his servant a hearty clap on the back that nearly had him on the floor. "And now we must go carefully. For we are suspected—and rightly. Only the lack of evidence prevented us from ending the night in the dungeons. Our only safety is in behaving as innocently as possible until the letter comes with Grahame's pardon.

"After that, who knows? We must act as the occasion demands, and that we do not yet know. And in the meantime, we trust no one, for we have no means of knowing who are friends, and who are enemies."

Chapter Nine

"**M**ake way! Make way!"

Swords uplifted, horses foam-flecked with hard riding, a party of horsemen galloped madly across Antwerp's main square towards the Town Hall, its citizenry running to escape being mown down.

"What is it? What is it?" was a cry raised by many. One of the riders, lagging behind the others because his horse was falling lame, called out to them, "The French are coming! The French are coming!"

This threw the people in the square into a worse terror than before. A woman near Tom and Catherine—who were walking to the post office to see whether any message had come from London—fell on her knees and began to pray. The dreadful sack of Antwerp by the Spanish nearly a hundred years earlier was a folk memory that remained strong in the consciousness of its citizenry.

She was not the only one who felt the need to call on God to save them. Many others began to run in the direction of their homes, ready to abandon them as refugees if the French marched on the town. Catherine clutched at Tom's arm for support. "Can this be true?"

"I fear so. It would be a master stroke for the French if, while the Dutch are concentrating their forces and their treasure on fighting the English, they could conquer Flanders. For then Holland lies before them, another possible conquest—and a richer prize than Flanders even."

He said this coldly, like a scholar considering a mathematical problem. Catherine shivered. "What shall we do if they reach Antwerp?"

Tom put a large reassuring hand over hers. "That I will tell you when we have collected our post—if there is any. But one thing, I'm sure, is certain. I don't think that the French can be very near to us yet, for if they were, we should have heard the sound of their cannon by now. But you are right to be afraid. At present, the French are the best soldiers in Europe and their leader, Turenne, is Europe's greatest general.

"On the other hand, it is also possible that, threatened by the French, the Dutch may be driven to offer us peace at Breda. They cannot wish to fight us both. But that is for the future. The present is murky."

Catherine's shivers arose from the fact that this adventure of theirs was growing more and more dangerous. The notion of flying before an invading army was not an attractive one. But Tom was right. They must collect their post and then decide what to do. She had awoken this morning feeling happy for the first time since the magistrate had questioned them. There had been no further word from him, nor from Grahame.

She and Tom had spent nearly a week visiting various shops and booths where beautiful glass, lace, silverware, leather goods and pottery were sold. Tom had ordered various items and paid for them from what seemed a bottomless purse. They were to be delivered to London Docks by packet boat. Catherine wondered what Tom would do with them all when they returned to London.

If God did allow them to return to London. This was a litany Catherine constantly repeated, not daring to be too hopeful lest she tempted Fate to punish them for having an overweening faith in their own ability to survive.

Tom had also stopped trying to get her into his bed. In one way this was a relief, but oddly enough, Catherine found herself regretting his cheerful advances, and the merry glint in his eyes that told her when they were coming. He had been much more serious in his manner to her and to Geordie since their arrest. After his first lengthy discussion with her about their mission when they had been allowed to return to the inn, he had refused to refer to it at all.

"We have claimed that we are merchants here on business. Let us behave at all times as though that is true. Walls have ears. Geordie, do you be careful in what you say. Particularly when you have been drinking. But I do give you permission to gossip about my success as a merchant whenever you please."

"Oh, aye, master, trust me. I never say nothing, and that's the truth. I don't ask questions, neither. Not even to know where you went yesterday when you left me and the mistress alone."

He dodged the light blow Tom aimed at him. "You

know perfectly well, man, that if I tell you and the mistress little of some of my doings, it is in order to protect you both.'' He didn't add, and myself, in case either of you should care to betray me. No, he didn't really believe that either Catherine or Geordie were traitors, but as his old nurse used to say, What you don't talk about, others can't know.

What Catherine also did not know was that she had suddenly become a temptation so great that Tom dared not so much as touch her lest he fall upon her and brook no refusal. And that she did not deserve.

Since his last mistress, a pretty little widow, had deserted him to marry a City merchant, he had been continent—a state to which he was not used. Always before when he had lost his mistress he had made it his business to console himself immediately with another. He had vowed never to take a wife, having been a sad witness of his father and mother's unhappy marriage.

Unfortunately, having reached the age of thirty-five as a bachelor, he had suddenly grown tired of the free life that he and his fellows about Charles's court were following.

Not only the fear of disease, but boredom and a feeling of weariness at the prospect of chasing yet another woman who would fill his bed for a time—and then depart—were overwhelming him. When he had first watched Catherine on the stage, and afterwards when she had joined him in his mission, he had seen her simply as yet another woman with whom he might amuse himself.

What was it that he wanted of her—and from her? He and his friends, The Merry Gang, were contemptuous of women, viewing them as either light-minded toys or mere milk cows one married solely to produce heirs—and to neglect. But he could not persuade himself that Catherine fitted into either of these categories.

She was witty, spirited, amusing, clever and brave. He could talk to her as though she were a man, and she would respond to him in the same way. He had been surprised by the depth of her replies to him when he had discussed the problems of their mission with her. And even when confronted for the first time with sudden and violent death, she had not fainted, had a fit of the vapours, or needed to be comforted and consoled.

She had more than held her own with the magistrate when it would not have been unnatural for her to be overwhelmed by his ruthless inquisition. For all these reasons he could not dismiss her as he had been in the habit of dismissing most women. That she held him off also intrigued him, for he was used to conquest and had been spoiled by his successes.

He could not, dare not, believe that he was falling in love with her. For love was an illusion believed in by fools. A beckoning dream which could never come true. And he was not a fool. Lust was all. But was it enough?

Undoubtedly he was a fool for allowing himself to be distracted by such unnecessary and untimely considerations when he was on a mission rendered more difficult by her presence.

Reaching the post office after threading their way through the growing crowd—for after the first flight from the square of many of the citizenry, others had flocked to it to discover what further news, if any, was to be heard—ended Tom's musings.

And there *was* a letter waiting for them, which he handed to Catherine to carry, saying loudly, "This must be from my clerk in London, telling me the latest news of my enterprise. Do you guard it well, wife."

Back at the inn, Catherine settled down to the laborious business of deciphering what was apparently an innocuous letter, documenting the day-to-day occurrences of Tom's supposed shop near the Strand. What she found in it was dismaying, and so she told him when she finally handed it over to him to read.

Tom flung the paper down in disgust. "Reasonable enough, in all honesty," he said sadly, "but it does not move us a whit further forward. I cannot believe that Grahame will accept this."

He read aloud from the letter. "At this moment, matters being as they are, it would not be wise to forward the actual pardon for Grahame, but you may assure him most heartily that a pardon awaits him once he returns to our shores, having given us those assurances about the Dutch which he has promised and we expect."

He looked across at Catherine, who sat opposite to him, her quill pen in her hand, her face as disappointed as his own. "I fear that he will give us nothing when he reads this. I understand why my masters have acted so—but will he? The peace discussions at Breda, and the possible knowledge that the French intended to invade have caused their caution—but has left us with no carrot to offer the donkey and persuade him to oblige us."

Catherine laughed, and said demurely. "I don't think

that Master Grahame would be happy to learn that we see him as a donkey.''

''I don't give a damn for Grahame's happiness,'' growled Tom, ''only for any information that he may care to give us. Now we must go to Amos Shooter straight away and ask him to tell us where Grahame may be found—or, if he will not do that, then arrange for us to meet Grahame at his home.''

This was no easier to accomplish than Tom had expected. Shooter was not at home, but at his warehouse on the banks of the Scheldt. He was not pleased to see Tom and Catherine arrive.

''What now?'' he asked, his manner surly. ''The French may be here at any time; they are well over the border and are besieging Lille. They will soon be on their way to Ghent and Brussels. This is no time for me to be seen with those under suspicion of being agents of the English government.''

So Amos knew that they had been arrested. And the question was, how? But this was no time to consider that.

''We need to see Grahame at once, and the sooner we see him the sooner we leave Antwerp and you are free of us,'' said Tom shortly. ''Can you arrange a meeting for us?''

''Not at my house, no.'' Amos was no longer the friendly host who had eaten, drunk and laughed with them. ''I can tell you where he lodges and you may find him yourself. He is at The Oriflamme, a hostelry by the river, not far from the Town Hall. It is not difficult to find. And now you have learned that, I bid you good day.''

"Something—or someone—had frightened him, that is plain," Catherine said to Tom as they walked away, unnecessarily, she knew, for he surely was aware of that without her telling him! But he was obviously pleased that she had grasped that, as well as the need to go to The Oriflamme without delay. For if there was any danger of the French taking the city—and rich Antwerp must be one of their main targets—it would be well if they had left before the French arrived.

It was true that The Oriflamme was not difficult to find. What was difficult, though, was that when they reached it, Grahame was not there. He had left his rooms the day before and had gone, the landlord thought, to Amsterdam, though he could not be sure.

"He must have learned of the French invasion," Tom told Catherine, "and decided that discretion was the better part of valour."

"What do we do now?" Catherine asked him, although she already knew the answer.

"We make for Amsterdam, of course, and try to find him there. A useful turn, perhaps, for at one stroke by leaving Antwerp, we avoid the French and the possibility of further trouble with the magistracy. We must go to the inn and pack immediately."

If Catherine had been surprised by the cleanliness and order of life in Flanders, she was even more struck by what she found in Holland.

"It's as though the whole country is scrubbed clean every morning," she told Tom as they sat eating bread and cheese and drinking strong ale for breakfast in a tavern near Utrecht on their way to Amsterdam. "I thought that I was clean, but these people, and their clothes, look as though they were new-minted every morning. Look at this floor.''

Mirth on his face, Tom obeyed her. ''Yes, wife, what is it that you wish me to admire?''

He was mocking her, but Catherine was too full of what she was seeing to take any notice of that.

''Look,'' she told him gravely, pointing at the spotless black and white tiles, ''imagine what this floor would look like in a London tavern. The filth of weeks of neglect, spilt ale, dogs' droppings, straw—and worse. But here...''

Even as she spoke, a burly peasant sitting in the corner of the room accidentally knocked over his pot of ale. Almost before it reached the floor a little serving maid appeared, her cap, collar, cuffs and apron snowy white, a mop and bucket in her hand, and began to restore the floor to its pristine condition.

''There!'' she exclaimed triumphantly as the girl ended her task. ''They can't leave the place dirty or untidy for a moment.''

''Yes,'' agreed Tom equably, looking around him, apparently admiring the remarkable cleanliness of the Dutch. What he was actually admiring was not Dutch hygiene but the sharp wits and knowing eye of his supposed wife. She was becoming a true helpmeet to him because she had all the best instinct of an agent: an intense curiosity about the life around her.

Catherine could have told him that her success as a playwright was based on her observation of life and her fellows, for one cannot write convincingly without being acutely aware of the passing show that makes up

the world. It was that talent that Betterton had seen in
the play she had given him, and that, he was sure,
would make her future plays worth staging. It was a
talent he had found surprising in so young a woman—
or in a woman at all.

Tom had watched her watching Geordie, and—like
a true actress—even imitating his walk and gestures,
but never when he was by. For she also had a delicacy
about her that made her unwilling to hurt people and
animals unnecessarily.

On their ride north, Geordie and a packhorse trailing
behind them, she had always refused to eat the food
and drink that they had carried with them from the inn
where they had stayed the night before, until he had
caught them up. She also insisted that he supped with
them in the evening, instead of being consigned to the
yard or the kitchens to eat his meal.

Now she was offering Geordie the ale she could not
finish, which he took from her gratefully.

"You are spoiling him," Tom told her lazily.

"No, indeed. A happy servant is a good servant. One
of my father's maxims."

"So you say," Tom drawled back at her, still lazy.

Geordie looked from one to the other of them. They
might not be married, or even share a bed—yet—but
they were beginning to behave like a happily married
couple, freely laughing and talking together. Even
when they argued they remained cheerfully friendly—
except when the master was trying to get her into bed,
that was.

He spoke, and what he said surprised him as much
as his hearers. "I wish you were my true mistress, for

a kinder lady never breathed. Remember that, master.''
He put the empty pot of ale down and strolled off into
the yard. ''To find the necessaries,'' he grumbled, for
here, in Holland, one did not use the nearest wall as a
privy. Stinking back alleys were few.

''Great God,'' exclaimed Tom, amused. ''I thought
Geordie despised all women since his wife ran off to
live with the Turks.''

''He has been with you as long as that?''

''All my life,'' said Tom, before finishing off his
own ale, and following in Geordie's wake. ''I suppose,'' he added, a little surprised at the thought, ''that
he is my oldest friend, one on whom I can always
depend, despite his never-ending wailings. Geordie enjoys being miserable.''

It was apparently a day for revelations, for sitting
alone, finishing her bread and cheese, Catherine had
seen a side to Tom that was new to her. It struck her
that, unlike many men with their servants, he was never
actually unkind to Geordie. She had never seen him
beat, or even strike him in anger.

Oh, he might rail at him, but that was all, and she
had never seen Geordie cringe away from him as many
servants did with their masters. He took Tom's sar-
casms for granted, and rode over them. As she was
beginning to.

''How do we find Master Grahame?'' she asked
Tom later in the day, when they sat by the roadside
eating the inevitable bread and cheese and drinking water from a skin refilled that morning.

''We ask.'' Tom was being uncharacteristically

brief. He looked about him. Holland was flat and there was little shelter or comfort to be found near the road—which was itself nothing more than a dirt track. Once or twice a wagon or a farm cart jolted by. Nearer to the towns through which they passed the roads improved and coaches, large clumsy things, rolled along them.

"But surely that will draw attention to us—and we cannot want that."

"Not at first. I have kept careful watch and we are not being followed. One thing the French have done for us is to give the authorities in Flanders more to worry about than possible English spies. It may take some little time, I trust, for the Dutch to become suspicious of us. Unless we have been betrayed."

"And we go on pretending to be merchants?"

"Indeed, and it is not only pretence. The goods we have bought in Flanders and shall buy in Holland will be shipped to London to be sold there. I might as well gain some profit from this adventure."

Well, that certainly answered her question as to what was to become of the beautiful things that she and Tom had bought. On one of their last buying excursions in Antwerp, they had bought bolts of exquisitely patterned cloth that Tom had held up against her to see whether or not it matched her eyes.

"Is that what you do now that you are no longer a soldier?" she had ventured.

Tom had smiled one of his secret smiles. "Not exactly, but the wise man takes advantage of any situation in which he finds himself. Do you do the same."

The only advantage Catherine could think of arising

out of her present adventure was that it was providing a great deal of material to help her to write future plays. But she could not tell him that.

Amsterdam, she found when they at least reached it, was not as large as Antwerp, but was much more compact, being built round a series of canals, often parallel with the cobbled tracks along which they rode in search of a suitable tavern.

The narrow streets and the bridges across the canals were full of people who took little interest in them. Strangers, she knew, were easily identifiable in small towns, but not in large ones. This would help them in their wish to be anonymous.

''Here, we'll stop here,'' exclaimed Tom, pointing to an inn whose sign board showed the portrait of Piet Hein, the Dutch admiral who had captured the rich Spanish silver fleet thirty years earlier.

It was set at the corner of a lane that opened off a long road on which stood some of the most splendid houses Catherine had ever seen. That they were narrow, terraced and many-storied, added to their rich splendour rather than took away from it. She was later to discover that they had been riding down one of the richest streets in Amsterdam, the Herengracht, where many of Holland's great merchant princes lived.

Tom turned into the inn yard, Catherine and Geordie following him. They had not hired any servants to accompany them, partly because Dutch roads were safe, and partly because the less anyone knew of them, the better.

Their rooms were even cleaner and, although

smaller, were more impressive than the ones they had occupied in Antwerp. The window looked out on a view of the bridge, the canal, the Herengracht and the distant road leading to it.

"A soldier," Tom announced, looking out of it, "would say that this was a splendid vantage point, since no enemy could advance on us without being seen."

"Unless they came by the back way," Catherine announced naughtily.

She was less amused on exploring their quarters to discover that the great four-poster bed in their room dominated it forbiddingly. Geordie was housed in a minute ante-room off theirs, which boasted a narrow bunk bed in a niche in the wall. There was no way in which Tom could sleep in either room other than by lying on the floor: they would have to share the great bed!

"Did you arrange this deliberately?" she demanded of Tom who, sprawled in a large armchair, was watching her, smiling at her agitation and knowing what was causing it.

"No, *wife,*" he said, laying emphasis on the word wife. "This is, alas, the only room left."

"I told you," she said frostily, "that I did not intend to pose as your wife other than in public. In private is quite a different matter. May we not move to another inn?"

"Amsterdam, dear wife, is not Antwerp, and the inn-keeper assures me that we are fortunate to find a good room at all. We could, of course, try our luck in the seamen's alehouses on the waterfront, but I fear that you would like their attentions even less than mine.

"But do not trouble yourself; the bed, as you see, is large, and we may put the bolster down the middle to preserve your honour, for I have no intention of sleeping on the floor."

"It's not my honour I'm worried about," Catherine told him bluntly, "but yours."

"Very wise of you. As Geordie will inform you, my honour is a fickle thing—it comes and it goes, but do not fear, I have never forced a woman yet, and I do not intend to begin now."

Oh, damn his smiling impudence! And why did she find such an unhandsome man so attractive? Why should a craggy face, a grim mouth and a shock of red-gold hair undo a poor girl so?

Later, alone, for Tom went drinking with Geordie, reeling from tavern to tavern to try to find news of Grahame without drawing too much attention to themselves, she found herself remembering him and his taking ways all too often. Pray God they took not her! These days when she was composing impudent speeches for her dashing rake, Lovewell, he grew more like Tom every time she wrote of him!

"Do not think that your last declaration makes me feel any happier," she told him.

"Oh, wife, if you wish to feel happier, then let us remove the bolster, and we can fly to heaven together."

Best to say nothing to that, for whatever she said, he would be sure to cap it with a witticism that would be difficult to refute. A plain and straightforward villain

he might call himself, but he was as slippery as an eel
and possessed a tongue as sharp as Satan's.

Catherine was still thinking of him later that night
after she had finished writing another scene of *The
Braggart, or, Lackwit Married,* and was carefully putting her manuscript back into her pack. It had grown
dark outside and the noise of the revellers leaving the
inn to stagger home had died away.

She lit the candle beside the bed and decided that it
was time for her to retire. Tom had been adamant that
they share the bed, and she had reluctantly given way.
She put the long bolster down the length of it and
stared at it hopefully. She knew that when men married
young children who were not old enough to become
their true wives, they shared the bed for a night with a
bolster between them to signify that the ceremony had
been performed.

But I am not married, and if I am truthful I fear
myself as much as I fear him. Catherine put this uncomfortable thought at the back of her mind and tried
to forget it as she dressed herself for the night. Her
nightgown was of cotton and covered her even more
than her day dress did since it had a high neck, a collar
and was tied demurely under her chin with a drawstring.

But she was naked beneath it and she was going to
share her bed with a man who attracted her strongly,
but of whom she knew nothing: not even whether he
was married.

He was also a man who was somewhere outside in
the streets, or rather the inns and stews of Amsterdam.

Was he pleasuring another woman because she had forbidden him to pleasure her? The thought of him with a woman distressed her when she finally entered the bed and pulled the sheets up to her chin. She had already decided that she would not lie down or go to sleep until he returned. She wanted to be fully conscious when he did.

Time passed. Occasionally in the distance she heard the sound of merrymaking. A woman laughed once, beneath her window. A man's voice said something to her, she laughed again and they moved away. Drunken singing in the distance came nearer and nearer. Catherine found that her eyes were closing, and that sleep was claiming her; it had been a long day. Resolutely she fought to stay awake.

The drunken singing was now just outside the inn. Then, thankfully, it stopped. The candle was beginning to gutter: it was as weary as she was. Footsteps on the stairs had her sitting up again. They reached the door and she heard it open, and a man's voice cursing as opening it seemed to prove difficult. It was Tom and Geordie. Geordie began to sing again in a tuneless voice until Tom shushed him.

They both fell into the room, flushed with drink and God knows what else. Tom, swaying and smiling foolishly at her, mumbled, "There's a good wife, Geordie, awake and waiting for me to come home. Do you go to bed, and leave us to celebrate my return."

"Don't want to go to bed," moaned Geordie, "want another drink."

"There's no more to be had tonight."

If Geordie was a miserable drunk, then Tom was

evidently a cheerful one. He pushed Geordie, still complaining, into his ante-room and shut the door on him, before beginning to tear off his clothes.

Unwillingly fascinated, Catherine watched him strip for a moment, before saying in an acid-sweet voice, "Forgive me for asking but, during this merry evening's drinking, did you manage to find anything out about William Grahame?"

Tom shook a bleary head and winked at her. He threw his breeches on to a chair—which left him standing there only in his shirt. "Alas, no, woman, and a fine night we made of it while trying to catch our bird. All's to do again. And now your hard-working spouse has come for his reward."

So saying, he staggered to the bed, heaved the bolster out of it and himself inside it, and took Catherine in his arms, giving her a smacking, beery kiss before she fully understood what he was at.

Horrified, for in her wildest reveries she had never thought to find herself in bed with a happy, drunken man, who was stroking and caressing her, Catherine realised that the time had truly come when she needed to fight him off if she were to retain her maidenhead. This proved difficult, for he seemed to possess as many arms and legs as the proverbial sea monster, and no sooner had she pushed off one arm, than he trapped her legs with his.

Impossibly, Catherine found herself wanting to laugh; Tom's erratic and drunken good humour was beginning to have its effect on him for when, now thoroughly roused, he tried to kiss her, his aim was wildly off, and he embraced her pillow instead. Which had him saying despairingly to her, desire subsiding a little, "For God's sake, hold still, wife, and let me at you, you and the room are going around together."

"You shall not have me tonight," Catherine told him, recovering her common sense again, "nor ever— and certainly not in this condition."

He gave a low sigh when she spoke and she suddenly realised that, being as drunk as he was, his desire might outrun his ability to perform—at least she hoped so—but when he finally struggled himself on top of her, even that hope seemed a desperate one.

"Thass better," he mumbled happily, aiming a kiss at her, which this time found its target on her lips. Oh, how betraying the body is! Catherine thought, when the mind is no longer controlling it, for she could not prevent herself from kissing him back. Far from repelling her, his state of cheerful drunkenness made him seem vulnerable since it had silenced his caustic tongue.

"So soft, so warm," he sighed, holding her loosely in his arms, "what a comfortable woman you are, wife." Smiling down at her, he laid his spinning head in the crook of her shoulder, and heaving a great sigh of "nice," fell asleep as sweetly and swiftly as any babe.

To go in one moment from being on the point of half-willing ravishment, to holding a sleeping and heavy man quiescent in her arms in the next, was strangely enough an anticlimax so stunning that Catherine, of all things, found herself disappointed. Her whole body was throbbing and thrumming in the oddest way—and the desire to cry was as strong as the desire to laugh.

She shifted Tom's weight so that he rolled away from her to lie on his side of the bed. Dead to the world, he showed no signs of waking up. Catherine restored the bolster to its proper place between them, and blew out the candle, which was on the point of expiring anyway.

Before she did so, she could not help looking at Tom. He was now lying in a posture of complete abandon. His shirt was rucked up above his knees showing long, strong legs and beautiful narrow feet—the ones with which she had recently struggled. His shirt strings had loosened and it had fallen open to the waist to reveal a massive chest decorated with whorls of red-gold hair.

His head lay on one strong arm and his relaxed face wore an expression of complete and happy contentment, as though he had truly succeeded in having his way with her. Catherine wondered what he was doing in his dreams.

Altogether he was—half-naked—as splendid a specimen of manhood as you might hope to see. Lying awake in the dark, Catherine was asking herself a question. Do I regret that the drink overwhelmed him before he could have his way with me? She could not call it ravishment, for after the first few moments she had never truly tried to fight him off.

And if so, is it because I would prefer him to take me when he is in his senses rather than as tonight, when he is half out of them?

Either way, she could not find an answer.

Chapter Ten

His head throbbing as though the devil were trying to beat a tattoo on it, Tom Trenchard woke up to find himself in a strange bed in a strange town. Memory was lost to him as he flung out an arm to encounter…a bolster!

''What the devil!'' Heaving himself up, his head hurting and his stomach revolting against any movement, he looked down to find Catherine sound asleep on the other side of the bolster.

Memory—or rather part of it—returned. Enough to have him feeling a sickness that had nothing to do with drink. For all that he could remember was falling gleefully upon her—and after that, nothing. Great God, had he drunk so much that he had ravished a woman who had consistently held him off, and then had no memory of having done so?

He had always prided himself on having more conscience than most of his sovereign's courtiers where women were concerned—or his sovereign himself. It had always been his boast that any woman who lay with him did so willingly. Oh, he had the right to sweet

talk her into agreement, but not to force her. He gave
a groan that hurt his head. Had he, in his drunken folly,
allowed the desire he felt for Catherine to drive him
on to do the unthinkable?

He gave another groan and dropped his aching head
into his cupped hands. For was it not the frustration
her constant presence was causing him that had set him
drinking like a madman the night before to try to forget
her?

He felt Catherine stir. What would she say to him?
What could he say to her? If only he were Rochester
or Sedley, the task would be easy enough. For both
regarded all women as prey, but he had never been able
to bring himself to be quite as hard as that. Which was
one reason why he had never married.

He groaned again.

"Tom?" queried a worried voice from the other side
of the bolster.

For very shame he must answer. He turned his poor
head, oh so gently, in order to look at her, and winced
as he did so.

"You look ill," she told him, and then, kindly,
"Shall I wake Geordie and send him for a restorative?"

"Good God, no." Unwisely, Tom shook his head,
before turning it away again. "He'll be in no better
case than I am, and will probably need restoring himself."

"Oh, how stupid I am. I hadn't thought of that."

Through blear and red-rimmed eyes, Tom looked her
full in the face for the first time.

"Catherine," he began. "About last night..." He

stopped, not knowing how to go on. For a woman whom he thought he had ravished not many hours earlier, she seemed remarkably composed. Perhaps she hadn't minded, had changed her mind about lying with him. This little seed of hope had him asking her, "You feel well this morning?"

Catherine looked at him, puzzled a little by his odd manner, which, now that she thought of it, matched his sad condition; eyes bleary, blue shadows under his eyes, his face yellow, and a hangdog manner very unlike his usual cheerful brashness. Whatever was the matter with him? He had been a cheerful drunk last night. But this morning, now that he was sober, he was as dismal as Geordie had been.

And then, as she met his worried eyes, understanding flooded in. The only drunken man she had known well had been her father after her mother's death. And one of his symptoms the morning after had been what he called his "forgettory". He frequently forgot everything that had passed in the later stages of a night spent in drinking.

What more likely than that Tom remembered nothing after he had leaped into bed with her, and had lost all knowledge of what had passed before he fell asleep. His owlish, worried look was most likely caused by his worrying over whether he had finally had his way with her against her will.

"About last night," he began again. "I didn't... frighten you, did I?" His expression was a pleading one.

She was right. He *had* forgotten. She would punish

him a little both for forgetting what he had done, and for starting to do it—and failing.

"Frighten me? Oh, no. Why should I have been frightened?" And then the devil seized her tongue and spoke with it. "Why should I be frightened when you asked me to marry you? That flatters a woman, not frightens her."

"Marry you!" Had he been so far gone in drink as to say anything so foolish, even in the act of persuading her to lie with him?

"Yes, marry me. You said, most distinctly, that you would marry me if I lay with you. Surely you haven't forgotten?"

Tom licked his lips. What the devil should he do now? He had wanted to bed Catherine, not to marry her, even though she had begun to intrigue him more and more and rouse strange longings in him. And now, by all the devils in hell he had gained what he wished—apparently with the help of a spurious proposal of marriage—and gained no benefit at all from it because he couldn't remember a thing!

For once the sophistical and sophisticated courtier who was one of the leading lights of Charles II's entourage was rendered speechless.

"I must have been mad as well as drunk," he muttered at last.

Must he, indeed! What a fine compliment to pay a single young woman whose maidenhead he thought he had enjoyed, to tell her that he was mad to wish to marry her! He deserved to be teased. Catherine decided to prolong Tom's torments a little longer.

Her enjoyment was given spice by the contrary fact

that, whilst she was teasing him, she wanted to kiss him and tell him that all was well. Through no access of virtue of his own, quite the contrary, she was still untouched. But if the thought of marrying her was so abhorrent, then he deserved to be punished.

"You were so happy afterwards," she told him, "that you spoke of our wedding being celebrated as soon as we returned to England, under the auspices of Sir Thomas Gower, who had indirectly caused to bring it about."

"I did?" groaned Tom. The feeling that drink had driven him mad grew stronger, as did another feeling. Well, if he had promised her marriage and she had given in to him, then his conscience informed him that he ought to marry her. He had never, ever, proposed such a thing before.

As he worried over this like a dog worrying over a large and strange bone, trying to decide whether to chew on it or not, he looked across at Catherine to discover that she had both hands over her mouth, trying to smother the laughter that his tormented expression was provoking.

What the devil was she laughing at? Enlightenment dawned. He leaned over the bolster to grab her to him.

"What game are you playing with me, wife?" and he kissed her. Not as he had done the night before, but gently and ruefully.

Held against him, her soft cheek rubbing against his rough unshaven one, Catherine said into his neck, "Oh, Tom, I cannot go on deceiving you. Nothing happened last night. True, you did get into bed with me and tried to lie with me as a husband lies with his wife, but before you did so drink overcame you and you fell asleep. Not a very flattering thing to happen, I do assure you. Particularly now that you seem to have forgotten everything that passed.''

Tom held on to her for a moment before letting go of her. Was this strange feeling that overcame him when he did so regret that he had not offered her marriage? It had him muttering, ''I am sorry that I behaved so badly as to try to take you against your will. That is not my way. All I can remember is walking through the door, seeing you…and falling on you. After that, nothing.''

He looked wryly down at his shirt. ''I suppose that I must have undressed myself, unless you or Geordie helped me.''

Catherine was enduring some strange feelings of her own, for she could have continued with the lie and perhaps blackmailed him into marriage. Whether he would have allowed her to do so was quite another thing, and a thing she would not like to have tested.

No, it was all a joke, in which for once she had turned the tables on Tom for a change. ''No,'' she told him, ''you stripped yourself. Geordie was too far gone to help himself, let alone you, and I was too…''

''Transfixed,'' offered Tom helpfully. He was beginning to recover his usual comic sang-froid now that the dread word marriage was to be forgotten.

''Scarcely,'' riposted Catherine in her best Will Wagstaffe manner, ''for if I had been transfixed, we should be discussing our wedding vows by now!''

She was well pleased with this swift reply and decided to write the exchange down as soon as she had a private moment that would allow her to turn into Will Wagstaffe.

Tom's shout of laughter at her naughty jest had him holding his poor abused head, and brought Geordie through the door to stare at their amusement.

"You wanted something, master?" he asked mournfully.

"Yes, ale and water at the double, and for all three of us. And some dry bread for you and me, and cheese with it for the mistress."

"I'm glad some on us is happy this morning," grumbled Geordie as he went to do Tom's bidding, "seeing as how my head's banging like the bells of St Martin's in the Fields during the Great Fire."

Whether it was her teasing of him or the ale which Geordie brought him which did the trick, Tom was soon his normal cheerful self again. He took himself off into Geordie's ante-room to dress, leaving Catherine some privacy. He held what he called a council of war once they were all decent.

"I cannot see myself," he told Catherine with a cheeky grin, "staggering in and out of every alehouse in Amsterdam trying to find Grahame. I am alike to die of a syncope brought on by drink before the month is out."

"Then how shall we manage to find him in a city of a hundred thousand people?" asked Catherine anxiously, for Amsterdam was not only the richest city in Europe, it was also one of the most populous.

"Never fear, dear wife," said Tom, putting his forefinger beside his nose like a trickster from Alsatia in London where the rogues and vagabonds lived.

"Before we left England, Sir Thomas Gower gave me the name of a Dutch merchant in Amsterdam, one Hendrick Van Sluys, who has passed on some useful information to us in exchange for Sir Thomas preventing two of his cargo ships being impounded and their contents sold when they were compelled to put into Portsmouth in a storm. He said that I was only to use him if we were at *point non plus*. Time has gone by and we have now reached that destination!

"I propose that we put on our finest clothes and pay him a visit. He lives but a short distance from here on the Herengracht. We shall present ourselves as merchants—and then decide how to play him when we have discovered his true kidney—as the London cullies would say."

So it was that once again, splendidly accoutred, Tom and Catherine, Geordie in attendance, stood outside the door of a fine house, in Amsterdam this time, not Antwerp.

"If you begin by posing as a merchant," Catherine had said before they left the inn, "will Master Van Sluys not be surprised that you are calling at his home, not his place of business, and that you are bringing your wife with you?"

"Not at all," replied Tom, who was busy trying to tie his lace cravat, and who was debating whether to ask Catherine to help him. "Mijnheer Van Sluys's place of business *is* his home. His cellars will be the storehouse of his merchandise.

"Sir Thomas Gower told me that he sells luxury goods of all kinds, glass and pottery being his specialisms. And his home will be full of treasures, too, because he has a portfolio of other interests, everything from cattle, land and dealings in the Stock Market. Dutch luxury is becoming notorious, and Sir Thomas told me that he is very wealthy.

"Your presence will not seem odd, for the Dutch allow their women far more freedom than we do. They are partners in their husbands' businesses and they form committees to run old peoples' homes and hospitals. The only area of life from which they are barred is that of government in any form."

"'Tis a pity that all women do not live in Holland," said Catherine pertly, "since their lot seems so much more preferable to our own. If I were to marry, my property would become my husband's to do with as he would, even though he had done nothing to earn it."

Tom gave up the unequal struggle with his cravat. "Do you tie this for me, wife," he told her, handing it to her, "and let us discuss the condition of women at a later date. I wish to call on Mijnheer Van Sluys today, not tomorrow!"

Sir Thomas Gower had been right about Van Sluys's wealth. Catherine had thought that Amos Shooter was living in extreme luxury, but it was as nothing to the splendour to which Hendrick Van Sluys was accustomed. She was also growing accustomed, after a different fashion, to Tom's extraordinary range of knowledge, far beyond that of your usual mercenary captain—which had at first surprised her.

Another surprise was that Van Sluys agreed to see

them immediately when his servant took Tom's request for an audience to him. They waited in a lobby whose walls were hung with splendid maps of Dutch possessions in the Far East, as well as a bewildering variety of still lives, seascapes and landscapes.

"More cows," whispered Catherine irreverently to Tom. It had already become a shared joke with them that, after ships, nearly every Dutch and Flemish painting had a cow in it. Catherine had begun to count them, and had decided that her next play would contain a rich Dutchman who constantly boasted of his painted cows.

Presently the servant returned and, the house being long and thin because of the Dutch desire to save land, he led them through a series of the most splendidly furnished rooms with still more pictured cows in them, to a drawing room at the back that was the ultimate in splendour.

No less than twenty paintings hung on one wall, and three superb tapestries on another. Twelve leather-seated chairs were stationed around the room. A harpsichord stood in one corner. Marquetry tables with Chinese ivories on them stood about. Four armchairs faced a giant hearth, a wall of books behind them. A long sidetable held bottles, glasses and pewter dishes of sliced lemons and small round biscuits.

Through an open doorway could be seen an oak dining table large enough to seat twenty people, surrounded by twenty red velvet-covered chairs. The huge sideboard was of ebony and was loaded with Delftware and fine silver.

Mijnheer and Mevrouw Van Sluys were equally

magnificent, both in their dress and their manner. He was large and majestic in sober black velvet; she was small and dainty in silver-blue satin. So magnificent were they that they quite eclipsed Tom and Catherine. This must be a mistake. Mijnheer Van Sluys would be sure to send them packing when he discovered what their true errand was. Such a grand gentleman could hardly be engaged in sordid transactions with English agents.

"Master Trenchard," said Van Sluys musingly after bidding them sit in the splendid armchairs. "A relation of Ned Trenchard, perhaps?"

"A distant cousin, no more," admitted Tom. "I am but a humble merchant."

"Ah, you would prefer to talk business! You will take a drink with me before we do so, will you not? Are you the kind of Englishman who only drinks ale? Or would you and your good lady prefer wine—as we do."

"Wine," said Tom. "We prefer the grape to the grain, do we not, wife?"

Catherine nodded, amused. Tom had certainly preferred ale last night! Perhaps that was why he was insisting on wine this morning.

"Well, very well," agreed Van Sluys, motioning to a footman to serve his guests and himself. A footman placed the lemons and biscuits reverently on one of the small tables together with plates, knives, forks, snowy-white damask napkins and four exquisitely chased wine glasses. The Dutch seemed to make a small ceremony of everything.

They began to talk business. Tom had primed Catherine beforehand and several times she smiled prettily and qualified what he had said.

"Oh, no more paintings. Dear. China sells far better. After all, we do have to eat, but looking at paintings is a diversion, nothing more, and once seen, often forgotten."

"A clever lady, your wife," commented Van Sluys approvingly. "Every good businessman should have one, eh, my dear," he ended, putting a hand on his own wife's arm.

They were committing themselves not only to the purchase of china and glass, but fine damask tablecloths and hangings.

"Later," Van Sluys said, after dishes of oysters and prawns had been brought in, together with a loaf of bread, and his footman had been sent away again, "we will go to the cellars, and you may show me what you prefer. You have no clerk with you to make an inventory?" Geordie was obviously no clerk, and was being entertained in Van Sluys's vast kitchen.

"My wife is my clerk, I need no other. And the secrets of business are best kept in the family, eh?"

"It does my heart good to meet so sensible a member of your country," said Van Sluys enthusiastically. "You Englishmen are usually not clever enough to use the talents of your women to best advantage. Why pay a clerk when you have one in your bed?"

"You have had a deal of business with Englishmen, *Mijnheer?*"

"Indeed, indeed. Very much." He winked. "I like the English—unlike those who rule us and are not wise enough to see that we need your help to keep out the French and those who would enslave us.''

''Well said, sir. And did you tell Sir Thomas Gower that?''

Dead silence followed. Catherine, watching Van Sluys carefully as Tom had instructed her, saw the faintest flutter of his eyelids, the sudden stillness of his hands and the firming of his mouth when Tom mentioned Gower's name. The brute power of the man, concealed by his fine manners and his elegant home, briefly shone through the veneer of charming civilisation that he offered the world.

''You know Sir Thomas?'' he asked, after slowly spearing an oyster, squeezing lemon on it, and swallowing it carefully.

''Intimately,'' said Tom. ''Intimately.'' His own eyes were as hard as Van Sluys's had become and were focussed on his face. His wife said nothing, but she too, Catherine saw, shared in the tension which had suddenly gripped her husband.

''What do you want of me, Master Trenchard? Besides glass and other trumperies. You do wish to buy them—or is that a blind?''

''No blind.'' And if Tom was surprised by his quarry's bluntness—which he was—he gave no sign of it. ''And what I want is simple enough. I need to know where to find William Grahame.''

Tension visibly ebbed out of Van Sluys. ''And that is all? I can easily tell you where Grahame lodges, and shall do so before you leave. But you said two things, and that is only one.''

Tom smiled. He was beginning to enjoy himself. He

thought that Van Sluys was more shaken by his sudden transformation from simple merchant to an English agent than he ought to be. Time to turn the mental thumbscrews.

"I mistook," he smiled artlessly. "Three things. The second may also be simple. Do you know aught of Giles Newman?"

"Only that he is dead. I am told that he tried blackmail—and paid for it. Something you should remember, Master Trenchard. Next?"

Catherine could not but admire Van Sluys's coolness under fire. And Tom's as he directed the fire.

"What do you know of your country's dispositions that your friend and benefactor, Sir Thomas Gower, might like to know?"

Van Sluys was not in the least put out.

"Oho, so you *are* his intimate. One sees that well. I know nothing that the whole world does not know. That we intend to drive you from the seas. Except..." and he paused tantalisingly.

"Except?" Tom repeated.

"Except that William Grahame knows as much as I do, and I would prefer him to tell you what we know, rather than speak of it here. Here I am a simple merchant."

Tom looked round the splendid room, paid for by the wealth of the East Indies and Holland's gift for trade and commerce.

"Simple!" scoffed Tom derisively, Catherine echoing him internally.

"As simple as you are, Master Trenchard. No more and no less." He smiled engagingly, looking Tom up and down. "You see, Master Trenchard, a man of power can always recognise another, and I suspected what you were from the moment that you and your pretty wife entered this room. Does she know you, Master Trenchard? And do you know her? But let us leave that, and finish our business. Later we shall dine, and toast our two agreements."

"So, I ask you again, wife, for I have come to value your judgement—what did you make of Hendrick Van Sluys?" It was late afternoon and they had not long returned from dining with Van Sluys and his wife after they had inspected his vast and crammed storerooms.

Catherine pondered a moment before answering. "Why, I thought that he was a cheerful rogue—unlike either Amos Shooter or William Grahame." She stopped, wondering whether to continue, for what she might say of Amos Shooter could possibly distress Tom. After all, they had once been companions in arms.

As usual Tom missed little. Slight though her hesitation had been, he had seen it. "Go on," he told her. "You have not finished."

"No. I think that I do not trust either Van Sluys or Amos Shooter overmuch, but of the two I would trust Amos Shooter the less."

"Why?" Tom was being provoking and knew it. He was leaning against the wall, facing her where she sat and was twirling a small parchment windmill, a child's toy that he had brought from a stall set up not far from the inn. "Is it because Van Sluys was more cheerful and has the prettier face?"

"You are pleased to mock," returned Catherine stiffly, "and I confess that I have little enough evidence on which to make such a judgement, but there is something about them both on which I cannot lay a finger but which leads me to believe that what I have said is true."

Tom bent down and handed her the windmill after setting its miniature sails spinning.

"And again," he said, his own face so near to her that she could see plainly see the red-gold hairs of his beard along the lines of his strong chin, "we are in agreement. And I cannot give you any good reasons for my judgement that Amos is less trustworthy, either. It is a feeling, no more, but to such feelings I have often owed my life when others around me have lost theirs. I think, sweeting, that your instincts are sound."

He finished his sentence with a light kiss on the corner of her mouth before propping up the wall again.

Catherine had already noticed that he called her wife when he was teasing or provoking her, and sweeting when he was praising or trying to seduce her.

"Geordie tells me," he continued, "that they keep a good kitchen for their servants—unlike some whose riches are reserved for the drawing room. He has also discovered that Van Sluys is a burgomaster and is therefore a Regent, a member of one of the ruling families in Amsterdam. Which makes his dabblings in treason more interesting."

He paused, waiting for Catherine to comment. She held up the little windmill and set it spinning again, before obliging him.

"I suppose that he is playing both ends against the

middle. That is, he believes that the French are more of a danger to Holland than we are, so he seeks to ensure that any victory the Dutch might achieve over us will not be so great that it might make us a weak ally in the future. Also, by telling Grahame to pass information to us, he is not personally committing treason by telling us himself.''

''Oh, bravo,'' exclaimed Tom. ''And tomorrow you shall visit Grahame and find out what Van Sluys thinks is important enough to hand over to Sir Thomas Gower.''

''I!'' exclaimed Catherine, startled into losing her usual composure. ''On my own, without you?''

''Oh, you may take Geordie with you, and if aught went wrong he would protect you. Do not be deceived by his complaining and miserable exterior. Geordie's skill with a small sword is remarkable. Besides, he has taken a liking to you, believes that I am overharsh with you, and from thinking that I ought to seduce you on the spot, now thinks that I ought not to seduce you at all! Quite a chaperon is our Geordie.''

''Which does not explain why you wish me to go alone. Why so?''

''Because William Grahame will be less wary with you than with me. Charm him. Allow him to think you foolish and that you might not even remember correctly what he tells you. More than that, I think that he might believe you over the matter of his pardon, rather than me.''

Catherine played with the little windmill again, her face troubled.

''Believe me, sweeting, I would not ask you to do

this thing if it were not that I think that you will manage him better than I could. Remember what Van Sluys said about the Dutch trusting and using their women, particularly their wives."

He came over to her and took the windmill from her to lay it gently on the big bed before he knelt beside her. "I trust you, sweeting, and I vow that I would not send you into danger."

Tom cursed himself inwardly, even as he spoke, remembering poor dead Giles Newman. They were playing a dangerous game, but he, Gower and Arlington had coldbloodedly decided to use Catherine against Grahame because it was known that he could easily be influenced by the charms of a pretty woman.

But he had not met her then, and as he took her hand to kiss it, he was blessed—or was it cursed?—by a sensation he had never thought to experience. He suddenly knew that, of all inconvenient things, he had fallen in love with her. He swore to himself that he would follow her and Geordie, and watch Grahame's lair as carefully as he could so that she might not come to any harm.

All that he wanted to do was to protect her, to keep her from danger, to lap her in silk, to lie her in his bed, and...and... But he had sworn an oath to Gower and Arlington and he had to keep to it, as she did, for there was the matter of her brother whom they had used to blackmail her into going on this venture. A matter of which he was beginning to feel ashamed.

He had fallen so strangely silent that Catherine looked into his hard, suffering face and said gently, "What is is, Tom?"

''Nothing,'' he said roughly, and crushed her to him, not to try to make love to her, but to hold her safe. ''Nothing, and believe this, I shall not allow any harm to come to you, this I swear.''

Oh, if only he could go back in time, to London, to that night at the Duke of York's Theatre, he would— knowing and loving her as he now did—have gone back to Gower and told him that she was not suitable, that they would have to find another wench.

For this wench had become too dear to him for him to want to risk her. And when and how that had come to pass he did not know.

Chapter Eleven

"So, wife, you know what you have to say and do. Geordie shall be your footman and I shall follow you at a suitable distance and keep watch outside Grahame's lodgings. Between us we shall do our utmost to protect you."

Remembering Giles Newman's sad fate, Catherine nodded her thanks. Well but not ostentatiously dressed, Geordie behind her, she set off towards the far side of the Buttermarket where the New Church, Amsterdam's pride, stood. It was mid-morning and the huge square was full of people. A boy rolling a hoop dashed by her, and she also had to dodge an advancing coach, a great clumsy thing carrying one of the Regents and his fat wife.

On one side of the square an impromptu stage had been erected and a group of players were performing on it, watched by a crowd of well-dressed burghers. Catherine regretted not having the time to stop and watch them, but she needed to press on. She dodged a sledge on rollers, piled high with parcels, being vigorously pushed along by a stout young man—only to be nearly knocked over by yet another boy vigorously chasing a hoop.

Looking wistfully back towards the stage, she was surprised to see Amos Shooter standing before it. He was not watching the players but was talking earnestly to a large man in country clothing.

What was he doing here? He had said nothing to her or Tom about a visit to Amsterdam. She must be mistaken. After all, she was only seeing him at a distance, and when she looked again to try to make sure whether the man *was* Amos or not, he, and the fellow with him, had disappeared.

This odd sighting of a man she thought to be many miles away disturbed Catherine, but she said nothing to Geordie, and walked silently on through the rich and bustling scene, richer indeed than any she had ever seen before.

It was only when she was out of the square and making her way down a back street by a minor canal that the almost universal prosperity of central Amsterdam disappeared. She was suddenly confronted by beggars in rags, some apologetic, some bullying, but all were pushed away from her, cursing, by Geordie's staff.

The house in a side alley where Grahame lodged was similar in design to Van Sluys's superb home, but on a smaller, dingier scale. The landlady who answered the door took them up to his room by a flight of steep stairs smelling of recently cooked food.

William Grahame betrayed no surprise on seeing her. He welcomed her in with a smile and offered them both a seat. Geordie refused in his usual put-upon whine, and took up a standing position, with his back to the door of Grahame's small living room.

"Mistress Trenchard, I vow that I did not expect to see you here in Amsterdam, but now that I do you are a sight to please any man's eyes." He looked around. "Your husband is not with you?"

"No, alas, he has a megrim today so I have come with our servant Geordie. He particularly asked me to give you his good wishes and to tell you that we have had a letter from London regarding your proposed offer."

Catherine coughed prettily behind her hand and added, "We called on you in Antwerp and found that you had already left for Amsterdam. Despite suffering from an attack of ague, my husband insisted on leaving Antwerp at once in order to tell you the good news— and he has sent me here on my own so as to waste as little time as possible."

She offered him Belinda Bellamour's best blushing smile and William Grahame blossomed before it, forgetting as he did so, to ask how she and Tom had known where to find him.

"Exceedingly kind of you, Mistress Trenchard—and of your husband, of course."

"Of course, sir," and Catherine blushed again. "You would wish to know what the despatch from London said?"

"Indeed—at your leisure, mistress. The walk from the Herengracht is not a short one." He was aware at once that by saying this last he might have given something away—for someone must have told him that they were lodging just off it since Catherine herself had not said where she and Tom were staying. Such an admission meant that either they were being watched, or someone to whom they had spoken had passed on the news to him.

Looking at Catherine, Grahame decided that she was too innocent a newcomer to the dangerous game she was playing to pick up such a slight reference. She appeared so young and charming that he underestimated her age, believing her to be barely twenty when she was almost twenty-five.

Grahame was wrong to believe that Catherine was as naïve as she seemed. Well used to all the nuances of speech both by being an actress and also by writing plays where such ploys were often used, Catherine had grasped immediately the inner meaning of what Grahame had said. She betrayed no sign of this when she answered him.

"Quite so, sir, but I am used to walking long distance in London and made nothing of this. I still have my breath. My husband told me to inform you that our masters have agreed to give you an unconditional pardon, but dare not send either the pardon or an open letter to you saying so. Such a move would be unwise, and the letter we received was, of course, in code.

"But we have the power to assure you that London will play fair with you—if you will play fair by us by giving us the information about the Dutch fleet's intentions of which you spoke in Antwerp."

"To you, mistress, or to your husband?" He looked across at Geordie. "And will your servant be present when such high and mighty secrets are passed to you?"

Catherine turned to say to Geordie, "Oh, I'm sure

that my faithful footman will consent to leave the room—so long as he is in such earshot that while he may not hear exactly what we say, he will be aware that nothing untoward is taking place between us.''

She almost felt Geordie bridle at the mere idea of leaving her alone with Grahame, but she was sure that it was a necessary ploy. She shook her head prettily at him. ''Oh, Geordie, I am sure that I am perfectly safe with Master Grahame. Especially if you are near.''

''I shall go no further than the other side of this open door,'' he growled, indicating the one behind him.

''If Master Grahame agrees to that, as I am sure he will, then you will agree, I trust, that you are still able to protect me from there—although from what danger, I cannot imagine.''

Belinda Bellamour's smile was for both of them. And both men fell before it—although it would be more true to say that Geordie had already fallen, and that Grahame was about to do so. But their intentions towards her were quite different.

The moment that the door was left ajar with Geordie behind it, William Grahame rose from his chair on the other side of the room to come to sit near her. ''For we must not be overheard by anyone,'' he murmured urgently.

''No, indeed, Master Grahame.'' Seeing that he proposed to move even nearer to her, she told him hurriedly, but keeping her voice honey-sweet, ''I can hear you quite well if you remain where you are. I would not have my servant think wrong things about us whilst we are alone. I am sure you understand, sir, that a young wife must guard her reputation at all times—as you guard your secrets!''

He nodded, and then said, his voice very low, ''I am still a little troubled that London might not play fair with me.''

''Never say, sir, that you doubt my word.'' Catherine primmed her mouth and put on an expression of great and earnest concern. ''I lay my hand upon my heart, and assure you that Sir Thomas Gower himself, even before we left London, swore to me that your services to the State he serves were so great that your reward would be equally great. In the face of this, and the letter I carry with me, would you call me false or a liar?''

William Grahame would have done well to do both since not a word that Catherine had just uttered was true. The ring of righteous indignation in her voice owed everything to her career on the stage of the Duke's Theatre and nothing to honesty. Only the knowledge of the number of Dutch and Englishmen whom the man before her had callously sent to their deaths was making her so double-faced. She owed him nothing—especially since Tom had told her that he believed that Grahame might also have killed Giles Newman.

Moved, Grahame put out a hand to take hers. He knew very well that what Gower had told Catherine before she began her mission might have been a blind, designed to influence her, as well as him. But her patent sincerity affected him.

''Of course I believe you, my dear,'' he told her, still holding her hand in his, and looking into her beautiful violet eyes. ''And to prove what I say, I will tell you what I have learned of the Dutch Navy's intentions.

"They plan a frontal attack on your naval base at Sheerness. They intend to sail up the Medway and destroy it, and Chatham, and the ships at anchor there, leaving England crippled and unable to fight at sea. This would be an almost mortal blow, coming on top of the financial damage caused by the plague and the Great Fire of London last year."

Catherine withdrew her hand sharply and stared at him. "Are you sure of this? That is as bold a stroke as I have ever heard of. Can I believe you?"

Nothing that Tom, Gower or Arlington had told her when they had briefed her before they left London had suggested that the Dutch would attempt anything quite so daring.

"Believe me, Mistress Trenchard, that is their battle plan. And I have more information about what the Dutch wish to gain in the peace talks at Breda. Information that would help England to negotiate a better bargain than they might have hoped for—seeing that this war has not gone their way since their victories in the plague year."

All this was even better than she and Tom had hoped. Now, if only Grahame would give her the information about the Dutch War aims that he believed to be so valuable, they might notify London of it at once—and then set out for home themselves, their mission safely over. Rob would be freed and she could take up her life again.

And say farewell to Tom Trenchard, a little voice said. Do I really want that? She tried to ignore the voice, to concentrate instead on persuading Grahame to give her this last vital piece of information.

''If what you have to say of Breda is so important, sir, then why not tell me of it now?''

''What! And give away both my bargaining counters? Nay, mistress. Send the first to London, and then you must bring me a letter containing my pardon. And come alone, if you please, without that tall oaf, your husband, who is not worthy of you, as I hope to prove when you visit me. And leave your servant behind, too.

''And after that, why, after that, I will give you what you wish—having gained from you what *I* wish.'' He placed his hand suggestively on her knee, pressed it, and winked at her.

Every hair on Catherine's body rose. *She* had only one wish. To push his desecrating hand from her knee and tell him to keep his damned information if the price of it was her virtue.

But the memory of Rob's predicament held her still and steady. She and Tom had promised to deliver Grahame, and Grahame's information, to Gower and his cohorts in London and she would try to keep her promise.

So she smiled Belinda's seductive smile at Grahame again. Only her talent for acting made it possible for her to pretend that what he was demanding from her as the price of his information was one that she was willing to pay.

''I hear you,'' she told him through stiff lips, ''and when I have the further letter that you require I will bring it to you.''

''Oh,'' he said softly, ''I am sure you will. We understand each other, you and I.'' In proof of this mistaken belief, he placed his large hand on her breast and squeezed it. ''An earnest of what is to come,'' he told her.

Catherine stood up, and removed his offensive hand. ''Not now, dear William, not now. My servant is but a step away and will doubtless be thinking that you are giving me the entire plans of the Dutch government regarding not only the navy, but also their intentions towards the Spice Islands and their regaining of New Amsterdam! I am sure that we do not want him to report to my husband that our rapprochement is more than a business one.''

''What a clever doxy you are,'' was Grahame's only, and admiring, reply.

Catherine made him no further answer but called to Geordie, ''You can come in now. Our business here is over, and so we may go home and tell your poor ailing master of our success. The news should have him out of his bed and well again!''

''He suggested what?'' Tom's voice rose to a drill sergeant's roar. ''And Geordie not even in the room with you!'' From venting his fury on Catherine, he now turned it on his servant. ''Damn you, Geordie, didn't I tell you to stay with her at all times. Do you never do as you are bid?''

Geordie stuck out his lower lip and glared back at Tom. Catherine rode to his rescue. ''And damn you, Tom Trenchard, for railing at poor Geordie when he was only doing *my* bidding.''

They had returned to the inn to report on their meet-

ing with William Grahame. Tom, after first congratulating Catherine for persuading Grahame to pass on the
plans of the Dutch Navy, was now half-mad with rage
on learning that the price of further information was
that Catherine should agree to be Grahame's mistress!

Her intervention on Geordie's behalf did her no good
at all; it merely served to fuel his anger the more.

"Your bidding, mistress, was it? *You* sent him out
of the room in order to sell your body to Grahame."
When Catherine tried to reply, to explain, he crossed
the room to grasp her by the elbows and stare into her
face. His own was suffused with blood. Catherine suddenly knew what he looked like in battle, and an awe-
some sight it was.

"No," he cried, shaking her, "I'll not have it. I'll
not be cuckolded."

Silence followed this remarkable statement.

Geordie gave a cackle and Catherine said numbly,
"Hardly that, surely. I am not your wife. What's more,
I know quite well that your plan, aye and that of Sir
Thomas Gower, was that I should play the whore with
Grahame if that were necessary to gain the information
he holds. So why are you complaining now? Why re-
proach me when I am merely following orders—to
save Rob."

Tom stared down at her, to see that for all her brave
words to him, fear of him was written on her face. The
moment she had told him of her final conversation with
Grahame, he had suddenly run mad with rage and jealousy. And the devil of it was that everything she had
just said was true. She was not his wife, they *were*

using her as bait, and he had no right, no right at all, to speak to her and Geordie as he had done.

But the thought of her in Grahame's arms, doing with him what she would not do with Tom Trenchard, had unmanned him quite. He suddenly knew why Othello in old Will Shakespeare's play had murdered his wife. The saying from The Song of Solomon, that jealousy is as cruel as the grave, took him by the throat to remind him what horrors he might be tempted to commit if he allowed his passions to run away with him.

As gently as he could he let go of her and stood back. Not only Catherine let out a sigh of relief, but Geordie also. Tom would never know that his servant had been ready to attack him if he attacked Catherine.

"Forgive me," he said humbly, which had Geordie staring at him. Tom Trenchard humble! Here was a turn up! "I should not have spoken as I did, but you cannot…"

Catherine did not allow him to finish. "Of course not. Even to save Rob." She shuddered. "How can I say that? I do not know what I might, or might not, do to save someone I loved."

"Nor do any of us." Tom's voice was as shaky as hers. "Let me recover my good sense. We can then discuss quietly what we *are* to do. Did Grahame give you any hint of what he might have to tell us? Or of whom he is dealing with in Amsterdam?"

Catherine shook her head, happier now that Tom was his usual controlled self again. For the last few minutes she had watched him, fascinated, as he had rivalled

Betterton himself in giving vent to his rage. Betterton's stage rants were famous.

"There was one odd thing, though. I thought that I saw Amos Shooter when I was crossing the Buttermarket, before the play actors' stage. I could not be sure that it was he."

Tom looked at Geordie. "Did you see aught of Shooter?"

"Nay, master. I was too busy guarding the mistress—as you had bid me," he finished soulfully.

Tom ignored this piece of impudence. "I came through the Buttermarket in your wake, but I saw nothing of him. Which does not mean that he might not have been there. You have sharp eyes, sweeting."

There! She was forgiven. She was sweeting again, neither wife nor you.

To mollify him she said quietly, "As for Grahame, I was too busy holding him off at the end—whilst seeming to lead him on—to try to coax further information out of him. Nor, I think, did he wish to give it."

Tom thought for a moment before saying, "You did well, very well. What we must do next is encipher this information and send it to London tomorrow by the morning's post. For the rest, we must avoid suspicion by going about our business and loudly lamenting that old Noll Cromwell's successors are not ruling England."

"And if the letter comes back with no more concessions for Grahame, what then?" Catherine's voice was anxious and Tom put a consoling arm around her shoulders.

"Why then, we shall devise a plan. Do not fear, sweeting, whatever they would have you do, those who sit on their backsides in London, and leave the dirty work to us, you shall not sell yourself to Grahame, my word on't."

How warm it was, how safe to be held thus, to see Geordie grinning approvingly at them, so that the danger that they were running disappeared for a moment from her consciousness. She was alive as she had never been before.

Catherine remembered something that Betterton had once said to her about his experiences in the Great Plague: "One is never so truly alive as when one faces death at any moment." She had never thought that there might come a day when she would be in a position to test the truth of this observation!

Chapter Twelve

"Now what do you make of this?"

Sir Thomas Gower tossed across the table to m'lord
Arlington a decoded copy of the letter containing the
news of the plan to raid Sheerness. He was seated at
the head of a long table in the Navy Office. Sam Pepys
was there to take the minutes. He was flanked by Buckingham and Lord Clifford. George Villiers, Duke of
Buckingham, was in one of his flighty moods and
yawned ostentatiously as Arlington silently read the
document through twice.

"I must apologise for springing this matter upon you
without warning," Gower said, "but it reached me
only last night and the matter is urgent."

"Truly so," agreed Arlington, handing the letter to
Buckingham to read, "if we can give any credence to
what is written here."

Buckingham tossed it across the table to Sam Pepys.
"Read us what it says," he commanded. "I've a
woundy sore head and have no mind to decipher some
clerk's cramped script!" Although in many ways the

cleverest of the men around the table, he was capricious to a degree.

Pepys did as he was bid and read out Catherine and Tom's letter, informing them that Grahame had handed over details of the Dutch plan to raid Sheerness and sail up the Medway.

Dead silence followed before Clifford spoke.

"We are expected to believe this?"

His tone was so sceptical that Sam Pepys looked up in surprise. He alone of the men there thought that the letter told the truth. But he was only their secretary and consequently held his tongue.

Clifford picked up the letter and waved it about. "Was your fellow in Holland drunk that he concocted such a cobweb of moon madness? He doubtless seeks to earn his money by sending you a tale that would sound well on the boards of the theatre rather than in the halls where statesmen need to make decisions."

Arlington nodded. "I trust our man in Holland," he said slowly, not telling them that "our man" was an intimate of them all. He would say and do nothing to put Stair Cameron in danger, and he knew only too well that Buckingham had a reputation for being indiscreet. "But I agree with you that this plan is fanciful, to say the least."

"A pity that the Duke cannot be with us," said Sam Pepys as tactfully as he could. He was referring to the Duke of York, the King's brother, who was an efficient naval commander. "His opinion would have been invaluable."

"As it is," said Clifford, ignoring Pepys's contribution, "I submit that no action need be taken and that we allow this letter to lie on the table. Even the Dutch are not so harebrained as to dare all on such a risky venture."

Several heads nodded. Of all the great men present, only Sir Thomas Gower frowned. Like Arlington, he trusted Stair Cameron and he thought that what he had written to them had been sent in good faith, but like the others he also thought that it was most likely a trick by Grahame to gain the pardon he wanted.

"And for the rest? The second matter promised?" he asked.

"I propose that we send Grahame renewed assurances of a pardon in exchange for further information, although judging by this it may be worthless," suggested Clifford. "We can determine what to do about that when we have examined it."

And so it was agreed.

Afterwards Arlington, frowning, said to Sir Thomas, "It would not be like Stair Cameron to send us nonsense, but I am also of the opinion that this information is worthless.

"Nevertheless, we will do as Clifford suggested and give Grahame another chance to pass on something useful. Which means that Stair and the woman are not to be sent word to return home until after they have forwarded to us Grahame's second offering."

Sir Thomas agreed. They walked out of the room, leaving the letter on the table, where later, at Sam Pepys's bidding, a minor clerk filed it away, to be lost in the State Archives for the next three hundred years.

So far Tom and Catherine had dared all for nothing.

* * *

Unaware that London had dismissed their hard-earned information as worthless, Master Tom Trenchard and his wife were discussing more urgent matters.

After the first few nights, both of them had become accustomed to sleeping with the bolster between them. That was not to say that Catherine was not uncomfortably aware of Tom's large presence so close to her. Worse, he frequently walked through her dreams, jolting her awake whenever, in the dream, he approached too near her—which was often.

She wondered how well Tom was coping with sleeping so near to her. Matters were helped—if that were the right word—by his not coming to bed until some time after she had retired.

He and Geordie usually ended the evening in the taproom. Tom played a wicked game of chess and was constantly being challenged by the other patrons of the inn. She was often asleep when he finally climbed into bed, and he and Geordie were considerate enough to make as little noise as possible so as not to disturb her.

In the morning, Catherine usually awoke to find him gone. He washed himself at the pump in the yard behind the inn: she had been warned never to go there before breakfast since he was only one of many men making themselves ready for the day, parading around half-naked—or so Geordie had told her.

She was not to know that Tom's sleep was as disturbed as hers was. If he woke during the night to hear her steady breathing, he had to use all his self-control not to push the bolster aside and treat her as lustily as a healthy man should treat a desirable woman.

What kept Tom from falling on her was his growing respect for her as the days flew by, and the unfortunate fact that not only was he in love with her, but that he also loved her. He did not want any harm to come to her, and he was daily more and more amazed at the turmoil of mixed feelings that she roused in him.

Perhaps it was that that made him clumsy when he walked upstairs on the night of the day on which Grahame had sent word to Catherine that he was ready to pass on his latest, and most important, piece of news.

Tom had just played a hard and lengthy game of chess that he had won—a great relief to Geordie, who had staked his week's pay on him—and was more tired than usual. For once he lit a candle, but still managed to stumble as he climbed up the high steps into bed. He fell forward heavily on to the curst bolster.

Forgetting Catherine's presence and decorum generally, he roared in exasperation, "Oh, hell and all the devils preserve me from bolsters!" With that, he hurled the bolster to the floor.

The noise of his anger woke Catherine. Startled, wrenched from a dream of Tom and herself walking happily by the Amstel River, she sat up, alarmed.

"What's that?" she asked, having no idea what Tom had actually said, only that he had said something. "Is anything wrong?"

"Very wrong. It's this damned bolster. I've ridden us of it," Tom announced proudly. "We shall be more comfortable without it."

"What!" Catherine leapt out of bed and ran round to his side of it, to pick up the bolster and hold it to her as though it were a shield. "No such thing! We agreed."

"Well, I'm tired of the agreement. I disown it. The Dutch aren't the only people who can play skittles with agreements. Down with all bolsters and up with comfort in bed, I say!"

"And I say I shan't get into bed again until you agree that the bolster shall lie between us."

Tom lay back lazily on his high pillows. Standing there in the half dark, the candlelight illuminating her, Catherine looked more beautiful than ever. Her black hair was down, her violet eyes were flashing, and the white linen of her nightrail with its deep lace-edged collar gave her the appearance of an angel in an old painting. Only the halo was missing.

"Lovely though you look, my sweeting," he told her cheerfully, "I shall not agree to your terms. By all means keep the bolster—and spend the night on the floor."

Catherine looked at him, and her treacherous heart fluttered in her breast. In Van Sluys's superb home, she had seen an old Italian painting of the god Apollo lying on a cloud, his arm around a nymph no more remarkable in her perfection than he was in his.

Tom Trenchard, unshaven, muscular, his body golden in the candlelight, his red-gold hair about his shoulders, might have been the model the artist had chosen for his image of masculine beauty. Never mind that his face was neither as soft, nor as pretty, as the god's, his body was a perfect match.

Anguished, her own body trying to deny its primitive instincts that would have had her jumping into bed to lie as close to him as she could, Catherine said stiffly, "You are no gentleman, sir, to suggest any such thing."

"I have never claimed to be one," returned Tom naughtily, "so that makes no matter. Your choice, sweeting, your choice. The bed without the bolster, or the floor with it. Your choice, always your choice. I know what mine would be."

Catherine's temper was up. She stamped on the floor. "You are a bully, Thomas Trenchard, a bully, a very Mohawk. Have you no shame, to leave me on the floor whilst you lie on the bed?"

"*I* am not leaving you on the floor." Tom was sweetly reasonable, a grin on his face. "*You* are choosing the floor. I refuse to take the blame for your decisions."

Catherine wanted to fling the bolster at him, to wipe the grin from his face. "It is no choice at all, and well you know it. It is there to protect me."

"You'll be even better protected on the floor, for I shall not be there," Tom pointed out. "Which should be some comfort to you—if not much."

Before Catherine could reply—she was being rendered speechless by his impudence—the door to Geordie's ante-room opened and he put a weary face around it. "Cut the cackle, will you? Some of us want to get a bit of sleep, even if you two don't. Give me the bloody bolster if that's what's causing all the noise, my pillow ain't comfortable."

This was really the last straw! Angered beyond reason, Catherine spun round and flung the bolster at Geordie. Catching it and clutching it to his breast, he whined cheerfully at her, "Thankee, mistress. And a good night to the pair of ye now that's settled." He closed the door gently behind him.

What had she done? Now if she lay on the floor she had not even the bolster to ease her tired body. Stricken, Catherine made the mistake of looking at Tom. He was, as she might have expected, laughing at her.

"You! You!" she raged, walking to the bed, her hand raised. It was, though she did not yet know it, another mistake.

Tom began to sit up as she approached. "Me what? Catherine, my sweeting? I didn't throw the bolster at Geordie. *You* did."

She must hit him, she must. Frustration, anger, lust, nay, the desire to love him and be loved by him, all fuelled by the nights that they had spent with the denying bolster between them, had Catherine bending over him, threatening she knew not what.

Tom did not threaten, he acted. A wicked look upon his face, he leaned forward, quick as a snake striking, or a leopard pouncing on its prey, and scooped her up bodily so that she landed in the bed beside him.

But not for long. For now he turned her on to her back so that he might look down at her, as she panted with rage beneath him. Until he laid his mouth on hers and, quick as a flash, rage vanished and she melted beneath him...

Oh, the wasted days and nights when they had been apart! Tom had her nightrail off in a flash and she was pulling at his. Afterwards, Catherine was to think how strange it was, and yet how right, that she knew exactly what to do when they began to make love, as though she had been loving him all her life. His hands roved her body and hers roved his. Her hand stroked the golden down on his breast and his stroked her breasts, so small and yet so perfect.

Tom had always before admired buxom, large-breasted wenches, so how was it that Catherine's delicate perfection of form and feature so entranced him that even in passion's thrall he held back to treat her as gently and carefully as he could?

Tenderly he stroked her face and the long elegant lines of her body, which were even more lovely than he had imagined them to be when he had watched her move, fully clothed, about their room.

Catherine moaned and sighed beneath him. His lightest touch set her on fire where roughness would have repelled her. His very worship of her, the gentle brushing of his lips on her mouth, the cleft in her chin, the hollow of her throat, her breasts, the slight mound of her stomach, as he wandered lower and lower, had her writhing beneath him, crying for fulfilment.

Nor was this one-way traffic, for Tom, too, was roused beyond belief by the ease with which he brought her to fulfilment. The few weeks they had spent together, so close and yet so far away—the bolster being a symbol of everything that had kept them apart—only served to add to the fever in the blood now that the symbol had gone. Tom's hurling the bolster out of the bed, followed by Catherine throwing it at Geordie, had freed them both.

And then, as they came closer and closer and Catherine's legs, of their own accord, clasped him, the fever they shared grew and mounted. Until at the last, when she fully opened herself to him, Tom achieved what he had always wanted since he had first seen her as Belinda Bellamour, dancing on the London stage. He became Catherine's lover in every sense of the word.

Only to discover that he held in his arms that rare thing in the London of King Charles II, a beautiful young virgin, who gasped and cried as he entered her. But it was too late for remorse, for even as his brain told him that he must stop, his body achieved the most powerful fulfilment he had ever known. Tender consideration had brought him a pleasure that lusty carelessness had never conferred.

His love was shuddering and crying in his arms. And whether her cries were of pain or pleasure, Catherine hardly knew. But when he tried to draw away from her, to ease her pain, she only wound her arms around him the more tightly.

"No! no!" she panted. "Stay with me. Ah, God, I never thought such pleasure existed."

"But, sweeting—" and now the word was a very caress, not a mockery, and accompanied by the gentlest kiss "—I have hurt you. Oh, I should have known, but how could I?"

How could he, indeed? Innocence was such a rare commodity that men, aye, and some women, too, mocked at the mere idea that it could exist. But it did, and beneath him lay the living proof. And he had violated it.

"You should have told me," he said gravely, lifting his weight from her, but leaving them still united.

Mischief rode on the face that looked up at him. "Would you have believed me had I done so?"

His half-laugh in reply was rueful. "Aye, you have me there, sweetheart. I constantly jeered at your virtue, believing that, like most women, you had none. And now I have robbed you of it."

Catherine shook her head. "No, I cannot have that. I was your most willing partner. You could not have seduced me on your own. It takes two to make love— and you never needed to force me. Strange it was that from the moment I flung the bolster at Geordie I was lost."

Her words, and her loving face as she said them, had the strongest effect on Tom. He grew inside her, which would never do. To love her again, so soon after robbing her of her maidenhead, would be truly to hurt her. He must play the man and let her go, not play the selfish cur and think only of his pleasure.

Even as Tom decided this, he suffered the strongest pain of all. For was she not bound on the morrow to visit Grahame? Grahame, who thought that she was not virtuous and was his for the taking. The anguish he had suffered when she had told him of Grahame's proposed bargain had him by the throat again, and now it was doubly hateful to think of her lying with him.

He could not allow it, he could not—and he would not. When he had agreed that she should be recruited as the bait that might be necessary to achieve their mission, he had believed that she was any man's for the taking—or the paying.

And now he knew better.

He released her, so that they might lie side by side.

He held her so that she rested on his shoulder, and he kissed the top of her head in lieu of kissing anything else. Even that small token of his love had his body protesting that it wanted more. He rebuked it.

After a moment he said, very slowly, "Catherine, I do not think that I can allow you to visit Grahame tomorrow."

So soon after their loving Catherine did not want to contradict him, but she must. They had their mission to fulfil and Rob's life might depend upon it. "Surely I must go," she said, "not to do so would be to break the promise I made back in London."

Passion ringing in his voice, Tom shook his head. "No, I forbid it. For he will not give you the information he has promised us unless you lie with him. That I am sure of. I know his kidney. And that you must not do. For your own sweet sake, you cannot become his mistress."

He did not say, And for my sake, too, for I cannot bear to think of another man touching you. You are mine, and you are precious to me. I have never felt this way about a woman before. I have taken my pleasure where I found it, and never heeded the morrow. When this mission is over, and pray God it may be so soon, I shall take you back to London with me.

Even now Tom could not quite bring himself to think of marrying Catherine. The habit of years still held him in its bonds, and although day by day these bonds were weakening, they had not yet broken.

He could not move her. Duty was more than a word to Catherine, as honour was. It was something by which she had always lived. Her father had believed in

both and had lost all because of it. "No, not all," he
had said once. "For I have never compromised my
honour, nor broken my word, and that is more precious
to me than land and money."

Holding her tightly to him, petting her rather than
making love to her, for he was fearful of hurting her
any more, Tom at last gave way.

She finally said the one thing that could make him
agree that she should meet Grahame. "I shall not lie
with him, Tom. This I promise you."

"But if he refuses to pass on his information without
that?"

"Then I must accept that I shall have failed—but,
at least, I shall have tried. Besides, we have already
sent the most vital news of all to London. They should
be ready for the Dutch when they come. They cannot
ask for much more than that."

Tom nodded thoughtfully. "We can always tell them
that Grahame was tricking us and had little more to
give."

"Oh, Tom, that would be a lie," said Catherine
gravely.

"But a lie in a good cause. Sleep now, sweeting. We
must be ready for the morrow."

Sleep they did, in one another's arms, leaving the
candle to gutter low, giving light to Geordie when, after
silence had fallen in the next room, curious, he entered
to see them lying there, entwined.

"And about bloody time too," he muttered as the
candle expired and he returned to his own lonely bed.

Catherine insisted on following Grahame's instructions to the letter. She had awoken the next morning,

a trifle sore, but happy beyond belief. She had no regrets over her lovemaking with Tom, and was resigned to the fact that he might have no intention of marrying her. That would be to believe in fairy stories and Catherine was, above all things, a realist.

She would never marry now if she could not have Tom, and what roving soldier and adventurer would wish to be hampered by an actress wife? True love would mean that she must grant him his freedom, however much it might cost her. And she had had her perfect night with her lover, which was more than many women ever had.

As for the possibility of a child, we would not worry about that until her courses were due and did not arrive—and not much after that. It was commonplace for actresses to bear bastard children, and she would be commonplace. Nor need she fear that she might not be able to support a child. She could always write some more plays, and perhaps even the story of the fairy Morgana in King Arthur's time, an idea of which she had already spoken to a London bookseller.

Armoured in love—however brief the time of loving might be—Catherine walked across Amsterdam again, Geordie behind her, Tom trailing them in the distance. Geordie was to wait for her outside Graham's lodgings, and Tom would keep watch on Geordie. It was all rather like a child's game, she thought. But then, her life since Rob had been arrested seemed to have turned into a rather nasty child's game.

But at least the game had brought her Tom. She would live for the day, and count each happy moment and paste it into her book of memories, which she kept in her head, not on paper.

The landlady gazed at her sourly when she answered the knock on her door.

"What, another visitor for him?" and she jerked her thumb towards the stairs. "I'm not taking you up, and that's flat. You're the third he's had this morning. First there was a shabby little dwarf, next a showy gentleman in fine clothing—we don't see many of those round here—and now you. His door's always open—and don't trouble me when you leave. I've more to do than wait on him," and she flounced off, leaving Catherine to mount the stairs alone.

She knocked on Grahame's door twice before she realised that he was either out, or was not going to answer. But the church clock had sounded the hour of twelve as she had crossed the Buttermarket and Grahame had insisted that she come as soon after mid-day as she could manage.

Catherine was tempted to return to the inn, and tell Tom that Grahame had not been at home after all, despite his message. That being so, they could forget the whole sorry business and go home. Something stopped her. The landlady had said his door was open. If it were not, then he had gone out. If it were, she would go in after knocking again. Perhaps he had not heard her, was dozing on his bed.

Further pounding on his door produced no answer. Catherine turned the iron ring on it that served as a handle—and it opened.

She walked in, gently calling Grahame's name as she did so. The room was empty. It was also in a dreadful mess. Books had been swept from their shelves; crockery from a dresser lay in shards on the floor. Every drawer had been wrenched from a tallboy and their contents strewn about the floor. A cupboard door hung open, and papers from it had been thrown over the smashed crockery and glass from the dresser.

Afterwards, Catherine was to wish that she had left at once, but curiosity and shock held her stock still. She looked around her, was about to bend to pick up a paper from the floor when the half-open door to Grahame's bedroom swung fully open and he came through it.

It would be more accurate to say that he staggered through it. His face was grey and a thin trickle of blood was running from his mouth. He had something clutched in his right hand. For a moment he steadied himself to stare at her before he fell forward on to the floor at her feet, still clutching the paper.

Catherine put both hands to her mouth to stifle a scream. Given what she and Tom were engaged in, she must not be found here with a dying man. She was sure that Grahame was dying, especially when she saw the dagger sticking out of his back. The blood from the wound it had caused had covered the whole back of his body and was still running slowly down to soak his breeches and his stockings.

She had never liked him, but sheer pity had her kneeling beside him on the floor in order to help him. She baulked at pulling the dagger from his back. But before she could as much as touch him, which she afterwards thought was just as well, because had she done so she would have been covered in his blood, he turned his head as it lay on the floor and croaked at her, "Mistress, you came." She could scarcely understand what he said.

Catherine nodded, said numbly and pointlessly, "Yes. I promised."

His head still turned towards her, agony on his face, he writhed, trying to raise his body, the effort causing him to gasp in agony.

"No, no," Catherine exclaimed fiercely. "Try to lie still."

He shook his ghastly head at her and finally succeeded in wriggling his right arm and the hand that held the paper towards her, saying something unintelligible. Catherine thought that it might be "For you."

Light dawned. He *was* trying to give her the paper. In her shock and distress she had not been thinking clearly.

She bent to take it from him, murmuring, "Lie still and I will fetch a doctor for you."

This time his words were clear, "No, no, too late. Go!"

Before she could contradict him, beg him to hold on until help came—even though reason told Catherine that he was right—Grahame's head fell sideways. A torrent of blood gushed from his mouth, and he lay still.

Death had claimed him.

Catherine never knew how long she knelt there. It seemed hours at the time, but Geordie and Tom later told her that very little time at all had passed between the moment that she entered the house, and the moment that she left it. She wanted to hold him, to close his staring eyes, to move him away from the broken crockery and the soiled papers amongst which he lay.

Self-preservation said no. There must be no blood on her if she should chance to meet his sullen landlady on her way out. He was dead. He might even have earned his death, but no man should die like that, and to leave him warred against all her better instincts. But there were Tom and Geordie to think of, as well as herself, and the paper to take away, which he had been so determined to give her.

She rose to her feet, and tried to control her shaking hands as she stowed the paper in the bag she was carrying. Grahame had seemed to think that it was important. Now there were only the stairs to negotiate, the landlady to avoid, so that she might be far away before the shock she was experiencing overcame her.

Carefully, Catherine picked her way on shaky legs out of the ruined room, leaving behind its ruined owner. She walked silently down the stairs and out of the front door to where Geordie was waiting for her.

He was about to make a light remark on the lines of "Well, that was quick, mistress, and no mistake," when he saw her ashen face, her white lips and her shaking hands.

"What is it, mistress? What's happened? I'll kill him for you if he's hurt you!"

Catherine shook her head, and smiled a ghastly smile. "Too late, Geordie, too late. Find Tom and let us go home, and there I will tell you all. But quick about it, we must not be found here."

Chapter Thirteen

"A dwarf and a well-dressed man, eh? Van Sluys, perhaps? We'll discuss that later."

After they had returned to the inn, Tom had given Catherine a glass of brandy, and made her lie on the bed before she told them what had happened in Grahame's room. Geordie had already reassured Tom that she had not been molested by Grahame. Tom had asked her to tell them everything that had happened in as much detail as she could remember.

Catherine drank a little more brandy. Tom said, "I shan't interrupt you again. Go on." She had already informed him when he had joined them in the Buttermarket that Grahame was dead, but had given him no details.

She told her dreadful story lucidly and well, much better than any junior officer had ever reported his tale to him, Tom noted.

Finally, she reached the point where Grahame had given her the paper. She stopped to fetch it out of her bag and handed it to Tom.

"He was absolutely determined to give it to me,

even though he was dying. I think that he was attacked in his bedroom, left for dead, heard me arrive and then, somehow, revived sufficiently and briefly to stagger in and live long enough to pass it on. It's in some sort of code, not ours. After that he died,'' she ended, taking another swig of the brandy.

The drink was making everything seem distant and far away, as it had done on the packet when they were at sea. It was as though what had passed had happened to someone else, and not to her.

Tom was examining the paper. She said hazily, ''It must be important, but it's not very useful if we don't know the key to the code, is it?''

He gave her a wolfish grin. ''But I think we do. A moment.'' He crossed the room to where his trunks stood against the wall, sorted through one of them and came back with Giles Newsman's prayer book.

''I didn't tell you at the time,'' Tom said, ''but reading through it I found this paragraph near the beginning which had apparently been used as the basis of a cipher. Suppose we try to decipher this letter using Newman's code? We lose nothing if we can't, and gain everything if we can.''

Catherine sighed lazily, ''Oh, Tom, I'm too drowsy to be able to decipher a letter. You shouldn't have given me so much brandy. All I want to do is sleep.''

He came over to the bed, sat by her, put an arm around her and kissed her. ''No need to worry, my brave girl. Try to rest. Today I'll be the clerk. If I'm right about the code, we must send a letter to London tomorrow, telling them what we have discovered—if we have discovered anything useful, that is.''

''Who could have killed him, Tom? And why?''

''Not the dwarf, I think. He may have given Grahame the letter. The better bet is the richly dressed man. That could be Van Sluys, but I wouldn't have thought that he was the kind to do his own dirty work. Of course, the murderer might have broken in after the rich gentleman left. Whoever it was, was almost certainly looking for the letter. I wonder how Grahame hid it from him. We shall never know.''

''Shuppose it were Amos Shooter, Tom.'' Catherine was so sleepy that she had begun to slur her words.

Tom considered. ''We don't rule anyone out. It might be someone we don't know, who thought Grahame a danger to him. We also have to ponder on why Grahame should have gone to such lengths to give you an enciphered letter when he couldn't know whether we possessed the key to it. Unless...'' and he paused.

''Unlesh what?''

''Unlesh, my schweeting,'' said Tom, tenderly mocking her, after kissing her cheek, which was now rosy again, ''he was somehow sure that I was the stranger who went to Newman's rooms after his death and recovered the book with the key in it.''

''Thatsh a jump in logic, Tom,'' Catherine told him. She yawned prettily. ''May we discush this later? I'm going to shleep now.'' Which she did as sweetly as a young woman could, and Tom, kissing her as she closed her eyes, prayed that Grahame would not walk through her dreams.

The key to the code *was* in Newman's book. Tom deciphered Grahame's letter while Catherine slept, which she did until early evening, when she awoke with a yawn to find that Tom had now begun to write the letter to London, passing on Grahame's information.

Halfway through the afternoon he had run out of ink. He pondered for a moment whether or not to send Geordie to a stationer's to buy some more. He decided not to go himself because he did not wish to leave Catherine in case she awoke distressed and needing comfort.

An idea struck him. Catherine had on one occasion fetched a stoppered bottle of ink from the trunk she had brought with her. She would surely not object to him using it, seeing how important it was that the information in Grahame's letter should reach London as soon as possible.

He opened the trunk. Like everything connected with Catherine, it was in perfect order. Lying above her carefully packed clothing was the large leather box from which she had lifted the ink bottle. He opened that too and found that the bottle was held steady by straps fixed to the side of the box so that it should not fall over.

The box also contained two quill pens, a penknife to sharpen them with, a small glass bottle containing sand to dry the ink, and a great sheaf of paper, much written on.

Tom had not set out with any intention of prying into Catherine's private belongings—and so he had intended to tell her when she woke up. But he was only human and the sheaf of paper intrigued him. What was it that she was busy writing—presumably when he oc-

casionally left her at night and in the day? More than
that, why had she taken such great care never to be
seen working by either himself or Geordie?

He now had a reasonable excuse to examine her papers, for their contents might concern the mission they
were engaged on. Was she somehow secretly sending
information about their mission to the agents of their
enemies? And was that why everybody seemed to be
beforehand with them?

The idea seemed far-fetched, but Tom, as he had told
Catherine earlier, had more than once saved his own
life by not dismissing far-fetched ideas and taking
nothing on trust.

He looked across at the bed. She was sleeping so
sweetly, a smile on her face, that he felt a cur for mis-
trusting her. Nevertheless, it was his duty to check what
she had been doing. He picked up the papers and began
to read them.

Catherine had obviously written at speed, but her
hand was a clear and clerkly one and Tom was soon
astonished to find that he was reading the text of a play.
Even more astonished to find on the first page that the
leading character was the self-same Lackwit whom he
had seen Betterton impersonating on the stage of the
Duke's Theatre.

He riffled rapidly through the thick sheaf of paper.
There was no doubt that he was reading the work of
one Will Wagstaffe, of whom he had so often joked
and who was none other than the pretty woman who
was sleeping in his bed.

Any final doubts he had vanished when he reached
the last of the handwritten pages on which Catherine

had scrawled proposals for the play's title, crossing all of them out except the last one which read, *The Braggart, or, Lackwit Married.*

Could it really be true? Could the witty and impudent Will Wagstaffe, whose bawdy jokes he had so enjoyed, really be his supposed wife, Catherine Wood, known also as Cleone Dubois? Had she yet another name to add to the two that she already possessed? He read through the first page again, and as he did so her voice was in his head, reading the lines to him.

It was the self-same voice with which she had sparred and jousted with him, silencing him, or spurring him on to fresh heights of impudence himself, so that they had often ended by laughing together, drunk with their own wit.

Another thing. Was there no end to her? She had shown herself to be uncomplaining, untiring, brave and resourceful, so why be surprised at this new revelation? Were not these the characteristics that would enable her to write her plays, call herself Wagstaffe and persuade Betterton to put them on? The characteristics that were enabling her not only to survive, but to keep her brother whilst he studied for the law.

Tom carefully put back the ink bottle, the bottle of sand, and the papers, trying to remember exactly how they had been arranged, before closing the trunk. She must not know that he had discovered her secret. Thinking that, he remembered how she had replied with a double tongue when she had answered his question about whether she had known Will Wagstaffe. "I know no such he."

Of course she didn't. He was a she.

Tom laughed soundlessly, poked his head around the door into the ante-room where Geordie was having an afternoon nap, woke him up and sent him out to buy ink and a new quill pen so that he might finish his work.

Thus it was that Catherine awoke to find him smiling at her, and putting the finishing touches on his letter to London. A pot of tea, cups, plates and some little Dutch cakes—they called them cookies—were neatly arranged on the table before him.

"Awake at last, sweeting. See what Geordie has brought for us. He told the landlady that you had a megrim, and this is what she produced to cure it. Tea is a restorative for everything, she told Geordie."

"Aye," agreed Geordie, "but you look better already, mistress."

"I feel better," returned Catherine, rising and walking over to sit opposite Tom and the tea. "What did Grahame's letter have to tell us?"

"Something important, my dear wife. But do drink your tea before I tell you. I wouldn't like you to disappoint Geordie and the landlady by leaving it."

The tea did act as a restorative. The events of midday began to fade a little from Catherine's mind. The cookies were excellent, and the three of them emptied the plate at "double quick time", Geordie's words.

Tom picked up the letter, and the one he had written to send to London. "The letter tells us that, in their negotiations at Breda, the Dutch do not wish to cede us any concessions in the Spice Islands in the Far East. They wish to retain their monopoly there.

"On the other hand, they have little interest in the

settlements in North America that we conquered and took from them, renaming New Amsterdam New York. They see little profit or future in them. They will thus try to persuade us that the New World settlements are what *they* really want, and that the Spice Islands are secondary in the belief that we shall then think that they know something about the New World that we don't, and that this will change our minds about wanting the Spice Islands, and make us bid for North America instead.

"Now I know that our own government thinks that the trading future of the world—and thus of England—lies in developing the vast resources of the New World and the trade routes to them. But if the Dutch realise this, they might haggle with us, and if we can make them believe that they have won the diplomatic game by our—very reluctantly—accepting the North American territories, and relinquishing any claim to the Spice Islands, they will think that they have tricked us into doing what they want."

Catherine put her hands to her head. "Oh, dear, that sounds very complicated, but I think I grasp what you are saying. That the Dutch will think that they have gained everything if they keep the Spice Islands in the Far East, and will let us have most of what we want at Breda, thinking that they have bested us.

"In other words, usually the old saying is, The bird in the hand is worth more than two in the bush, but you are arguing that the Spice Islands, the bird in the Dutch hand, will in the long run be worth *less* than the birds in the English bush, that is North American and New York."

"Exactly, you clever girl. After this fashion are negotiations won and lost. This will be invaluable news for our people in Breda. Nearly as much so as the news of the plans of the Dutch fleet."

Catherine wondered briefly how Tom came to know so much about so many arcane matters, but dismissed the thought. "And you have written of this to London?"

Tom waved his letter at her triumphantly. "No need for you to trouble yourself over the matter, dear wife. It is already enciphered and we shall post it tomorrow. Our mission is over. After that we shall pack our bags and depart for home. Van Sluys has sent word that our goods are already on their way to England. You may soon see your brother free again."

Over, it was over. Catherine should have felt delighted to learn this, especially after the horrors of the morning, but strangely the strongest feelings of anticlimax stole over her.

"And Grahame," she asked, "what of him? I suppose now that it does not matter who killed him?"

"Not if we are to go home immediately. We shall, I hope, leave our enemies behind. Believe me, the latest news that the French are drawing nearer and nearer to the Dutch borders will make them wish to arrange a peace with us as quickly as possible."

Home! After the horrors of the morning it had never seemed more attractive. As to what would happen between Tom and herself when they reached there—well, she would think about that then.

Alas, on the following day, just when they were about to pack, a courier arrived with a letter from London addressed to Master Tom Trenchard. He was a servant of Sir Thomas Gower's and the message, he said, was urgent. It was also untimely. Had they been able to leave an hour earlier he would have missed them, and they would have been safely on their way to catch a packet for England.

As it was, Tom read the letter with a glum face, thanked the courier before paying him and dismissing him and telling Geordie and Catherine its unwelcome news.

''It says that London is sending two envoys to meet us here. They should arrive within the next forty-eight hours and we are to cease all operations until then. They are not satisfied that the information we sent them about the intentions of the Dutch Fleet is accurate, and they wish to talk with us and then question Grahame themselves—''

''Aye,'' interrupted Geordie rudely. ''They may visit him in Hell and take up residence there themselves! Is this what we risked our lives for, master? Not to be believed by them as sits at home on their fat back-sides!''

Catherine felt the same. Last night, in bed, she and Tom had celebrated not only a mission safely accomplished, but their return home as well and now it seemed that they were not to leave after all and London considered their mission a failure.

''I don't like it,'' Tom said suddenly. ''We are putting you at risk, sweeting.'' He picked up the letter. ''Sir Francis Herrold and James Vaux. I don't know the second and I don't like the first. Let's make for the harbour and take ship.''

Catherine said through numb lips, "I have no wish to stay, either, but might they not argue that by leaving after we received their instructions I have broken my word to them, and therefore Rob's life is still forfeit."

Tom swore an ugly oath. "Damn them, yes. If only we'd already left and consequently never received the letter... But 'if onlys' butter no parsnips. You're right. We must stay and hope that nothing goes awry because of Grahame's death."

"The mistress could leave with me," offered Geordie. "And you could deal with the two popinjays yourself."

Sadly Catherine shook her head. "No, Geordie. I made a promise and gained Rob's life in return. I cannot break it, and thereby put him at risk."

And so it was settled. "They may not take long to arrive," Tom told Catherine when Geordie had gone to inform the landlord that they would not be leaving Amsterdam today after all, "and until they do you must not leave the inn, nor must we do anything to arouse suspicion."

He put an arm around her and drew her to him, to kiss her tenderly on the cheek. "Never fear, sweeting. I am here to protect you, and to take care of you in the future also. I cannot allow any harm to come to you now, when I have just found you. Besides, luck may be with us—it has been so far."

Tom tried not to think that luck might change. Catherine was so soft and sweet in his arms, as no woman had ever been before. He wanted to tease her about being Will Wagstaffe, but this was not the right time, nor did he wish her to know yet that he had rummaged among her private belongings. Later, when they had returned to England and safety, they would have time enough to get to know one another.

Nor was he alone in hoping this. Held in the circle of Tom's arms, Catherine tried to tell herself that all would be well, but from the bitter experience of her changing youth she knew that—like the little windmill that Tom had given her—time's whirligig spun so quickly that from one day to the next nothing was sure.

Chapter Fourteen

"Waiting is one of the most damnable things there is." Tom was standing at one of the windows of the inn early one morning, looking out into the yard at the back, which was occupied at the moment by a large coach.

He swung round to smile at Catherine who was sitting in one of their room's most comfortable chairs, engaged in stitching a rose on a small piece of canvas. He had brought it home for her three days ago, together with the wool, to occupy her time, for she had said that she was not used to idleness. She wasn't idle in his absence, for she was nearing the end of writing *The Braggart* and was determined to finish it before she left Holland.

The picture that she presented, her head bent over her work, was a touchingly domestic one, fit to be recorded in one of the many paintings in Holland being commissioned by the rich bourgeoisie to celebrate their comfortable life. He was minded to buy some of them himself when this wretched business was safely over.

A week had gone by since the letter keeping them here had arrived. A week in which nothing more had been heard of Grahame and Catherine was beginning to feel safe.

She and Tom had been living as husband and wife, and were still at the stage when they could hardly bear to be separated, when to be with one another was to want to touch and be touched. Only Geordie's possible interruptions during the day stopped them from behaving like a nymph and satyr let loose in Amsterdam.

The nights were for celebration, and if at first Catherine had regretted their enforced stay, now she was beginning to enjoy it. For she had Tom, and how long she might have him was unknown, so *carpe diem,* "Seize the day", was her motto.

She smiled as Tom idly kissed the top of her head. "I must go out," he told her. "It's the only way to discover what is happening in the great world. The French are marching north, 'tis said, and they are still talking at Breda—but going nowhere. Our news might remedy that."

They had agreed that Tom must not stay in their rooms all day, even if Catherine did. She was not well, Tom told the landlord. The landlady asked if she were breeding, and Tom replied, "Mayhap," with a significant smile.

The notion that Catherine might be breeding pleased him mightily. He had never thought much of owning a small Tom before, but now he found that the idea held him entranced.

"Will you miss me when I'm gone, Mistress Trenchard?" he asked her, going down on one knee beside her, taking the embroidery from her hand and beginning to kiss her. From there it was but a short step to pulling down the bodice of her dress and beginning to kiss the treasures beneath. But when Catherine would have loosened the strings of his breeches, Tom stayed her hand.

"Not now, sweeting, Geordie will soon be back." His voice was thick with desire denied and he buried his head in her lap so that she could stroke his waving red-gold hair. "You said, Catherine," he told her, his voice muffled, "that you could not believe that such pleasure existed, and for all my wicked life before I met you, I have never felt such pleasure as you have given me. If I should give you a bairn in return, would you be unhappy?"

"Never, never." Catherine's denial was as passionate as she could make it. "I can think of nothing better than to have your child."

He dropped his head again, and groaned, "Ah, you do me too much honour, sweeting. I am not worthy."

Which was nothing less than the truth. He thought with distaste of the manners of Charles II's court and the sheer savagery with which the courtiers pursued pleasure. He had been one of them, but never again, he swore to himself, never again.

I am growing too old, I have found a woman to love, and I want a child, undamaged by the carelessness of loving. He knew only too well that promiscuous love brought disease in its train, and he had never been quite as reckless as many of his fellows, but reckless enough.

"We shall soon be home," he said and, forgetting his pose of poor mercenary captain become merchant, added, "I shall dress you in silks, we shall eat lark's tongues, and make love on a bed of flowers in a wood I know."

Catherine stroked his head again, saying gently, "You turn poet, sir. Rochester shall have a rival, and Etheredge, too," for she thought that his extravagances were mere imaginative licence, not the truth.

"Soon, soon," he said, rising. "This I promise you," but did not say what he promised, for Geordie's step was on the stair, and he had come to take turns in guarding her.

"I shall not be long gone," Tom assured her as he put on his plumed grey hat and his short leather jacket. "When I return, you shall come downstairs with me and give me another game of chess," for he had been teaching her to play and had found her an apt pupil.

He kissed her goodbye, passionately. Catherine, stroking the cheek he had caressed, walked to the window to watch him cross the empty inn yard, before picking up her stitchery again. In his little ante-room, Geordie was whistling tunelessly and cleaning Tom's new boots, bought in Amsterdam's market. Shortly he would go downstairs to arrange for their mid-day cold collation to be waiting for them there when Tom returned.

Catherine felt mindlessly happy after the fashion of those who have been well and truly loved the night before. So happy that she was beginning to fall into a light sleep over her work when she heard the tramp of booted feet on the stairs.

The feet stopped outside the door, and someone rapped smartly on it, shouting. "Open, in the name of the law!"

Geordie shot out of his room to open it and stand before Catherine, for there was nowhere where she might hide. She held on to her embroidery as though it were a talisman when three men entered, one of them obviously an important official.

"Mistress Catherine Trenchard?" he questioned her.

Useless to deny, for the landlord, who stood behind the men, jaws agape, must have told him her name. Geordie, undaunted by such authority so blatantly displayed, for all three men wore breastplates and helms as though they had come to arrest a nest of dangerous criminals, said defiantly, "What the devil are you doin' here? My mistress is a peaceable lady, as you may well see."

Number One waved him aside. "Mistress Trenchard I have come to arrest you for the murder last week of one William Grahame in the city of Amsterdam, and to take you to the Town Hall for questioning and from thence to prison."

"No, you ain't," bellowed Geordie. "I'll not have it!"

Number One negligently threw him against the wall, took Catherine by the arm, and handed her over to the two men behind him. "Another word from you, my man, and I'll take you in with her."

Catherine said swiftly as Geordie squared up to the man again, "No, Geordie, no. You cannot help me this way. Wait here and tell Tom when he returns what has happened. He will know what to do."

Geordie nodded sullenly, howling after them as they marched Catherine down the stairs, her embroidery still clutched in her hand, "Look after her, damn you, she's as good a lady as ever breathed, that she is."

Which might have relieved his feelings a little but had no effect on Catherine's captors as they matched her through the streets to the Town Hall.

* * *

Tom returned to the inn carrying yet another present for Catherine, a posy of spring flowers brought from the flower market, which was situated by a bridge over one of the canals. He was enjoying the thought of the pleasure on her face when he bounded upstairs. It occurred to him that never before had he behaved like a boy carrying fairings to his first sweetheart. He couldn't even remember having a first sweetheart.

But he had a sweetheart now.

He knew instantly that something was wrong when he walked through the door. Geordie was standing opposite to him, his face even more miserable than usual. There was no sign of Catherine. He put the posy down on the small table by the bed and said hoarsely, ''Spit it out, man. What's to do?'' Somehow he knew that the worst had happened.

Geordie didn't prevaricate. That was not his way. ''The watch came and took her to the Town Hall for Grahame's murder.''

''Damnation! I thought that by now we were safe.'' He made for the door, his head on fire, tears in his eyes—to do he knew not what. Geordie, insubordinate, caught him by the shoulder. ''Not that, master. Think before you act. You cannot help her if you end up in prison too. Not like you to be an impetuous fool—sir!''

Tom's rage and despair subsided a little. ''True, very true. I suppose the landlady talked and there are not so many strangers in Amsterdam that they were not able to track her down. Did they ask for me?''

''No, nor took note of me, neither. I thought that strange, master, but mayhap they believe it to be a quarrel between a man and a woman he tried to force to be his doxy. Remember that the landlady never saw you, and I only went in with the mistress once.''

Tom nodded. ''Belike they think that she killed him with his own dagger. They would scarce believe that she had gone there as a British agent.''

He turned his suffering face away from Geordie, struck his clenched fist against the closed door and swore a violent oath. ''I told her that I would protect her always. A poor protector I turned out to be! There is only one way out of this and that is to find out who did kill Grahame and turn him over to the authorities.

''Do you scour the alehouses, dens and stews around the harbour, and I will go to Van Sluys to see if there be any help or information to be found there. Ask about a dwarf—and I shall question Van Sluys, who might or might not be the richly dressed gentleman.

''After that I shall go to the Town Hall to find out what is happening to her—and try not to get arrested myself. That way I could do nothing to help her.''

He picked up his hat, which he had gaily tossed upon the bed, and tried to avoid looking at the posy of flowers with which he had thought to please her.

The worst had happened and he was in hell, who had so recently been in heaven.

Van Sluys was in, and received Tom in the room where they had dined. He listened to his story and inclined his head in sympathy.

''Alas, I have no direct help I can offer you, *mijnheer*, would that I had. Of the small network of agents who work in Amsterdam I knew only Grahame. That is common practice, for the less one knows of others, or they of you, the less they can betray you.

"As for your wife, as Regent I can enquire about her, vouch that she is of good character and try to see that she is justly treated. But the case against her is a strong one, as you must see. Your best plan is to try to discover who did murder Grahame—which may be difficult.

"One thing I can tell you. Amos Shooter is in Amsterdam. He is not to be trusted, and will bear watching. You say your man is scouring the drinking dens for information. That, too, might prove fruitful. I wish you luck."

And that was all. Tom thanked him and left. He was not sure that Van Sluys was being wholly truthful with him, but he believed that he might try to help Catherine. And so he would tell her when he saw her. For that was his next errand, and one that would cost him dear. He had never thought to love a woman so much that the loss of her had him nigh running mad—and that was, as the old philosophers truly said, to give a hostage to fortune.

"Yes, I visited Master Grahame, sir, but no, I did not kill him, and that is all I can tell you, but it is the truth."

Catherine was being questioned by a magistrate who was the exact opposite of the one in Antwerp. He was burly, brutal in face and figure, and was possessed of a hard dogged manner. He was leaning across the table to question her, his cruel eyes avid.

"The landlady, as you have seen, swore that you were his last visitor, which leaves you, madame, in the position of being his most likely murderer."

"But sir," ventured Catherine, trying to keep her wits about her, "you also know that I visited Master Grahame around noon, and the landlady did not find him dead until six of the clock. Any number of persons might have secretly visited him during that time."

The magistrate smiled. "Oh, you may be sure that the landlady would have heard anyone who came in. She has the ears of an owl and the sight of an eagle where preserving the respectability of her home is concerned. No, you were the last to visit him."

Catherine and Tom had already decided that, if it came to her being questioned, she would claim to have left Grahame alive. To tell the truth, that she had found him dying, would never be believed—since she had informed neither the landlady, nor the authorities, of his death. Those two facts alone, would, in their eyes, seal her guilt.

"Come, mistress, tell us the truth. Why did you visit him, and did he, as the landlady thinks, for he had a bad reputation with women and many visited him, try to assault you? If the last, then your guilt is not so great and will be thus considered at your trial."

"I *am* telling the truth: I did not kill Master Grahame. I visited him to give him news of his relatives in England. He was growing unhappy in his exile."

Well, at least the first sentence and the last were the truth. The one in the middle wasn't. But I can hardly confess that I am here as an agent dealing with another agent, and both of us engaged in activity designed to damage the country Grahame was living in, thought Catherine wryly.

"Now why do I not believe you, mistress?" said the magistrate softly. "For I do not."

Catherine's brave front almost cracked. "I would wish to see my husband, sir. He will be greatly troubled by my arrest."

"Indeed, madame. Perhaps you might care to explain why you visited Grahame twice, and on neither occasion did he accompany you. Why was that?"

"He is trying to make his way as a merchant and he had other appointments on the days of my visits."

"Twice, madame, twice? Go to. I wonder if he knew what you were doing. He may visit you, that is if he wishes to see you after your involvement with Grahame, but only in the presence of a tipstaff. Take her to the cells, and leave her there to contemplate her sins and then she may tell us the truth."

The cell was a bare room, with stone walls, a straw bed, and a chair. A wash basin stood on a stand, a pail beneath it. Light came from two slits in the thick walls. Fetters were attached to the wall, for unruly prisoners, no doubt. Her guards made no attempt to chain her, simply locked her in.

Once alone, Catherine put her head in her hands and tried not to cry. She could see no way out—except that Tom, ever resourceful, might think of one. She found that she was still clutching her stitchery but, with no wool and little light it was of no comfort to her. A Bible stood by the wash basin and she began to read that to try to find some solace in it.

How long she sat there before they brought Tom to her, she did not know. For a bare second when he entered his face told its own picture of shock at her capture.

Ignoring the cold stare of the guard who stood at the open door he took her in his arms, murmuring, "Forgive me, my dear heart, for not protecting you better, and allowing you to be dragged to this dreadful place. When you are out of it I shall protect you always, be sure of that.

"All I can say now is that Geordie and I are trying our best to discover who did murder Grahame so that you may be freed as soon as possible. I visited Van Sluys this afternoon and he has promised to intervene on your behalf. Oh, I blame myself for this—for bringing you to Holland at all!"

"Foolish Tom," said Catherine tenderly, "for you did not bring me here, I was sent by others more powerful than either of us. And had they not coerced us into going on this mission we should never have met, and never have loved."

"My darling, it is like you to try to comfort me when it is I who should be comforting you. What a brave gentleman you are, Mr Wagstaffe! No wonder you write such remarkable plays. God send you may be freed from this place to write many more."

These betraying words flew out before Tom could stop himself. Catherine stepped back out of the circle of his arms.

"You know! How do you know?"

"Forgive me, sweeting," he said, taking her little hand and kissing it, "but I looked in your trunk for the ink you carry and I naughtily examined your papers— to discover that I loved a bright genius. I have been intrigued by the man who wags the shaft, or shakes the spear, ever since I saw you as Belinda. I never thought that he was a she who would be my love and that I should tell her that I knew her secret in a Dutch prison.''

'''We know what we are, but we know not what we may be,''''' Catherine returned, kissing his hand, and damn the watching guards, "as Master Shakespeare wrote in *Hamlet*. I played in it once, and shall ne'er forget it.''

"Forgive me for spying on you, my brave heart.'' He had never thought to ask forgiveness of a woman before.

"Of course I forgive you. I am sure that what you did was not deliberate. Besides, I should not have liked you to have run out of ink!''

To think that she could jest so bravely when she was in such danger.

"Time's up,'' snarled the guard suddenly. He took Tom by the shoulder to lead him away.

Tom shook off the man's hand and said hoarsely, "I shall come to see you tomorrow. With better news, I hope.''

"Give my love to Geordie, too,'' Catherine called after him.

"What, has your wife cuckolded you with another as well as Grahame?'' chuckled the guard coarsely. And never knew how near he came to death, as Tom restrained himself from doing that to him which would have had him in prison, to be tried alongside Catherine. He must remain free to help her.

Chapter Fifteen

Neither Tom nor Geordie's investigations that afternoon or evening bore any fruit. They discovered nothing that might lead them to Grahame's murderer.

"Tomorrow," said Tom morosely as they wandered home nigh upon midnight. "We'll try again tomorrow."

They had heard further news of the French advance towards the Dutch border, which had Tom hoping that a truce between Holland and England might soon be declared. Such a development would be sure to help Catherine. May was about to pass into June, and the negotiations were still continuing.

Morning saw him sending Geordie out for further explorations. He stayed behind to write a letter to London, telling them of Catherine's arrest and asking what had happened to the envoys whose supposed arrival had placed her in such danger by their late arrival.

He was halfway through enciphering it when there was a commotion in the yard outside as a fine coach rolled in. Such a commotion that Tom went to the window to see what was about.

It was the envoys from England arriving at last—and in some state. First came Sir Francis Herrold, overdressed as usual, and full of wind and importance. Accompanying him was his toady, James Vaux, who would be Herrold's echo, Tom was sure. He cursed them both. Without their intervention, he and Catherine would now be safe in London.

He told them so when they came in, curled, prinked and pompous as though they were still at Whitehall, both ambitious for advancement. Herrold he had always disliked and the feeling was returned ever since Tom had succeeded with a Maid of Honour who had refused Herrold's clumsy advances.

"I wonder that you came at all, seeing that you have taken so long," he began. "And what is so important that you were sent to instruct me? God knows, I need no instructions from you, Herrold."

"I might have expected this from you, Cameron," returned Sir Francis Herrold, looking disdainfully round the small room, letting his greedy stare rest on the big bed that dominated it. "London thought that you might need help, seeing that you have taken so long, and all that you have sent us is a rigmarole about a supposed Dutch invasion that would not have deceived a child.

"When we received your latest letter about the Dutch intentions at Breda, Sir Thomas Gower was of the mind that you had found something definite at long last. My instructions from him are that you pack your doxy off home at once—her work having been done—

and that you set off for Breda this very day with Vaux here, there to turn yourself into a gentleman again—if that be possible—and do your duty in the negotiations. I shall look after your doxy."

Red rage held Tom in thrall. His doxy, indeed! Pack her off home, indeed! Like a bale of soiled goods! The desire to take Herrold by the throat, to squeeze the life out of him and throw the body out of the window to join Newman and Grahame's was so strong that it took all his will-power to resist it.

"Damn you, Herrold, for your foul tongue," he began. "Know that my doxy, as you call her, has proved as good as any man on this accursed expedition. And for her pains she is languishing in a Dutch gaol on a charge of killing Grahame, of which she is totally innocent. And, for your information, I shall not travel a yard with you, to Breda, or anywhere else until she is out of the prison into which her devotion to duty has landed her."

"Bedded her, did you?" sneered Herrold. "So hot for her you cannot wait to bed her again—" He got no further, for with an enraged roar Tom sprang on him and took him by the throat.

James Vaux, who had so far remained silent, protested feebly, "Steady on, Cameron, you'll do him a mischief."

"I should have done him one long ago," roared Tom, but sanity returning, he reluctantly let go of his victim, and stood back.

"Your face looks prettier coloured purple, Herrold," he growled. "You can be off, both of you. You heard me. I don't leave here without the lady."

"Be damned to that," snarled Herrold. "I have my orders, and so have you. Sir Thomas foresaw this. He told me to tell you that if you refused to go to Breda, or to allow her to return home without you, then we should hand her over to the Dutch as a spy.

"Seeing that she has already landed herself in gaol, I shall make no attempt to free her unless you travel with Vaux to Breda. I shall remain here to arrange her release and send her back to England before travelling to Breda myself."

"And be damned to you," Tom returned without thinking. "I shall go the gaol myself and tell them…" He stopped.

"That you are English agents? Come, come, what would that do but condemn you both to hang, when if you do it my way, she will be freed today, for I can give them the name of the man who killed Grahame. She will be safe in England and you will be safe in Breda, with no suspicion attaching to either of you."

He would kill Herrold one day for this filthy piece of blackmail, he most surely would, and have it out with Gower and Arlington for their high-handed treatment of Catherine. But for the present the swine had him on the rack. He was helpless, and Herrold knew it. If he could be believed, Catherine would only be saved if he went to Breda. And there was another thing.

"Who killed Grahame—and how do you know?"

"Amos Shooter killed Grahame. He has been playing everyone off against everyone else. He has spent his wife's fortune, and is in desperate need of money. As to how we know, you must ask Sir Thomas yourself. Since he is as close-mouthed as ever, I doubt whether he will oblige you.''

James Vaux said in his pleasant and reasonable voice, ''Come, Stair. Surely you can see that this arrangement is in the best interest of both of you.''

''I promised to visit her today,'' returned Tom. ''At least allow me to delay my journey until I have seen her.''

Herrold was delighted to be able to say, ''Those are not my instructions, Cameron. You are to leave at once—or the doxy is thrown to the wolves.''

Geordie! Where was Geordie when he was wanted? He should have been back long ago. ''I shall wait until my servant, Geordie Charlton, returns. He can accompany Catherine home.'' At least he could do that for her: see that she had a protector on her long and difficult journey back to London.

Herrold sighed. ''By no means. You are to leave at once. I can pass on your instructions to your man if he does not return before you are ready to go. But make all speed, man, we waste time.''

They had him by the throat and there was nothing for it but to follow orders. He could not help Catherine by staying.

''I shall delay long enough to write a letter to her, explaining why I am leaving her alone in Amsterdam, and you will do me the honour of delivering it,'' Tom said. He hated to have to beg anything from the swine before him, but he had no alternative. ''And if Geordie does not return before I leave for Breda, you will be sure to tell him to look after Catherine for me.''

''Of course,'' said Herrold, gracious in victory. ''By

all means, write your letter. Vaux's man will help you to pack.'' He gazed patronisingly round the room. ''Not that you appear to have much of value with you!''

Tom resisted the impulse to strangle him. Instead he sat down and wrote his first love letter to Catherine; the first, indeed, that he had ever written to anyone. He poured his heart and soul into it, telling her how much he loved her, and how wretched he felt at having to go to Breda without her.

''But I know that Geordie will look after you, and, God willing, we shall meet again soon, never to part.'' He sealed it carefully and handed it over to Herrold with a heavy heart.

''I shall be sure to see that your doxy receives this, Cameron. I have to say that I never thought to find you in such a pother about an actress who doubles as a whore. More like you to enjoy the night with her and be off.''

Oh, he was well aware that he had Tom on a chain as though he were a dancing bear, and could not resist jerking the chain. That he would pay for this one day soon, was the only thing that kept Tom from despairing altogether. He would make sure that his revenge was sweet when he took it. The knowledge that Catherine would wait in vain for him to visit her would haunt him all the way to Breda.

''And you will give her this purse. It has enough money in it to provide her and Geordie with an easy passage home.''

''You may depend upon it, Cameron,'' Herrold said

and, taking it from Tom, he placed the purse on the table beside the bed.

While Tom was downstairs settling his account with the landlord before he and Vaux set off, Herrold took Vaux on one side. He gave him brisk orders, enjoying his power over his friend. And then he took Tom's letter to Catherine from his coat pocket where he had stowed it, after promising Tom on his honour as a gentleman that he would give it to her as soon as she was released from prison.

He held it up in the air, saying regretfully, "No time to read it, alas, before he returns," and then slowly, laughing as he did so, he tore it to pieces, before tossing it into the small fire which burned in the grate.

"You promised to deliver it, Francis, on your honour," wailed Vaux, as the fire reduced Tom's letter to ashes.

"Honour! To Cameron, to a wench any man might have for a small fee? Who will doubtless lie with me tonight if I make it worth her while. Come, come, my friend, you know better than that."

He saw Vaux begin to hesitate, leaned forward and said to him, quite jovially, "Inform him of what I have done, Jem, my lad, and I shall tell the world of your little adventures with the pretty boys in Southwark. So, mum's the word, and all's well."

Vaux closed his mouth and shrugged resignedly. Cameron would have to take his chances if the wench thought that he had deserted her.

A thought that echoed Herrold's own, as he watched the coach containing his victim roll out of the inn's courtyard on its way to Breda. Next to deal with Cameron's man: another pleasure awaiting him.

Geordie had had a hard morning. He had been patiently wandering through the stews of Amsterdam searching for anything that might lead them to Grahame's murderer. He had told Tom that it might be a dangerous occupation, and so it proved.

At a stinking grog shop near the poor end of the harbour he had asked after a dwarf who might know one William Grahame. The landlord had professed no knowledge of any such dwarf. A dirty seaman had sidled up to him as he had left muttering hoarsely that he knew of a dwarf who lived nearby—a whole family of them, he had leered, refugees from one of the travelling fairs that toured Europe.

"Turned away for drunkenness and lechery," he had offered piously. "Give me a groat, master, and I'll take you to them."

All this in broken English. Geordie reluctantly handed over the groat and followed the seaman down a squalid alley, tripping over ropes and odds and ends of broken ships' chandlery. At the far end of it the seaman whistled, and the next thing that Geordie knew was that he was propped up against the wall of the alley, his money gone, and a dirty great headache blurring his sight.

He had no notion of how long he had been unconscious as he staggered back to the inn for succour, hoping that his failure would not distress his master overmuch.

But he found no master there. In the room that Tom

and Catherine had occupied, he found a stone-faced gentleman in fine clothes who stared at him as though he were a cockroach who had lost his way from the cellars.

"One Geordie Charlton, I presume?" asked Sir Stoneface. He had a right nasty expression.

"Aye, that I am. Where's Master Trenchard?"

"Gone. I don't know where. Took off with a friend of his and mine who came for him from London."

Geordie stared malevolently at him. "And who the devil be you, when you're at home?"

Sir Stoneface rose negligently to his feet. He was wearing red-heeled shoes and stank of some fancy perfume. "Show a little respect for your betters, my man," he drawled, "or I'll have my footmen trash you."

"And where's Master Tom? Did he leave me a message?"

"Nothing. Just a couple of groats for your pains."

Geordie clutched his aching head. This was not like his master, not at all. But the whole world knew how capricious were the great ones who ruled it.

"And Mistress Trenchard? Where be she? Never say he left her behind."

"That's the usual way of dealing with doxies, my man, as you should know. She's in Amsterdam gaol still—until I free her and pack her off home. And now, be off with you."

There was something wrong here, very wrong. But whether it was Master Tom or Sir Stoneface who was wrong, Geordie did not know. His head hurt him so much that it was difficult for him to do any hard thinking.

Sir Francis picked up a fat purse from the table by the bed. He opened it and took two coins from it.

"Your master left you two groats, I'll make it four, so long as you take yourself off forthwith. You understand me?"

"Aye, sir, that I do."

Geordie took the groats. He thought of Tom and Catherine and their loving. Of how Tom had always been true to him, and he didn't like this one bit. To be turned off with such a trifling sum after all the years he and Master Tom had spent together! He would not go away, not he. He would haunt the inn, try to discover what Sir Stoneface was up to, and replenish his empty purse by some means or other—fair or foul.

And keep a watch for poor Mistress Catherine when she was freed from gaol. From what Sir Stoneface had hinted, she might be in need of a protector.

Catherine was waiting for Tom. She had been taken before the magistrate again that morning after being given bread and water for her breakfast. He had questioned her sternly, but he had not been able to shake her. Her sincerity in denying that she had murdered Grahame was so patent that the magistrate was beginning to doubt her guilt.

On the other hand, she could not prove that she had not done so, and until then he must hold her. His men were making enquiries about Grahame, but had found no one who would confess to as much as knowing his name, let alone him. He sent her back to her cell.

And still Tom did not come. But she did not repine, for was there not the afternoon to look forward to? After mid-day, one of the guards brought her some gruel and a slice of coarse yellow bread to eat with it. She was drinking the soup when he returned to say, "That magistrate wishes to see you immediately. Leave that."

Hungry though she was, Catherine did as she was bid, and he led her back to the room where the magistrate had twice interrogated her. As usual, he was seated behind his big table.

Opposite to him, in one of the big armchairs that the Dutch favoured, was a fine gentleman, sour-faced and thin-lipped, who stared at her, stripping all her clothing from her as he did so. Catherine found herself hating him on sight and wondered what he had to do with her. She was soon to find out.

"This is Sir Francis Herrold from England," the magistrate said. "He is on his way to the diplomatic mission at Breda, but he also brings good news for you."

Sir Francis Herrold. Catherine found his name familiar. She said nothing. He rose and bowed to her, she curtsied back at him; she could do no less.

"Sit, mistress, sit," said the magistrate, his manner to her as polite as it had been peremptory. "Sir Francis has brought us proof that the murderer of William Grahame is one Amos Shooter, who has been spying for every state in Europe in turn. He was the fine gentleman seen by the landlady that morning before you arrived.

"We believe that he returned later, by a back staircase, and killed Grahame so that he should not betray his treachery. Only the French invasion of the Austrian Netherlands saved him from arrest in Antwerp. He fled to Holland in the confusion caused by the French attack in order to ply his wicked trade here.''

He paused. ''Sir Francis has told us that he was bankrupt, having wasted his wife's fortune and his own. We are trying to find him in order to arrest him. This news, mistress, means that we will release you immediately, and apologise for having detained you. Sir Francis will be only too happy to escort you to your lodgings.''

Sir Francis inclined his head at this, and said coolly, ''My pleasure, mistress.''

Catherine wished that she liked the look of him more, for was he not her saviour? ''Thank you, Sir Francis,'' she managed to say, and then, ''Tom, my husband. Is he not with you?''

''Alas, no,'' replied Sir Francis, sadly, ''but all shall be made known to you when you return to the inn where you have been living. We may go now, *mijnheer?*''

''Indeed, indeed.'' The magistrate rose and bowed them both out. He evidently considered Sir Francis a great man, and the coach he had arrived in, the liveried servants who accompanied him, all bore out that belief.

As though to emphasise her lowly station, Sir Francis was handed in to the coach by an obsequious footman before the same honour was offered Catherine. His air of consequence, his fine clothes, his silver-topped cane, and his lordly manners were overwhelming. He scarcely deigned to acknowledge the magistrate's farewells.

Nor did he deign to speak to Catherine as the coach rumbled along. When they reached the inn, his footman handed her out after his master, and he preceded her mannerlessly up the stairs to their rooms.

Tom! She was going to see Tom. She had not known how much he had twined himself round her heart until she had been arrested and lost him. And Geordie, too, had become part of her life. She had gained a new family, who had so bitterly lost one.

But there was no Tom and no Geordie waiting for her. The big room was bare of them and their possessions. Tom's coat, his hat, his two trunks, and his nightrail flung carelessly across the bed, all, all of them, were gone. The door to Geordie's ante-room was open and he was not there.

She turned to Sir Francis, who had rudely seated himself in the chair that Tom had used—although she was still standing—spread her hands and asked, like a bewildered, bereft child, "Where are they, Tom and Geordie? Have they gone without leaving me a letter—or even a message?"

Astonishingly Sir Francis began to laugh. She stared at him, and said haughtily, although the rapid beating of her poor heart was making her breathless, "What amuses you, sir?"

"You," he choked at her, raising his lace handkerchief to his mouth. "Think you, that once your value to him was gone, both as to your performance in bed with him, and with Grahame, that Sir Alastair Cameron would trouble with such as you any further? You deceive yourself, mistress.''

''Sir Alastair Cameron? What is he to me?''

''Come, come, mistress, do no try to cozen me! Surely you know with whom you have been living since you left England? You must know as well as I do that Tom Trenchard is none other than Sir Alastair—or rather Stair—Cameron, one of the King's favourites because he never asks him for money, and occasionally does his bidding on such little adventures as these, changing his name when he does so.

''It must have pleased him mightily to find such a willing little doxy as yourself to pass the time with. Which is probably why he sent that nonsensical despatch about the Dutch Navy's attack! No doubt he was thinking more about your shopworn charms than of the work he was sent to do! But all that is over for you now. You are to go home at once.''

For one terrible moment Catherine thought that she was going to faint. Tom, her Tom, was Sir Alastair Cameron, who had made such a brouhaha and nuisance of himself when she had been playing Belinda in *The Braggart!* He was not a poverty-stricken mercenary of relatively low degree, but a rich and powerful magnate who had the ear of the King and his Secretary of State, Lord Arlington!

It was no wonder that he had abandoned her without a word and left her to the tender mercies of this cold-blooded fop who plainly saw her as prey! For had not Tom seen her as prey, too? He had not meant one of the loving words that he had showered on her over the last few days, not one. He had simply been passing the time agreeably with yet another easy conquest.

The room began to spin about her. Sir Francis Herrold was leaning forward and murmuring slyly, "You need not go home at once, my dear, we could pass a pleasant few days together, here in Amsterdam, and you could earn yourself a nice little fee. I warrant that Stair Cameron has not given you anything for the odd tumble in his bed."

He moved towards her, his face aglow with lechery. "We can begin now, if you so wish."

"No," Catherine said, recovering herself, pushing back the awful faintness and putting her hands out to fend him off. "No, never, and if you come any nearer to me and try to force me, I shall go downstairs and tell the landlord what you are trying to do. They treat women more kindly here in Holland than they do at home, and it would go ill with you if you were to assault me."

She had her hand on the door knob, for he had been foolish enough to leave the way to the door open. He glared at her, and growled haughtily, "A stupid doxy, then. Well, well, you may have your way. Pack your bags and I shall pay for your passage home, but nothing more, if you refuse to earn it."

Could Sir Thomas Gower have meant this to happen to her? Could Tom? Could the man she had thought she knew have left her in prison to be insulted and mocked by a fellow courtier? Could he have agreed that she should be turned away, to find her way home alone and virtually penniless, with not even a word of thanks for work well done?

Instead, she had been offered only a sneering comment that what the three of them had discovered, and sent to London at great risk, was worthless. The feeling of faintness overwhelmed her again, and again she pushed it back. She would not be overset by this, she would not.

And where was Tom? Where had he gone? Without a word, and why should she be surprised that he had abandoned her? After all, had she not half-expected such an ending to their short idyll? She had had her pleasure with him, and he with her, and if she had been foolish enough to fall in love with him, that was her fault, not his.

But she could not forget that he had held her in his arms and promised to take care of her always. And always had turned out to be a few short days, and when, as this unpleasant man had said, her usefulness to him was over, he had left her behind and passed on to his next adventure, his next woman.

"And Geordie?" she asked, for Geordie had become her friend, too. "What of Geordie?"

"The ill-favoured servant? Why, he was turned away too—after being liberally paid. But this is none of your business, mistress. Come, prepare to leave, the packet departs on the evening tide and the sooner you are back in London, the happier we shall all be."

Mechanically Catherine packed her trunk, and dressed herself for the journey whilst Sir Francis went downstairs to eat a hearty meal. She sat on the bed, numb. So, Tom had turned Geordie away as well. She would not have thought that of him—but, after all, she had never really known him, only the man he had pretended to be.

Sir Francis offered to have food sent up to her, but she refused it. She had not eaten properly since she had been arrested, but the thought of eating anything made her feel ill.

A footman came upstairs to carry her trunk down and take her to the coach. "I shall come with you to the packet," Sir Francis had said, speaking to her as though she were an under-servant, "to make sure that you board it. We have no mind to leave you plying your trade in the Netherlands. You can do that at home."

"I am an actress," Catherine told him, "not a whore," but he merely laughed at her.

He was true to his word and watched her go aboard, the footman carrying her trunk. The last she saw of Holland was of him watching the packet sail towards the open sea. Behind him the spires of Amsterdam's churches ran like a tall fence on the long skyline.

The slow tears slipped down her face until, the harbour behind her, a familiar voice said, "Do not cry, mistress, I have come to take you safely home since he will not."

It was Geordie.

It was Geordie who saw her trunk safely carried ashore when they reached England, who made her shelter from the rain on the packet when she stood helpless beneath it, since she seemed to have lost the power to look after herself. It was Geordie who arranged her journey back to London and Cob's Lane. All the drive and resolution with which Catherine had run her life since her parents' death had leached out of her since Tom—no, Sir Stair Cameron—had deserted her.

She had thought that she had found the other half of herself, that consequence of true love of which all the poets sang. The dream had beckoned and she had followed it gladly.

She had been wrong. Today she was weak, but to-morrow, oh yes, tomorrow, she would be strong and let no man who protested his love for her ever come near her again, for all men were tricksters. For the present she had Geordie. Geordie who had caught her when, at the sight of him, the world had turned around her, and faintness had overcome her at last.

He had sworn an oath, sat her down on the wet deck and fanned her face until she had recovered.

"Bear up, mistress! You have been a brave lass so far. Never say die."

"No, indeed," she said, looking up at his face, more miserable then ever at the sight of her distress, "but who would have thought that he would have abandoned us both? For he has abandoned you, has he not?"

Geordie squatted beside her, and nodded agreement. "Aye, and 'tis not like him at all. I have been with him man and boy and all he left for me was two groats and no message—nor any hint of where he has gone."

"Nor me, either, Geordie. We are partners in misery, are we not?"

"That we are. I would never have thought that Master Tom would serve me so. But who knows what the mighty of this world may do to us, so long as they get their own pleasure? Poor folk like us are nothing to them. I saw yon Stoneface fetch you from the gaol, and I followed you to the harbour. One of his servants told me that they were sending you home. They thought it a fine joke.''

He did not tell Catherine that he had stolen the fellow's purse for his pains, and that it would help them to get safely home again.

''Master Tom?'' Catherine heard him use the false name and wondered whether Geordie had been deceived over that as well. ''Do you not know what his real name is?''

''A 'course I do. Sir Alastair Thomas Cameron Bart. His mother was a Trenchard. Called himself Tom Trenchard, he did, when he were a young lad in exile when we soldiered against the heathen for a living. Allus been Master Tom to me, he has.''

Catherine gave a great sigh. ''He's gone, Geordie, and he has done the greater wrong to you.''

''Aye, and still I cannot believe it. We live and learn.''

After that, nothing was said between them except on matters pertaining to the journey. Catherine felt too helpless to check Geordie when he told her that he intended to see her home. For once he did not appear to be enjoying his misery.

''I cannot pay you, Geordie,'' she told him as he carried her trunk into her small house in Cob's Lane. ''I have been left virtually penniless. I need to go to the Duke's Theatre to earn somewhat to make an honest living.''

''No need to worry about that, mistress. I have enough to keep me for some little time, and will, if you so agree, rent a room from you and serve as your footman until you are settled again.''

Catherine's eyes filled with tears. She did not deny him, for until Rob returned home—if he returned home, that was, for what had so recently passed with Sir Francis Herrold had made her doubt Sir Thomas Gower's honesty—she had no masculine protector in a cruel world.

''You are sure that you wish to do this, Geordie?''

''Oh, aye. Give me a home, it will.''

And so it was agreed. And of all strange things, Catherine thought ruefully as she composed herself for sleep and a future without Tom, she had acquired not the master, but his man!

Chapter Sixteen

All the time that he was in Breda, richly dressed, one of the major figures in the discussions that were daily leading towards a hoped-for peace, Stair Cameron thought constantly of his lost love, wondering what she was doing.

Stair had spoken to Sir Francis Herrold when he finally arrived in Breda, asking him for news of Catherine. Herrold assured Stair that he had seen Catherine safely out of gaol and on to the packet. He did not tell him that he had turned Geordie away and kept the purse that Stair had left for them—nor that, through a bribed clerk in Breda, Stair's letters to Catherine were stolen and destroyed.

His revenge on Stair had taken long to ensure, but it was satisfyingly complete. He was too stupid to worry over what might happen if and when Stair discovered his duplicity.

Stair had expected Catherine to reply to his love letter when she reached England, but no word came from her, which surprised him. He wrote several times to her at Cob's Lane, but nothing came back.

After a little time he began to worry that something untoward might have happened to her and Geordie. He consoled himself with the thought that, owing to the war, the post had become erratic, and made up his mind that he would apply for leave to return home as soon as he decently could...

May passed into June. Stair spoke to Arlington, who had arrived in Breda for a brief visit, asking that he be relieved of his duties and be allowed to go home as soon as possible.

"I have done the state some service," he argued. "What I learned from Grahame about Dutch demands for peace, and the information I passed from him to you about the raid on Sheerness..."

Arlington interrupted him, "Oh, you must know, Stair, that no one gave that business about the raid any credence. It was simply Grahame's daydream designed to get him a pardon—which, of course, we would never have granted him whatever he sent us. It was a piece of luck for us that Shooter disposed of him."

Stair gave him a deadly glance. "I offered him his pardon in good faith. I am sorry to hear that you were prepared to cheat him had he lived."

Arlington laughed. "Oh, come, Stair, you know that no one trusts anyone in this business! And you had your payment in the company of the little actress we provided for you, I trust."

Stair saw red again, but controlled himself. "She did the state some service, too. I hope you saw her well rewarded. And was it necessary for you to order Herrold to send her home so abruptly?"

''No doubt she was paid,'' returned Arlington, who had not the slightest idea whether Catherine had been rewarded or not. ''And confess, you could scarcely have arrived at Breda masquerading as Trenchard with your little doxy in tow. We did you a favour.''

''Hardly that, but no matter,'' said Stair drily, containing his anger at Arlington's light-minded references to Catherine. There was no point in making an enemy of a man who was more useful as a friend. ''She will gain a better reward than money, I trust, when I return to England.''

Arlington was too tactful to enquire what that would be. His old friend seemed a trifle hipped where his little doxy was concerned. And who could have foreseen that? He, too, decided that silence was always the best policy.

Nor did he have much to say two days later when the dreadful news from England was delivered to him by a grim-faced courier. It dealt a shattering blow to Arlington's hopes of defeating the Dutch and being able to lay down peace terms from a position of supremacy.

Stair was present when Arlington opened the despatch in the privacy of the offices assigned to them. George Downing, the British Ambassador to Holland, and the rest of the peace delegation were present, waiting for the day's orders.

Arlington's face lost its ruddy colour. He threw the paper down on to the table before him, and stood silent before them all, trying to regain his composure.

''The devil's in this war,'' he announced at last. ''I

have just been apprised of the gravest news a man could well receive. On June the twelfth, De Ruyter burned down Sheerness, sailed up the Medway and raided Chatham, destroying much of our fleet and capturing *The Royal Charles,* its pride.''

He tried not to look at Stair as he spoke, knowing that he must be thinking sadly of the disbelief accorded to the accurate information which he and Catherine had sent back to England. Before Arlington could continue, he was interrupted by the sound of cheering in the street outside. The news had reached Holland and all Breda was rejoicing.

The advantage given to England in the peace negotiations by the French invasion of the Austrian Netherlands was destroyed by this humiliating defeat. The glum faces of everyone in the room told their own story.

''The only thing we may be able to salvage from this dismal business,'' Arlington said heavily, ''is that we shall appear to add to our humiliation by ceding all our interests in the Pacific and accept instead the territories in North America in lieu of them. Territories that we want.''

Heads nodded. The peace talks would soon end, and they could all go home, their tails between their legs.

Stair said nothing. He would not compound Arlington's misery by speaking of the lost opportunity to defeat the Dutch that he, and his advisers, had thrown away. At least this news meant that he would soon see Catherine again, although he wished that some means of bringing that about, other than a stunning defeat, had been necessary.

Once the others had left, he remained to speak alone to Arlington. "I would not say so in public," he announced hardily, "but if you had heeded the information we sent you, we would have been waiting for the Dutch when they arrived—and the consequent humiliating defeat would have been theirs.

"Because of that, I ask you again to allow me to return home at once. The talks will end soon, in any case, and you will not want my presence at them further, seeing that I am in possession of what you can only regard as the most unfortunate information!"

He smiled winningly. Arlington had spoken lightly of cheating Grahame and had intimated that blackmail and cheating were part of the rules of the game. That being so, he had no hesitation in blackmailing Arlington.

Let me go home, he was saying, or I will tell the world that you had news of Dutch intentions, and not only ignored it, but mocked at it and the senders!

He knew he had won by the wry expression on Arlington's face. He laughed abruptly. "We shall make a statesman of you yet, Stair. That was as well done as anything I have yet experienced. Your knife went between my ribs so sweetly, I hardly knew that I was injured. Yes, you may go home, to enjoy your little actress. Herrold seemed to think that you had enjoyed her already."

Stair smiled again. He would not tell Arlington that he would soon make Herrold pay for all the insults that he had heaped upon him in Amsterdam. He had been an honest soldier once, but had for the last few weeks played the dishonest diplomat and spy in his country's service.

But that was over now and when he got back to England—well, he would be an honest soldier again—and make Herrold pay his dues. Nor would he ever be a spy again: the experience had left a bad taste in his mouth.

But he was not able to leave as soon as he had expected. The negotiations began to proceed at such a pace that Arlington begged him to remain until they ended. "I need your support, Stair," he argued, "against such as Herrold, who do not understand the long view, and I conceive it to be my duty to claim it and yours to give it. In any case, you would scarcely have time to take ship before the rest of us are ready to leave."

"You are demanding a great deal of me," Stair told him gravely, "and when and if the time comes when I need something from you, I shall not hesitate to ask it."

Arlington looked at him knowingly. Stair Cameron had changed, no doubt of it. It might not be anything more than the inevitable alteration brought about by time, giving men a gravitas and a responsibility that they had not possessed in early youth. Stair was in his middle thirties, a time when most men began to take stock of their lives.

But it might also be, improbably, the influence of his little doxy, for Stair had privately confessed to him that he wished to marry her and settle down.

In that he was unlike some such as George Villiers, Duke of Buckingham, Arlington conceded wryly, who remained a permanent youth even though he was now in his middle forties. But Stair Cameron was proving himself to be of a different kidney. He had been a useful member of the negotiating party, unlike Herrold, whose open dislike of Stair warped his judgement, since he opposed automatically everything which Stair suggested, however wise and reasonable.

Stair had avoided Herrold and his crony Vaux whilst at Breda, but on their last evening before they left for home the entire delegation took the opportunity to drown the memory of the defeat at Sheerness by indulging in a wild drinking party.

In the middle of it James Vaux staggered up to Stair, who had remained comparatively sober, and sat down opposite to him. "Thought you were leavin' Breda early, Cameron."

"Hal Arlington asked me to stay on," Stair replied coolly. He had no wish to talk to Vaux, and rose to leave. Vaux leaned forward to seize him by the elbow, saying earnestly and drunkenly, "Was never happy with the way Frank Herrold treated your little doxy, Cameron. Want you to know that, whatever happens."

Stair pulled his elbow out of Vaux's restraining grip and said, surprised by Vaux's words, "Whatever happens, Vaux? Why, what could happen—to me and mine?"

Vaux opened his mouth to speak, but no words came out. An arm in scarlet satin took him by the elbow and lifted him to his feet.

"Take no note of poor Vaux here," murmured Sir Francis Herrold, pulling Vaux towards him. "He scarce knows what he is saying. 'Tis merely the drink talking, eh, Jem, my lad? Should know better than to take too much, always a mistake.''

Stair watched him walk Vaux away, hissing into his ear. What had Vaux been about to say that Francis Herrold did not wish him to hear? Unease rode on his shoulders again. He had half a mind to pursue Herrold and try to discover the meaning of Vaux's drunken hints. The only thing that prevented him from doing so was the certainty that he would become so heavily involved with the man that his departure from Breda would be delayed.

No, best to let it go. Tomorrow he would be away, and he could scarce wait to see Catherine—and England—again.

''Thought I saw Amos Shooter in the Strand today, mistress. He's like a ghost haunting us—you were certain that you saw him in Amsterdam.''

Catherine handed Geordie his dish of soup, before giving her brother his. On the day that the naval defeat at Sheerness had been cried in the streets, and the London mob had rioted, screaming for somone's blood, Rob had been released. He had arrived at Cob's Lane, unshaven and gaunt, swearing that, after his experiences in the Tower, he would never meddle in politics again.

''And a good thing too,'' Catherine had told him briskly, ''for my life since I last saw you has scarce been a bed of roses.'' She gave him an edited version of her time in the Low Countries, speaking little of Tom and not telling Rob that he was, in reality, that noted courtier, Sir Alastair Cameron. Nor did she tell Rob that she had gone there to save him from hanging.

Fortunately, she had already warned Geordie to guard his tongue when Rob came home, for one of Rob's first remarks when he had been fed and watered was aimed at him.

"So, we seem to have acquired a footman. Where the devil has he come from? And can we really afford one?"

Catherine had risen to Geordie's defence, although he needed none, for Rob's doubtful reception of him had merely served to confirm his melancholy view of life.

"Tom Trenchard abandoned both of us, and Geordie was so kind to me after that, and saw me safely home that it would have been a brute thing for me to have turned him away as well. Besides, he's more of a lodger than a footman, seeing that for the first week I was back his rent kept me in food before I found work at the Duke's Theatre again."

Catherine had told neither Rob nor Geordie that Betterton had been delighted with *The Braggart, or, Lackwit Married,* which was currently in rehearsal and being advertised on bills about the town. She was already working on a new play.

Neither she nor Geordie had told Rob that the government had ignored the information that they had sent back from Holland, for neither of them wanted him to be spurred into unwise political action again.

Since then Rob and Geordie had become unlikely friends, occasionally grumbling at one another. Imprisonment had turned Rob into a silent man and he and

Geordie were happily silent together. There were quite
a number of secrets being kept in the little house, for
Geordie did not tell either Rob or Catherine that he had
followed Shooter to his lodgings and discovered that
he was known there as Master Harris.

They had just begun to drink their soup when a
knock came at the door. Rob flinched at the sound.
Since the day of his arrest any sudden noise distressed
him.

"Never fear," said Catherine gently. "They can
scarcely be coming for you again."

Geordie reluctantly put down his spoon, and grumbled his way to the door. He opened it—and then shut
it again immediately. Whoever was outside now beat a
rapid tattoo on it.

"Who the devil was that?" Rob demanded.

"Someone you don't want to know," returned Geordie morosely, sitting down again.

Catherine was seized by a terrible suspicion. She
rose and pushed by Geordie who was attacking his
soup with relish, and opened the front door.

She had been right to be suspicious, for it was Sir
Alastair Cameron, also known as Tom Trenchard, who
was standing there, a bewildered expression on his
face. Before he had time to as much as utter a word,
Catherine shut the door on him, saying smartly as she
did so, "No pedlars wanted here today."

Rob, who had briefly seen a fine figure of a man
standing outside who was certainly no pedlar, said impatiently, "What silly game are you two engaging in?"
Before either Catherine or Geordie could stop him, he

opened the door himself. This time an angry Stair Cameron, his eyes blazing, stepped into the room.

"What the devil are the pair of you playing at that you should refuse me entry?" he exclaimed in a deep voice. There he had been on the doorstep, dreaming of seeing Catherine again, and of the joy with which she would greet him, and instead she had shut the door in his face, and turned him away! And Geordie had been no better. He had been prepared for his man's usual litany of complaint at life, but not to be denied absolutely.

"That," said Catherine, staring him down, "we might ask of you, Sir Alastair Cameron! What the devil are *you* doing here, expecting to be welcomed after you turned the pair of us away in Amsterdam without so much as a word of farewell or any notion of where you might have gone?"

"And only four groats between us," grumbled Geordie, "and half of that given to me by your fancy friend; a fine reward after years of faithful service."

Catherine saw Tom—for she could not yet think of him as Stair, however hard she tried—turn his face away from them both for a second.

So *that* was what James Vaux had been trying to tell him. Herrold had destroyed his letter to Catherine, and stolen the money he had left for her and Geordie, leaving them penniless. Mingled shock and rage at such treachery combined to silence him—coupled with the belated knowledge that he should never have trusted the man.

Catherine interpreted his silence as guilt. "Oh, you

may well look away from us, sir. My only wonder is that you have dared to come here at all.''

''Just a moment, Catherine,'' said Rob, his face bewildered. ''What in the world is going on? I thought you said that you were both in the Low Countries with an ex-soldier called Tom Trenchard. Now you have named this man as Sir Alastair Cameron. Were you there with two men?''

''Yes,'' said Catherine.

''No,'' said Geordie.

''Which?'' cried Rob exasperated. ''Which of you is telling the truth?''

''Both of us,'' announced Catherine. ''For Tom Trenchard was the name I knew him by until Sir Francis Herrold enlightened me as to his true identity before I was packed off to England at short notice like an inconvenient parcel. And Tom Trenchard and Sir Stair Cameron are two very different beings.''

''Enlightened you, did he?'' said Stair in his best sardonic mode. ''I could think of a better word for what Sir Francis Herrold did, but you would not like it.''

''Why don't you leave us alone?'' Catherine told him passionately. ''Please go. You know where the door is.''

''No!'' exclaimed Rob, suddenly turning into a lawyer. ''There's something damned odd going on here, and I want an explanation.''

Stair thought, irrelevantly, that Catherine had never looked so lovely. Her eyes were shining, her cheeks were glowing, and fiery indignation informed every line of her body. His busy mind had quickly worked out what Sir Francis Herrold had done to the pair of them, and he could not blame Geordie for his indifference or Catherine for her anger.

He would appeal to her brother, who seemed to be a more commonsensical man than he might have thought him from his knowledge of the conduct that had landed Rob in the Tower.

''If we could all sit down together, and talk quietly, without anger or passion, I can explain to you why you think that I betrayed you both. I assure you that I did not.

''In the meantime, you might offer me a glass of ale.''

Catherine let the hurt feelings and the memory of betrayal, which the sight of him had revived again, subside a little. She saw that he had not come finely dressed as Sir Stair Cameron would have done, nor was he as plain and shabby as Tom Trenchard at his worst. He simply looked like a pleasant gentleman, not a courtier at all.

''Very well,'' she conceded grudgingly. ''But tell me what I am to call you.''

''Stair will do,'' he told her, smiling at her for the first time. ''May I sit down?'' Without waiting for permission other than a nod from Rob, who appeared fascinated by him, he pulled out the empty chair next to Geordie and accepted the tankard of ale that Rob had already poured for him.

''Your good health,'' he announced gravely, toasting the three of them.

Catherine let out an exasperated sigh in return. Geordie merely grunted. ''We are waiting for your explanation, Sir Alastair,'' she said coldly.

"Stair," he said, grave again. "Tell me what happened when they let you out of gaol, Catherine, and you, Geordie, tell me how Sir Francis Herrold treated you when you finally returned."

"Sir Francis Herrold treated me as though I were the merest doxy who treads the London streets," Catherine told him bluntly. "He said that you had had your fill of me, and ordered me to leave by the next boat. He even took me to it as though I were his prisoner. He paid for my passage home in the packet, and that was that. I was left without any money to enable me to travel from the docks to Cob's Lane.

"I thank God that Geordie followed me to the harbour and then boarded the packet. He paid for me to reach home safely, and has been serving me ever since. He even kept me until I found work again since I had left Holland penniless. Are you surprised that we do not want to see you?"

And then, through the tears that she had never shed after he had abandoned her and which were threatening to fall at last, she choked, "Oh, Tom, I never thought that you would treat me after such a cruel fashion, never. To leave me without a kind word, or any message to comfort me on the lonely journey back to Cob's Lane."

"And if I told you that I never treated you so, what then?"

Catherine stared at him. "He said, that fine gentleman, Sir Francis Herrold said..."

Stair interrupted her, swearing an oath so dreadful that all three of them shuddered, and Geordie said reproachfully, "Master!"

"That fine gentleman must have destroyed the love letter that I left for you, explaining why I was leaving for Breda without saying goodbye to you after he and London blackmailed me into going there immediately by threatening your life if I did not. This I swear."

Catherine put her hands up to cover her face and began to cry at last. She hardly knew whether she was crying for sorrow or for joy.

Stair moved swiftly from his chair to kneel on the floor beside her, and put a loving arm around her. "No, do not cry, sweeting. You could not have known. Why should you not think that I was willing to desert you when the time came? Many would have done, but once I knew you and came to love you, I would not have hurt you for the world.

"I could not have believed that even Herrold would destroy my letter and lie to you so brutally. And what of my letters that I sent you from Holland? Did they never arrive either?"

Catherine put her hands into her lap. She was shivering. "No," she told him, her voice little more than a whisper. "No, nothing came. Oh, I hoped so much that you might relent and wish to see me again—and Geordie, too…who had been so kind to me, and so faithful to you."

He kissed her gently on the cheek, for a brief moment ignoring Geordie and Rob. "Oh, my dearest heart, I would have done anything to spare you this."

He lifted his head again. "And Geordie, too. You said that I had left you nothing but two groats for your pains, and turned you off into the bargain. When you returned to the inn, what did Sir Francis say and do?

For besides the letter I left for Catherine, I also left a purse of money for you both so that you might get safely home.''

''A purse of money!'' and now it was Geordie who swore. ''Tell me, master, was it left on the table beside the bed? For Sir Francis gave me his two groats from that. I thought that it was his purse.''

''That was where he placed it after I gave it to him,'' Stair said.

This provoked an instant reaction of, ''Oh, the villain! The vile sneaking villain! He lied to me and to the mistress. He stole your money and turned my mistress away without so much as a groat! I'll cut his throat for him, that I will!'' from Geordie, who was so incensed that he made for the door straightaway.

''No,'' exclaimed Stair commandingly, his arms still around Catherine. ''I'll not have you hang for the swine. In due course he'll gain his just reward for what he did to you both. This I promise you.''

''If,'' announced Catherine spiritedly, ''I had written of Sir Francis's villainy in a play, everyone would say that it was not possible!''

She shivered at the thought that what he had done might have parted her and Stair forever. She hugged him to her all the more tightly for having wronged him over the last few weeks when she had thought him a villain who had deserted her. To have him back again, cleared of all guilt, was like a dream come true and it was enough for her to grant him whatever he wished from her—whether it be marriage or no.

Rob, who had been listening closely to them, his eyes swivelling from one to the other, said in his new sober manner, ''A question for you, Sir Alastair. What are your intentions towards my sister? As the man of the family I ought to know. Are they honourable?''

Three pairs of eyes surveyed him, bemused. Catherine because never before had Rob said anything half so commonsensical about anything. Stair because Rob's questions had put him squarely in the dock, and Geordie because he had never before heard any one question his master's behaviour to his face.

Stair rose slowly to his feet, leaving Catherine gazing up at him almost fearfully. During the three weeks that they had spent apart, his anguish at not hearing from her had told him how much he loved her. It had brought him squarely before the knowledge that he would not, could not, lose her. Nor, in honour, loving her so, he could not, must not, debauch her.

The man who had sworn that he would never marry was ready to marry the virtuous woman who had sacrificed her virtue only because she loved him. That he was sure of. At the age of twenty-four she had come to him virgin, having resisted all the temptations of a life in the theatre—that hotbed of immorality.

Because of that, even if he had not loved her, it was his duty to love her. But he did love her, and duty did not enter into it.

He was silent for so long that Rob said irritably, ''Well, sir, well?''

''Well, very well,'' replied Stair almost absently, his eyes still on Catherine. He saw her lips quiver and knew by the empathy that lovers share that she was fearful that he was about to refuse her; that Rob had spoken out of turn.

He had never thought that he would ask a woman to marry him. Even if he had ever done so, he would never have thought that he would propose to her before an audience consisting of her brother, and his servant— who stood unwontedly quiet behind him.

Stair sank to his knees before his dear love, took her small hand in his and looked deep into her beautiful violet eyes, which were shining at him, assuring him of her love.

"My darling," he said, "my dearest heart, will you do me the honour of marrying me, of becoming Lady Cameron?"

Catherine took a long breath, and then asked anxiously, "You are sure that you really mean this, Tom…I mean, Stair? That you do not consider that you are compelled to marry me because of…" and she searched for a suitable word, ending with "…everything?"

"It is precisely because of 'everything' that I wish to marry you," Stair told her, gently kissing the palm of each of her hands. "I want you for your wit, your courage, and your steadfastness. Because I love you, and only you, and above all, perhaps, because I cannot think of a better way of having Master Will Wagstaffe in my bed to amuse me!"

"Will Wagstaffe!" exclaimed Rob. Stair noted at once that Robert Wood was no fool, he had picked up the allusion at once. "What does he mean by that, Catherine?"

Catherine coloured, released Stair's hand, and said reproachfully, "Oh, Tom—" for it was difficult to re-

member that he was really Stair ''—you have given
my secret away!''

''You cannot keep your secret forever,'' Stair told
her, ''particularly if you marry me, although I must
remind you that you have not yet given me an answer
to my question. Now that I have disposed of the 'everything' that troubled you, perhaps you will do so.''

''Do you intend to allow me to continue to write
plays for the theatre? Are you willing to play the Duke
of Newcastle to my Duchess?''

Stair recognised at once this reference to Margaret,
the Duke of Newcastle's wife, whose eccentricity consisted of writings plays and poems and expecting them
to be published as a man's would be.

''I have not the slightest intention,'' he assured her,
''of allowing myself or the world to be deprived of
Master Wagstaffe's wit. The Duchess's does not hold
a candle to it. But I fear that you must cease to be an
actress. You will have no time to be one when you are
my wife.''

It was Rob's turn to sit down, clutching his head. ''I
am quite bemused,'' he announced, ''first Tom Trenchard, the penniless adventurer, turns out to be Sir
Alastair Cameron, whom even I know is one of the
King's counsellors. Then he proposes marriage to my
sister instead of making her his mistress, and finally
my sister turns out to be Will Wagstaffe, whose plays
are the talk of London. Either I am drunk—or run mad.
Which?''

''Neither,'' Catherine said, ''for I had to become
Will Wagstaffe in order to earn us a living—being only
an actress was not enough—and the rest seems to have

followed. It will not trouble me to retire from acting—when I have finished my current contract with Betterton, that is.''

Geordie said, ''Make the most of it, Master Rob. For this is the eighth wonder of the world—that Master Tom should marry. He always vowed he never would. Alas, I think that our adventuring days are over.''

''Not quite,'' said Stair, laughing. ''For Master Wagstaffe here has still not given me my answer, and there is another matter or two to settle. Come, mistress, yea or nay. Do not palter with me, my darling heart.''

''Oh, Tom, I mean, Stair,'' sighed Catherine hanging her head and blushing, ''you already know the answer, and this is the strangest proposal a woman could receive—being made before two other people.''

''Only,'' said Stair, feasting his eyes on her, ''because I wish to be absolutely certain that you are fully committed to me, before witnesses. There has been enough confusion between us already. And still you have not answered me.''

''You know the answer. It is yes, it was always yes, and always will be. Will that do?''

''Splendidly so! I call upon all here present,'' Stair declaimed grandly, ''to witness that Mistress Catherine Wood, who like me has more names than one—indeed, exceeds me by having three!—has consented to be my wife. Is not that so, sweeting?''

Catherine rose and curtsied. ''Exactly so.''

''Well said.'' Stair looked around the room, particularly at the table set for a meal that had not been eaten. ''And as token,'' he announced, grave for once, ''that you are now *my* family, let us break bread together.''

* * *

Catherine was beginning to feel that she was living in one of old Will Shakespeare's plays, *All's Well That Ends Well,* except that her intuition told her that Stair—she really must learn to call him by his proper name—and Geordie seemed to have something else on their mind.

It was when she asked Stair, after their meal, whether he had discovered who had killed Giles Newman and William Grahame that she first became suspicious of him. "Oh," he told her airily, "about the only useful thing Sir Francis Herrold did was to inform me that Amos Shooter, who was playing a double—nay, a treble—game had disposed of them."

"Geordie thought that he saw Amos Shooter in London recently," Catherine said. "You remember that I thought that I saw him in the Buttermarket in Amsterdam.

"A much-travelled gentleman," remarked Stair, still airy, and left it at that.

"I am also beginning to think that it was he who betrayed us to the authorities in Antwerp," she added.

"Perhaps," Stair said, "but that is all over now, sweeting. Let us forget it," and he kissed the top of her head in lieu of anything more personal, seeing that they were now drinking coffee with Rob and Geordie.

Geordie was later to tell Stair that all that Rob needed to put him on the right path in life was a firm fatherly hand.

"Such as yours," said Stair.

"Aye, you may well laugh." Geordie was a trifle bitter. "But it is the truth."

"I am not laughing," Stair told him. "For you offered me a firm elder-brotherly hand—to some effect,
I believe. If you can make Rob Wood less of a hothead,
then that is all to the good. You will save me the trouble!"

He had evaded Catherine's questions about Amos
Shooter for a good reason, and when she had also said
to him in an earnest voice, "You won't try to punish
Sir Francis Herrold for what he did to me and Geordie,
will you, Stair? He didn't succeed in destroying what
we had between us, and that is his real punishment,"
he never gave her a firm answer—which, of course,
she immediately noticed.

No sooner was he alone with Geordie after Catherine
had set off for the theatre and Rob had retired to his
room to study, than he pursued the matter of Amos
with him.

"You are sure that it was Shooter whom you saw in
the Strand?"

"Quite sure, master. I followed him to his lodgings.
He is known there as James Harris and his wife is not
with him."

"Gone back to her family, no doubt." There was
something on Geordie's face that made Stair ask,
"What is it, man? You look as pregnant as a woman
nearing her term!"

"I wants to serve Shooter as he has served others,
that's all, Master Tom. You've got your hands full with
Sir Francis. Leave Shooter to me. No call for you to
be suspected of dealing with two. Mum's the word,
eh?" And he put his finger by his nose. "Less said the
better, even between the pair on us."

Master and man looked at one another in perfect agreement. Stair said, "You're sure you want to take this on, Geordie?"

"Aye, master. He served the mistress a nasty turn, so he did, and he deserves what he's going to get for that alone." He hesitated and added, "You be careful with Sir Francis, I wouldn't want her to be hurt any more than she needs. She's a brave lady, that she is."

"I'll be careful, Geordie. Trust me, no heroics. And no comebacks from the authorities either."

To make sure of this, after bidding Catherine farewell—for they were remaining chaste until their marriage—he made his way back to Arlington's lodgings at Whitehall.

"A word with you," he said, and when Arlington bade him sit down and speak he told him of Sir Francis Herrold's treachery to Catherine, and that she had agreed to become his wife.

"A remarkable lady," Arlington said at last, "if she can trap you into marriage! No, Stair, do not be angry with me. I respect the lady, too. If for no better reason than that, between you, you sent us the news that might have given us the beating of the Dutch—if we had heeded you. But you said that you wanted something from me?"

He waited for an answer. Stair said shortly, "I wish to deal with Sir Francis at once, and I don't wish to find myself in gaol before I even have time to marry. I shall not seek him out in the precincts of Whitehall, but corner him somewhere where duelling is not a crime—as it is in the King's neighbourhood. And I shall try not to kill him, but humiliate him, instead. I have no mind to be the centre of a scandal when I am about to be married.''

''Very wise,'' approved Arlington. ''You may rest assured that any punishment that you hand out to him for so mistreating your lady will not be looked ill upon. Believe me, he far exceeded his instructions when dealing with you and your lady. Neither Sir Thomas nor I gave him leave to blackmail you as he did. True, we wanted Mistress Wood to come home without you, but not after the cruel fashion which he arranged.

''I would not like you to think that I gave orders that you—or she—should be dealt with so scurvily—or that I would ever be a party to betraying you to our enemies! Quite the contrary. As for Herrold, there are many of us who will be happy to see him humiliated— if that is what you succeed in doing. But wise of you to check with me, Stair, that such a move as you propose would be acceptable. You are growing cautious in your old age.''

''A wife and the hope of a family in the not-so-distant future changes a man's character more than a little, I find. But I grow didactic. And I never was as rash as Rochester and the rest of The Merry Gang are. At least grant me that.''

''And more, Stair, and more. I wish you luck—in all your enterprises.''

Stair found Sir Francis Herrold, his toady, James Vaux, by his side, in the Great Coffee House, not far away from the Poultry and Cornhill, well away from the palace of Whitehall, and much frequented by those about the King and court. Sam Pepys, the Clerk to the

Navy Board, was often there, and was present that night.

Sir Francis had drunk more than coffee. His face lit up when Stair walked in. "Ah, Cameron, you are back, then? And your doxy, is she back? Has she found a new keeper yet?" Discretion was never his middle name, and Stair blessed him for it. At least it would never be said that he had begun the quarrel.

"I have no doxy, Herrold. I assume that you believe all men are as loose as you in their habits or—" and he swung his gaze significantly towards James Vaux "—perhaps even more so."

"And what the devil do you mean by that, Cameron?" bellowed Sir Francis, ignoring James Vaux's hand pulling at his arm to try to quieten him.

"You must make what you will of it yourself," returned Stair negligently, "for I cannot tell what is going on in the lump of pig's swill that you call a brain!"

Sir Francis made to lunge across the table at his taunting enemy, who was only too happy that he had diverted Sir Francis's innuendos away from Catherine. He had no wish for her name to be flung about in public. Several of Sir Francis's court tried to hold him back. They were successful, but they could not make him hold his tongue.

"By God, Cameron, I'll call you out for that, damned if I don't."

"And damned if you do," returned Stair agreeably, in no whit troubled that the other man was the aggressor who might name his weapons. "Where shall we meet—and when?"

Sir Francis hesitated. He had meant merely to provoke, not to find himself in a duel with a man whose courage and skill were a byword.

"Can't think, eh?" riposted Stair, amused that he had neatly trapped his man. "Now? At Leicester Field? My second shall be Buckhurst—if he so pleases," for that gentleman was lounging against the wall, amused by what was passing.

"With pleasure, Stair. Can't stand the man m'self. Few can. Do the world a favour by ridding it of him."

Several present who were not Herrold's toadies muttered their approval. Someone shouted, "Let's to Leicester Field and have done with it."

"A splendid notion," approved Stair, and nodded familiarly at Sir Francis. "Settle it now. With small swords, I suppose—although it is your choice. Vaux to be your second, I presume?"

Vaux's anguished face showed that Stair might presume, but Vaux could not approve. But neither he nor Herrold could back down without losing their place in society. Leicester Field it was to be, and presently. Herrold fancied himself with the small sword and agreed to that, as well.

"It's too dark to fight," was James Vaux's only—and desperate—contribution.

"Nonsense," said Stair pleasantly, "there'll be enough light to kill a man by, I'm sure." He had no intention of killing anyone, there would be too much trouble for the survivor afterwards, and he would tell Buckhurst to spare James Vaux, and hope that he would.

So it was decided. Leicester Field it was. A small crowd followed them, which grew larger when interested passers-by learned that four fine gents were about to have a set-to in the usual place for such activities.

Stair would have preferred to have finished Francis Herrold off for good and all, but wisdom said no. Wisdom also said short and sweet would be better than long and drawn out, which would have added more to Herrold's humiliation, but might not be wise. There was his future with Catherine to think of.

But humiliation it still was. Stair toyed with his enemy for a brief space before he finished the bout by inflicting on him the *coup de Jarnac* of which he had told Catherine. Herrold fell to the ground, moaning with pain, and unable to rise. The bout between the two seconds was brought to a close by Stair, who swung his sword up between Buckhurst and Vaux's. He had no wish to see Vaux dead, and Buckhurst was flighty enough to kill him for the fun of it.

"Damn you, Stair, I was just about to inflict the *coup de grâce* as you inflicted the *coup de Jarnac*." He laughed heartlessly at Herrold who was being held up by two of his servants. Stair handed his small sword to Geordie and walked over to where Herrold was sitting, his face drawn.

"Note this, Herrold." Stair's voice was as hard as he could make it, as hard as the soldier he had once been. "If I ever learn that you are insulting me and mine as you have done this evening, and lately in Holland, I shall finish off the task I began today. Next time I shall not cripple you, but kill you. Do you understand me?"

Herrold made no reply.

Stair repeated what he had said. "Yes, or no, Herrold?"

"Yes, Cameron, I understand you." The words were groaned out with difficulty.

"Good, and see that you continue to do so."

Stair turned away, vengeance having been done. Geordie handed him back his cloak and sword, and said softly. "Your task done, master, mine is yet to be fulfilled," and slid away into the growing dark.

Stair, with Buckhurst's arm through his—he had forgiven Stair for not allowing him to kill Vaux—walked back to Whitehall. He was sure that he had silenced Herrold for good and all since his downfall was already being cried in the streets by the many who had witnessed it.

He would never revile or insult Catherine again.

Geordie's target was Amos Shooter. He walked briskly to Shooter's lodgings; all his usual dallying was missing. He was in luck, Shooter was there. His appearance and his rooms were both a pale shadow of all that had surrounded him when he had been a wealthy merchant in Antwerp.

He stared suspiciously at Geordie. "What the devil do you want of me?" he demanded. "You are Tom Trenchard's man."

"No longer," replied Geordie, lying in his teeth. "We have had a right falling out, and I am hot to be no man's man. Also, I would wish to do him an injury, seeing that he has turned me off after many years of faithful service. So I have come to give you information."

"Why, what have you to give me?" Shooter was plainly still suspicious.

"You must know that my late master is high in the King's favour, and is privy to the secrets of state through his other friendship with Lord Arlington. Come, I hear that you, too, have lost all after such noble service to the state."

Geordie was careful not to say which state, for he was not quite sure of all of Shooter's many and varied treacheries.

"Aye, that I was and did their dirty work for them— only to be betrayed."

Geordie might have felt sorry for him had he not known of the trail of dead and ruined men Shooter had left behind him. Worse, he had put Catherine in danger and, after Tom Trenchard, Catherine was his guiding star. He had no relatives, few friends and Tom had rescued him from servitude when Tom had been a lad starting out in the world and Geordie had been a poor young man already scarred by life.

Shooter looked narrowly at him and sighed. The man before him might have something to tell him, and if he did not, or was trying to trick him, well then, he could be easily disposed of, like many before him.

"Speak on," he ordered grudgingly.

Geordie smiled cunningly at Shooter and said, "I shall require little from you other than a promise to pay me for my information. As a start, you may buy me a tankard of ale at the nearest tavern and after that I shall tell you my news."

For a moment Shooter hesitated. "Why not here, where we may be private?"

"Where more private than a noisy alehouse? We shall appear to be drinking companions, no more, no less. Best that I am not seen at your lodgings. Landladies have long tongues." He hesitated, before half-turning away, saying, "If you do not want my information, then I may as well try to sell it elsewhere."

His prey was desperate. He was alone, the agents of three governments were pursuing him because he knew too much, and he thought Geordie a sly fool because he was, like many before him, misled by his careless dress and his servile manner. A fool who would sell himself for a mere tankard of ale!

"Very well then, lead on. There is a tavern in the next street. We may reach it through an alley a few doors from here."

Excellent, thought Geordie with a grin. It was a dark night, with a pale sliver of moon. Exactly what he might have wished. He and Shooter reached the alley where Shooter, talking to a man he imagined to be a lesser villain than himself, was taken completely by surprise when Geordie caught him by the arm, swinging him round so that for a brief moment they were face to face.

Before Shooter could grasp what was happening to him, Geordie, in one subtle movement, slid his dagger into Shooter's ribs whilst murmuring, "This is for the mistress."

Shooter fell dying to the ground, and Geordie, transformed into a flying elf rather than a dawdling goblin, slipped out of the alley and made for Cob's Lane, Catherine and his supper, his vengeance accomplished.

* * *

"And where have you been?" Catherine asked him when he returned to Cob's Lane. "Misbehaving yourself with your master, I suppose." For Rob had come home not long before, telling her that it was already being cried about the streets, the coffee houses and the inns, that Sir Alastair Cameron and Sir Francis Herrold had fought a duel at Leicester Field and that Sir Francis had been disabled for life.

To her amusement, Geordie performed his most artistic cringe. She shook her head at him. "Do not lie to me, I know that your master defied me by risking his life to punish Sir Francis for his treachery towards us. I suppose that you have been celebrating his naughtiness."

Something in Geordie's face made her suspicious of more than that. Oh, she trusted neither of them, they were a scaly pair of rogues and whether either of them would ever settle down into being good honest citizens she begged leave to doubt. She was not sure that she even wanted them to.

"No," she told him. "Say no more. I have no wish to know what the pair of you have got up to. I most certainly should not like it. Go to bed without supper, that shall be your punishment."

Catherine laughed ruefully to herself as Geordie scuttled out of the room and up the stairs. One thing was certain, life as Lady Cameron was never going to be dull! She took that thought to bed with her in lieu of Tom—no, Stair!

And as she drifted into sleep she knew that, once they were married, there would be many more nights for them, and all as joyous as those she had already spent with him in Amsterdam.

Epilogue

Two men from the court of King Charles II at White-hall sat on the side of the stage of the Duke of York's Theatre in the summer of 1667. One of them was short and plump and was wearing a monstrous black curled wig. The other was tall and muscular, he was not wearing a wig, but his own waving red-gold hair. Neither of them were sporting masks.

They were watching a play called *The Braggart, or, Lackwit Married,* by one Will Wagstaffe, which was rapidly reaching its end. The chief actress, one Mistress Cleone Dubois playing Belinda, was on the stage being reconciled to her husband, Amoroso, after having discomfited Lackwit in no uncertain fashion.

Betterton, who was playing Lackwit, lay at the back of the stage, groaning, after being assaulted in a vital part of his anatomy by Belinda.

In a moment, the play over, they would all jump to their feet, join hands and move to the front of the stage to accept the applause of the audience. *The Braggart* had been a riotous and bawdy success, and many were asking who the author was. The name of Wagstaffe was, all were agreed, a pseudonym.

"D'you still favour her legs, Stair, now that you are married to them? And are you going to join in the play?" whispered Black Wig to his companion, who on this visit to the theatre had behaved himself rather better than he had done in the spring.

"Yes to the first question and perhaps to the last," whispered Stair.

"Pity that, about the last," returned Arlington. "I rather enjoyed your part in the action when we came here in the spring. Has your inventiveness finally run out?"

"By no means," said Stair, who had not relished the sight of Catherine being kissed by another man, even if that man were simply a mummer, a mock hero pretending to be violently in love with a mock heroine. "As you will later discover."

"And shall I then discover who Will Wagstaffe is?"

"Ah, you must wait to learn that!"

Arlington fell silent. The play ended. The applause was lengthy—this was the first night and it was plain by the audience's enthusiasm that the play would run for at least a fortnight, making it a most notable success.

Catherine, standing between Betterton and Jack Hayes, the actor playing Amoroso, found that her eyes were filling with tears. Oh, it was not that she wished to continue as an actress, far from it. She had only become one in order to earn a living and the pains associated with being a female player had been greater than the pleasure.

She had spent a large part of her time avoiding forced seduction. Many thought actresses fair game—the equivalent of whores. No, her real dedication was given to becoming a playwright whose work would be ranked with the best.

She looked towards Stair, who had risen to his feet and was applauding her loudly. That look told him of her love. "No, no regrets," she had said to him earlier, for he was worried that she might regret having to leave the stage. She hoped that he had believed her.

Betterton released his hand from that of the woman on his right, and Catherine let go of Jack's. Together she and Betterton walked to the front of the stage. Applause broke out again.

At length Betterton raised his right hand and announced, "My friends, Mistress Cleone Dubois has something to say to you, but before she does so I have a piece of news for you. I have frequently been asked who Master Will Wagstaffe really is and I have always told you that I had not permission to give you his true name. But tonight I may do so for, my friends, Master Wagstaffe is none other than this same Mistress Cleone Dubois, who tells me she will write many more such as *The Braggart* to entertain you."

Astonishment reigned for a moment before renewed applause broke out. Stair tossed a posy in Catherine's direction, which she picked up and waved at the audience. Those few, like Arlington, who knew that they had been secretly married earlier that day, redoubled their enthusiasm, began to cheer, and to tell their neighbours the happy news.

Betterton raised his right hand again. "Pray silence

for Mistress Dubois who will now speak her own, and the play's, Epilogue.'' He stood back to allow Catherine to hold the stage alone.

For the first time in her life stage fright threatened to overwhelm her. Before her was a sea of avid faces, alight with the knowledge that it was a woman who had written the comic masterpiece that they had just enjoyed.

Stair's voice broke her temporary trance. ''Courage,'' he said, in his best mocking manner. ''*Le diable est mort*—the devil is dead—so you need not fear him.''

The spell of fear was, indeed, broken. Suddenly Catherine wanted to laugh instead. She gave the audience a vast curtsy before she spoke the Epilogue that she and Stair had written between them that very morning.

> ''Friends, I reject the buskins and the mask
> In favour of another, harder, task.
> For Hymen calls, the marriage god, no less,
> His call so strong my answer must be yes.
> Yet absent though I be, I shall not quite
> Desert my other Muse, since my delight
> Is still to comment on life's varied scene;
> To write with passion, true and bold and keen,
> More plays in which to celebrate our time
> In words and music, dancing and in mime.
> So now farewell, forget me not, I trust
> 'Til theatre, actors—and myself—are dust!''

Silence followed, and then more applause, led by Betterton. Stair, still applauding, moved across to her to see that her eyes were full of tears. "Weep not, sweeting," he murmured in her ear. "This is but the mime of which you spoke. Outside is the real world where we shall walk together."

And then he took her hand, and bowed, with Catherine beside him falling into the actress's farewell curtsy.

"Friends," he announced, his voice as resonant, and as powerful as the actors who had preceded him. "I have but lent my wife to you for this night and for a few more. But rest assured that I will see that she keeps to the promise that she has just made you. Will Wagstaffe will write again. And now, I, too, will append mine own Epilogue to the play."

Amid cheering he began to do just that.

"An orange, a posy, a perfumed glove,
Were the three presents I gave to my love,
When on these very boards I first met my wife—
And that was the end of my bachelor life!"

He bowed as the cheering broke out again, and took Catherine by the hand, saying *"Adieu, adieu, adieu."* Walking backwards, he escorted her from the stage.

One of the King's courtiers had provided the audience with yet another night's entertainment. To make matters even better, this time the courtier had married his actress, not simply made her his mistress.

Stair did not allow Catherine to pause in the green room. Tonight was theirs, and neither the players nor the audience would share in it. Holding her tightly by the hand he led her through it, through the stage door, and into the street, to where their coach waited. Geordie, clad in a resplendent new livery, handed them in.

"Still no regrets?" he asked her as the Duke's Theatre fell behind them, for he was more than a little troubled that she might not have wished to end her career as an actress.

"None," said Catherine, whose dreams had come true that day, for was she not married to the man who had featured in them from the moment that they had met?

"Good," said Stair, leaning forward to kiss her as the coach drove into the night and into the future, where as man and wife they were to share in that contentment that many wish to achieve but few do, but whose magic beckons us all towards a distant dream.

The Lost Princess

PAULA MARSHALL

Chapter One

She was lost in a forest, at night. But she was not alone. Her hand was in someone else's. A man's hand. Large and strong and warm. He was urging her along, almost running her through the trees. What man was this? Why was he being so urgent with her? There had been other men with them once, but they had been sent away some days ago. How did she know that?

Did she know the man whose hand she held—or, more accurately, whose hand grasped hers? More importantly, did she trust him?

She stopped suddenly, so suddenly that he stopped too—and spoke to her.

For some reason she could not see his face, but she could hear his voice.

"Do you trust me, Marina?" he asked her urgently.

"With my life!" she told him. "With my life."

Even as she said the last word everything swirled away into the dark—the moon, the forest, and the man—and she was awake again, remembering everything which had happened to her since the morning when her uncle Ugo, the Marchese of Novera, had unexpectedly sent for her to end for ever the peaceful life which she had been living as Novera's lady...

"Marina, my child, the lord your uncle wishes to see you at once."

The lady Marina Bordoni, princess of Novera, looked up with a sigh. She was seated in front of a tapestry depicting the rape of the Sabine woman, which she had designed and was stitching for the great hall of the Castle in which she lived. She might be almost twenty years old, the nominal lady of the city state which her uncle ruled, but to her middle-aged companion, Lucia Capponi, she was still the child whom she had come to serve fifteen years ago.

"Immediately, he said," murmured Lucia anxiously; the lord always frightened her, if he did not frighten his niece.

"It is always immediately with my uncle," remarked Marina with a smile, "but his bark is worse than his bite. You should know that by now, Lucia."

Lucia looked her disbelief. Ugo Bordoni, now in his middle sixties, had been a *condottiero* of note, a mercenary captain of great panache and ruthlessness in his long-gone youth, and Lucia could never forget that.

"So you say," she muttered, as Marina rose gracefully from the tall stool on which she had been sitting.

Lucia noted with approval that however urgent the lord's commands, Marina always did everything gracefully. She invariably moved slowly with great confidence, possessing a natural dignity and a graceful stately walk. The whole charming effect was heightened by her calm golden beauty, that of a Madonna painted by Fra Lippo Lippi. Her hair was caught behind in a large knot, her eyebrows were dark and fine, her eyes a translucent grey, her nose was straight, and only a beautifully shaped, generous mouth hinted that there might be a passionate nature beneath her lovely placidity.

Even the knowledge of why her uncle was so wishful to speak to her on the instant was not allowed to disturb Marina's perfect self-control. He had returned from a short trip to Florence, Novera's great and powerful neighbour, the day before, an expression of extreme self-satisfaction on his face.

Marina knew only too well what had put it there. The one thing which she did not know was to what decision concerning her future her uncle had finally come. But her walk was as stately as ever, and when she entered the great hall of the Castle where Ugo sat in state in a high-backed chair, Father Anselmo beside him, and old Benedetto Spano, his one-time lieutenant, now the Captain of his Guards, standing at his back, no-one could have guessed at her inward misgivings.

She leaned forward to kiss Ugo's wrinkled old cheek, a surge of affection running through her. Whatever he had done, or was about to do, was being done with her best interests in mind, she was sure.

He had gone to Florence to find her a husband—he had not told her so directly, but he had spoken often enough of his desire for her to marry, and now the time had come: he had made his decision.

He had done so without consulting her—and that, she told herself ruefully, was because she had so often refused to discuss her marriage with him.

"I would wish," she had told him, "to be the lady of Novera, the Marchesa without a Marchese. You have taught me the art of governance, why am I not to be allowed to practice it? You know as well as I do that any husband whom you find for me will see me only as the mother of my children, his superior chattel. I would wish to be more than that. I thought that *you* wished it, too. There have been other great ladies who ruled fiefs, and ruled them well."

"Oh, Marina," her uncle had sighed at her. "Those days are gone, if they ever existed. I was wrong to raise your hopes. You need a husband, not only to protect you, but to protect Novera from the greedy claws of Florence, or even of Milan. And not only from them: you must know that every lordship left in the hands of a woman is also at the mercy of every ambitious rogue who sees a way to ennoble himself by conquering the lordship and marrying its lady.

"No, do not argue with me, child. Events have determined this, not I. I should have seen you married long ago, but, alas, I did not want to lose you, as I lost my brother—your father—when he died fighting for Milan. You are the last of the Bordonis of Novera, and the future hopes of the lordship rest on you and your husband.''

And that had been that. Marina had hoped that he might have heeded her wishes. But shortly afterwards he had gone without her to Florence with the most magnificent train he could summon to stay with their distant relatives there, leaving only old Benedetto behind to guard the lordship until he returned.

Now he was back to tell her whom he had chosen, what plans he had made for Marina Bordoni, who could make none for herself. But however much she might have wished to argue with him, Marina knew only too well the truth of what her uncle had said to her. She also knew that it was true that he did not wish to part with her. Childless himself, his own wife long-dead, and her father gone, too, he had treated Marina more as a grand-daughter than a niece.

She straightened up, and as she did so, he snatched at her hand. ''Sit, sit, my child.'' He hooked a stool towards them with his right foot. ''Sit here, where I may hold your hand as I speak.''

To do as he bid was a small thing, for he was showing his affection for her, where many a man would have made his arrangements without any thought for her, would have roughly shouted at her to do as she was told, or get herself to a nunnery, whilst he found a young mercenary captain of promise whom he could trust, in order to adopt him as a son to be lord of Novera when he died.

Once she was comfortable, her small soft hand in his rough large one, he told her his news.

''Dear child, you know whereof I am about to

speak. I went to Florence to find you a husband, determined that whoever I chose would be one to treat
you kindly. There I met, as arranged, my old friend
and companion in arms, the Duke of Montefiore, who
has a son, Leonardo, in need of a wife—as you need
a husband. He is a man of good repute. We arranged
the marriage on the spot, for such an alliance is most
propitious. It means that not only will Novera's future be assured, but by adding to Montefiore's lands
and riches, you will enable that duchy to hold off the
Florentines when they turn covetous eyes on Montefiore itself—''

Marina could not prevent herself from interrupting
him. Usually hard-headed, and prepared to agree to
her uncle's wishes, and fully understanding the politics of the matter, there was one question which
needed to be asked, for something was missing in
her uncle's story.

''You have met my future husband, then?''

''Alas, no.'' Her uncle shook his head a trifle ruefully. ''He did not accompany his father to Florence,
but he assured me that Leonardo is a fine young man,
learned as well as brave, and most fit to be the husband of a Bordoni.''

''It is hardly likely that his father would say anything else,'' returned Marina quietly. Her happy life
at Novera was at an end, she was to be married to a
man whom she did not know, go to live in a place
which she had never visited and Novera would become an appendage to another family's duchy. However expedient this was, however necessary to secure
Novera's future, it was all to be done at her expense.

She released her uncle's hand, rose, and walked to the narrow window which overlooked the beautiful valley below the rock on which the Castle of Novera stood.

"You know, uncle, that you promised that you would never do this to me. You said that you would never marry me, sight unseen, but that I should have the privilege of meeting my proposed husband, and having the right to refuse him if he did not please me. Besides, I might not please him!"

"No likelihood of that, my dear," exclaimed her uncle fondly, looking at her golden beauty, enhanced by the deep blue and white of the gown which she wore. He thought that she resembled one of the statues of beautiful women left behind by the old Romans who had conquered Tuscany long ago. They had been dug up recently when the town of Novera was being enlarged. "A man would be a fool not to wish you for his wife, and I firmly believe that Leo di Montefiore is a man whom you can respect."

Marina shrugged. "That is for me to find out on the day I am married—but, no, uncle," she cried, impulsively for once, as she went on her knees before him. "Do not look at me like that. Of course I will do as you wish. I must remember that I am a Bordoni of Novera, and what I do must be done for the lordship, not myself."

Ugo Bordoni smiled in relief. "There, my niece, I always knew that you would do your duty. You will not regret it, I am sure. Duty done leaves one fit to meet one's Maker when the time comes to do so.

I have told the Duke that we shall travel to Montefiore for the wedding. It must be done in fine style.''

Well, she would have to be content with that but,
in an unusual burst of inward rebelliousness, Marina
could not help but think that the Lord God was asking too much of her, to give her to a man who, for
all she knew, would mistreat her for the rest of her
life.

She must hope that what his father had said of Leo
di Montefiore was true.

This thought buoyed Marina up in the days which
followed as the preparations for her to travel to Montefiore for the wedding went ahead. Dresses were
fetched from the great painted chest in Marina's bedroom, and the jewellery which had last been worn
by Marina's mother was taken from the strong box
in which it had long been kept. At the last moment,
a few days before they were due to set out, when she
was stitching at the great tapestry, so soon to be left
behind for one of the sempstresses to finish, Lucia
came running into her room.

''Oh, lady, the lord is ill. They say that he fell
after he came from the chapel, and could not rise
again. Father Anselmo is with him, and a physician,
and he is asking for you.''

Her uncle ill! On the one hand Marina felt sick at
the very thought, on the other a treacherous voice in
her brain was saying to her, Perhaps this will mean
that the wedding will be put off. She silenced the
treacherous voice, and made her way to her uncle's
bedroom.

For the first time, seeing him there, propped up

against cushions, she realised how frail he had become, and why he was so insistent that she should marry. She felt ashamed that she had temporised with him for so long. He gave her a weak smile, murmured painfully, "Oh, Marina, do not be distressed. This is nothing, a passing malaise…"

At the bedside, unseen by him, the Castle's physician shook his head at both of them. "No, lord," he intoned repressively, "for while your illness does not as yet threaten your life, it is imperative that you rest."

Ugo sat up, for a moment completely the lord, before he sank back again, exhausted on his pillows. "Silence, man. I have a duty to perform. I must escort my lady niece to Montefiore for her wedding."

The physician shook his head again, his face severe. "Set out for Montefiore in your present condition, lord, and you will die on the way. My life on it, if you do."

"The journey and the wedding can be delayed until you are fit to travel, uncle." Marina's voice was as tender and loving as she could make it. "I know how much it means to you and to Novera, but…"

This time when Ugo sat up, he remained upright, although the effort cost him dear.

"No," he commanded. "Listen carefully, Marina. It comes to me that I might never be able to make such a journey again, and this wedding must go ahead without me, if the Lord God so wills. I wish to live until it is accomplished. The journey will be made. Benedetto and Father Anselmo shall escort you—your worldly and spiritual guides as they have been mine.''

"But, uncle," Marina began to remonstrate with him, although she knew that the matter was hopeless.

"But me no buts, girl. I have spoken, and so it shall be done. You shall be Montefiore's bride before the month is out. This is no time to delay.''

Marina could not argue with him. She could see the effort that he was making, even to speak to her in a low and broken voice. To oppose him might be to kill him. She saw by the physician's expression that he wished her away. She must agree, and endure—for was not that woman's lot?

"Come, lady," ordered the physician as Ugo's eyes closed, the effort of speech having almost exhausted him. "The lord your uncle needs to rest. You may see him later when he is a little recovered.''

And later on, thanks be to the Lord God, he was somewhat better, though still insistent that Marina should set out for Montefiore without delay—"so that I may know that you are safely married before death claims me.''

His counsellors, grave and reverend men all, supported him in his wish. Indeed, the most senior of them, Cola da Rimini, insisted that he would lead the party so that Novera's heiress should be supported with all due ceremony and solemnity when she arrived in Montefiore.

Ugo, against his physician's orders, had himself carried down to the courtyard in a chair mounted on poles to see his niece begin her journey. Marina clung to him, as she bade him farewell, hoping against hope that it was not for the last time. Ugo was almost as much affected and, kissing her on the cheek, he murmured, "Go with God, dear niece, and the blessings of an old man who loves you."

Pain on his grey face, he watched her enter her sumptuous litter, beautifully gilded and painted, with curtains to protect her from the sun of early summer. For her to travel in this fashion rather than on horseback would slow the party down, but Ugo had insisted that she must in order to demonstrate to all the world that she was a lady of high degree. Afterwards Marina was to wonder how different her life might have been if she had travelled on horseback as she had wished.

At the time it seemed little enough to do for him to agree to her uncle's orders without argument. After they had travelled beyond Novera's walls, she opened the curtains to look out at the smiling countryside, and to wave to the occasional staring peasant who rarely saw such a prosperous and splendid cavalcade. Opposite to her, Lucia fanned herself and complained vigorously of the heat, of having to go to Montefiore at all. "I am growing too old for such jaunting," she told Marina. "The lord should have sent a younger woman with you."

Later when they sat eating in a shady copse, just off the crude road, she changed her tune. "The lord said that your future husband is noted as a handsome young man, a soldier and a scholar, too." She gave an arch giggle. "Such a man should be an excellent bedmate for you, lady. You are blessed among women.''

Marina, who was eating good bread, butter and cheese vigorously, for the fresh air had made her hungry, shivered a little at Lucia's words. A bedmate! For the first time she forced herself to contemplate the realities of marriage. For the first time, also, she acknowledged that her opposition to marriage was because she was strangely fearful of the whole business of getting into bed with a man, and the love or lust, call it what you will, which went with it.

Living as she had done, the favoured child of an elderly uncle, she had had little to do with any young man, and now was frightened of all men. They were strange brutal beings who laughed and belched and swore and stared frankly at one's breasts with hot eyes. They might say that they obeyed and feared the Lord God, but their actions certainly didn't support any such belief.

And now she was going to belong to one of them. The only way in which she could have avoided such a fate was to have declared that she had a vocation and wished to become a nun, renounced the world, and retired to a nunnery. That, however, would have been a lie, and Marina prided herself that she never lied—and besides, one should never try to cheat the Lord God.

Perhaps her uncle and Lucia were right. She would have the good fortune to marry a handsome, meek and kind young man, who was more of a scholar than a soldier, and she would live happily ever after with him. Well, she would soon know the truth of the matter for each slow day was bringing her nearer and nearer to her fate.

But the fate which was awaiting her as they left Noveran lands, and entered the great forest which covered much of the territory of the neighbouring state of Verdato, was not the one which she was anticipating. Her party was not expecting any trouble when they passed through Verdato since its tyrant, Gentile da Cortona, had recently visited Novera, and had made a pact with Ugo that neither should attack the other. He had been a *condottiero*, a one-time friend of Ugo's, but his reputation, unlike Ugo's, had not been good.

It had been rumoured that, more than once, Gentile had sold the lord who had hired him to the lord's enemy, because that enemy had secretly offered him a large sum to betray his master. Nothing had ever been proved, and finally, in early middle age, he had won his lordship and settled down into something resembling respectability.

Marina remembered him as a large man, middle-aged, running to fat, with a blowsy wife who had died suddenly, shortly after his visit to Novera. She remembered, too, that he had been another of those lecherous men who had looked at her with hot eyes, and that those eyes had made her shudder.

They were halfway through the forest, their speed still at the same steady pace which they had kept up since leaving Novera, several days earlier, when disaster struck. The forest had become broken, with clumps of trees alternating with scrub through which the wild boar roamed, so the rider leading the way was keeping a look out for danger, when danger of an entirely different kind was upon them.

Marina and her companions had heard the steady approach of thundering hooves for some time, the noise of a large party of men riding towards them. Their small column drew to a halt, Benedetto turned in his saddle to speak to Cola da Rimini when a crossbow bolt struck him in the chest so that he fell, dying, to the ground. da Rimini, a peacable man who had never seen war, wrenched his horse's head around to flee from what was now apparently a body of heavily armed men, intent on attacking the Noverans. He had only galloped a few paces when the bolt which killed him struck him in the back.

A crossbow needed to be rewound each time that it was used, and that was only possible on foot, so the oncoming cavalry were restricted to loosing off one bolt each but, owing to the advantage of surprise, these bolts were deadly enough to deprive Marina's escort of any chance of defending themselves. That the attack was carefully planned became clear when Father Anselmo was the only male member of the party to be left alive, apart from those underlings who had managed to ride off into the forest.

At the sound of men shouting and cursing, of galloping hooves, of neighing horses, Marina pulled back the curtains of her litter—to reveal a scene of carnage as their attackers mercilessly slaughtered those of her party who had not had the time, or the good fortune, to escape on horseback.

Marina, in the grip of a desperate belief that she might somehow escape, although how she could not imagine, climbed out of the litter, Lucia following, crying and wailing at the dreadful sights around them. Any hope that Marina might have entertained of salvation was dashed when the leader of the assassins, a big man accoutred in splendidly chased armour, and wearing a steel helmet with a beak like a swan's, dismounted, removing his helmet once he had done so.

She recognised him at once. This was no leader of rogues who haunted the badlands of the lonely borders between the city states, preying on hapless travellers, but the lord and tyrant of Verdato himself, Gentile da Cortona in all his monstrous glory.

He ignored the wailings of Lucia and the remonstrances of Father Anselmo, who had been pulled from his horse, and pushed roughly to his knees before him, to say with dreadful jocularity to Marina, who was trying to control her fear at the sight of him, and the massacre he had perpetrated, "Welcome to Verdato, lady of Novera. We are well met. Allow me to escort you to my humble home, which shall be yours for a space—or perhaps for ever, the Lord God willing."

Chapter Two

⟨flourish⟩

From the window of the turret room in which she had been confined Marina could see the road leading from the small town of Verdato towards the forest where she had been captured. The view was beautiful, but she was in no condition to enjoy it.

She had expected immediate rape, or worse, but Gentile had proved far more subtle than that. She had been thrown up on to a horse behind one of the men-at-arms, her litter left behind, and a wailing Lucia was compelled to ride pillion behind yet another grinning soldier. Father Anselmo had been treated equally roughly whilst protesting his priestly station and his noble rank. All he earned was a buffet for his pains from the tyrant himself.

"Be quiet, shaven-head! Did I not need you to take a message to the lord of Novera, I would have left you dead with your companions. Be thankful that you have been left alive and cease trying me with your puling." He followed these unkind words with yet another blow.

To Marina he had been grotesquely polite, after a manner which made her skin crawl. He had walked towards her once they were in the great hall of his stronghold and he had laughed to see her shrink away from him.

"Have no fear, lady. I am of no mind to take your maidenhead yet. You are worth more to me as a virgin, if that is what you are, than as damaged goods. The priestly sniveller who accompanied you, and the noisy shrew who is your woman shall take my demand for your ransom to your uncle and through him to the Duke, whose son you are marrying. A refusal will mean that I marry you myself, although I would prefer the treasure your ransom would bring me, for I have no wish to provoke a war with Novera and Montefiore."

"Oh," blazed Marina at him, showing open emotion for the first time in her life, to the astonishment of Lucia who was cowering behind her. "But I would prefer that they went to war to rescue me, if only to disoblige you!"

She had thrown her head back and spoke to her captor in as arrogant a manner as she would have used to discipline a grossly disobedient servant. Far from annoying him, Gentile seemed to be pleased by such a show of defiance.

"Oh, the pretty princess who looked at me so loftily when I visited Novera has spirit, has she? I thought you were made of milk and water, lady, more fit for a convent than a palace. I see that I was wrong. I am of a mind to hope that your uncle refuses me a ransom so that I may marry you, if only to have the pleasure of taming such a vixen.'' He put out a hand to her and Marina dashed it away.

Afterwards she was to wonder at her own daring in baiting and defying such a monster, but anger at her treatment and at the cruel deaths of so many whom she had known since childhood overcame her fear. Once alone in the room he had assigned her in the tower she had wept bitter tears, but she would not show fear before him, even though she quaked inwardly.

Because he said that he admired her spirit, Gentile had allowed her to make her farewells to Lucia, who accompanied Father Anselmo on his journey to Novera carrying the letter containing the demand for her ransom. ''I don't wish you to have any allies whilst you are in my castle, lady,'' he told her. Instead for a tirewoman and companion, almost a gaoler, he gave her a grim-faced woman, Letizia, who was barely polite to her.

All that she had to do was wait. Each evening Letizia escorted her to the great hall to eat dinner with Gentile and his companions. He treated her with a politeness which was almost grotesque, and when one of his minions spoke a little disrespectfully to her, knocked him from his stool with a blow which half-stunned him.

''Due deference to the lady,'' he bawled, when the man slowly rose from the floor. ''She may yet be the mistress of this castle.'' He favoured her with a smile which was meant to be kind, but which had Marina shivering in her shoes. She, who was used to having everyone obey her lightest command, had never felt so helpless.

But as time slipped by, Gentile began to lose his deference to her. One afternoon, seated before the window, an illuminated missal on her knee, her only reading matter, the door opened, and Letizia entered, delighted to be the bearer of bad news.

"Up, my girl, up on your feet—at once! The lord wishes to see you immediately." When Marina moved a little slowly she was treated to a buffet on the ear. "I said at once, girl, the lord is in no mind to wait for you."

This time Gentile greeted her with a frown. He was pacing up and down the long hall, and his chamberlain, who was his chief adviser, was running after him, attempting to placate him. As he had dealt with the unfortunate henchman earlier, so Gentile did with him. He silenced the poor wretch with a blow which set his ears ringing, and caused him to stand back, alarmed and silenced, after stammering, "I had not meant to offend, lord. Your pardon."

Gentile waved him on one side and advanced on Marina. This time his anger was written so sharply on his face that she retreated before him.

"You do well to fear me," he told her, his voice high and furious. "It seems that your uncle, and your future husband's father, set so little store by you that not only do they palter with me by informing me that they are *still* debating whether to pay me a ransom, but they have offered a reward to any chance-met reckless fool who might be stupid enough to try to reft you from me! They are demanding more time whilst they consider the conditions in my letter. Well, *my* demands have changed, and they shall pay the price of their folly. I shall marry you tomorrow and then advance on Novera to wrest from that old fool your uncle, not a ransom, but Novera itself, which I shall claim in your name—he being incapable of ruling it.''

''I cannot believe that my uncle would leave me to your tender mercy, Lord Gentile, knowing that you have none.''

Marina heard Letizia give a great gasp behind her as she came out with these brave words, and no wonder, for Gentile advanced on her, his huge fist raised, ready to chastise her. And then, as he drew it back for the blow, he checked and smiled a cruel smile.

''No, lady. You must wait for your just punishment for your insolence until after we are wed. You may spend the time between now and our wedding night pondering on what exactly it will be. I want a wife, but I require a meek one, not a termagant. It will be a pleasure to tame your haughty spirit, lady.''

Marina had never felt less haughty in her life, but as before, she would not show her fear. Instead she simply bowed her head before him and turned to leave. He caught her by the arm and swung her round to face him, his eyes shooting fire and his teeth showing. He looked like a wild animal, ready to attack.

''By God, lady. I have a mind to take you here and now, on the floor before all my court. You will not leave my presence until I bid you go. Understand me, by the time I have finished with you you will crawl before me to lick my feet, if I so will.''

From whence came the courage which enabled her to stare back at him, even as he threatened her, Marina never knew. She was discovering in herself reserves of strength and determination which until now she was unaware that she possessed. All the same, by the time that she was back in her room, she found herself shaking at the very memory of what she had risked.

But before then Gentile had roared at her that he would have her robed on the morrow as befitted the bride of the lord of Verdato. "Letizia shall dress you in finery suitable for a princess, and you will be ready by morning to wed me in Verdato's cathedral. I am determined to celebrate our union with nuptials fit for a Prince."

By cathedral Gentile meant the small church which stood in Verdato's main square, but he made it sound as though she were going to be married in the superb confines of Florence's Duomo at the very least! No-one could say that Gentile da Cortona was other than grandiose in his pretensions. As Marina had half-expected, the "suitable finery" turned out to be the beautiful dress which had been pillaged from the baggage which she and her party had been carrying with them for her wedding in Montefiore to the Duke's son.

Letizia brought it to her room, together with the headdress, slippers, and cloak which had been made to go with it, as proudly as though she had stitched them herself, and laid them reverently on the painted chest at the end of Marina's bed, ready for the morning.

"Sleep well, lady," she bade Marina as she prepared her for the night, slipping one of Marina's bedgowns, made for her wedding over her head: yet another garment from her baggage. "It is not every woman who has the privilege of wedding the lord Gentile." And then, she added with a sly wink, "Oh, he is a lion in bed, is the lord, as well I know. Oh, the lucky girl that you are!" She blew out the candle and Marina could hear her laughing all the way down the tower's winding stair.

Sleep well! Marina could not sleep at all. Fear had her in its grip. She would, she knew, have been a little apprehensive on the night before her wedding to Leonardo di Montefiore, but the very thought of being Gentile's unwilling bedmate had her sitting up and gasping for breath.

"May the Lord God give me strength," she murmured at last, "and may the sweet Virgin bless me by saving me from such a fate." It only seemed fair to give the Deity and His mother the chance to save her, but how? She was trapped in Gentile's eyrie and from what he had said no-one, not even her uncle, seemed anxious to save her. But to give up hope seemed as bad as to surrender life, and at length Marina slept.

Her dreams were strange and uneasy. Waking, she could not remember them, only that at the very end she had been in a glade in a forest, like the one in which she had been captured by Gentile. There was a man with her. She could not see his face. She knew that he was speaking to her, but she could not hear his voice. He seemed to be encouraging her. He took her hand and began to run with her, and when she felt that she could run no more, he stopped, swung her towards him, and bent his face towards hers.

In her fear Marina still could not make out his features: she was not even sure whether or no it was Gentile who was with her. She was only aware that the man was about to kiss her, but as his mouth neared hers, she was suddenly sharp awake, panting, sweat pouring down her face, although whether from fear of the unknown stranger in her dream, or of Gentile, she could not be sure.

Dawn was breaking. There was a lovely apricot light in the sky, making long lines across the deep blue of the dying night. Her wedding day! Like all young women Marina had often wondered what her husband would be like, but never, in any of her dreams of the future, could she have imagined herself marrying such a one as Gentile, and after such a hugger mugger fashion, far from family and friends, and everything she knew.

She found a sad amusement in the fact that three weeks ago she had baulked at the very thought of marrying Leo di Montefiore because he was unknown to her, even though he was supposed to be a handsome young man from a noble family. Yet here she was preparing to be married to a monster who was famed throughout all Italy for the cruelties which he had committed.

Perhaps the Lord God was trying to teach her a lesson. Marina could almost hear Father Anselmo telling her that God's ways are mysterious, and that what He does for and to us, is always for our own good. "We may be sure," he was fond of saying, "that if He is harsh to us, it is meant to be a punishment for our sins." But if so, surely the lesson was a harsher one than any sin of hers deserved!

But what can't be cured must be endured, and whilst Letizia was dressing her, and exclaiming how lovely the lady looked in her cream silk dress, embroidered with carnations, with a silk wreath of them set on her blonde head, Marina was telling herself that endure she must and would. So much so that when she arrived in his great hall Gentile was almost awed by the lovely calm with which she greeted him and took his hand. He bowed low to her and kissed it, saying "Come, lady, we must away to the church, the priest awaits us, and all Verdato is in the streets to see us go by and cheer our union."

Letizia was nodding and bowing beside her, before standing back to take her place immediately behind her, level with Gentile's chamberlain whose face still bore the evidence of the great blow which Gentile had given him the day before.

It was as though she were living in a dream from which at any moment she might wake up to find herself back in her bed in Novera. But it was no dream, it was harsh reality. Still holding Gentile's hand, a few members of his guard and a herald preceding them, Marina walked out of the castle and into the main street lined with Verdato's citizenry.

Gentile had proclaimed the day a holiday and all had been bidden to be present to cheer their lord on his wedding day. The herald, brilliant in his particoloured clothing—one of his legs was green and the other yellow—was blowing his small trumpet, and between blasts was shouting, "Make way, make way for the most noble lord, Gentile da Cortona and his most noble lady, the princess Marina Bordoni."

Calling him a great lord was a bit much, Marina thought, trying not to giggle hysterically. It was said that like Francesco Bussone, the great *condottiero* known as Carmagnola, whom the Venetians had put to death for treachery, Gentile had started life as a swineherd. But he would not, she knew, be the first mercenary captain to begin life as a peasant and end it by ruling a great state, as now looked likely once he had married her and could claim Novera because he was her husband. And as for calling her a princess, well, that too was something of an exaggeration: nobility she could claim, but little more.

Still as in a dream, she and Gentile walked up the steep street until they stood before the steps of Verdato's "cathedral". At the top of them, immediately before the open doors, the herald was intoning something which, at first, she could not properly hear because of the noise of the crowd assembled in the large square which fronted the "cathedral".

He was reading from a scroll, and presently she grasped that it was Gentile's military victories which he was celebrating. The crowd cheered as each battle and siege was named. Then he read out her name and the roll of honour of her ancestors so that all might know what a noble wife the lord Gentile da Cortona was acquiring. The crowd cheered again, but somewhat less loudly than they had applauded Gentile.

The press of people was so great that Marina began to feel overwhelmed by them. Fortunately, after a few more moments of vainglory from the herald, he at last stood aside, bowed low, and allowed them to enter the blessed cool of the church away from the cheering throng.

Inside, after the golden splendour of the sun, it was as dim as though dusk had fallen. There were a few candles already lit, whose flickerings cast giant shadows on them as they processed in. A party of boys was lighting more, so that by the time they reached the waiting priest, standing before the altar, she and Gentile were in the centre of a great pool of yellow light. The congregation standing behind them was a small one, consisting mostly of the leading citizens of the town. Letizia had told Marina before she left her room that Gentile had summoned them there to bear witness to the coup he had brought off in marrying such a great heiress.

In a few moments she would be Gentile's wife. The priest was bowing to the altar, Gentile was turning to face her, and now that the irrevocable moment had come, Marina found that her unnatural composure was about to crack. She was on the verge of falling on her knees before him and begging him for mercy, begging him to send her back to Novera, or forward to Montefiore.

Whether she would have done so, she would never know, for even as the priest began to speak, the great doors of the church were thrown open again, and a small party of armed men advanced up the aisle towards them. They were dressed in the uniform of mercenary soldiers, leather jerkins and woollen hose, heavy boots, and steel caps. Some of them were armed with broadswords which they unsheathed as they walked up the aisle; others held crossbows wound up and at the ready as though they were about to do battle at the sounding of a trumpet.

They were led by their captain, a tall, broad-shouldered man, also in military uniform, but wearing a steel helmet with a nasal, a broad bar which covered and protected the nose, but which also hid the features of whoever wore it. He was carrying not a sword but a long dagger, which he swung negligently at his side. The whole party resembled nothing so much as a group of *banditti*, mercenary soldiers who had left their *condotta* to prey on everyone and everything which they came across.

At the sight of them, the priest began loudly objecting to naked swords and other weapons being displayed in church. Behind him Gentile's chamberlain was bleating, "What's this, then? What's this?" while Letizia confined herself to wringing her hands and wailing.

Gentile, forgetting he was on holy ground, roared at the sight of them, "In hell's name, what have we here?" Turning to the captain of his guard, he asked, "What in the name of Satan, Cecco, were your men outside thinking of to let this armed rabble in?"

"Armed rabble!" exclaimed the leader of the *banditti* reproachfully. "Oh, I do object to that. We're a very well disciplined body as you are about to find out."

With the speed of a striking panther, before anyone could stop him, he launched himself on Gentile, seizing him by the neck and holding his dagger to his throat. So sudden was the attack that neither Cecco nor any of his men, let alone Gentile, was expecting it.

He was now so near to Marina that she could see that his eyes were a brilliant, blazing blue, although the rest of his face was shadowed by the nasal and the side of his helmet.

Cecco bellowed orders at the guards behind him, at which they began to draw their swords, which had the captain saying, still in the same reproachfully mocking voice, "Oh, I shouldn't do that, Cecco, for if you do I shall be compelled to cut Gentile's throat for him, and order my crossbowmen to shoot your men down—starting with you. And what would the survivors do for pay day then? Besides, we outnumber you, the citizenry in the church are unarmed, and I've been looking forward to committing a massacre for days—life's been damnably dull lately."

As Cecco hesitated, he pulled the dagger across Gentile's throat so that a thin line of blood ran from it, before continuing conversationally, "Tell them to behave themselves, Gentile mine, or I shall finish you off before the high altar, and enjoy doing it."

Gentile, caught in a death grip, croaked, "Do as he says, Cecco. We'll kill him later—slowly."

"Oh, bravo," drawled his captor. "Now, Marco," speaking to the leading crossbowman who appeared to be his lieutenant, "escort the lady of Novera to the church door, while I follow you with Gentile

here, and remember, Cecco, a false move from any
of you, and he's butcher's meat.''

Marina, who had been silent and motionless from
the moment the armed men appeared, and who had
been trying to work out how they could have entered
the church so easily that they were able to surprise
Gentile, allowed Marco to take her arm. If she was
going from one ruthless captor to another, then so be
it. At least this one seemed to be younger and leaner
than Gentile, if equally as bloodthirsty. Looking forward to a massacre, indeed! Could he possibly have
meant it?

The whole party, Marina included, retreated to the
church door behind Gentile's captor, who was still
holding Gentile, the dagger to his throat, and was
crooning in his ear, ''The lady is an even better prize
than I thought. I shall enjoy relieving you of her.''

This had Marina quaking inwardly all over again.
Any hope that her new captor might be a mercenary
trying to claim the reward which her uncle had offered for her return was beginning to fade. More
likely that he was imitating Gentile and was either
going to marry her forcibly, or was going to hand
her back only after a much bigger ransom had been
paid than the one offered.

By now they had reached the church door, and she
and Marco and the men in front of them, swords and
crossbows at the ready, were through the door and
beginning to walk down the steps—and what would
happen once they were in the open again?

Having merely exchanged one monster for another—and a more efficient one than Gentile at

that—there was still the problem of how this new monster thought that he could get away without a pitched battle in Verdato itself. When Gentile's men outside the church and at the castle realised what had happened, they would surely attack him and his followers with all the strength at their command. And if these were all the men whom he had brought with him, how could he hope to escape with her?

No time to think of anything more, for as he reached the top of the steps the man holding Gentile flung him into the church and banged the doors shut behind him, shouting, "Key, Dino, quickly!" Whereupon one of the burly rogues produced a key and locked Gentile, his men and the congregation in the church. Other men trotted up with a stout piece of timber which they ran through the door handles to imprison the lord of Verdato and his men more securely. They could hear Cecco's guards hurling themselves unavailingly at the doors.

In the square a further line of *banditti* was holding the townsfolk back without much difficulty. For the first time Marina realised that if Gentile ruled Verdato with such careless brutality as she had seen him display, then its citizens would not enthusiastically defend him against any man or group of men who proved that they could defy him. They might, indeed, see such a band of men as saviours—a new master might prove kinder than the old—or so they could always hope.

Even when the invading banditti began to retreat they made no effort to remove the timber from the doors.

"To horse," shouted the captain briskly. Without more ado he took Marina by the hand, and shouting, "Hurry, lady, hurry, before the doors give way," he ran her down the street so that Marina thought that she was back in her dream again. She saw the remnants of Gentile's small bodyguard which had been left outside the church lying dead and wounded in the steep roadway.

Unhindered by the townsfolk they tore through the great arch which led out of the town, and there, beyond it, were a few more men who were guarding the horses which belonged to her rescuers.

Marina was panting with the unaccustomed effort of running. She felt as though her legs were giving way even before they reached the horses. Her captor, ignoring her gasping cries, flung her up on to the first horse which they came to, and shouted, "Astride, lady, astride," before he mounted the one beside it.

Once astride her horse—something which she had not been since she was a child—Marina struggled to pull her incongruous wedding finery down to hide her legs.

Ignoring her futile efforts at modesty, her new captor cut his whip across her horse's flanks so that it bounded forward, almost unseating her. Shouting, "Follow me!" he galloped his party down the cobbled road beyond the gate, which soon turned into a track which they left to make for the forest in which Marina had been captured.

Even as she struggled to control her horse, Marina noticed that not all of the men with them had horses, and that some of them, once they were through the gate, had disappeared into the scrub which lined the road. They took the opposite direction from their captain's party which was now reduced to some ten in number.

Well, she was escaping from Gentile, whose very touch had revolted her, but she was now at the mercy of an arrogant swine who bawled peremptory orders at her as though she were her own waiting woman. The sooner she found out who he was and what his intentions towards her were, the better. She had a horrid feeling that they were not benevolent, but for the moment all that she could do was follow him, and hope not to fall off her lively horse...

Behind them, in the town, the church doors burst open when Gentile's maltreated citizenry belatedly pulled out the timber which held them. Cecco, Gentile and his men streamed after Marina and the *banditti*, to find horses and to take up the pursuit.

Chapter Three

"Well, lady," drawled the mercenary captain, offering her his hand to help her dismount. "The forest is not as comfortable as Gentile's castle, but at least you don't have to share it with him."

Hot, tired and sore, Marina made him no answer. She could barely think, let alone speak. As her feet touched the ground her knees gave way and she would have fallen through sheer exhaustion had not her captor caught her to him to steady her. For a moment, before he released her, she could feel the hard strength of his long and shapely body, the strength with which he had held and controlled the massive Gentile so easily. It came to her that she ought to fear him even more than she had feared Gentile.

"No need to assist me," she told him haughtily; it was time to put him in his place. "It was a mere passing weakness, that's all."

He smiled at her for the first time, showing excellent white teeth. "If you say so, lady, but I thought that you might be tired after your unaccustomed ride.

I doubt me that you often venture out of Novera's castle, wearing a wedding dress, and riding astride— but perhaps I am mistaken.''

Oh, the insolence of him! Marina had never been rude or unkind to her inferiors, or those who served her, but she had hardly spoken to this man, or he to her, and she already resented him, resented most of all his air of effortless superiority.

''No mistake,'' she informed him coldly, grey eyes frosty. ''But the lady of Novera would be a poor thing if she allowed such a trifle to discommode her.''

His helmet hid the look of admiration which he unwillingly threw her. Exhausted by having been kidnapped, not once but twice, having ridden hard across country and then wound her way painfully through that part of Verdato's forest which climbed into the mountain beyond it, she was still showing a haughty, froward spirit. Unable to see his expression, Marina mistakenly thought that he held her in despite as a useless great lady, fit only to be coddled.

So she walked away from him to sit on a fallen tree, her legs trembling and her whole body vibrating after the rigours of her ride. She wondered why he had chosen to take them all so high that she could look across the valley which divided Verdato from them, and see it on a hill below them, blue in the distance. His men were too absorbed in looking after their horses, in unstrapping their saddle bags, in making a small fire, and preparing themselves to remain for a time where they were, to take any notice of views, however beautiful.

Not that Marina was registering its beauty, either.

She was too engaged in watching her captor. He had taken off his helmet to hang it from his saddle, beside the broadsword which he had not taken with him into the church, so that she saw his face for the first time—and it surprised her.

By his easy command and his tone of ruthless, effortless impudence she had not thought him to be young, but she could see at once that he had barely thirty years to his name. And he was handsome also, after a fashion which she had not expected. His blazing blue eyes she had already seen, but not the curling waves of his black hair worn long, nor the perfect oval of his strong face with its straight nose and shapely, amused mouth. It was not by any means the face of a coarse and brutal bandit. The only thing which kept him from being an absolute Apollo was a scar beneath his eye on the right side of his face. It was not large enough to mar it: in an odd way it enhanced the general impression he gave off of careless assurance, based on the kind of superb athleticism which she thought that her uncle Ugo must have possessed as a young man.

His men were obedient without being servile. He gave them orders which he obviously expected to be carried out on the instant—as they were—but now that the urgency of their escape was over, he neither bellowed at nor struck them, as Gentile had so often done. He saw her watching him—did he see everything?—and called to her, "Lady, we are about to eat. We have not done so since dawn, and I doubt that you have, either. Afterwards, we will talk, but not before. Decisions taken on an empty stomach are rarely wise. I advise you to join us.''

Marina's answer was a brief nod. Speech, for the moment, seemed beyond her. Too much had happened to her since morning, but yes, astonishingly, she was hungry for the first time since Gentile had captured her. The wretched man was right again.

He ordered two of the men to reconnoitre the neighbourhood. Marco cooked their meal. Another looked after and fed the horses. Two of them set up a small improvised tent. When the reconnoitring men returned he spoke swiftly and certainly to them after they had made their report to him, gesturing with hands which were as long and shapely as the rest of him.

In some odd way, he was beginning to fascinate her. She had never met anyone quite like him before. The men around Ugo had been old and grave; such smiling insouciance as he was displaying was foreign to them—and to her. A stately gravity had been the order of the day in the court of Novera and she had been a willing party to it.

How would that serve her here? Were all the lessons she had so painstakingly learned to be of any use to her? No doubt she would soon find out!

His lieutenant, Marco, a burly man nearing middle-age, who reminded her a little of poor Benedetto came over to her with water in a small pewter cup. ''Drink, lady, drink. Your day has been hard and long.''

She was drinking it gratefully when *he*, for so she was beginning to think of him, still having no knowledge of his name or rank, walked towards her. She looked at him over the rim of her cup, murmured

"Yes?" and managed to make the brief word a haughty command as much as a question. She must never forget that she was the lady of Novera and that he was some nobody who had rescued her. Worse, she was not yet certain whether she ought to be grateful to him for that—he might be a worse master than Gentile.

He sat beside her on the log, and looked frankly at her as—apart from Gentile—no man had ever done before. She had become used to deference, but it seemed that there was little of that on the mountain beyond Verdato.

"My men tell me," he said, "that there is a waterfall and a small pool some hundred yards from here where you might be able to refresh yourself after your hard ride. I have some clothes in my saddle bags which are more suitable to your present condition than the frippery which you are wearing. You could take them with you and change into them. I guarantee that neither my men nor I will molest you while you do so."

He hesitated, and then with a wicked smile, added, "And, of course, you will do nothing so foolish as to try to run away. You have no notion of how to survive in such conditions as these, and there is always the possibility that Gentile's men might find you. You will behave yourself, I trust, and save us all a deal of trouble."

Marina flushed angrily. "I am not a fool," she informed him frostily. "You have no need to bully me. I have no intention of trying to escape, the mere idea is ridiculous." In reality, she was grateful to him for his suggestions, but she was not about to tell him so. Not only did the notion of exchanging her soiled and sweat-dampened clothing for something cleaner and warmer attract her, for it was cold here, high in the thin air, but he was also solving another problem for her, which she had been fearful of mentioning through very modesty.

''So happy to learn that we understand one another, lady,'' was his only reply to that, before he went over to his horse to collect the clothing which he had promised her from his saddlebags. He had obviously thought of everything which might be needed when he had set out to capture her, and the knowledge infuriated rather than pleased her. It added to his air of infallibilty, and made her feel even more helpless before him.

The clothes he handed to her were of a rough coarse frieze, brown in colour, and the dress was so made that she would be able to ride astride without the loss of modesty which her light wedding gown with its tight skirt had forced on her. There was also a length of black ribbon with which she could tie up her hair which had fallen down. A pair of scuffed heavy boots completed the unlikely ensemble.

Nevertheless, it was with real gratitude that she carried them all to the waterfall, laid them on the ground, and retreated into the scrub where she was at last able to answer the call of nature. After that she washed herself, took off her tattered and stained wedding dress, and changed into the rough and ready garments which meant that no-one looking at her could conceivably imagine that she was the missing lady of

Novera. Her long blonde hair she arranged into two plaits which she wound round and round her head, trying to see herself in the troubled waters of the pool to check that she was as neat and tidy as a woman could be who had endured the kind of day which she could not have dreamed of before she left Novera.

Her reward when she returned was to have *him* stare hard at her, and remark, "Excellent, lady—you have exactly the look of the miller's wife at Monreale. We have a chance of escaping alive if only the rest of us are able to appear as harmless. Marco, hand the lady her share of the rabbit, and a piece of bread to eat it on."

Beforehand Marina would have sworn that she could never have sat at the end of a day spent in the open, wearing rough clothing and enjoy eating coarse yellow bread and rabbit's meat tinged with the smoke of the camp fire over which it had been cooked. But the meat tasted like manna, and the rough red wine which Marco poured into her pewter cup from a skin which had hung from his saddle, tasted even better.

She found that she was so hungry that she licked her sticky fingers in appreciation. She caught Marco looking approvingly at her. "You enjoyed my cooking, lady?" he asked her with the kind of directness which told of the camp rather than the court.

"Delicious," she told him truthfully, and he rewarded her with another joint which she attacked as hungrily as the first. His master was seated opposite to her, cross legged on the ground, hardly distinguishable from his men. His gaze on her was sardonic, but he was eating his share of the food as greedily as she

was, and had he said a word of criticism to her she
would have told him so. Perhaps, she thought, as she
stared aggressively at him, it was the change of clothing which was making her assertive after a different
fashion from that of the lady of Novera.

"We need to talk," she told him abruptly once the
meal was over, and the fire had been extinguished so
that it might not give their presence away.

"Indeed, we must." He smiled at her, and came to
sit closely by her on her log.

Marina, avoiding his impudent eyes, moved away
from him and went straight to the point. "I do not yet
know your name, ser captain, or whether I ought to
thank you."

He showed his excellent white teeth again. "Very
wise, lady. I am not sure whether you ought to thank
me, either."

"That is a matter of opinion," she returned, "on
which I shall make up my mind when I not only know
who you are, but what your intentions are towards me.
Am I to suppose that you will escort me safely to
Montefiore and claim the reward from the Duke and
my uncle, the Marchese?"

She said this with all the arrogance which she could
summon up to remind him who she was—and who
he was.

He was not in the least put out, but said lazily, "I
am a mercenary captain, Niccolo da Stresa by name.
I heard of the reward offered for your return, but now
that I have met you I am not sure that I want to hand
you back to Montefiore and Novera." Having thrown
this dart at her, his smile grew more brilliant still.

"Why should I not make my fortune as well as another, by marrying the heiress of Novera? Tell me that."

He put his head on one side, and said, still in that lazy impudent voice, "You are passably good looking, have a haughty temper—but that is of no moment, marriage to me would soon cure it. I shall need to keep my options open, lady, and shall put off any decision until we are safely out of Gentile's clutches. Does that satisfy your haughtiness?"

Marina tried not to betray her agitation and dismay as he justified her suspicion of his motives. "You must know that it does not," she told him, trying not to provoke him in any way, for she had been right over one thing, if nothing else: he was as dangerous, if not more so, than Gentile. "I will make sure that you will be well rewarded if you take me to Montefiore, and I am sure that my future husband, Leonardo di Montefiore, will also reward you highly, too."

He looked at her from under hooded eyes. "Tell me, lady, is it true that you have not met your future husband, the heir of Montefiore?"

"That is true, yes, but what is that to you?" Marina was rather proud of the coolness of this answer, and the sentence which followed it. "Between the three of you, you, Gentile and Leonardo, there is little to choose, for I am being taken against my will by all of you, and in the end what matters it but that you are men, and I but a hapless woman?"

Niccolo appeared to consider for a moment, then said gravely, "Very true, lady, but does that mean that you have no care for which of us you wed? Does the fact that Leonardo di Montefiore is the heir to a duchy mean nothing to you?''

''Only that he offers me a more settled life than either you or Gentile can, and that by marrying him I obey those who made the match for me. In any case, it is as the Lord God wills, not I.'' She folded her hands and looked at him with a composure which she did not feel.

The blue eyes were blazing at her now. ''You show a singular meekness in action, lady, which contrasts with the fieriness of your language. I would enjoy making the one match the other.''

Now this was a two-faced statement. For what did he mean—that he wanted her fiery in action, or meek? And in any case, did what he meant matter to her? He was certainly looking as grave as Father Anselmo had done when discussing a problem in logic with her. But this was no problem in logic: they were discussing the disposal of her body.

And then Marina made her mistake. She said, as grandly as she could, ''Seeing that I am indifferent towards all men, whether they be dukes or bandits, it means little to me personally whom I marry, so to please both God and my uncle I must do my duty and marry Leonardo di Montefiore.''

The blue eyes blazed at her harder than ever. He leaned forward and said softly, ''Say you so, lady, say you so. I pity the poor devil whom you do marry. Indifferent to all men, eh?'' His fine black brows rose. ''I shall test that one day, not here, not now, but soon,'' and his hard stare was for her and no-one else.

Marina did her best not to quail before it. She might

be at his mercy, but she would neither shrink before him, nor beg anything of him. She would be as cool and distant with him as she had been with Gentile. Her dignity was all that was left to her, and she was determined not to lose it.

His eyes hooded again, Niccolo rose in one swift and supple movement. He was like a great cat, stretching and enjoying the power and grace of his superb body. He was done with her for the moment, having made his none too veiled threat. He was once again the soldier and organiser, urgently calling Marco to him, saying so that all might hear him, "We must have a counsel of war, and make plans for the morrow before we sleep."

Marina watched him as he talked, watched him listen also to what Marco had to say. Again there was the contrast with Gentile, who went his own way without consulting others. There was something formidable about him. He reminded her of a young *condottiero* who had visited Ugo when she was still little more than a child. The Leopard he had been called, and he had possessed the same leashed power which Niccolo unthinkingly displayed.

Marina shivered. Handsome he might be, and young, but where she was concerned he was only Gentile writ large, after all, and she was more in his power than she had ever been in Gentile's. For who would rescue her now—from him?

"The devil is in it," raved Gentile da Cortona at Cecco Fioravanti, his captain of the guard. "And who the devil was he?"

Cecco shook his head. "I know him not, lord. One of his men, yes. Marco Despini. He was with Gattemelata in his youth. A sound man in a tight corner, I do know that."

"Which is more than I can say of you," snarled Gentile, still raving, "after yesterday's bungling. Half of my personal guard dead or wounded, and my bride snatched away from me while some nobody treats me like a bale of rotten goods. I have a mind to send you to the stranglers were it not that I have none fit to put in your place until Braccio returns from his errand. Though God knows, my youngest page might have done better by me than you have done. One more mistake like that and I'll have you gutted on the instant!"

"But who could have guessed at such impudence?" returned Cecco desperately—he knew his master's wicked temper. "To come into the church—and with so few men—and to disappear so quickly."

"The devil was in that, too." Gentile ceased raving. "Before I do aught else I'll round up a few of those who stood in the square and took so long to open the doors for us, and hang them up in the church for all to see what the reward for treason is."

"But the church is holy ground, is sanctuary," yammered Cecco, who was beginning to wonder whether the pay he was getting from Gentile was worth what he was being asked to do for him.

His reward was a blow in the face from Gentile's mailed fist which sent him reeling. "By the living God, man, did the fiend who stole my bride away and cut my throat for me care about holy ground or sanctuary? If it were not that he has done me a mortal harm, I had better find him to make *him* my captain rather than carry on paying such a bleating sheep as you have proved to be.''

He swung about to bellow at his chamberlain, who cowered at the very sight of his scarlet, angry face. ''Send out heralds and messengers to offer a reward to any who will either capture the foul fiend who has my bride, or will give us news of where he is. I'll have him on the rack to entertain us all before the week is out. He cannot have gone far—wherever he has gone.''

Gentile had just returned empty-handed from a fruitless chase after Marina and her new abuctor— fruitless because the trail was lost shortly after Verdato's limits had been reached. Pounding far into the night along the track which ran northwards had brought them nothing but tired horses and repeated cursings against fate from Gentile himself.

There he had been, decked out like a bullock for slaughter, standing in the church, one of Italy's richest heiresses by his side, his future seemingly assured, and the next minute she was gone, snatched away by God knows who, gone God knows where, his throat and body aching and his guard half massacred. He would be the joke of all Italy—as he suspected he was the joke of the townsfolk who lived under his brutal and tyrannous heel. Well, some of them would pay a nasty price for their laughter, he would make sure of that before the day was over.

Meantime he set in train the further pursuit which would surely net the man who had humiliated him, and return the woman who, having gone meekly with him to church, had left equally meekly with her new owner.

"When and how did they arrive?" he snarled at Cecco, who was nursing his bruised mouth which would no longer allow him to speak clearly.

"Yesterday, lord," he lisped. "Half of them put up at the inn, and said that they were a small company making for Florence where they had been hired by the Signoria. The other half slept in the open. When they saw that the day was given over to carnival by reason of your wedding, their leader said that they might as well stay to see the fun before they left for Florence."

"See the fun!" Gentile was raving again. "I shall teach Messer bandit what fun is before I have done with him."

Cecco said nothing, for he was thinking of the old French maxim regarding the killing of a flea… "First catch your flea…" Wisely he said nothing, but began to organise the search for the lady of Novera and those who had spirited her away. To spirit himself away from Gentile once this unfortunate episode was over was an even better idea—but that would have to wait until he had recovered the lady. To desert Gentile now would mean that Gentile would hunt him to his death with all the savagery of which he was capable.

Cecco called his lieutenants to him and began to give them orders urgently. After all, his own pride was at stake here, too.

"They will be after us, no doubt of that," Niccolo was telling his remaining men and Marina, who had just breakfasted, and were seated before him. "And if I know Gentile, he will have sent messengers, heralds and envoys to every quarter of Verdato telling everyone to be on the look out for us—and offering rewards for information which proves fruitful as large as the one which Montefiore offered for the lady and which brought me here."

He paused. "And, mark this, we shall not be safe even when we're out of Verdato's territory until we reach Montefiore's lands—if that is where I decide to go. What I *have* decided is this. Gentile will be looking for a large party and it was for that reason that I paid off most of my company *before* snatching the lady away, and told them to make for safety at once, once the raid on Verdato was over. The rest of you, who have served me in the past, I retained until we were safely out of Verdato's immediate bounds.

"Marco will pay you off—handsomely—for the excellent way in which you backed me up. I know that I can trust you not to run to Gentile and betray me—but if you do, no matter, you have no idea where Marco, the lady and I, are going, nor in what guise we shall travel. And I would advise you to trust Gentile even less than you might trust me!"

There was a general laugh at this, which Niccolo joined in. Men! thought Marina disgustedly, there was no knowing what they might find amusing. Niccolo had not finished.

"If any of you wish further employment, then make for Florence and the house of Giannini Belforte. Tell him that you have been serving under me—show him as proof the paper which Marco will give you, and he will find a captain for you to serve under. Never let it be said that da Stresa neglected the fortunes of those who served him well.''

One of the men said, ''I would rather stay with you, Captain. I have served you before, and know you to be a fair man—if hard. I may not be so lucky in my Captain again.'' Several of his companions nodded as he finished speaking.

Niccolo said gravely, ''What you say pleases me, Enzo, but if the lady and I are to avoid Gentile's traps, then we must travel light. Perhaps in the future we may be comrades in arms again?''

The man was clearly disappointed. What he had said had thrown a new light on Niccolo, confirming her belief that, for all his ruthlessness, he was not simply another brute like Gentile. But she was going to be alone with him and Marco. The thought troubled her. But the thought that Gentile might recapture her troubled her even more.

''Ser Niccolo.'' She spoke a little peremptorily to him after the meeting had broken up and Marco had begun to hand the men their money and their papers.

''Lady?''

''Ser Niccolo. You said, if I mistake not, that you had not yet decided whether you would take me to Montefiore. Did you mean that? Remember that Montefiore and Bordoni will reward you well for my return, and I should beg them to raise the reward as a bonus for returning me when you were tempted to do otherwise.''

Niccolo looked steadily at her. She stood straight and tall, not quailing before him, quite emotionless.

He had not once seen her display emotion. She was like a beautiful living statue which was more stone than woman. What would it take to break that lovely calm? Even when she was a little fierce with him the fierceness was measured, controlled.

Would passion ever rule her? If she were in a man's arms, in the throes of love, would she still resist love's pangs and be as cool, as measured, as she was now? Was she essentially cold, or was the coldness a mask beneath which the currents of passion swirled and boiled? For no reason at all, Niccolo thought that the mask existed and was there to be torn away.

What if *he* were to tear it away? What transports would reward him? His eyes dilated at the very thought. His expression changed.

The woman before him knew that something had happened, some balance which had lain between them had been tipped in a direction which she might not like. How she knew was a mystery. She said, "You heard me, Ser?" because he was as still and silent as an animal which had scented danger.

"I heard you, lady, and I will say this. I have not yet made up my mind what I shall do with you. I shall make no decision until we are safe out of Gentile's clutches—and then—" he smiled tantalisingly at her.

Marina could not stop herself. "And then?" she queried almost despairingly.

"And then," he told her gaily, "why, lady, you will have to wait—until then!"

Chapter Four

"Where are we going, Ser Niccolo? Or do you not intend to tell me?"

Niccolo looked up from his work. He and Marco were busy erasing all traces of their overnight stay from the small glade where his party had camped. They had restored ruffled grass as much as possible, and had just begun to drag fallen branches and other debris over the fire and the disturbed ground where the tent had been erected so that none might know that anyone had camped there. Marina had slept in it, sheltered a little from the full rigours of spending a night in the open. He had been considerate about that, if nothing else.

He straightened up, stretched himself frankly, and remarked, "You would learn little if I told you, lady, for it is no place you have ever heard of, or would be likely to visit. We are heading for a small farm some few miles from here, off the road to Ver-dato—"

"Off the road to Verdato! How far from Ver-

dato?'' Interrupting him, Marina was trying not to
betray her agitation. ''Why should we go anywhere
near Verdato at all? I thought that we were trying to
escape from Gentile's territory, not making it easy
for him to find us.''

He was giving her that infuriating smile again, all
white teeth and patronage. If anything was calculated
to annoy her, that smile was it.

''Precisely, lady. And that is why we shall be near
Verdato. It is often better to hide things in plain sight
where no-one will expect to find them. Gentile will
assume that we are making for safety as quickly as
possible and all his efforts will be bent on trying to
cover his borders. He will not be looking near home
for us, you may be sure of that. And then, when he
begins to weary of the chase, we shall make our slow
and careful journey to safety.''

Marco was nodding as he spoke, but Marina was
still doubtful. ''Yet we are conspicuous, are we not?
Two soldiers and a noblewoman, strangers travelling
through territory where people are looking for strangers...'' Her voice died away as he smiled again.

''True, lady—if that were how we shall seem. But
that is *not* how we shall seem.'' He stood back, and
looked her over. ''A lady, hmm... So long as you
keep that lovely mouth closed, and don't deluge all
those about you with orders and questions, we may
yet pass you off as something other than you are.
Come.'' Without more ado, he took her hand and led
her over to where the ashes of the fire were awaiting
their covering blanket of branches, leaves and scrub.

''This is how we shall transform you. Kneel, my

lady Marina, kneel.'' Uncomprehendingly, wondering what was to come, Marina did as she was bid.

''Now, do as I do.'' He placed his hands where the fire had been and began to rub them hard among the cold ashes, before lifting them to his face to smear it so that he was covered in soot and grime. He repeated the action and smiled at her again, his teeth showing whiter than ever through the dirt which surrounded them.

''Thus we disguise ourselves. We shall appear to be a travelling pedlar, Gianni of the roads, a jack of all trades, his wife Angela, and his assistant, Beppo. Fortunately, Marco and I came this way on another errand some years ago, and none will think it odd that I return with a wife, as grimy as myself. For we must hide that splendid hair as well.'' He began to smear his hands over it, saying regretfully, ''Only the direst need could compel me to commit such a sacrilege, I do assure you.''

It was now the turn of Marina's grey eyes to blaze at him: a feat in itself it being difficult for grey eyes to blaze.

''On the contrary, Ser Niccolo,'' she gasped under his ministrations. ''I have the feeling that you are enjoying yourself, rather than regretting your actions.'' The stroking motions of his hands were more in the nature of a caress than anything else.

Niccolo took his hands away and looked sadly at them before plunging them into the ash again, Marco joining him.

''Very well, then, lady. But now you must do to yourself as Marco and I do, and presently we shall dress ourselves to match you.'' His wicked eyes mocked the peasant's clothing which she was already wearing.

There was nothing for it. If she wished to escape Gentile, she must do as he bid her, but Marina murmured angrily as she smeared earth, grey ash and soot on herself, and her clothing. ''But a pedlar travels in a cart, Ser Niccolo, not accoutred with broadsword and helm, and he has his farings with him. Where are your farings and cart?''

''Patience, patience,'' he told her, thinking that, as usual, she was showing herself willing to demean herself, provided the cause was good. Whilst she might argue with him at first, sweet reason from him usually had its way with her in the end. ''We shall acquire them all before we are on the road out of Verdato, I assure you.''

Oh, he had an answer for everything! And, whatever else, it was plain that the whole scheme to rescue her had been most carefully planned. So that when, presently, they rode down the mountain to come to a small farm in the foothills, she was not surprised to discover that the peasant who farmed it was an old soldier of his, and that hidden in his barn was the pedlar's cart and equipment of which he had spoken. There were rough peasant's clothes for him and Marco, too, and in the cart a strong sack where his and Marco's broadswords could be hidden away.

The other military accoutrements which they were wearing were to be left behind, but not before Azzo, the farmer, had fed them, and had given them, in return for more money from Niccolo, a supply of food to start them on their way. It was plain from the manner in which he spoke of Gentile that he had no intention of betraying them and helping him.

Niccolo improved the occasion by remarking sententiously to Marina, "You see how important it is, lady, not to be over-tyrannous in your rule. To be so means that you lose hearts, not win them. Remember that."

It was plain that he thought they were going to escape, for such advice could only be of advantage to her if she were to become the lady of Novera and Montefiore. Not, she thought resentfully, that she needed it. Ugo's rule had always been benevolent, and he had been her teacher.

When they had eaten they were on their way again. Marina and Niccolo bumped down the track towards the road which led from Verdato behind a spavined horse which bore no resemblance to the splendid steeds which they had left with Azzo. They were an extra payment to him for the risk he was taking in helping his one-time commander. Marco was riding a mule on which more of their possessions had been packed, including a lute—though which of them was going to be playing it, and why, remained a mystery for the time being.

Both Marco and Niccolo, like Marina, looked as though they had not washed for weeks, and Niccolo bore no resemblance at all to the dark Apollo whom Marina had first seen at Verdato. He was wearing a dirty scarf around his neck, and when he walked he sported a spectacular limp. They had eaten food heavily spiced with garlic at Azzo's and they all reeked of it, adding to the odour of sweat on the old clothes which Azzo had given them.

Marina had been given a soiled piece of white cloth to tie round her head, and she could not help but think of the fastidiousness which she had always practised when she had been the pampered lady of Novera. The daily bath in scented water. The oils which Lucia had rubbed into her skin to keep it sleek; the clean clothes, smelling of the herbs which had been placed between each layer of them in the painted chest at the bottom of her bed. She felt as though she had truly turned into the peasant which she now looked.

Except when she said so to Niccolo, his answer was a dry, "Best not let anyone see your hands, lady. Your nails are unbroken and your palms and fingers have none of the callouses which a true *contadina* would possess. But think nothing of that, a week's cooking of our meals, washing clothes occasionally, and helping me unload the wagon and sort the simples will soon change all that."

"Cooking your meals!" Marina could not prevent her voice from sounding hollow. "I cannot cook your meals. I have never cooked a meal, I should not know how to begin."

"Lady, you seem to me to have some intelligence, and that being so, you must learn to cook, and do all the other necessaries of our life. I cannot be seen to have a wife who does not know the duties of a wife. That would be to give us away, at once. Marco and I will tell you what to do, but yours must be the doing. There is no escape from that—unless, of

course, you would prefer to surrender yourself to
Gentile? If so, say the word—not that I should necessarily do as you bid me, but it would be useful to
know where I stand.''

Oh, he was hateful! Had he no idea how difficult
this masquerade was for her, coming as it did on top
of all that had happened to her since she had left
Novera? Apparently not, for he began to deluge her
with information about cooking, washing clothes,
making a fire, and all the other duties expected of a
pedlar's doxy—''for I doubt me anyone will think
that you are truly my wife, marriage and giving in
marriage not being the custom of those who travel
the roads.''

His doxy! Did he mean it?

And performing all the duties of being his wife!
Could that conceivably mean that he expected her to
share his bed? Having escaped Gentile's assault on
her person, was she now to endure his? She looked
sideways at him, at the strong profile, at the mocking
twist to his long mouth, and found no reassurance
there. That shapely mouth with its full lower lip had
doubtless kissed many women, and doubtless they
had taken pleasure in being kissed. But she, Marina
Bordoni, had no wish to be kissed by him, and would
certainly take no pleasure in it if he forced her to kiss
him…or worse.

Only to think of it had Marina going hot all over,
and a slight sweat, not wholly attributable to the
growing heat of the day broke out on her upper lip
and forehead.

It did not help matters that he suddenly looked at

her, and said in that annoying slight drawl of his, "You are well, lady? You look a little feverish."

What to say to that? I am feverish at the mere idea of being kissed by you, for that would give him entirely the wrong idea. She should be shuddering at the notion, surely, not running a temperature! So she answered him as coolly as possible. "No, I am not feverish, it is merely that I am not accustomed to travelling outside of a litter in the heat of the day."

He nodded gravely at that and said nothing more. Well, at least by her reply she had stopped him from continuing his long catalogue of all that she was expected to do whilst they were fleeing from Gentile. And once they were on the road from Verdato, Niccolo remained silent whilst he concentrated his whole attention on driving the cart.

Marina felt uncomfortably conspicuous, even when they shared the road with no-one but the odd boy driving geese. What did surprise her a little was the number of travellers whom they passed, both then, and later in their journey. When they approached a village through which the road ran, she thought that the whole world must be looking at her, and thinking, There is the missing lady of Novera. How much will the lord Gentile reward me with if I capture her and take her back to him?

But no such thing. The whole world or, rather, that part of it through which they were travelling, apparently saw what Niccolo da Stresa wished it to see. A pedlar who had visited them at sometime in the past and who had returned, to unpack his cart after he had lowered its rude leather canopy, and set out his wares

in the village's little square, which had at one corner
a chapel with a tiny bell tower.

Marina had often visited such small settlements
when she had been moving about Novera, but she
had never before stopped in one, other than to look
out of her splendid litter and be handed a cup of the
coarse local wine, which she drank to please the
giver rather than because she needed it.

Niccolo first stopped the cart before the inn, which
stood at the other corner of the square from the
chapel, and bade Marco fetch them all a drink.
Marco, who looked, if possible, even more villainous
than Niccolo, for his clothing was so ragged and elderly that it barely fitted him, showing great expanses
of sun-burned chest, arm and leg, grumbled loudly
and surlily at them both before making his way into
the inn. Even when he was inside it, Marina heard
his curses still being hurled at them out of the door
through which he had disappeared. It was plain that
he and Niccolo had practised their deceits before, so
that they had become second nature once they had
exchanged their military clothing for a peasant's
garb. Marco, from being gravely obedient, had turned
into every surly under-servant whom Marina had
come across in her previous life.

Niccolo's reply was to hurl curses of his own after
Marco before driving across the square to take up a
position before the church steps. He jumped down
from the cart, threw the reins to Marina and in a
brusque voice ordered her to "Look after the horse
and cart for me, wife, until I have gathered us a
crowd." He then unstrapped the lute from Marco's

mule, which had ambled after them, and walked to the centre of the square where a small well with an ornamental wall around it stood.

Look after the horse and cart, indeed! Marina had never done such a thing before, and it was fortunate for her that the horse was a weak, tame creature, quite unlike the lively chargers who graced the court of Novera, and stood meekly before her as though Niccolo still held the reins.

Meantime Niccolo sat himself on the wall around the well, crossed his legs, tuned the lute and began to sing, ogling and winking at the first few curious housewives who had already made their way over to him. His song was one which Marina had never heard before, but which the women obviously had, because they all began shrieking with laughter, poking one another, and waving their hands at the singer. They made so much noise that men, too, crossed the square to listen to him, and to throw small coins into his small round hat which he had doffed and placed on the ground before him.

The song over, Niccolo graciously acknowledged their applause by bowing his head, and launching into another ditty, apparently even more scandalous than the first. He was singing in a lowish voice so that Marina could not distinguish the words, other than the occasional amore which floated over. Before he began the second song he called over to her. "Go and help Beppo—" Marco's new name "—carry out our bread and wine. Look to it, Angela, don't dawdle."

It was becoming less and less difficult to remember that Niccolo was Gianni, she was Angela, Marco was Beppo, the horse was Nello, and the mule was "Hey, You" or "Damn Your Eyes", apparently not being considered worthy of a name. It was also difficult to believe that Niccolo was drawing attention to them quite deliberately, and that everyone was taking the three of them at face value, three gypsy-like pedlars making a sparse living as they travelled the roads.

Muttering rebelliously to herself, Marina took from Marco the wine, bread and cheese which the innkeeper's wife had cut for them, and placed them on the steps of the chapel, behind the cart. Marco began to set out the bits and pieces of the pedlar's trade, which had the women ignoring Niccolo's songs, in favour of haggling over a new broom or a fine scarf. "All the way from Florence for your delight, ladies," half-sang Niccolo, who now put his lute away in favour of money making, rather than entertaining to gain a crowd to whom to sell his wares and make a few coppers.

Marina continued to help Marco by showing off the few pieces of women's finery they carried by holding it up, or draping it round her shoulders, remembering Niccolo's admonition that she was to speak as little as possible.

An old grey beard who had hobbled over to see the fun was so entranced by this silent woman—all the village women apparently being singularly noisy—that he congratulated Niccolo. "Hola, Messer pedlar, you have a treasure of a wife there. Dumb, is she?"

"Not exactly," riposted Niccolo with his most impudent grin, as he sold one of the village women a trumpery comb decorated with small glass beads. "She has a fine turn of speech when she thinks it necessary." He turned his grin on Marina. "Is not that so, wife?"

Marina could not help herself. She did something which no lady of Novera would ever have contemplated doing. She was holding a ladle in her hand, a copper one, to show to the group of housewives who were admiring Niccolo's wares. Without even thinking about her dignity as the lady of Novera, but only of her anger at his insolence, she cracked him smartly on the top of the head with it. That would teach him not to make fun of her in public!

All of the women, and the old greybeard, let out joyful screeches at the sight, and Niccolo, holding his head, jumped backwards with such a comical expression of alarm on his face that Marina, who had begun to advance on him, ladle upraised, dropped the ladle and started to laugh.

For the first time in her sheltered, dignified and ordered existence she was letting fly with a full-bellied roar, the sort of roar she had heard the older ladies of Ugo's court give when a crowd of mummers came to perform a masque for them, and did a suggestive comic dance. She had always turned her nose up at such a coarse and vulgar lack of reticence, but here, in the square of an unknown village, dressed like a fishwife, answering to a name which was not her own, and at the mercy of an impudent scoundrel who apparently did not give a ducat for her rank, she was laughing as she had never laughed before. Side-splitting laughter, which presently Marco joined in, and then Niccolo himself, still holding his insulted head, so that the little square rang with their mirth.

She was weeping tears of joy when Niccolo came up to her, and pulling a battered square of linen from his pocket began to wipe her eyes, and murmur gently, "Enough, wife, enough." He could hear that the unforced joy was beginning to turn into the hysteria of someone who had been sorely tried for a long time, and he wanted her to say and do nothing which might betray them.

Marina was in the circle of his arms, and oh, it was pleasant to lean against his strength, and be gently petted by him, for he was crooning something to her, and it was the naughty song which he had been singing. It was as though she were a child again, and she fell into a pleasant stupor and let him lead her to the church steps where he held the flagon of wine to her lips for her to drink, and oh, it was so delicious after the hardships of the day that it tasted better than the finest Falernian.

He was being kind to her—for the first time.

Later, they made their way to the stable at the inn's rear. They had eaten the remains of their own food, given to them by Azzo, and each drunk as much wine as they wished, the gift of the landlord, who had admired Niccolo's singing, and had rewarded them accordingly.

"You may sleep with the horses, Messer pedlar,"

he had roared at them. "And free, though many would charge you."

"Oh, the generous fellow that you are." Niccolo had bowed to mine host, staggering a little, for the wine had been strong, and they had drunk hard and deep. "Blessings upon you, and may the Lord God reward you as you deserve!"

Marina thought that this was perhaps a little fulsome, but did not say so. Her own balance was not all that it should be, and she needed Marco's steadying arm to steer her into the stable, and to help her to make a comfortable bed in the straw. She had tried to refuse to drink the freely offered wine, but Marco had whispered into her ear, "You must, Angela, if you are to play your part correctly. This is no time to court suspicion."

So now she was sitting in the straw, her head whirling, and Niccolo was throwing himself down beside her in the straw, staring at her, his blue eyes feral. Marina found herself shivering beneath the hypnotic blaze of them and, flown with wine, ready for sleep, tired as she had never been in her old life, she only thought that like her he wanted to rest. Instead, he leaned forward and tried to pull her down beside him. Even through the haziness caused by the unaccustomed amount of drink she had taken, some instinct for self-preservation had her trying to push him away, saying faintly, "No, Gianni, no. I wish to sleep."

Only to have him throw an arm about her, and say, his voice hoarse between drink, singing and laughter, "Come, wife, a good wife lies with her

husband, does she not? And you are my good wife."
Now she was fully underneath him and his mouth
was on hers. Marina tried again to push him away,
but Niccolo only lifted his mouth from her enough
to whisper, "Do as I say, wife. Do not fight me,"
before his lips were back on hers again, and he was
teasing them open with his tongue.

Gasping, she felt the full weight of the length of
him until he lifted himself above her a little—but he
kept his mouth on hers whilst his hands roved her
body. He had pulled down the bodice of her dress
and was beginning to caress her revealed breasts,
which had her gasping again, and lifting her body to
meet his, giving a little throaty cry as she did so. She
had ceased to resist him, and the pleasure he was
giving her.

Yes, he was about to make her his wife, there was
no doubt of that. Her senses reeling, giddy with drink
and the delightful feeling induced by his roving
hands, Marina found that her mouth had also taken
on a life of its own, and was responding avidly to
his kisses, as her body was responding to his ca-
resses.

And then, even as some warning bell began to ring
in her mind, she heard above them a coarse voice
bellowing, "Hola, Messer pedlar, I came but to see
you comfortable. Alas, I am too late. You are comfortable already, could not even wait to pleasure your
doxy, so I bid you goodnight—and may the nightingale sing for you until dawn!" Suddenly struck
stone cold sober, Marina heard his muffled laughter

which only ended when the stable door shut behind him.

Niccolo rolled off her at last when he was certain that the landlord had gone. He sat up, and Marina was left lying alone and bereft, as his mouth and his body retreated from her. Instead of relief, shamefully, she felt that she had been deserted. And then, sanity returned. What could she have been thinking of? She, the lady of Novera, had been willing to be tumbled in the straw like a very whore, by Messer Nobody, who had kidnapped her as cruelly as Gentile had done. Almost, at the end as he had left her, she had been ready to beg him to come back into her arms again and end what he had begun.

Something of what she was thinking and feeling shone on her face. Niccolo da Stresa cursed to himself a little, not only because he had roused her, but because he had roused himself. He had drunk just enough to inflame desire, not cool it. Pulling himself away from the sweet and soft body beneath him, which he knew by Marina's response had suddenly become a willing body as well, was one of the hardest things he had ever done.

He rose, bent down towards Marina, and taking her hand he pulled her into a sitting position, saying gently, "Forgive me, lady, for handling you so freely, but none must suspect that we are not husband and wife, or lover and doxy. None do now, and none will, if we behave as though we are what we appear to be. Remember that at all times, and now, sleep."

He moved over towards Hey, You, who had been put in his stall for the night, beside Nello their horse, and fetched a blanket for Marina to sleep on, so that she should not be prickled by the straw. Her eyes filled with tears. His kindnesses to her, because they were so rarely given, had the effect of moving her powerfully. And looking at him in the dim light of the stable, she acknowledged to herself that he was also beginning to affect her after a fashion which she could never have foreseen when she first met him.

His strength, the power of his shapely body, the brilliant looks which she knew were hidden beneath the grotesque disguise he had assumed, were working a strange magic on her. A magic which Marina did not fully understand, which frightened her, but which she was beginning to be powerless to resist if he turned it on her as he had done this night. She had never before wanted a man to as much as touch her hand, but Niccolo had touched much more than her hand, and her whole body throbbed pleasurably at the memory of it.

What she did not know, but which the vigilant Marco did, was that Niccolo was beginning to feel exactly the same about her—and that was no part of the plans he had for her!

Chapter Five

"Kidnapped! Again!"

The messengers who had unwillingly carried the unwelcome news to Ugo that Marina was no longer in Gentile's hands, but had been carried off by an unknown adventurer, whether to claim the reward which was being offered for her return, or to keep her for himself, no-one knew, cringed before his anger. What was known, they told Ugo fearfully, was that Gentile was running mad looking for her, and that she and her new captor had vanished into thin air.

Ugo, normally a kind and equable man, was nearly as choleric as Gentile himself on hearing this latest piece of bad news.

"No-one!" he roared. "No-one? Some nobody pulls off such a coup against a man of Gentile da Cortona's known capacity, and neither Gentile nor any of his lieutenant's recognised him?"

"He wore a helm with a nasal," said the leading messenger, "and all that could be seen was that he was young and dark. His lieutenant was recognised as Marco Despini, but who he has worked for lately is unknown.''

"Unknown, unknown," raved Ugo, sounding as fierce as Gentile for the first time in his life. "And my poor niece is at his mercy! The Lord God has countenanced a bad month's work, first allowing Gentile to abduct poor Marina, and now in allowing some *nobody* to carry her off. At least whilst she was with Gentile, bad though that was, we knew *where* she was. Now we know nothing, nothing. Would to God that I had agreed to Gentile's demands at once, however monstrous they were—at least I would know her to be safe.''

Ugo had risen from the couch where he had been resting, and his face ashen, he began to shout for Rinaldo, the man who had replaced poor slaughtered Benedetto as the captain of his guard. Rinaldo came at the run, saying fearfully, "Yes, lord. What want you with me, lord?''

"Make up a goodly troop of men and, without fear or favour, enter the territory of Gentile and any other lord where you think my niece may have been taken, and try to recover her for me. If you do, bring back this nobody who has made off with her, and he shall die slowly before me. I shall give you a paper authorising you to act in my name. Quickly, man, for who knows where she may now be, or what she may be doing. Oh, my poor niece, it was a bitter day when I agreed to marry her to Montefiore, and the devil take me if ever I let her out of Novera again, if the Lord God wills that she is restored to me.''

"Yes, lord, at once, lord." Rinaldo went running into the courtyard, calling for his lieutenants, his sergeants, to make the necessary arrangements to carry out his lord's orders. And if he thought that he and his men were going into danger to enter Gentile's lands at such a time, he did not say so.

Never before had he seen his kind and considerate master so desperate. And no wonder; like Ugo, he dared not think what might be happening to the most gracious and gentle lady Marina Bordoni.

The most gracious and gentle princess, Marina Bordoni, was seated between Marco and Niccolo on a bench in the inn at Ostuna, a small town ten miles down the road from the village where she had been baptised into the life of a travelling pedlar's wife. She had never found out its name, but as they left the villagers came out to wave them goodbye and bid them return—with more wares to sell them next time. They, at least, had no inkling that the lady of Novera had stayed among them for a brief space.

Seated beside Niccolo and behind the spavined horse, Marina watched the poor road unfold before them as they ambled north-east through wild and beautiful country. Alas, like Marco and Niccolo, she was suffering from a thundering head, a noisy witness to last night's drinking. She had woken in the small hours in a strange cold sweat, shuddering not only at the memory of the wine she had drunk, but at her own shameless wantonness in Niccolo's arms. How could she have virtually offered herself to the monster who was at present ruling her life?

It had taken some time for her to fall asleep again, and then she had woken up unrefreshed. Well, at least she had the satisfaction that Marco and Niccolo looked no better than she felt! Marco even grumbled at the bright sun, and when the time came to eat and take their siesta, they camped by a stream and drank the pure water from it. Niccolo made her eat the bread, cheese and slices of cold meat which they had bought from the innkeeper, telling her that she would feel better when she had done so, even though the mere idea of food had made her feel quite ill.

As usual he had been right—which Marina was beginning to find boringly predictable. It would be a pleasant change to prove him wrong for once. The road climbed into the foothills of the mountain above them and they could see in the distance a small town, clinging to its sides.

"Ostuna," announced Niccolo reminiscently, tickling their poor horse gently with his whip. "I remember Ostuna, they made us welcome. I wonder if they remember us, eh, Marco?"

Marco turned and looked at them from Damn Your Eyes's back. The mule was Damn Your Eyes today, because when they had left the village he had refused to move, however much Marco had kicked, cursed and sworn at him. And then, without warning, he had kicked his heels into the air, throwing Marco on to his back in the small square and had trotted away to bray evilly at him, before allowing Marco to mount him again, walking away as though he were the most docile beast in Italy.

Marina had found herself laughing heartlessly at

poor Marco on his back, his legs in the air, looking like an upside-down, stranded, black beetle. It had occurred to her as she gasped into silence at last that she had never before enjoyed herself so much as she was now doing, roving the roads of Italy, dirty and in danger.

Something of that remembered joy was on her face as Marco told Niccolo that, yes, he remembered Ostuna, and that there might not only be a welcome there, but that no-one would possibly identify them as Gentile's fugitives. "And, yes, lady," he finished, forgetting to call Marina "Angela" for once. "I heard you enjoy my downfall in the village square, but patience, patience, our journey may be long, and I may have the pleasure of the last laugh."

"Hardly likely that I shall be unshipped by Damn Your Eyes, though," returned Marina pertly, and heard Niccolo's laughter at her quick retort.

"You might suffer an even worse fate, wife," he told her. "Pride goeth before a fall."

"And tall trees may be cut down as easily as small ones," she reminded him, quoting a saying of Lucia's, designed to remind her that the great and the tall may suffer the same fate as the weak and small. "Remember *that*, husband."

And then he surprised her once more by leaning sideways and planting a kiss on her blushing cheek— the pallor caused by her sheltered life was rapidly disappearing. "And impudence is sometimes rewarded, wife." His bright blue eyes were shining at her again, and Marina registered that they were an indication of his feelings. He was pleased with her, and she wondered why.

No need to wonder had she been privy to Niccolo's thoughts. He had thought her a cold, haughty piece when he had first seen her in the church by Gentile's side. He had felt some fear that rescuing her might be difficult given his plan of campaign, which depended on its success for her willing co-operation in disguising herself as a peasant's wife.

What he had not bargained for was that she would enter so wholeheartedly into the spirit of the thing after her first misgivings. The change in her had come when she had struck him with the ladle. It was as though she had been liberated: that out of the stiff cocoon of haughty propriety in which she had been wrapped, a mischievous butterfly had emerged. He thought that the odds on them all escaping alive from this risky venture were much better than they would have been if she had been as stiff-necked as he had at first feared. What was still to be discovered was how she would react if they were ever in any real danger...

And so they rode into Ostuna, where, as at the unknown village they had just left they received what was almost a royal welcome. Ostuna was larger than the village and richer. The church in the main square was beautiful, showing signs of wealth, and the steps which led up to its noble doorway were high and wide. The church door itself was of bronze on which episodes from the lives of the saints had been hammered in low relief: it reminded Marina a little of the door which adorned the Duomo, Florence's giant cathedral.

She was not given much time to admire it. As she stared interestedly in its direction Niccolo smacked her smartly on the backside, bellowing good-naturedly, "No day dreaming, wife! Work awaits you. Help Marco to unpack the cart whilst I entertain the good citizens of Ostuna."

For the first time Marina understood why the maids who served her were given to flouncing and tossing their heads if she were a little peremptory with them. She found herself behaving in exactly the same way as she obeyed Niccolo's orders and joined Marco in laying out their stock of knick-knacks and necessities. Her tormentor wasn't idle, either. He was singing the same ballad with which he had begun their huckstering at the village. This time his audience was larger and better dressed, and not quite so free with their laughter—but they were more free with their money, so that Niccolo rewarded them with more songs than he had sung before.

The inn, again situated at the corner of the square, was larger and better appointed than the one at the village had been, and presently the landlord walked over to where their cart stood. But he hadn't come to buy anything: instead he listened intently to Niccolo playing and singing, and when he stopped, flung a coin into his cap before saying, "Messer pedlar, you came this way a year or so agone. I remember your voice and your impudence. I would have you entertain us tonight and then stay tomorrow to play for us at our early summer festival. Our own musician has fallen ill and we need one to take his place. The Lord God knows that since Captain Gentile began to rule us, we get but small pleasure in our lives. Do as I ask and your reward shall be that I will not charge you for the bed and board of your woman and your servant whilst you stay here.''

He hesitated, looked dubiously at Marina, and then asked, ''Does the wench dance, too? Give her a good wash and a decent gown and she might be passable looking.''

The voice with which Niccolo answered him was full of laughter. ''Why, let me but command her, ser innkeeper—for I remember you, too—and she might perform a rondo for you, if she feels so inclined. Wife!'' He bellowed at her again as he had done a moment ago. ''How say you? Would you dance for the townsfolk—and help us to earn our supper?''

Oh, the insolence of him! To suggest that she, the lady of Novera, for whom other people danced, should be reduced to cavorting to entertain peasants! Marina began to open her mouth to tell him so—and then she caught his eye, remembered the danger she was in, that Gentile was doubtless at this very moment scouring Verdato to find her, kill Niccolo and Marco and take her back to his eyrie—and held her tongue.

''Wife?'' queried Niccolo gently, but there was steel in his eye and in his voice.

She faltered, ''If you so will, husband, but I have no fine clothes to perform in—as well you know.''

''Oh, there's no minding that,'' roared the innkeeper. ''She may borrow the dress that Primavera, the Lady of the Spring, wears when we celebrate Easter—after you have washed her, of course. The gown must be handed back in good condition for next year's procession.''

Oh, this was impossible! She was to be washed and decked out for all the world to see—and what would that do to the anonymity which Niccolo had said that he wanted to retain? And she was to dance for them, who had never danced on her own before. Just let her corner Niccolo on his own for five minutes and she would tell him exactly what she thought of him! But not now.

The townsfolk were drifting away, and the innkeeper was urging them over to the inn. He was promising them wine and a hearty meal and room for the night. Marina's treacherous stomach was telling her that was exactly what she needed as the sun sank in the sky. Oh, and a wash. However much she might regret the danger being clean might place her in, the thought of being so was attractive.

This time the innkeeper was showing them to a room for the night—and not the stables; they were left for Nello and Damn Your Eyes, and their cart. Marco was pulling their bags from it and carrying them in. He had been given a straw palliasse on the corner of the landing, but she and Niccolo were led with some ceremony into a room with a big bed in it, and a chest on which stood a large earthenware pitcher and some coarse towelling.

A bed! One bed! For the pair of them! For were they not man and wife? Marina opened her mouth to protest, to say that this would not do, then closed it

again as she caught Niccolo's eye. The worst of it
was that the innkeeper chose to twit them about it,
turning back the sheets and poking Niccolo jovially
in the ribs. "The nightingale will sing all night, Messer pedlar, now that you are bedded in such comfort!" They could hear him roaring all the way down
the stairs.

But the moment that he had left them, Marina
hissed at Niccolo, "No, ser Niccolo, we cannot sleep
here, nightingales or no."

Niccolo, engaged in untying the scarf which he
wore around his neck on their travels on the road,
swung round, his face innocent, to ask, "And why
not, wife? Has the room not a bed, and a fine one,
where three might sleep in comfort—and there are
only two of us."

"Oh." Marina wrung her hands at his wilful mis-
understanding of what she was saying. "I am not
your wife, as well you know. Neither am I your
doxy. *You* must sleep on the floor."

"Oh, no," murmured Niccolo softly, advancing
on her. "It is I who am doing all the hard work
necessary to keep us fed. It is I who am risking my
life to rescue you from Gentile. If anyone is to sleep
on the floor, then that anyone must be you. And there
is no need for you to do so. The bed is big enough
for us both. And now, cease to nag me. My mind is
quite made up, and I cannot have you scolding me
like a fishwife—" this as she began to open her
mouth again "—that would never do. None in these
parts respects a man who cannot keep his wife in
order."

"But I am not your wife!" Marina, glaring at him, stamped her foot.

"No, but the world must think so—as you agreed with me when we began this masquerade."

"I never thought…"

"No," he told her, his face suddenly stern. "You never thought. You have never had to think, lady. Others have always done your thinking for you. Now you must do your own. We are in desperate straits, and fortunate it is that the landlord takes us at face value, but he will not go on doing so if you insist on playing the fine lady with me. Do not worry about being recognised. When you have been washed we shall paint you as the mummers in the masques you have seen are painted, and we shall braid your hair and deck you out in a fashion that no lady of Novera would ever adopt. Does that satisfy you—or must I treat you as a peasant would treat his disobedient wife—and beat you until you do as you are told? Choose, lady, choose."

He meant it, by St Michael and all the angels, he meant it! And she was alone with him and helpless. She bowed her head and muttered sullenly, "I have no choice, and well you know it. I will do as you wish."

"Good, and in the morning we may tell them that the nightingale sang sweetly for us." As Marina looked her incomprehension at him, he laughed gently, blue eyes alight again. "Oh, lady, I forget how innocent you are. The landlord but echoes what Messer Boccaccio hath hinted. The nightingale sings are but polite words for the act of love itself, and as man and wife, he expects us to take our ease in the comfortable bed he has provided for us, instead of making do with the hard earth.''

Marina's cheeks flamed, and she turned her head away from him. It was not the only part of her which flamed, and oh, how she hated him for affecting her so. Being close to him, sharing in the intimate acts of living, if not yet loving, feeling his strong hands on her as he helped her in and out of the cart, were all combining to let her know that she had a body and that body was demanding satisfaction whether she willed it or no.

He must be in league with Satan himself to make her forget so easily who and what she was, and oh, somehow, sometime, Marina raged to herself, she would pay him back for all that he was doing to her—and that included the attraction he was beginning to possess for her. But first there was the evening to be got through, and then the night, when she would be in the big bed with him...

Yes, the pedlar Gianni of the roads, his wife and his servant were good value for money, thought the innkeeper smugly. The inn was full of customers, the wine flowed freely. Niccolo sat on the bench provided him, singing whatever song his audience demanded of him. His voice hoarse from his exertions, he turned at last to Marina.

''Come, wife, I know that you can sing. Let me play whilst you entertain our friends.'' When she would have demurred, shaking her head a little, he turned to the waiting drinkers, winked slyly at them, murmuring confidentially, ''Oh, but yestereve as we prepared for rest, I heard her sing *The Blackbird's Song* so sweetly, I would have sworn that it was the blackbird himself singing it.'' He began to play, gently and lyrically, the song which she had sung all unconscious that he had heard her.

There was no help for it, sing she must. And had he not said that it was he, and he alone who was earning the money for them to live? His own store had soon been spent, and she would like to show him that he was not their only provider.

She stood up, as she had stood up to sing for her uncle and his little court, her sweet, true voice ringing out to the sound of the lute. Never mind that she was in a smoky inn, full of the fumes of drink and sweaty bodies, for a moment as she sang she was back in what now seemed a lost paradise, an improbable place which she must have imagined, not truly experienced, so far away did it seem.

As the last notes of the song hung in the air, the lute following them faithfully, until it, too, was silent, there was silence from the roystering drinkers. It was as though, for a space, they had been in a forest glade, and the blackbird had truly sung for them… Marina bowed to her audience, as though to Ugo, and life began again. A rough voice shouted to Niccolo, ''Oh, aye, pedlar, bravely done, and what betting but that the nightingale sings for thee tonight.'' The coarse allusion which would have passed Marina by earlier that day, set her cheeks flaming once more.

Coins were thrown to them, and several called for her to sing again, at which Niccolo whispered in her

ear, "If it be too much for thee, Angela, then rest,"
because he knew what strain she must be under and
wished to spare her. Marina, however, rejected his
offer. She would show him, that she would, that even
a great lady used to ease and comfort could play her
part, if needs be, as well as any man. She shook her
head vigorously, and asked him if he knew *Lucia's
Prayer*. He immediately began to play it, and she
sang again; this time the song was short and sad,
telling of love lost and never regained.

For the first time Marina sang it with deep feeling.
Why, she knew not, but since her abduction the calm
passivity with which she had always met life had
disappeared. It had depended, she was beginning to
understand, on the knowledge that she was sheltered
from everything that the ordinary people whom she
was meeting on her travels experienced. It had begun
to crack when Gentile had abducted her, and her safe
world had disintegrated around her. Her snatching
away by Niccolo, and the plan he had devised to
rescue her, had carried the process on further.

These new emotions which she was beginning to
experience wrote their message in her voice, which
broke in the last verse telling of Lucia's despair and
death after she had lost her love. The song had never
moved her before, but as she ended the tears were
falling, unbidden, down her cheeks.

They did not go unnoticed by Niccolo. This time,
after she had finished and the drinkers had roared
their approval, he pulled her gently down beside him,
and muttered, "Rest, wife, rest. Your labours are
done for this night."

The landlord brought her a goblet of wine, and bade her drink it. "You must sing tomorrow, Angela, as well as dance," he told her. "Such a voice must not be wasted."

The drink tired her. She was content to sit back and watch the passing show. Niccolo, his voice recovered a little, sang again, but even as he launched into his last song, Marina's eyes were closing. The strain of the escape, the new experience of living most of the day in the open air, the novelty of the evening which she had just spent among carousing farmers and peasants had all taken their toll of her.

The man who had jested to Niccolo of the nightingale singing looked down at her as she slept against his shoulder. "You have a treasure there, pedlar, and not ill-looking beneath the dirt, I'll be bound." He threw Niccolo another coin, and joined his rustic fellows who were falling out of the door, singing a bawdy song, the one which Niccolo had ended with. He could hear the echoes of it floating behind them as they straggled down the narrow road to their beds. The landlord was collecting pewter pots, Marco was helping him, and Niccolo, an odd smile on his face, was bending over Marina.

She was so deeply asleep that she made nothing of his lifting her and carrying her upstairs. A sweet smile curved her mouth as she dreamed that she was a child again, playing in the palace garden at Novera. Her second song had brought back old memories, and she was roving among them. Even when he carried her into the bedroom to lay her down on the big bed which had so affrighted her, she did not wake.

He pulled back the covers, took off the peasant's sandals which Azzo had given her, before stripping off his own clothes to leave himself only in the long shirt which he wore whose points fastened into his hose which he also removed.

Then, with a wry and rueful expression painted on his face, Niccolo climbed into the bed beside her, pulled the covers over them both—and tried to sleep. But sleep was long in coming, not the least cause of its absence being the temptation which Marina presented to him, lying unconscious beside him in the bed. Finally he too, bone weary, slept...and the nightingale never sang for them once.

"Sit still, wife!" Niccolo's voice was exasperated, and no wonder. He had spent the last hour helping Anna, the innkeeper's wife, to dress Marina for the festival. Between them they had laced her into a heavy blue dress, stiff with tarnished gold embroidery and dressed her hair for her in the most outlandish fashion which Marina had ever seen. To her astonishment the wash which she had been promised turned out to be nothing but a rub with a damp towel which removed most, but not all, of the grime from her face. Her hair had not been touched. Washing in the town of Ostuna, it seemed, was very different from what it was at the court of Novera.

So was hairdressing. After a perfunctory combing, Anna began to plait coloured ribbons through her hair so that presently it did not matter whether it was its usual brilliant gold or the duller ochre shading towards brown into which her travels had transformed it; the ribbons hid it completely. The plaiting completed, Anna placed a chaplet of fresh flowers on Marina's head before standing back to appraise her work. Marina could only marvel at what she might look like, but Anna had no doubts about her own artistry or the improvement in Marina's appearance.

"What a pretty child you are, Angela," she exclaimed, "and will be prettier still when we have painted you. You will rival the ladies of the Signoria in Florence, no doubt about it! Is not that so, Gianni? Does not your wife look even more lovely than the ladies of any court you may care to name?"

"Oh, indeed, Signora Anna, she looks as beautiful as the Virgin on the wall of Ostuna's church," was Niccolo's enthusiastic response—but he took good care not to catch Marina's eye whilst he was making it. Lacking any sort of mirror she could not judge exactly how she looked, although she thought that no-one at Novera would have agreed with them—but she kept her opinions to herself, safer so.

The promised painting she endured. Anna smeared various strange substances on to her face—they were coarse and vivid, nothing like the delicate cosmetics used by the ladies of her own court. A brilliant scarlet for her cheeks and lips, a bright blue smeared on to her eyelids, and a piece of charcoal to emphasise her eyebrows were all deployed by Anna with more enthusiasm than skill.

"And now," she announced proudly, when her work was done, "all may see and admire the lady of the fiesta, however far away from her they are." She turned her charge about and about for all the spectators who had gathered around them to wonder at, just as Marina's own waiting woman did after she had made her mistress ready for some great occasion such as the arrival of an envoy from the Florentine Republic. For the first time in her sheltered life, Marina became aware that in matters of dress and display, all women, whether high or low, tended to share the same interests and mannerisms.

No time to think of that now, for Anna was poking Niccolo in the ribs and shrieking joyfully at him, "Kiss your wife, Gianni. So lovely as she is, she deserves a reward from you."

Marina had no time to protest for Niccolo, taking Anna at her word, leaned forward to kiss her on the lips, his eyes closing as he did so. Not that Marina saw that, for her own eyes closed as his lips touched hers, and they stood for a moment, twined together, all in all to one another, before Niccolo stood back lest he become aroused before all the world.

Stars in her eyes, her mouth a little open, Marina stared at him. The scarlet from her lips was now smeared on his, and without thinking, she put forward two long and shapely fingers to brush the betraying colour away. So intimate in nature was this lightest of touches that Niccolo drew in his breath with a hissing noise and Marina, stunned by her own daring, defied him with her eyes and put the traitor fingers to her own lips.

But this served only to compound what she had done. Not only was the taste of him on her lips and in her mouth, but it was as though she had kissed him by proxy as it were, as children blow kisses at one another to tell their love. She had not willed this thing, but she had done it all the same, and a profound shock ran through her whole body.

For the first time she had initiated a form of love play with a man, and like all the new things which she had experienced since Gentile had snatched her away and Niccolo had come into her life, it was telling her things about herself which she had not known—and which she was not sure that she wanted to know.

What she *did* know was that, for once, she had surprised the man who now owned her, for she was also coming to understand as she flowered and matured under the strain of living this dangerous life, that she had always been owned by some man or another. First she had been owned by her uncle, and then he had proposed that she should be given to another man, the heir of Montefiore. But instead fate had stepped in and handed her over to yet another man, Gentile da Cortona and, if that were not enough, she had next acquired a new master, the one who stood before her, who might be her saviour or her betrayer.

At the moment she had nonplussed him a little, which pleased her, and also told her that, though he might have one kind of power over her, she had another power over him. She had the power to make him tremble, to desire her, but this power was two-edged, for if she exercised it, she was in danger of giving him yet another power over her. Not simply to dispose of her freedom, will she, nil she, but the power to make her desire him…

So she gave him a dazzling smile and swept him a great curtsey which had Anna shrieking at her. "Oh, you have gained a lady's manner with a lady's face! Look to her, Gianni, lest she seek a lord for herself instead of a pedlar." Anna collapsed into bawdy laughter.

Once Marina would have moved away from, or reprimanded anyone who spoke so before her, but today, freed of all constraints, she laughed herself, and flung back at him and Anna, "Oh, tempt me not, *signora*, lest I take you at your word!"

It was as though, shedding her identity, assuming this new one, she had truly become someone else, a someone who could express her own feelings, not carefully stifle them in case they destroyed the mask of propriety which she had worn since she was a small girl.

Spontaneity had not been her friend.

It might be now.

As though he was aware of what she was thinking and feeling, Niccolo took her hand and gently led her away from the giggling Anna into the square, where he and the landlord began to explain to her what they wanted of her. That she was to walk behind the leading men of the town, who would be carrying wreaths of flowers to adorn the shrine to the Holy Virgin which stood at the entrance to Ostuna. An entrance which was also an exit; the gate by which she and Niccolo and Marco and Damn Your Eyes would leave in the morning, their tasks here completed.

Today Niccolo would walk at the head of the procession singing and playing. But before they left the square, she would dance before them all, a grave dance to honour Christ's mother.

"I have never yet danced alone," she wanted to say to them, but Niccolo had told her earlier, that he would have none of this. "You have danced often and often in the court at Novera," he had said in his most persuasive voice. "All that you are required to do is to dance on your own as you would have danced in company."

"But so many will be watching me…" she began, falteringly.

"And how many do you think watched you when you were the lady of Novera? Many and many, I have no doubt. Think only that once this is done, we may leave, and we shall have behaved in such a manner that none will doubt that we are what we say we are. Courage, wife," he had finished. "The devil is dead, as they say, and the devil which is Gentile cannot harm us if we remember that!"

Yes, she was remembering what he had said as the crowds began to gather in the square. The small crowd which was to walk in procession to honour the Holy Virgin, the larger one watching and cheering it, before they all returned to start the feasting and drinking which was designed to celebrate the longest day of the year.

"It is a small enough thing to ask of you," Niccolo had finally said, his eyes grave, before she had nodded her agreement. And now, suddenly, the excitement of the town was infecting her, and her feet began to itch, ready to launch themselves into the dance which was to start the celebrations.

Men—and women, too—propose, but God disposes. Marina was never to dance for the townsfolk of Ostuna, for even as Niccolo began his song, and she moved forward into the centre of the square, there was a great noise and a thunder of hooves. A party of horsemen, followed by men-at-arms, came charging through the crowd, driving them in all directions and striking at them, so that men, women and children were thrown to the ground, injured and dying.

Like Moses parting the waters of the Red Sea, they thundered into the square, to come to a halt directly before the steps of the church where the procession was still standing. One of the leading citizens, a goldsmith whose name was known throughout Verdato, moved forward to remonstrate with the leader of the horsemen. Even before he spoke, even before the leader raised his whip and slashed him across the face with such force that he fell to the ground, writhing, Marina, her heart sinking, recognised him.

It was Braccio degli Uberti, one of Cecco's lieutenants, a man as brutal as Cecco himself, and his master, Gentile da Cortona. Marina was in no doubt as to why he was here, and what he was about. He was in charge of one of the parties of Gentile's men who were searching for Gentile's lost prize—and here she was, standing in the square for all to see, immediately before him…

Chapter Six

Braccio degli Uberti's hard stare swept the crowd of townsfolk who were stunned by the sight of the dead and wounded, stunned by the ferocity with which their leading citizen had been struck down, denied even the right to speak. The stare passed over Marina, passed over Marco, passed over Niccolo, saw them as merely part of the herd of cattle who called themselves the citizens of Ostuna.

Satisfied that he had cowed them, as cattle should be cowed, he relaxed in his saddle, smiled a grim smile, and spoke to his herald who rode beside him.

"Do your duty, man. Tell this scum why we are here, and tell them that if I find that they have lied to me, why, I shall hang every man and boy in the town in the square, and hand the women over to my troops."

He needed no herald. His bellow had reached the ears of all. Nevertheless the herald dismounted, and standing in front of his master unrolled a scroll from which he read aloud.

"Know ye, that I speak for your lord, the most merciful and righteous Gentile da Cortona, and demand that all who may have knowledge of the whereabouts of the most noble lady Marina Bordoni, and the piece of filth who stole her from me at the very moment of our nuptials, shall at once inform those who stand before you of it. Your reward shall be my thanks. Your punishment, should you withhold that information from me, is death."

He fell silent and Braccio swung his fell head in an arc which took in all who still stood in the square.

"Well, you have all heard the herald. What have you to tell me? For sure, it must be that the lady and her abductor passed this way with their troop."

Silence fell on the square. In the distance a bird began to sing, its pure sound rebuking the dirty intrigues of man. Standing quite still, as though by doing so she might somehow vanish from Braccio's sight, Marina scarcely dared to breathe. His stare darkening, Braccio pointed his whip at an elderly man who had been standing at the front of the procession, and demanded imperiously, "You there! Answer me!"

"Most noble lord," stammered the man. "I have seen all who passed through Ostuna within the last week. None such as you describe have been seen here. Of what kind was this troop?—not that we have seen one, you understand, but should we do so, then we shall inform the noble lord your master, at once."

Braccio leaned forward, his grim face grimmer still. "Come nearer, yes, nearer." Paralysed with fear the man hesitated. "The troop comprised some twenty men-at-arms, as well as ten crossbowmen and their captain. The lady they have made off with is most delicate, blonde and as beautiful as an angel. The devil is with them for they have all disappeared. But at some time they must surely have passed through Ostuna. Remember, if you lie…''. He bent down and flicked his whip so that it curled round the man's neck. ''Your life is not worth a ducat—tradesman!''

Clutching at the whip which was strangling him, Braccio's victim gasped. ''They may have passed through in the night, lord…'' and screamed a little as Braccio tightened the whip.

''Passed through in the night, eh? And yet you heard nothing?'' Braccio's laugh at that was a snarl.

''I said *may* have passed through in the night, lord,'' panted the man. ''All here will bear witness that I speak true.'' He fought for words, for something to say which would placate the monster before him. ''The pedlar, Gianni of the roads, will confirm what I have said,'' he finished.

''Pedlar?'' Braccio's head moved as though he were a falcon about to stoop, to kill. ''Where's he? Let him come forward.''

Niccolo, his lute in his hand, limped forward until he stood before Braccio.

''Here I am, lord. I have been travelling the road these many weeks, and have seen none such as you have spoken of.''

Marina's inward trembling grew so strong once Niccolo had been called for that she was fearful that it might begin to show. Surely if Braccio looked hard

at her he would recognise Gentile's wretched captive,
the woman whom he had so nearly made his wife—
the delicate woman as beautiful as an angel… True,
she did not now appear to be either delicate, or an-
gelic, but if Braccio looked hard at her he would
surely see that…No, she must not even think it, the
very thought might betray her.

But Braccio's gaze swept over her, unseeing, and
now all his attention was on Niccolo. "Pedlar?" he
mused. "So, why the lute?"

Niccolo bowed his head deferentially, avoiding a
direct look at Braccio and replied as meekly as a very
priest, so that even in the grip of terror Marina could
only admire the cunning impudence of him. He
seemed as fearful of Braccio as his previous victim
had been, who was now nursing his neck, the red
weal around it a mute witness of Braccio's cruelty.

"Why, lord, I do but play and sing at the towns
and villages I visit to add to the little I make from
my trade. It is a hard life on the road." He bowed
his head submissively.

"No doubt." Braccio's lip curled. "And you say
that you have seen nothing untoward on the road?"

"Nothing, lord. For sure if I had I would not hesitate to tell you."

"No doubt." Braccio's lip curled again. "Look
me in the eye, man. I hate a coward."

"Yes, lord." Niccolo raised his head to stare Braccio full in the face.

Braccio's smile was ugly. Here was another
chance to cow the cattle who made up Ostuna's citizens even further.

"Why, man, you have the seeming of one doomed to hang. I'll improve your looks for you, so I will." He brought his whip down across Niccolo's face with such force that he staggered and fell.

Marina could not help herself. She screamed and fell on her knees beside him, to turn her heavily painted face towards Braccio, who was laughing at her distress, to cry at him, despite her fear, "Coward, to strike an unarmed man, not ready for a blow."

There was no doubt that this time Braccio's laugh was a genuine one. "The doxy is braver than her owner, I see. Were you a trifle cleaner I'd have you sent to the castle, but, faugh, my palate is a trifle dainty to need such as you. But should you wish to earn a few ducats, why, you may come up to the castle to entertain my men this night. I'll see you well paid. Hey, pedlar." He leaned forward to speak to Niccolo who, still dazed, was rising to his feet, helped by Marina. "Your woman may add to your exchequer for you, if you are so willing. I will not force her. Her courage deserves more than that."

Marina was not to know that this kind of twisted chivalry was common to such as Braccio. Niccolo was not so damaged by Braccio's blow, which had left a scarlet and bleeding weal diagonally across his face, that he was unable to understand that Marina's reckless intervention had, surprisingly, saved them both from worse mishandling. All the more reason, then, not to provoke Braccio or to attract further attention from him which might cause either of them to betray who they were.

"It is for Angela to choose what she shall do,

lord.'' The wound on his lips made speaking painful, but none listening would have guessed it.

"Say you so, pedlar? Well then, *signora*. Choose." His tone was imperious and he had gone from ferocious brutality to ferocious goodwill almost in the course of a sentence. Inspiration struck Marina. She bent down to recover Niccolo's lute which had fallen from his hand, and which was, miraculously, undamaged, before putting a tender hand on his arm.

"Why, most merciful lord," she faltered, bending her head submissively, as much to hide her face from him as for any other reason. "Of your mercy you will excuse me, for my husband will need me this night to nurse him, to tend his wound."

"Enough." He was pleased by her flattery. He was not to know that Marina was inwardly seething at his brutality and was regretting that she was not still the lady of Novera so that he could be punished for his cruelty as he deserved. Ignorant of her true thoughts, Braccio was prepared to be merciful.

"So," he waved a dismissive hand, "you may continue with your revels, but mark me, I shall visit the lord of Ostuna in his castle, and should either of us learn that you are keeping anything regarding the kidnapping of the lady of Novera from us, be very sure that I shall not be so merciful again, as I am now."

Marina bowed her head as he finished speaking, although inside she was screaming, "Merciful! You call yourself merciful surrounded as you are by those you have killed and injured for no reason at all. May the Lord God visit you with such mercy—and soon."

Niccolo had taken her hand. He could feel her trembling. He thought that it was fear which was moving her, but for once he read her wrongly. It was not fear, but red rage, an emotion which had never troubled Marina before, an emotion which had no place in her previously placid life.

And the cause of it, surprisingly so far as Marina was concerned, was not only the carnage about her which Braccio had created, but the vicious blow which he had struck at Niccolo. It was as though he had struck her, and had wounded her to the quick. Later, much later, she was to think that if there was one moment in her odyssey across Italy when she turned into Angela, and Niccolo and Marco into Gianni and Beppo, it was when Braccio struck Niccolo. The lady of Novera had disappeared, to be subsumed into the pedlar's wife. Marina Bordoni was no more.

No time to think of that then. Nothing to do but watch Braccio order his men to follow him up the slight hill which led to the lord's castle, high above the town. The lord was old and ailing, rarely seen, and was wont to leave the townsfolk to themselves. His nephew and heir lived in Florence, a rich merchant whose interest in Ostuna was small, seeing that it was but a fief of Gentile's, over-taxed and exploited by him.

Whatever Braccio said it was plain that the festivities were over. Once the last of his men had entered Ostuna's castle, the townsfolk began to gather up and tend their dead and wounded. Fortunately, the dead were fewer than had at first been feared, although several had been grievously wounded. But all thoughts of a day's pleasure had disappeared in the need to mourn the dead and to tend those still living. The festivities were abandoned.

Niccolo, or Gianni, as Angela now thought of him, took his lute from her and to test it ran his fingers over the strings, creating a melancholy sound. Beppo emerged from the crowd in which he had been hidden and began to examine Gianni's face.

He shook his head ruefully, then said, "Not a bad wound, but a nasty one. You were fortunate that the eye was not damaged. It may even leave you with a scar." The wound was open and bleeding across the cheekbone and temple where the lash had struck Gianni with most force. "Angela, best you take him back to the cart and dress it for him." When she opened her mouth to tell him that she had no notion of how to do so, he smiled kindly at her, and said, "Never fear, I will show you."

Trembling a little, still from anger, and not from fear, Angela did as she was bid. Gianni's expression was unreadable as she slipped her arm through his. He handed the lute to Beppo and was content to sit by the cart and have Beppo and Angela clean his wound and dress it. The landlord and landlady of the inn watched them: both had been fortunate not to have been among those cut down.

"Alas, Angela," murmured the landlady, throwing her arms around Angela, her high spirits dampened by the day's events. "Your dance will not now take place. The procession to the Virgin has been abandoned, so this year Ostuna will not be blessed by her. Oh, the devil is in it, for not only has Braccio killed our townsfolk, but he has taken our luck away!''

Angela freed herself from Anna's embrace. She was still wearing the chaplet of flowers which Anna had placed on her head in the early morning. Now she removed it, looked earnestly at them all and said, ''But if, Signora, you and your husband were to escort Beppo, Gianni and me to the Holy Virgin's shrine at the edge of the town, we could place my chaplet at her feet and we could all pray to her to take pity on us. We could explain to her that it was not the wishes of the folk of Ostuna that she remained unhonoured today, and ask her to accept this offering instead.''

Anna's response was to throw her arms around Angela again and impulsively kiss her on the cheek. Angela thought that she had received more open affection from this new met peasant woman than she had received from anyone in all the years in which she had been the lady of Novera!

''Oh!'' Anna exclaimed. ''You are a good girl, indeed you are. I'll never have a word said against those who travel the roads again. You have the right of it, Angela. Come, husband, and Gianni, too, if you are able, and Beppo, and let us go honour the Virgin as she says. Our holy Mother will surely not ignore our prayers, reverently offered.''

And so it came to pass. Their small procession, Angela leading and holding her chaplet before her, began its walk to the shrine. On the way they told those fellow citizens whom they met of their mission.

Many joined them. Some, who had been carrying flowers to take to the shrine before Braccio arrived, returned to their homes to collect them and follow Angela.

Under the bright sun, her face smeared with paint and perspiration, wearing her tawdry finery, holding a crudely made crown of flowers, the missing lady of Novera, hot and tired, but full of a fierce determination that the townspeople of Ostuna who had been kind to a humble pedlar and his wife should not have their day completely ruined by lordly cruelty, led them to the shrine which stood just outside the far gate of the town. Always before when she had taken part in such ceremonies, she had stood cool and aloof whilst others did the work and organised matters, leaving her only to smile graciously, to be above the throng, accepting the plaudits of the crowd, having done nothing herself. Never before had the lady of Novera initiated such matters or taken part in any ceremony in such a way that she felt and bled with those around her.

She was unaware as she walked along, her eyes fixed on a distant goal, that Gianni was watching her in some astonishment. Her expression of grave but enthusiastic determination was so different from her usual calm indifference that it might almost have been another woman who finally knelt to lay her chaplet at the feet of the Holy Mother. Others followed her with their offering. Some, who had no flowers to bring brought fruit. Finally, Father Francesco, who had been one of those leading the original procession, arrived, having been informed of what was toward. He had been looking after the spiritual affairs of the dead and wounded, but came at once when told what the pedlar's woman was about.

''My daughter!'' he said to Angela, who knelt before him for his blessing, after he had blessed the decorated shrine. ''I salute you for your determination to see that our shrine was honoured. May the love of the Lord God be with you always.''

''Well, lady,'' Gianni said, when at last they were back in the square again, forgetting for once to keep up the fiction of their false names. ''I think that the Lord God is also responsible for your transformation, for I cannot think who else is.''

''Angela,'' reproved Angela gently. ''My name is Angela. And as for my transformation, I cannot think of what you are speaking.'' Her surprise was genuine, not assumed.

My transformation? she queried to herself, as she helped Gianni and Beppo to pack the cart, preparatory to their leaving Ostuna before night began to fall. Although in pain from his damaged face, Gianni thought that they ought to be on their way. Whatever can he mean? For the one person least conscious of how much she was changing under the impact of her new life was Angela herself, late the lady of Novera.

They slept that night under the stars. Anna and her husband had begged them to stay the night at Ostuna, but had reluctantly agreed that under the circumstances they had best be on their way, even though Anna argued that Niccolo needed a night's rest in a good bed, rather than sleep by the side of the road.

His wound, whilst not severe, was painful and, as he had argued earlier, to do what one was expected to do disarmed suspicion rather than created it. They would be expected to fly from Braccio's persecution, so fly they did.

Gianni caught Angela's pitying eye on his injured face as she sat by him whilst he drove them along the road from Ostuna. He smiled painfully at her, and said, "Do not feel sorry for me, Angela. Remember that it is likely to make it even more difficult for anyone who might recognise me to do so! Looked at in that light, one might almost consider it a boon."

"Nothing so painful could possibly be considered a boon," was her spirited retort. Once, when she had first met him, she might have felt pleased that he had been so cruelly attacked. But in the short time which she had spent with him on the road, Angela had come to know a different man from the one who had mocked her in their earliest encounters. He was both brave and resourceful, and the affection displayed for him by those who had known him in the past, such as Anna and her husband, showed a different side of him from the one which she had first encountered.

Angela did not ask herself whether her own changed manner might have altered his to her, because she was not yet aware how much she had changed and was changing. Beppo's manner to her had remained constant. It was impersonally kind and helpful. He spoke little, either to her or to Gianni, but what he said was always down to earth and full of common sense.

It was he who persuaded Gianni to stop earlier

than he had wished to and persuaded him to rest. "Sleep now, and make an early start tomorrow."

So exhausted was she by all that had happened to her that Angela thought she would fall asleep immediately, despite the fact that her bed was a blanket laid on the hard earth. But sleep was long in coming. All that had happened during the long day ran through her head. Again and again she heard the screams of the townspeople as Braccio's men carried out their murderous work. Again and again she felt Braccio's fell gaze on her. Again and again she saw him strike Gianni. Again and again she saw Gianni fall to the ground… The litany of all that had passed was long and oft repeated.

And then when she did fall into a restless slumber she was awoken by Gianni calling out. He was lying not far from her, and she had heard him tossing in the night. He was probably finding sleep as difficult to achieve as she did. His cry was so piteous that she sat up, and when it was repeated she rose and walked over to where he lay.

Somehow he had become tangled in the blanket which Beppo had wrapped around him, and was struggling to release himself from it. He was not properly awake for when she knelt down beside him and whispered his name he stared blindly at her. Nevertheless she persevered.

"What is it, Gianni, may I help you?" She put out a hand to him, to have him seize it and pull her to him.

He was hot, his hair was wet, and his voice when he spoke was hoarse. It was plain that he did not know her, for he muttered brokenly, "Oh, yes, mistress. Only lie with me, and after that mayhap, I shall sleep without dreaming."

Still holding her in an iron grip, he pulled her down beside him. Angela struggled, but it was hopeless. She could not free herself and, once she was by him on the ground, he put his arms around her, saying, "What angel comes to give me rest?" and made as though to kiss her.

But the effort pained him, and he rolled away, putting his hand to his injured face. As swiftly as she could, Angela moved away, to sit from him at some distance, saying more loudly than before, "Wake up, Gianni, you are dreaming. Shall I fetch Beppo?"

This time he sat up, shook his head, threw aside the blanket and murmured petulantly, "I am as hot as though I were in hell. How far gone is the night?" Then, staring at her, he said, "What brings you here, lady? Are you one of the moon's servants, come to haunt a poor devil in his fever?"

"Angela," she said firmly. "I am Angela, remember. You rescued me from Gentile's clutches and now we are fleeing from him. Shall I fetch you water? There is a stream nearby if our skin is empty."

He was fully awake now, and he yawned and stretched. "I remember. Your pardon, Angela, I believe I nearly gave you an unwanted baptism into life! Yes, I should like a drink. Braccio's vile blow has made me feverish. But do not wake Beppo. He at least is sleeping. What made you come to nurse me?"

Angela rose in one supple movement. "I heard

you call in your sleep. I could not sleep, and it seems that your dreams were all evil, so you cried for help. A moment, and I shall bring you water.''

It was pleasant to lie there even though the fever gripped him, Gianni thought, and to watch her walk to the cart to find that the skin still contained water. She poured it into one of the metal goblets they carried with them. All her movements were as elegant and controlled as though she were still a great lady in the court at Novera, instead of walking barefoot, clad in a peasant's rude gown, her hair streaming down her back.

Pray God he managed to keep her out of Gentile's vile clutches even though she might have landed in his! He remembered how a moment ago he had thought to have her in his bed, not knowing who, or what, she was. More and more on their journey she was coming to tempt him, who at first had seemed so cold and distant that she could not be a temptation to any man.

He drank the water which she handed him and patted the ground beside him. ''Sit with me for a time, Angela. Neither of us can sleep this night, and perhaps if we talk a little you may forget what happened today, and I may be able to ignore my fever and the pain in my face.''

''Now, how did you know that I could not sleep because of Braccio, and what he did to Ostuna?''

Propped on one arm, Gianni was able to admire the planes of the perfect face so near to him. The moonlight softened her severe expression, and made her more of a temptation than ever. He swallowed, and then said, "Why, that is not difficult. I think that you have led a sheltered life, and have never seen cruelty inflicted before. Ugo Bordoni is reputed to be a kind ruler, and I suspect that he has never allowed you to see the inevitably harsher side of his rule."

Angela nodded thoughtfully. "That may be true, but I cannot think that my uncle would ever behave as Gentile and Braccio do."

"Alas," and Gianni's voice was heavy for once. "Those who rule men, and those who lead men may occasionally be constrained to order many things which would soil the ears of an innocent like yourself. Harsh decisions have to be made—and be carried out harshly—as you would discover if you were ever to rule Novera on your own. Even a princess, if she were not to lose her throne, would be compelled to behave like a prince—remember that."

Strangely, Angela did not wish to be reminded that she was in truth the lady of Novera, who might need to rule it alone if she never married. She could not imagine ordering men to carry out massacres for her, but she had read enough of Messer Plutarch to know that a great princess could be as cruel as a great prince. Sitting in the open in the balmy warmth of a night in late June, talking to a nobody of a *condottiero*, was making her face facts about the reality of the life she lived—a strange thought. For the first time she was not grateful to Ugo for keeping her so innocent of the world.

Another thought struck her. "I would like to ask you a question, Gianni. I hope that you will answer it truthfully." She paused to watch him nod his head.

He was already looking less feverish, so she pressed on. "How can it be that these peasants, aye, and even the townsfolk of such as Ostuna, the people I have met in our flight, be so happy and kind when they have so little? Anna and her husband would have let us stay for nothing at their inn tonight. I have not always found that those about me at Novera, rich though they were, were as kind."

"It would be untrue to believe that all the lesser folk are happy all the time," Gianni told her, "but, having little, they are grateful for the small blessings which life brings them. And not all are as kind as Anna and many of those we met at Ostuna and the first village, but again, having little, they know how hard it is to have less—hence their kindness."

This made her think, and thinking made Angela sleepy. Unselfconsciously, and forgetful in her tiredness that Gianni was a man—and therefore not to be trusted—she lay down beside him on the hard earth which was not nearly so hard as it had seemed earlier and, blanket-less, let sleep claim her. Before she did so she murmured drowsily, "What makes you so wise, Gianni?" But she did not stay awake for his answer, nor did she see his rueful expression as he picked up his blanket and covered her with it to sleep unprotected on Mother Earth himself.

Astonishingly and surprisingly, sleep claimed him, too, and the moon shone on them both as she sailed down the sky towards dawn.

Chapter Seven

"Two rabbits!" exclaimed Beppo gleefully. "And mushrooms—large ones. We shall eat well tonight."

He and Gianni had been foraging for food. They had told Angela that it would be many days before they came to another town or village, and at first, in her ignorance of what life on the road meant, she had not fully understood that once their small stock of food ran out, they would have to hunt and forage for it. For drink they had water from the many streams in the woodland and scrub through which the road ran.

While Angela helped Beppo to skin, draw and cut up the rabbits and prepare the mushrooms—he had begun instructing her in the art of cookery from the day on which she had been renamed Angela—Gianni was looking with distaste at the stained linen shirt which he was wearing.

"Even to keep up our disguise I am not prepared to wear this filthy shirt much longer," he complained. "It will shortly be walking away from me!

Tomorrow, Angela, I shall show you how to wash clothes. This afternoon, whilst I looked for mushrooms, and Beppo hunted our noble prey, the rabbit, I discovered that we are near to a small river, with a shelving beach. We can all wash our shirts at the very least.''

''And our feet as well.'' Angela was looking with equal distaste at her small feet, which were beginning to show the signs of their long journey…

She remembered the day, nigh on a week ago when Gianni's fever had returned, and Beppo had driven the cart instead, leaving Angela to ride Damn Your Eyes. The mule's name was well deserved, for when Angela tried to ride it, it would have none of her, either throwing her off or refusing to move at all. In the end she had walked along, leading it, slowing them down, which was just as well for any rapid motion of the cart disturbed Gianni. Fortunately his relapse was not lengthy. He was well again the next day, but Angela steadfastly refused to return to the cart, saying, ''Ride in my place until you are fully recovered. It will not hurt me to walk.''

''By the Holy Virgin, no, Angela,'' he told her forcefully. ''I will not sit while Beppo drives and you walk, and that's final.''

Angela did not relish another day's plodding along the rough track into which the road had degenerated, but she was determined to make him rest—at least for a day—in case the fever returned again.

''No, it isn't,'' she announced, in her most daunting lady of Novera manner, and sat down in the road before the cart. "There. I refuse to move until you agree to ride in the cart and allow me to walk."

Both men stared at her. Beppo began to laugh, his stern face amused for once, but Gianni was furious—*his* usually cheerful face was stormy.

"Get up at once," he roared, "before I lift you into the cart myself. Dear God, why have you blessed me with such an obstinate shrew?"

"It was you who kidnapped me, not I or God, so there is no use in blaming me or God," returned Angela incontrovertibly. "You have made your bed and must lie on it, as my nurse so often told me."

"Damn you and damn your nurse. You are the most obstinate…" Gianni paused for breath, red faced. He had jumped from the cart to advance on Angela where she sat in the dirt, the mule beside her idly cropping the grass at the road's edge.

It did not help matters that she smiled sweetly up at him, murmuring, "Wench? Is that the word that you were looking for, Ser Gianni? Or were you thinking of a worse one? If you try to lift me into the cart I shall resist you. I know that you will win in the end because you are stronger than I am, but it won't do your health any good, even so."

Gianni knew only too well that he had no wish to struggle with her, that was for sure. For one thing, ever since he had woken up to find her by him in the night, she had begun to present a very real temptation to him. And now, looking down at her as she sat in the road, her smiling face was provoking him in more ways than one. To pick her up, to hold her in his arms—and do nothing with her, except throw her into the cart like a bale of goods—was more than a mere frail and mortal man could bear...

"You tempt me, *wench*," he muttered morosely. "When I first met you, you seemed to be as orderly and dignified as a woman could be. And now look at you, sitting in the road, exchanging words with me like a fishwife."

The devil was in her, no doubt about it, and where he had been all her life, and why now, on this long and tiring journey he should choose to whisper in her ear, Angela did not know.

She smiled prettily up at her captor, saying, "Oh, Ser Gianni, and there was I, congratulating myself that I was acting the part of the pedlar's wife so well that I thought to earn praise from you, not blame. A fishwife is what I appear to be, and you," she put her head on one side, "look exactly like the fishwife's husband," for he stood before her, scarlet in the face and angry, his hands on his hips, head flung back and as dirty as...as...the...devil.

Yes, he was the devil who was provoking her.

He glowered at her.

She smiled sweetly at him.

Beppo was hard put to contain his sniggers. The irresistible force had met the immovable object. He had seldom seen his lord and captain so nonplussed.

"I will bargain with you," uttered Gianni at last and reluctantly, his distaste for the whole business plain.

"You will? Oh, bravo. And what is it, this bargain? Go away, at once!" This last was to the mule which had advanced on her and was licking her hand

appreciatively, as though in admiration of her outrageous behaviour—for it was outrageous, Angela
knew, no doubt about that. But it was all *his* fault
for being so domineering and disagreable.

"If you will agree to spend the morning riding,
whilst I drive, then this afternoon I will agree to rest
while Beppo drives and you walk."

"A very judgement of Solomon," replied Angela
approvingly. "The lord of Novera himself could do
no better. Yes, I agree."

"Sense at last," remarked Gianni sourly, rolling
his eyes to heaven as though imploring the Lord God
to pity him, saddled as he was with a contrary
woman.

Angela's response to *that* as she took her place
beside him in the cart, and Beppo mounted Damn
Your Eyes, who had turned into Hey, You again, was
to inform him cheerfully, "My old nurse used to say
that there was no pleasing men. I cannot say that I
had occasion to agree with her until I met you, Ser
Gianni."

Gianni muttered an oath beneath his breath, then
said aloud, "I can spare your old nurse's sayings,
Angela. Let her disappear into the limbo from which
you have chosen to summon her!"

"But she said so much that was wise." Angela's
pious face as she uttered this monstrous fable was no
reflection of her thoughts, for she had found her old
nurse both sententious and boring. She was proving,
however, a useful whip to attack Gianni with, he being so unattackable otherwise. "For example—"

She got no further. "By all the devils in Gehenna,

and those roaming the world, enough! No more. I feel a fever coming on,'' and Gianni clutched at his head.

''You do?'' He had delivered himself unto her, as Father Anselmo was given to saying when he played Benedetto at chess, and Benedetto had made a false move. He had given her a delicious opportunity to bait him again. ''In that case, Ser Gianni, I suggest that you surrender the reins to Beppo at once, and allow me to walk. We cannot be put to the trouble of nursing you again.''

She looked as soulfully concerned as she could for Gianni's health, and the success or otherwise of this whole expedition, which was taking her—where? Only Gianni and the Lord God knew, and neither of them was choosing to enlighten her.

Gianni stopped the cart. ''What Pandora's box did I open, lady, when I rescued you from Gentile? Report said that you were quiet, modest, would not say boo to a goose, and had hardly a word for anyone, man or woman. An ideal wife for a man who wanted an ideal wife. At first I thought that, for once, report said true. But look at you now... And do not call me Ser Gianni. Gianni will do, no pedlar is Ser.''

''Certainly, if you will refrain from calling me lady. I am Angela. As for reproaching me for my behaviour, you would do well to reproach yourself. For safety's sake, *you* said, I was to be Angela in word and deed. No one was to suspect that I was the missing lady of Novera. If you wish her back again, then I will gladly oblige you. You have only to ask.''

Even Angela was stunned by her eloquence. For,

of course, all he had said of her behaviour before he had arrived in Gentile's church was true. She was, at last, beginning to realise how much she had changed—as Gianni had already tried to tell her. And now he was glowering at her again, before suddenly laughing as though he were demented,

"Great God," he choked, throwing an arm around her, regardless of Beppo, or poor drooping Nello and Hey, You. "That should teach me not to argue with a woman, and a pretty one. Angela and wife you shall be. I think, after all, she is preferable to pious perfection—which is what you were." He gave her a kiss, which rated somewhere between the loving and the brotherly, and started Nello on his way again.

Pious perfection. Was that what he had thought of her? But, of course, he was speaking no less than the truth. Her cheek burned with his kiss, for every time he touched her, however lightly, Angela found herself quivering and shaking. Did it happen because she was turning into Angela, or would Marina, the lady of Novera, respond in the same way?

Now that was definitely not the kind of problem which she could discuss with Father Anselmo. Nor could she ask Beppo, who was looking at both her and Gianni in the most speculative manner, as though he were trying to decide whether to buy peaches or apricots in the market. And why was that? What were they doing which was both intriguing and amusing him?

But, of course, here was another thing which she knew. She was behaving like the ladies of her court when they flirted with the men who surrounded them! They teased and tormented, eyes shining, sometimes from behind their fans, sometimes more openly. She had always despised them. She would never do such a thing. Not she! She would never talk in their double fashion, taunting to gain attention.

But that is exactly what you have been doing, said a sly little voice inside her, and as though you have been doing it all your life. No wonder he is surprised at you—after all, are you not surprised at yourself?

And if I behave in this wanton manner with a...nobody, chance met, who means nothing to me, shall I do so with Leonardo di Montefiore? If I ever chance to meet him, that is. If Ser Nobody from Nowhere ever lets me out of his clutches. Suppose I only wish to behave like the lady of Novera with Messer Leonardo...? Suppose...suppose that I do not jump and quiver at his touch...what then...?

A sardonic voice broke in on her troubled thoughts. "Silent so long, Angela, and so thoughtful. What are you musing on to make you look so soulful? Trying to recover pious perfection?"

Oh, how wrong he was! At this moment, pious perfection was a long way from her thoughts. So far away that she actually jumped when he spoke—and he hadn't even touched her!

Angela turned her head to look closely at Gianni. At his strong and beautiful profile, at his arrogantly held head with its crown of curling black hair, at his long athletic body, his powerful hands, meant for the broadsword, but now controlling the reins of an elderly and ambling horse.

He should be wearing the clothes of a Leonardo

di Montefiore with a face and body like that, not the
threadbare canvas of a poor pedlar, or a mercenary
soldier's battle-worn armour. Never, in all her years
at Novera had she ever met anyone like him. So
young and so sure of himself. He was like the Greek
heroes of whom Father Anselmo and Girolamo Bor-
gioli, Ugo's secretary, had told her of. He resembled
Apollo himself...except that Apollo was fair like the
sun...

And now he was staring at her, his expression
quizzical. "Yes, Angela, you have something to
say?"

Did she? Have something to say? What she wanted
was something to do. To put out a hand to touch the
apricot of his warm cheek, gilded by living in the
sun. To stroke the one black curl which had fallen
across his brow. To touch his sun-warmed lips, and
gently soothe away the pain of the wound which
Braccio had given him, healing now, but which must
still be troubling him. To... She must be going mad!
But she was not. Angela knew at last what was
wrong with her, what had been wrong with her from
the moment he had lifted the helmet from his head.
No, from the moment she had heard his beautiful
voice taunting Gentile in the church at Verdato.

She loved him and was in love with him! She, the
lady of Novera, untouched by a man either physically
or emotionally, who had only enjoyed the intellectual
companionship of men, was in love with a nobody,
a mercenary soldier on the make, who was certain
sooner or later either to ravish her, or even to sell
her to the highest bidder.

"No," she almost stammered in her very real distress and confusion. "I was…thinking."

His beautifully arched brows rose higher still. "Thinking, Angela? Of what?"

"Of nothing, Gianni, nothing." All the charming self control with which she had defied him a few moments ago was gone. Her eyes wide, she was staring at him as though she had never seen him before. Which, in a way, she hadn't. To discover that she loved him had new-minted him for her. And even if it was proximity to him over the last few days which had undone her, delivered her to him, there was no going back.

"Nothing?" In the contest between them, which had begun from the moment they had first met, Gianni was now the winner, whom a little earlier had been the loser. "A strange nothing which has you frowning so hard."

"I was thinking—of something which Father Anselmo told me once," she lied desperately.

"Father Anselmo? You are sure you don't mean your old nurse?" Oh, he was enjoying himself, damn him, and somehow she must wipe the smile from his face.

"Yes, Father Anselmo." Angela searched her memory feverishly for something to say, then came out at last with, "We were debating whether it was ever permissable in the Lord God's eyes to commit a wrong that right might follow," she ended triumphantly.

"Oh, I would hardly call that nothing, Angela," was his deceptively soft reply. "On the contrary, it is a problem which has troubled mankind since the time of the ancients. No wonder your brow was so furrowed. I am surprised that it is not permanently so if you ponder often on such deep matters!''

"You are pleased to jest, Gianni.'' Angela's voice was stiff.

"Not so. I can only commend you for inwardly debating on such profundities when we are fleeing from your would-be ravisher, and are in danger at any moment of being discovered.''

"It helps me to forget.'' Angela was startled to discover that there was truth in what she said. She remembered her discussion with the good father vividly. With a sly glance at her companion, she remarked coolly, "I don't suppose that you have anything to contribute to the debate, Gianni?''

"Again, on the contrary, Angela. For it seems to me that, whereas in the convent or in the study one may spend hours considering whether to do a wrong that a right may be the result, in the real life of the state or the battlefield, poor wretches like myself may have to make a decision on the spur of the moment. It is only afterwards that the magnitude of what we have done may strike us.

"What seems to be the right and sensible thing in the heat of battle, or in a busy council chamber, may look quite otherwise afterwards. And sometimes, of course, we have no choice. We must do what is to be done, and to the devil with the consequences— and sometimes, it may in truth be the devil.''

He was being quite serious for once; all mockery had fled from his voice. His whole manner had changed. There was a bitterness, no, a sad resignation in what he was saying, which struck Angela so hard that she could make no light comment back.

On the contrary, as he had said. So now she spoke slowly and sincerely to him, her head bent. "You speak from experience, Gianni?"

It was a moment before he answered her. "Yes. Would that I did not."

Silence seemed the best answer to that. So silence Angela offered him, and for the next few miles they travelled slowly along the road until, as the sun grew higher and hotter in the heavens, they stopped for their afternoon siesta after a light meal.

And when the siesta was over he was mocking Gianni again, teasing her, but for a space he had shown her quite another man. A man to respect. Which made it harder than ever for Angela to tell herself that she must not, should not, love him. But all the same, she could not help but wonder at what busy council chamber or battlefield he had been present, so that he could remember that the decisions which had been taken there were bitter ones...

She was back in the present again, the smell of cooking rabbit strong and sweet in her nostrils. Beppo, whose turn it was to cook, had gathered herbs on his journey back to the cart and had smeared the rabbit joints with a little oil from the phial they carried with them and rubbed the herbs into their skin. He was holding each joint above the flames of the fire at the end of a small pitchfork and, as each was finished, he wrenched it free and handed it to Gianni or Angela. They were sitting, as always, at a little distance from the road, with a view before and behind them of a forest wilderness, the road they were travelling on now barely a track.

"How far to Burani, do you think?" Gianni was asking Beppo after he had demolished a second joint.

"A day, a day and a half," Beppo shrugged. "If we are lucky. Remember, there was a bandit king near here when last we passed this way. We should make speed to reach Burani before he finds us."

"We dodged him last time." Gianni was lying back, his hands behind his head, his eyes closed, the scar on his face still livid, but beginning to fade. "We have nothing to offer him in the way of plunder, so we should be safe."

"Such creatures are capricious, as well you know. No-one, high or low, is safe from them."

Beppo held out another piece of rabbit to Gianni who waved it away, saying, "Give it to Angela, she must keep up her spirits, and besides, we cannot have her growing thin."

Oh, dear God, after that taunt she would like to refuse the rabbit, but even after eating two of its small joints she was still hungry, and was already salivating when she took the third from the end of Beppo's pitchfork. She ate it with a relish she had never felt for the fine and delicate food which she had been served at Novera. How strange it was that rabbit, eaten in the open as she sat, bare legs crossed on the hard earth, tasted like the food of the Gods. Ambrosia, Messer Ugo had called it, and she had always wondered what that food might be. She had never thought that it could be rabbit.

"This bandit king," she asked Gianni. "Who is he?"

"He calls himself Guido Orsini, but you may be sure that no Orsini would claim him as either their legitimate, or illegitimate, get. He is young, dissolute and violent."

"Worse than Gentile or Braccio?" This with a shiver.

"Much like Braccio, but worse." Angela pulled a face. "With luck we shall escape him."

But luck was not with them.

They were still some miles from Burani when fate struck again. They had spent the night in the forest, well away from the road. Somewhere in the small hours, the waning moon already falling down the sky, they had been awoken by the sound of a troop of men and horses moving along the road. Their fire had long been out, and they were hidden from sight by the trees amongst which they had camped.

Gianni, apart from the one night when he had been troubled and Angela had reassured him, was a light sleeper, and on waking, all his senses were at once alert. He sat up, pulling a long dagger from under his improvised pillow, and rose in one lithe and silent movement to look in the direction from which the hoofbeats were coming. Beppo woke, too, and finally, Angela. She was learning to be wary, and in any case, found sleeping in the open more difficult than in her comfortable bed. The untoward noise had roused her.

She rose to stand beside Gianni and whisper at him, "What is it?"

"Soldiers," he told her, "and from what I can make out of their pennons and badges, Gentile's. They are still searching for the lady of Novera." He spoke of her as though she were someone none of them knew.

"But why at night?" Angela tried to keep her voice down.

"To surprise those whom they might meet, particularly if they think that they have found the lady. She and her captors have disappeared so completely that Gentile must suspect magic." He gave a low chuckle at the thought. "He needs to recapture her soon, for it is likely that both Novera and Montefiore have troops looking for her by now."

This was a new thought for Angela. Of course, both her uncle and the Duke of Montefiore—to say nothing of Leonardo—would be looking for her, trying to find her before Gentile did.

"Should we not look for them, and surrender to them?" she asked, as artlessly as she could.

Angela only knew that Gianni was laughing, soundlessly, because she could see his shoulders shake in the dim light. "By no means, Angela. I have no wish to share you with anyone. Once we are away from them all, then, and only then, shall I make up my mind what to do with you."

"You forget that I am promised to Leonardo di Montefiore and by now but for Gentile, and then you,

I would have been his bride and safe in a comfortable bed,'' was her tart reply. The noise of the soldiers had died down, and they were out of danger again, so she was not worried when her voice rose in honest indignation.

"On the contrary—'' Gianni's favourite and most mocking answer ''—it is something I rarely forget. But I am intrigued that you mention the lord Leonardo so fervently and wish to be 'safe in his bed'. I understood that you were not in favour of marriage to him.''

"And that is true. I wish to marry no man. But at least if I were with Messer Leonardo I should not be standing in a forest wearing the garb of a peasant woman, with a man who rarely shows me any respect and has not yet made up his mind whether to wed, ravish, or sell me!'' She shot this at him with all the venom she could muster.

His answer was to put one hard arm about her shoulders. "Oh, Angela, do but confess to me, as to your confessor, honestly before the Lord God, how much you have been enjoying yourself these last few days! How much you enjoyed yourself at Ostuna before Braccio arrived. Your cheeks have now the most charming colour which were formerly wan. Your manner is enthusiastic and brisk, which was cool, measured and indifferent. Your walk is lively, not stately. And you ate your rabbit with such gusto that I cannot believe that you wished it other than it was. Of your clothing—yes, that is a pity, I grant you. I have a mind to see you dressed as you should be. But if you were, then...'' and by the light of the waning moon she could see that his eyes were aglint with mockery "...then I should never have seen your shapely legs and ankles. For sure, fine clothes may conceal an ill-made body, but your clothes conceal little—to my pleasure."

"Oh...!" She tried to wrench away. "How dare you? I am sure that Messer Leonardo would not speak to me so shamelessly."

"Then the more fool he not to treasure what he sees, and let his lady know of it."

"Think you," came a weary voice from behind them, "that you could cease this verbal jousting and return to your beds? I, at least, wish to get some sleep this night. Between Gentile's men and a pair of flapping tongues, I am like to be awake until dawn."

"I do but seek to quiet a fractious woman," Gianni tossed over his shoulder.

"Ser Beppo, pray tell your comrade to cease from distressing me with his ill-considered remarks and I shall be only too happy to end my share of our conversation," was Angela's response to his plea.

"There is nothing to choose between you," grumbled Beppo, lying down and pulling a blanket over his head. "Cry truce and let a poor devil sleep."

"Truce," both parties cried together, looking a little guilty at their lack of consideration for Beppo, who ran their commissariat so well and so unselfishly.

Beppo lifted his head for the last time to proclaim sardonically, "Let us run up a flag to celebrate your rare accord—and sleep on it."

Sleep they did, later than usual and, after a drink

of water and a hard crust of bread—the last which remained to them of their supplies from Ostuna— they set off down the road again. Burani, Beppo assured them, was now but a day's travel away, at the very most. There they would find food and perhaps a bed to sleep in, for one night at least.

"For today, cold rabbit," Beppo exclaimed.

They made good time. Nello was friskier than usual. Gianni was less frisky than usual, Beppo was even more silent, and Angela was even more talkative. She was on the point of asking Gianni where he had been campaigning before he had turned up to kidnap her from Verdato, when they heard in the distance the thunder of hooves again.

She hardly had time to pray that it was not Gentile's men returned, and that neither Gentile nor Braccio was with them, when the troop came round the bend of the road and were upon them.

By their pennants, the badges on their surcoats, and by their general condition, it was plain that, whoever they were, they were not Gentile's men. For all his faults, Gentile's troops were well turned out and well disciplined. This small troop was as slovenly a crew as any of the three of them had ever seen before.

They were led by a young man as ill-turned out as his band. On seeing their little procession, he held up his hand and commanded his troop to stop. Which was just as well, thought Angela, who had for one dreadful moment been under the impression that he intended to ride over them.

He leaned forward on his horse's neck, as Braccio

had done, to demand of them, "Who the devil are you, and where are you making for?"

Gianni did everything but actually pull a forelock. "Of your mercy, lord, I am Gianni of the roads and this is my wife and my partner, Beppo. We are on our way to Burani to sell our wares there."

"Hmm…" The ill-favoured man on the seedy warhorse allowed his feral eyes to rove over Angela; Beppo was not worth a stare. "And what have you seen on the road, of which you might care to tell me, pedlar?"

"Seen on the road, lord? Why, what should I have seen? Only the birds, and the rabbits which infest these parts. And last night, a troop of soldiers broke our sleep—and that is all, most gracious lord."

If Angela thought that this was overdoing the humility somewhat, the man on the horse did not think so. He put his chin on his mailed fist and after a moment ground out with an evil smile, "Now, why do I not believe you, pedlar? I have never seen you before. You are a stranger in these parts?"

"Gracious lord, not exactly. Beppo and I came this way nigh three years agone, before I married Angela here. We but thought to come this way again, business was good last time."

The man worried his lower lip with his teeth, then asked, "Do you know who I am, pedlar."

"Not for sure, lord, but I would hazard a guess that you are Messer Guido Orsini of the great house of Orsini, and if so, I salute you, lord."

"You may do more than salute me, pedlar. You may follow my men and me to my castle, for I would have more words with you. My men's women would be glad to inspect your wares and," with a sideways glance at Gianni's lute, "I crave entertainment, so you may play and sing for me, and your wife may dance for us. After she has been washed, that is. You understand me?"

"Yes, lord, I understand, lord." Gianni twisted and turned as though he were in truth a cowed peasant confronted by one of the great ones of his world and not knowing quite what to do to please him.

"Good. Then follow my troop. To make sure that you do, one of my men will ride beside your cart. If you should try to escape from us, why, he shall have orders to cut you down on the instant. You understand me, pedlar?" His grin was evil.

"Yes, lord, assuredly, lord," Gianni gabbled. Not all his fear was assumed, for he could see the capricious nature of the monster before him. Even if he were only Braccio writ small, he was none the less deadly for that. More so, perhaps, for he was not as clever as Braccio.

Nothing for it but to follow Guido and his little band. They left the road which led to the north, and ultimately to safety, and were soon struggling along a lesser track up the hillside, for Guido's eyrie was perched on high so that he might easily see all who made their way towards him.

It had once been owned by another bandit lord, long dead, who had gone on to greater things than preying on passers by. He had ended up with a little state of his own—which Guido might do one day. Angela had heard of such rogues, but had never thought to be a prisoner of such a one as Guido. She remembered what Beppo had said of him the night before, and shivered inwardly. She would not show fear, for she was sure that Guido and his men thrived on the fear of others.

After an arduous climb they had reached his stronghold, or rather, they had reached the outworks and the small village which lay on one side of it, behind a strong, easily defended wall. It was less of a true castle, and more an elaborate version of the towers which the nobility of Tuscany had built in towns like San Gimignano, which lay in the hinterland between Florence and the North. In these more peaceful times the nobility had deserted them, but here, lost in the woods of the Appenines, Guido still lived as men had lived for the last few hundred years, before the order and civilisation which had been lost after the fall of the Roman Empire had returned to Italy.

There was a wall around one side of the tower, the other side stood above the sheer rock which fell away beneath it. Guido's soldiers and servants lived in the little village. His small garrison was quartered inside the tower with a guard house at its entrance, through which all visitors had to pass before being admitted to Guido's presence. His living quarters were at the top of the tower, so arranged that an invading force would be compelled to fight its way up the stairway and landings which led to it—a difficult proposition.

Few of the rulers of Italy's city states cared to try to rid the countryside of such minor bandits; it was easier and cheaper to allow them to live, unless they became too much of a nuisance—like the flies and wasps which plagued people in the summer.

"Drive your cart into the main courtyard, pedlar," commanded the soldier who rode with them, "where the lord may see it. There is a hut in the living quarters where you, your wife and comrade may sleep and eat. The lord will provide you with food in return for your entertainment while you stay with us. But before I take you there, he wishes to question the three of you further."

No help for it, again, but to do as they were bid. Guido had not yet treated them as foully as Braccio had treated the citizens of Ostuna, but he was even more frightening, Angela thought, than Braccio had been. There was a barely reined in savagery inside him, something which she had never seen before she had left the safe haven of her uncle's palace. She had never known that such human wolves roved the earth, but her education in the realities of the world in which she lived was growing apace.

They were not taken to Guido's apartments but to a great hall on the ground floor opening out of the guard house, where there was a huge fireplace, empty now that summer was with them, and a noble oak table which ran the length of the hall, benches on each side of it. Beyond it was a large open space before a dais on which stood an elaborate if battered carved chair, on which Guido had seated himself in morose state. He had pulled off his helm and his mailed gloves, and was now biting his fingers as he stared at them.

"Come closer!" he snarled irritably at them. "Now, pedlar, I would question you further. You say that you have seen nothing out of the way on your travels, but I know that such creatures as you do not betray at once all that you know. Listen carefully: has the news reached you of the spiriting away of the lady of Novera?"

Gianni, who had been nodding his head earnestly in time with every word which Guido uttered, and whose dragging limp had been at its most pronounced on his walk to the hall, said eagerly, "Oh, yes, lord. We learned of it at Ostuna. One of the lord Gentile's captains, Braccio degli Uberti, came to the town to question the citizens and my humble self as to whether the lady and those who had captured her had passed that way…" He paused, almost, thought the shivering Angela, as though he were tantalising the monster before him. Had he learned nothing from Braccio's treatment of him at Ostuna? Was he not putting all their lives at risk?

Apparently not, for the caprice which Guido so frequently displayed was of a different order from Braccio's. He laughed a little, bit his fingers again, and commented drily, "You are a teller of tales, I see, pedlar, and tell your tale after such a fashion as to keep the attention of those who listen. That is good, I await your entertainment this night with interest—but do not toy with me overmuch. This is a serious matter of which I speak. I have a mind to try to find the lady myself—to enrich myself, you understand. The ransom for her will be a goodly one, since both Novera and Montefiore will have to join

together to pay it. Did Braccio give any hint of where
his master thought that she might be? For the word
is that she has vanished, and the troop with her. What
magician, think you, has spirited her away?''

For one ghastly moment Angela, and Gianni and
Beppo, too, thought that Guido was toying with
them, had guessed who and what they were. But
Gianni, whose cunning brain was whirling, continued
as though all were well. ''Why, lord Guido, the thing
is beyond the understanding of a poor pedlar—as it
was beyond Braccio's and his greater master. Certes,
no party resembling the one which took her had
passed through Ostuna. Nor have we seen, or heard,
aught on the road but the troop which passed by us
yesternight—and that was one of the lord Gentile's.''

''Um…'' Guido bit his fingers again, leaned back.
Thanks be to the Lord God, thought Angela, whose
legs were almost failing her, he was not suspicious
of them. But, as Gianni explained to her later, he
plainly thought that they might be withholding what
they knew to gain a greater reward.

''No matter,'' Guido came out with at last. And
then, as a thought struck him, ''And the troop which
passed. Did they question you?''

''No, lord Guido, for it is our habit always to lie
well off the road, safe from any marauders except
four legged ones, you understand. They did not see
us.''

''Better the bears than the men? Eh, pedlar?''

''Exactly, lord, you have the right of it, lord.''
Bowing, Gianni's head nearly reached the floor.

This greasy humility from an inferior, which

would have revolted Ugo, appeared to be exactly to Guido's taste.

"Now, pedlar, had you information which I could use, I would have rewarded you, but seeing that you have none, then your only reward will be for the entertainment which you will provide for us this night."

Gianni smote his brow and appeared to think. Both Angela and Beppo gave him apprehensive looks. Oh, Holy Mother, what was the rascal up to now?

The unholy rascal on the dais leaned forward eagerly. "What is it, pedlar? Has the sound of gold refreshed your memory? What have you to tell me?"

"Nothing much to the point, lord, but a packman we met on the road outside Ostuna, after we left—he was making for Ostuna, you understand, lord—told us of something strange which he had seen."

He had? What packman was this? Neither Angela nor Beppo remembered meeting a packman. Beppo gave a silent inward groan which was, had he but known it, echoed by the one Angela was internally emitting.

Gianni put his hand to his head, and closed his eyes as though trying to recover a memory almost lost. It was a gesture which Angela had seen deceitful servants make time without number. Had their condition not been so dangerous she could almost have laughed at it.

Finally he muttered so that Guido had to strain to hear him. "He said, lord, he said that he had passed a strange party of men by the roadside, who were arguing with one another, and a lady who was on horseback. When they saw him, the man who was their leader swore at him, and told him to be off. I remember, yes, that I do, that he said that the lady had given him a most piteous look, and that one of the rogues with her had turned her horse away, and shouted at him again, so that he travelled on, for fear of his life.''

"And that is all? In which direction was this party travelling?''

"Oh, lord, of your mercy, that I cannot tell you. Indeed, the matter had almost slipped my mind, until you jogged it.''

"Until the promise of a ducat jogged it. You've told me something, but little enough, and little is what you will get for it, you naughty rogue.'' Guido slipped his hand into the purse which swung at his side and drawing a coin from it, threw it on the floor at Gianni's feet.

With a delighted crow of joy, Gianni grovelled before him to recover it as the coin spun and rolled away from him. Guido laughed at the sight. "Be off with you. And Matteo," to the soldier who still stood guard over them, "bid your wife wash the wench and give her something fit to wear. She may help her rogue of a husband to entertain us this night. If his singing and playing are as good as his impudence, we shall have a splendid night of it.''

He flapped a regal hand at them and turned his head away to indicate that the audience was over, before bellowing at one of his sergeants to make up a troop to search along the road for such a party as the imaginary packman had seen. Angela could only marvel at Gianni's cunning. He had satisfied the monster, but he had not invented a story which would put the good citizens of Ostuna in danger. So she told him, when once they were alone together in the hut assigned to them, after she had been the recipient of another so-called wash, and yet another tawdry piece of finery calling itself a dress.

"How did he know that I could dance?" she asked Gianni, after she and Beppo had reproached him for his fertile imagination which had had both of them in a stew of fear that Guido might guess what he was doing. His answer to that was a shrug.

"I had to tell him something, you understand, to divert any suspicion that he might have had of us, and that was all that I could think of. It seemed to do the trick—for the moment, at least."

He went on to answer her question. "All those who travel the roads for a living have a myriad of such talents. Tonight we will play and sing for him, and pray God he will let us go in the morning—but with such a dangerous beast who knows what he might think to do with us? I did not like the way he looked at you, but at least he did not guess the truth."

The truth? What was the truth? Did Gianni know what telling the truth meant? He already had two names, Niccolo and Gianni. But, come to that, so had she—and Beppo. But it was at his behest that they had them. What was his real name? All that she truly knew of him was that he was a soldier, that when he was not disguised as a pedlar he was a most handsome man, that he was brave, foolhardy even, and had an inventive tongue. So inventive that truth and lies were inextricably mixed in what it said, so she could not fault Guido for not guessing that he was being lied to repeatedly.

The question was, and it was one which had plagued her since she had met him, could all of his talents get her safely out of Verdato—and then... what? She drew in her breath as she looked at him where he sat opposite to her, tuning the lute and singing beneath his breath, his face rapt, his whole shapely body at rest—and pray God that he did not forget to limp, for she thought that though he might have deceived Guido this afternoon, Guido might not necessarily stay deceived if he thought that there was something false about the pedlar and his household.

They were trapped in the eagle's eyrie, and had yet to escape from it.

Chapter Eight

Flambeaux painted shadows in Guido Orsini's great hall; there were no windows in it, only slits so that even on the long evenings of summer their light was needed to work and eat by.

The long table was heaped with food. Angela's mouth watered at the very sight of it as she, Gianni and Beppo were led in, to sit at the far end of it. Guido was seated on his dais: a table had been laid before him, and his lieutenants sat on either side of him, their women in between them.

Seated on Guido's right was a big-bosomed beauty, black-haired and black-eyed, magnificently dressed and bejewelled. Her headdress was a chaplet of gems which held down a filmy veil lifted away from her face, simply there to emphasise the glossy lustre of her hair, shining through it.

Even as Gianni and his company began to sit down, Guido spoke to his obsequious major domo and crooked a hand in their direction. It was thus no surprise that the major domo arrived busily before them to bid them attend on the lord Guido's pleasure.

"All of us?" demanded Gianni, a little insolently.

"As the lord wills it, yes."

Gianni took Angela's hand, and stood at a little distance from her, holding her hand high in parody of a great lord leading his lady into court, and processed down the room, a little slowly because of his limp, to stand before Guido. Beppo followed them, his hand on his heart, the parody of a perfect second-in-command.

Nothing escaped Guido it seemed. "You are pleased to mock, pedlar," was his grim comment. "Take care lest you become too insolent: a whipping might improve your manners, induce a due humility. For the present, I am content to allow you licence, but not for ever."

He turned to the woman by his side. "What think you of the rustic beauty, my lady Isabella?" Now it was he who was doing the mocking. His question was meant to provoke one woman, and perhaps humiliate the other.

Lady Isabella duly supplied the humiliation. Her eyes roved dismissively over the seething Angela. "Were she a little cleaner, my dear lord, she might be passable," she finally announced. "It is to be supposed that the Lord God has given her other attributes to make up for her lack of beauty."

"Do you say so?" Guido, it appeared, was bent on mischief making. "But I suppose it is too much to expect that one woman might be able to judge another's looks fairly. I see promise there, perhaps to be fulfilled when the pedlar's wife dances for us."

"Wife?" The lady Isabella's eyebrows rose dismissively. ''You honour her overmuch, surely? Such creatures do not marry, I understand. I see that the pedlar carries a lute. Do you play and sing as well as huckster, fellow?''

Gianni was suddenly greasily humble again. ''To please so fair a lady as yourself, I am willing to essay anything.''

This flattery patently delighted her. She turned to Guido. ''Now, my dear lord, had you asked me about the pedlar's claim to be well-favoured, rather than his wife's, I might have given you a different answer. Had he not such a bad limp, he would be as well set-up as any peasant might expect to be.'' She rewarded first Gianni and then her husband with a smile, toothy in its dazzling intensity.

Gianni could almost feel Angela's rage. The hand he still held was quivering in his. So, the lady of Novera had progressed from being a woman so detached from ordinary humanity that she could hardly be considered to be a woman at all, to one who could feel wounded pride and jealous rage! Wounded pride because of the lady Isabella's dismissal of her looks, jealousy because she was making eyes at Gianni! It was not conceit which told him this, but his knowledge of men and women. He also knew that the lady Isabella's dismissal of Angela's looks had angered him as much as Guido's lecherous eyeing of her.

Guido's answer to his wife was a stare of such malignity that Angela shuddered at it. ''Who do I reward for such a statement, lady?'' he finally snarled. ''The pedlar, or you? Or the pedlar's wife?'' And now the stare he turned on Angela and Gianni

was baleful in a different way from the one which
he had directed at his wife.

She seemed little troubled by it. Perhaps, thought
Angela, she was used to walking the tightrope which
had her husband's affection at one end, and his feral
temper at the other. But her principal fear was not
for the lady Isabella, but for Gianni and herself, who
had suddenly become two bones of contention between husband and wife.

Something else frightened her, a something which
she hoped Gianni was considering. How long would
it be before the two monsters before them began to
grasp that Gianni of the roads and his wife were
rather more than ordinary pedlars? The very fact that
each of them had felt attracted to a pair of peasants
might cause them to question why this should be so.

A short and silent prayer to the Lord God appeared
to be in order. Angela hastily composed one and inwardly offered it up to heaven. Surely the Lord God
was failing in His duty to mankind to allow such
creatures as these to hold power over helpless men
and women? This dreadful piece of heresy nearly
overset Angela, for never before had she had occasion to question the will of God—mainly because the
will of God towards Marina, the lady of Novera, had
been so unfailingly benevolent.

So overset was she that she missed Guido dismissing them, with a warning to Gianni not to let the
favour which the lady Isabella had chosen to show
him encourage him to commit more insolence. "Be
very careful," he grimly ended, "that you do not
provide entertainment for me and my men of a kind

which you may not like. The whipping post and the rack make men sing a different song from those sung to the lute.''

''I hear you but to obey,'' grovelled Gianni. ''Come, wife.'' As Angela, her mind for the first time fixed on the capriciousness of the Lord God, hesitated and stared blankly at him, he informed the closely watching Guido, ''Oh, great lord, my wife is so overwhelmed by your magnificent presence that she has been transported out of this world into contemplation of the next.'' A remark which was truer than he knew.

It was also true, and fortunate as well, that the lord Guido Orsini was sufficiently full of himself and his importance to take such grotesque flattery at face value, and he forgave Gianni his recent impudence, and lordly waved the pedlar, his wife, and his man back to the far end of the table where he bade them eat and drink their fill.

Even her fear of the man who was providing it could not prevent Angela from enjoying the good food set before them. Gianni, watching her frank pleasure as she looked around her, remembered the cold woman who had shown enthusiasm for little when she had first travelled with him. Now she was eating with even more enjoyment than she had shown when demolishing the rabbit which Beppo had cooked for them.

''Bravo,'' he whispered in her ear while consuming the boar's meat which rested on the manchet of bread before them. ''Alway's eat well when good food is provided in plenty is an excellent motto for a soldier and a soldier's wife. One never knows where the next meal is coming from. Drink the good wine, too, Angela.'' He poured it from the big earthenware pitcher which stood in the centre of the table into her pewter goblet.

Angela needed no further encouragement. When she had finished eating she looked around her at the motley crew which made up the senior members of Guido's household. She did not have long to look for they had barely finished their meal when the major domo was with them again. They were to go to the lord Guido's end of the room and play, sing and dance for him.

''What shall I dance, Gianni?'' asked Angela fearfully.

''Dance the dance with which you would have favoured the good folk of Ostuna. Remember that you are not at the elegant and civilised courts of either Novera or Montefiore, but in an outlaw's stronghold. They will not expect what would be expected there. Have courage, and all will be well.''

It was all very well for him to talk. He had obviously done this sort of thing before. While she had been prepared to dance for the good folk of Ostuna, she was not happy about capering before the greedy eyes of the lord Guido. But there was nothing for it but to do as Gianni told her, for she was as much his prisoner as she was Guido's, with the difference that he did not seem to be as cruel as Guido. She could only hope that she would perform well enough and not give the three of them away by her clumsiness.

Cross-legged on the corner of the dais, Gianni

tuned his lute and began to sing. The song he sang, and the manner of his singing of it, was quite different from the earthy songs he had begun with at Ostuna. His voice was as beautiful as the rest of him, when he was not disguised as a travelling huckster, and the love song he had chosen rang melodiously through the hall. After he had finished, even Guido's rough soldiers were quiet for an instant before demanding more.

He bowed his head in acknowledgement of the applause, and said, "Now my wife will sing *The Blackbird's Song* for you." He played the first bars of the introduction, looking encouragingly over at her where she stood, hands modestly crossed before her, her head bent.

As always, Angela found that while singing she forgot for a moment where she was, and who she was pretending to be. She could look away from them all, towards the flambeaux flaming in their glory and pretend that it was to her uncle that she was pouring out her song. She was transformed.

For a moment, watching her, Gianni was gripped by two strong and powerful emotions. The first was one of fear that those around them would see the transcendent beauty hidden by her poor clothing and uncared for face and hands. The second was the sudden untoward knowledge that she was beginning to wind her way into his heart. That he not only lusted after her, but was beginning to fall in love with the simple bravery which she was consistently showing.

Sheltered, spoiled, cosseted, thrown into a world so unlike her own that she must be in a state of constant bewilderment, she refused to show fear, or petulance, or any of the petty selfishnesses which he would have expected from her.

Her stoicism almost shamed him, if only because he had dismissed her before he met her as the worst sort of indifferent pampered beauty, who thought that the whole world only existed to revolve around her. But she had shown compassion for, and understanding of, the sufferings of the townsfolk at Ostuna, and once the first few days of fright and shock after his kidnapping of her were over, she had done her best to live her new and difficult life cheerfully.

And now he must be careful not to betray what he felt for her before Guido's band of rogues, lest he betray the pair of them.

The song drew to its end, and again, there was silence after its ending. Guido shook himself, leaned forward and said, "Enough of this maundering, pedlar. Let us have a song fit for soldiers first, and then your wife shall dance for us."

Gianni grinned up at him, and launched into a soldier's marching song of such surpassing indecency that the whole hall erupted with joy as the first words rang out into it. Titled *The Englishman and the Venetian Tart*, it ran through innumerable verses, each more filthy than the last. The lady Isabella put her fan before her face, and several of the women hid their faces in their hands—but took care to peep through their fingers at Gianni whilst they did so. The men hammered on the tables and stamped their feet at the refrain which followed each verse. Angela, standing before them all, was one vast blush, particularly when Gianni winked in her direction—and shouted, "Dance, wife, dance."

So she began to dance and realised that he was being kind to her, for concentrating on her steps she heard only the music. The women began clapping in time with it to drown the words, and the men shouted them out more than ever, so that the oak beams of the hall echoed with the sound. The lady Isabella dropped her fan in order to gain a better look at Gianni. Like his wife he would benefit from a wash but, Lord God, what shoulders he had, what thighs!

At long last it was over. Breathless, Angela sank down in a great curtsey, and Gianni, scarlet in the face, passed his hands gently over the strings, calling to Guido as he did so. "A rest, lord, I crave a rest. Let my comrade Beppo tumble and juggle for you before Angela and I sing and dance for you again."

Half drunk, as most of his men were, Guido nodded, and Beppo, who had been standing silently by, opened the canvas bag he had brought in with him, fetched out the clubs which he had been carrying in it, and began to juggle to the sound of Gianni's lute. Angela sank down on the dais by Gianni, who winked at her again, before rewarding her for her dance with an idle kiss. A kiss jealously noted by the lady Isabella, who was suddenly determined that if her husband had his way with the pedlar's dirty doxy this night, then she would sample the delights which the pedlar might have to offer.

Fortunately not privy to either the lord or the lady's thoughts, Angela was beginning to think longingly of her bed. Would this day never end? Her feet ached and her head was spinning as a consequence of the first rich meal which she had eaten since she had left Novera. The wine which she had drunk and the unaccustomed exercise she had been taking had also exhausted her. For the moment she was content to watch Beppo, who, having laid down his clubs, was beginning to tumble, bringing off a series of backward, forward, and twisting somersaults before he called on Gianni to help him with his final pièce de résistance.

Remembering to limp, Gianni laid down his lute, and legs apart, braced himself whilst he held out his hands to Beppo who, taking them, leaped lightly on to his shoulders. Beppo balanced there for a moment before throwing himself upwards into a double somersault which brought him to the ground some yards in front of Gianni, who maintained his own balance, just.

Both men bowed and, before she could check herself, Angela began to clap, shouting bravo and leading the hall's applause. Fortunately those around them only thought that she was acting as the tumblers' assistant and touting for approval, instead of admiring the trick for the first time. "Again!" shouted Guido and his lady, so they performed the trick once more, with a slight difference this time; Beppo facing in the opposite direction, landed behind Gianni—which allowed the lady Isabella to admire the pedlar's body all over again.

Beppo bowed to the lord Guido and, his part of the entertainment over, picked up his bag and his clubs and melted into the background. Unknown to

Angela—or to anyone else for that matter, other than Gianni—he slipped from the hall and slunk silently into the courtyard where he harnessed Nello and made certain that the uncertain mule—who was not sure whether its name today was Hey, You or Damn Your Eyes—was also ready for immediate departure. He liked the looks of neither Guido nor his lady, and thought that they ought to be ready for anything.

His activities went unnoticed, helped by the fact that Guido's men, secure in their eyrie, had become careless and, apart from the sentries on the walls, were nearly as drunk as their master.

And then he sat down to wait on events—and Gianni.

In the hall, Gianni was playing and singing again. But his audience was no longer attentive. Some had slipped to the floor, dead drunk, others lay with their face on the table, snoring. Still others had pulled serving wenches from their places at the back of the hall and disappeared into the shadows with them.

Gianni seemed tireless: helped no doubt, thought Angela sourly, by the nods and winks he was receiving from the lady Isabella as her husband descended towards drunken oblivion. He had earlier told Gianni that he expected him and his wife to wait on his pleasure at the feast's end, but it was becoming plain that by the feast's end he would take his pleasure with no-one.

Isabella prodded her husband, who had slipped sideways in his great chair and had begun to snore. Only one of his lieutenants looked even remotely so-

ber, and several of the ladies had forgotten themselves enough to join their lords in abandoning so-
briety and restraint altogether. The whole dissolute
scene was so different from anything which Angela
had experienced at Novera that she might be living
in a different world. She saw the lady Isabella looking mockingly at her and Gianni, and wondered what
new torments she was planning for them.

Nothing, apparently, for she leaned forward to say
to Gianni, who had stopped singing, and was idly
strumming his lute, the only sober man in a room
full of drunkards, "Enough, pedlar, take your dirty
doxy with you and leave. The lord, as you see, is too
far gone to entertain her, and I would not have her
stay here another day to be a temptation for him.
So—be on your way."

"And nothing tempts you, lady? And should I not
fear your lord's anger, if we disappear, incontinent?"

Oh, how dare he make eyes at such a…a…painted
maypol! Why, she was old enough to be his mother,
which was an exaggeration, Angela knew. But had
he no shame? For, after all, she was supposed to be
his wife, or his woman, or his doxy, and he was
looking at the lady Isabella as though he could eat
her—and she was doing the same to him. For no
reason at all, Angela wanted to weep.

She was not yet sufficiently aware of how the
wicked world wagged to know that one way of rescuing them all from the trap in which they were
caught in Guido's tower was if Gianni used the lady
Isabella's lusting after him to their advantage.

She heard Isabella laugh softly, then say, "Leave

now, pedlar, have no fear. One woman is very like another for Guido, and he dare not anger me too much for I have brought him wealth, and an alliance with my family. I was Isabella Attendolo—and,'' with a significant glance at him from her fine eyes, ''I do as I please.''

Attendolo! That explained much. For she was a member of one of Italy's most powerful dynasties which had provided great *condottieros*, dukes, marcheses, counts and lords to rule states without number. Why, the great Sforza himself, the Duke of Milan, was a member of this same family, and Guido would not gainsay a wife who had such power at her back.

But what would happen to a pedlar who gainsaid her?

No time to think of that, for she had arisen, stepped down from her chair of state so that she stood face to face with him, to throw insolently over her shoulder at Angela, ''Stand back wench, and look the other way. I would speak with your owner.''

For one shocking moment Angela was on the point of turning back into the lady of Novera, who would tell the Lady Isabella exactly what she thought of insolent bitches who annexed other people's husbands without a thought. No matter that Gianni was not her husband and never would be, praise the Lord God, the fires of jealousy raged within her. But prudence warned, Say and do nothing which might give away the game which you and he and Beppo are playing. And he is nothing to you. She says that he owns you and she speaks better than she knows.

What was the lady whispering to Gianni, her imperious voice low, the fan which she held in one begemmed hand tapping gently against his chest? Did she wish him to retire to her room with her? Even Angela knew that this would be a risky ploy. So, what was she plotting?

Isabella was laughing up into his face, was stroking it, and he had taken the gemmed hand which had caressed his cheek and was kissing it before she strutted away, the knowing eyes of the few who were sober, following her. She walked and behaved as though she had dismissed him, but Angela was not so sure.

"What do we do now?" she asked him anxiously.

He seemed at first not to hear her, then said at last, distrait, "She has dismissed us. We are to leave the tower at once. She wishes to thwart Guido by refusing him you."

Angela shuddered. "She does me a kindness, then."

"True, but that was not her aim. We will leave quietly, without undue haste. There may be some officious follower of Guido who might think to gain favour by detaining you for him."

"And that is all? We are to leave? Why should she agree to this? She seemed to want more from you than a public farewell."

Gianni waved an airy hand. "Who knows, dear wife. Such great ladies are capricious beings. Perhaps she felt sorry for us." He was urging her gently to the door with each word he uttered.

Why was it that she did not believe he was telling

her the entire truth? She was sure that he was not, for during their journey together she had learned to read him, and the tone of his voice told her that he was engaging in one of his deceits. But she could not question him further; they must use the respite which the lady Isabella had offered them to try to escape before Guido revived and called them back.

They strolled down the hall, Gianni whistling as though what he was doing was of no import, swinging his lute gently, his arm through Angela's as though he were intent on bed after a hard day's work. They passed the sprawled bodies of Guido's men lying below the sprawled body of Guido himself, only held upright by his elaborate chair. It was hard to tell how lost to the world he was.

Unbelievably, no-one stopped or challenged them as they walked through the guard house, where Guido's men, their superiors lying unconscious in the hall, were sleeping as careless as they. Hand in hand, they walked through the open door into the courtyard, where they could see the cart, Nello harnessed to it, and Hey, You standing by, Beppo's hand on his collar.

Angela's head was in a whirl. Was their escape to be as easy as this? After all her worrying about how they were to extricate themselves from between the lion's paws, had the lioness ordered the gates to be opened for them, and why? Not from the simple goodness of her heart, surely?

"Up with you into the cart, wife. You are ready, Beppo?"

"Aye, and you may tell me later how you performed this conjuring trick. Let us make all speed lest something untoward delay us.''

Gianni handed Angela his lute, but made no effort to climb into the cart himself. He seemed to be waiting for something.

Beppo called irritably from Hey, You's back. ''Get on with it, Gianni. This is no time to be standing about.''

True enough, and then the mystery was solved. Through the lighted doorway to the guardhouse and the tower a woman came, moving swiftly towards them. It was the lady Isabella! Her lustrous hair was down, she was wearing a plain black dress which fell just below her knees, all her jewels were gone, and her hair was tied back with a black ribbon so that she might be taken for one of the serving wenches roving the castle looking for satisfaction after an evening's entertainment.

In a voice as sweet as treacle, she addressed Gianni. ''Stay but a moment, pedlar. You owe me for allowing you to go free, and I would take my payment before you leave.''

So! This was what he had not told her. Angela set her teeth and stared at the lady as haughtily as she dare. To no avail. Her eyes were only for Gianni.

He turned to face her, his back to Angela. A flambeau set in a sconce in the tower's wall threw a flickering light over them. She saw that his fists were lightly clenched and that his whole body was at the ready, as though danger threatened. But when he looked full into the lady Isabella's smiling expectant face, Angela saw him relax, and when he spoke, his beautiful voice was as light and easy as a man's could be.

"Payment you shall have, lady. But surely you do not wish it here?"

Her laughter was honest and amused. "Why, pedlar. You surely do not expect me to receive you in my room. I want what you have for me now—and here. My husband is dead to the world—and I would not burn longer."

"But here—we are not private?" There was disbelief and a certain desperation in his voice.

"Why not, pedlar? Never tell me that you have not used a wall before to pleasure yourself. I have a mind to behave like the serving girl I appear to be."

Laughter still threaded through her voice, but Gianni knew that were he to deny her, her laughter would cease and condign punishment would follow. The lives of all three of them hung in the balance of the lady Isabella's pleasure. There was no help for it. In sight and sound of a woman whom he was coming to love and to respect, he would have to make love to another. He had counted on Isabella sending for him to go to her room—but she was maliciously intent on making him betray his wife in that wife's presence.

Now Angela was not his wife, but he could almost feel her distress as she listened to this exchange, could only imagine what she would feel when he began to pleasure the lady… Forget that.

He moved forward, said roughly, "As you will, lady," and seized her equally roughly. "You have chosen to have your pleasure this way, not I."

"Better and better," she told him blithely. "Your anger will fuel desire."

And there was truth in that, Gianni thought grimly, but not for him this time.

He dragged her to a niche in the wall, away from the light, out of Angela's view but not her hearing, and threw up Isabella's skirts. If the lady wished to play at being a peasant, then he would treat her as her kind treated peasants, roughly and without consideration. But, alas, that was what she wanted. And though, in the end, it might appear that he was raping her, she was raping him, for he had not the slightest feeling for her, and would never have touched her had not necessity demanded it.

His only prayer was that he would be able to satisfy her, for he knew as well as any man that it was not enough to will his body to arousal, for it had a will of its own.

And if he failed her, he had no doubt of the outcome. She would cast him off for not satisfying her and cry rape, and Guido's men would come a-running. The mere thought of that and what they would do to him before despatching him, and to Angela and Beppo afterwards, set him shuddering—and left his desire drooping still further.

Even her moans and sighs as his unwilling hands caressed her could not work the trick for him. The knowledge that Angela was watching him was like cold water thrown over him. Angela...! And there was his way out of this impasse. He could imagine that it was Angela pinned between him and the wall, that black-avised was fair, that black eyes were a clear and lucid grey, that lustrous black curls were blonde. To pretend that he held Angela in his arms revived his flagging self...

His last thought as he set about fulfilling the lady's wish was that either way, fail or succeed, he was dishonoured. But for once the Lord God was kind, even as he had at the last managed to coerce his unwilling body into submission. The sound of running feet, and a female voice trying to shout without shouting as it were, interrupted his desperate labours with the lady Isabella.

He heard her curse beneath her breath as her name floated towards them.

"My lady, my lady, come at once, the lord Guido is asking for you."

"Oh, Satan take the man and pitchfork him into hell where he belongs. I thought him dead to the world until morning, at least," exclaimed the lady Isabella, the milk of human kindness sadly lacking in every word she uttered. "Don't stop, pedlar."

"Oh, no, lady." Gianni stood back, trying to lace up his much darned hose again, and restore himself to respectability. "I have no mind to be cut off in my prime, and you may yet try him beyond reason."

By now Isabella's waiting woman was upon them. "Oh, lady, come at once. The lord Guido has asked for you, and will not be gainsaid. The drink hath made him wild." She turned her agitated face towards her mistress. "Delay not, lady, or worse will befall. He is raving." She was wringing her hands, and the tears were beginning to fall. What she dare not tell her mistress was that Guido had threatened her. "He thinks that you are with the pedlar, lady. Return, and prove him wrong."

Torn between wanting the pedlar to finish what he had started, and her fear of a man who was so capricious that he might forget his fear of her relatives, and punish her as he thought that she might deserve for her repeated faithlessness, the lady Isabella hesitated and was lost.

"Another time," she flung at Gianni, beginning to repair her own disarray, and then, with a flash of her old impudence as he walked away from her, "You have forgotten your limp, pedlar!"

He heard Angela's indrawn gasp at this taunt, and grinning, flung over his shoulder his final word for the lady Isabella, "Another night, lady, another time, and you might cure more than my limp for me."

She laughed at his impudence, showing white teeth, and called to the watching guard at the courtyard's gate, "Let them pass, man. They have entertained us enough for one visit."

Angela watched Gianni walk towards her, watched the lady Isabella run noiselessly back into the tower, her waiting woman behind her, still wringing her hands and wailing. No time to waste, though, for Gianni was in the cart, had taken up Nello's reins and was urging him on. Beppo was aboard Hey, You who was behaving well for once.

The yawning guard at the gate, who might have argued with them at their going, was too determined that once they were gone and the gate closed he would be able to sleep peacefully to stay them in their passing. Besides, the lady had given them permission to leave, and the Lord God knew, as did all the garrison, that in the end, the lord Guido always gave way to her—although one day he might not.

The pedlar's cart was being driven back down the road by which it had come, and Gianni's thwarted body was one vast ache for he had just reached the state required to pleasure the lady Isabella when her woman had arrived. Angela was quiet by his side, radiating fury. Between denied lust and his sense of shame at what he had been required to do to save them, he could not keep silent.

Once out of sight of the tower and when they were well on their way to the road he turned his head towards her, and ground out through gritted teeth, "Say it, then, Angela, say it! Do not sit there thinking it. The Lord God knows that I had no desire after such a hard day to please a female imp from hell such as Guido's lady!"

"Say you so! From the noise that you were both making I thought that pleasure was the one thing which both you and the lady were enjoying!"

"Body of God, Angela, I but tried to pleasure her to save us to get us out of Guido's clutches. It was my duty, woman!"

"Your duty, Gianni! God send us all such a pleasant duty! Sad it was that you were interrupted before pleasure became even more pleasurable."

Angela's voice was as acid as she could make it. Sitting in the cart, waiting for him to finish with the lady Isabella, consumed with jealousy, Angela had at last come to terms with the feelings which Gianni had aroused in her. The worst feeling of all was that she had but one wish: that it was she who was pinned against the wall, moaning beneath his ministrations, not Isabella. How dare he pretend that what he had been doing was his duty!

"Silent again," he snarled at her. "Admit that what I was prepared to do, much against my will, achieved what we wanted. Are we not on our way towards freedom, woman? It was a small price to pay, and you did not have to pay it."

"Freedom, Gianni?" Angela wanted to hurt him, yes, she did. Yes, she would. "Freedom? *I* am not free. You are free. Beppo is free, Nello is free, Hey, You is free, but I..." She was in full flow now, her voice soaring.

"Damnation and hell's torments, woman." Gianni's patience finally snapped. "Cease to nag me. There is no need to take the pretence of being my wife so far that everything which I do earns me non-stop reproach. Did you acquire that clacking tongue in Novera, only to save it to hit me over the head with it every time that I transgress your noble concepts of honour?"

"No, husband dear. I acquired it after I met you! When else? Know that I am your prisoner, that I have no notion of where we are, or where we are making for, or what you will do to me when we get to whatever destination you have in mind for me. And you prate to me of being free. By the Lord God..."

"By the Lord God, woman," began the incensed Gianni, to have Beppo, his patience exhausted, shout leather-lunged at both of them.

"By the Lord God, what has got into the pair of

you to make such a noise that Guido Orsini could hear you in his tower? Have you both taken leave of your senses? The lady has become a shrew, and you, Gianni, a fool. Save your breath, both of you. Let us get as far away from Guido's tower as we can, and then, why even then, you must cease your quarrelling. Survival is all.''

Chapter Nine

All that night Gianni's temper was no better than it had been on the day when he had quarrelled with Angela. They had stopped around dawn in order to sleep after they had travelled further at one time than ever before.

"Imperative that we get as far away from Guido as possible," Gianni had snarled at them earlier, after Beppo had taken one look at Angela's white face and suggested that they draw off the road and rest. "I am surprised at you, Beppo. We don't want Guido Orsini on our trail before we have put a good distance between him and us. We will sleep when we can see Burani, and not before."

Beppo held him to that, even though they were in sight of Burani's towers and its cathedral earlier than they had expected. They travelled further off the road than they normally did, and at last Angela could lie down. But not to sleep.

All that had passed during the last twenty-four hours ran through her head. She had thought herself hardened to her tribulations, but Gianni's cavorting with the lady Isabella, as she thought of it, had hurt her more than she could have believed possible. Which was stupid, because he was nothing to her as she was nothing to him, so how could she conceivably see his behaviour as treachery?

In the middle of her tossing and turning, for Angela found that it was difficult to sleep in broad daylight, she became aware that someone was sitting beside her and had taken her hot hand in his. It was Gianni. She brushed her hair out of her eyes, looked up at him and snapped, "Yes, what is it, Gianni? Has Guido found us—or his lady?"

The moment that the words flew out she regretted them, for he looked even more tired than she felt. As she finished speaking, he closed his brilliant blue eyes. If she had had a hard day yesterday, then he had a harder, and needed his rest.

He opened his eyes again, looked down at her, and amazingly, smiled. "Not long ago," he told her, "you comforted me at night when I was restless. I heard you cry out just now, and I thought that it was my turn to supply comfort. Send me away if I am wrong."

His voice was so kind that Angela wanted to cry. She turned her head away as the tears forced themselves out of the corner of her eyes, however much she willed them to stop.

He put out one of the shapely hands which Isabella Orsini had admired, turned her face towards him and began to speak earnestly to her. "Look at me, Angela. I know why you are unhappy and cannot sleep, and I know that it is my fault, doubly so, I admit. Imprimis, because in your presence I had to do something which should only be performed with love and in private, and I was compelled to perform in hate and publicly, before you. Secundus, afterwards in my distress, I was vilely rude to you, brutally ignoring *your* distress.

"For Secundus, I beg forgiveness. But for Imprimis, I do not. I only ask you to remember what we so recently discussed. That one might have to make decisions on the spur of the moment as to whether one should commit a wrong in order to achieve a right, and I told you how difficult it was to make such a decision. Rightly or wrongly, last night I agreed to what Isabella Orsini demanded of me in order to gain our freedom and to preserve you from rape by Guido—for that is what he intended. I am not proud of what I did, or so nearly did, but neither did I commit an act for which you, or any other, ought to reproach me. You see how difficult it is to make these important decisions in the heat of daily living, however easy it may seem when one is sitting comfortably in a garden or a study.

"Like you, I am finding sleep difficult, but if you can bring yourself to forgive what ought to be forgiven, and to understand why I acted as I did with Isabella, why then, perhaps we may both be able to sleep," and he kissed the hand which he was holding.

Angela did not pull it away. She let the tears fall freely now. He put out his other hand, wiped her cheek, then put his hand to his mouth and licked the tears away.

"Do not cry, sweeting. None of this is your fault."

"Oh, yes," she choked, "it is. I was cruel. I did not think of your feelings. Only of my own."

"Then we are quits, dear child, for when we quarrelled afterwards, I did not consider how outraged you must have felt, delicately reared as you have been. I thought only of my own shame, and I wanted to strike all the world in the face—instead, the face which I struck was yours."

He was being so magnanimous that the least she could do was not cry over him. "I forgive you both Imprimis and Secundus," she whispered, and now she was kissing *his* hand. "Quits, Ser Gianni, and let us sleep."

He nodded his head. "With this proviso, that I stay with you until sleep claims you, so that I may earn my own." When she opened her mouth to deny him, he shook his tired head at her, and said simply, "Do not argue with me. I am bone weary."

So Angela lay down and, as he had promised, sleep claimed her. When she awoke towards noon she found him lying beside her on the hard earth, still asleep, his hand held out towards her. Rising, she was careful not to disturb him, and when Beppo, who had been preparing a light meal for them came towards them to wake him, she put her fingers on her lips and shook her head at him.

"He is so tired, let him sleep." Beppo did not argue with her.

But when he awoke he was demanding, domineering Gianni again, and their early morning talk might never have taken place. He broke his fast impatiently, as though the food irked him, and said, before Angela and Beppo had time to finish their repast, "It is urgent that we talk. I have decided that we must change our plans and change them drastically. For one reason and another, we have drawn more attention than I had hoped." He paused, and Angela's glance at him was a worried one. What he said next added to her worries.

"Beppo knows that I had alternate plans prepared in case things went ill. It would be wise, I think, to implement them now." He walked over to the cart and began to haul out of it some of the packs which were stowed towards the back of it, and pull them open.

"From being three, we must become two, plus any servants whom we shall hire in Burani, in order to deceive any who might suddenly ask themselves who Gianni of the roads, his blonde doxy and his partner, truly are." He began to extract from the first pack a set of rich clothing which included a man's beautiful gold and emerald hose, and an emerald tunic to go with them, together with a fine linen shirt, lace edged around the collar. An emerald and gold houppelande with ampler skirts than was common completed the ensemble. Gianni followed this by fishing out of a second pack another set of men's clothing, darker and more sombre in nature, black with silver trimmings. Conical black hats and leather boots followed.

Gianni shook the beautiful clothing briskly, so that the creases began to fall out of it. He tossed the black suit at Beppo, bade him go to a pool nearby, wash himself, find shelter and then change into the suit. He plainly intended the glorious emerald suit for himself. With some amusement he watched Angela look down at her shabby brown dress, her bare legs and her crude peasant's sandals; an unlikely outfit, she thought ruefully, for a woman to wear who was travelling with such a pair of peacocks.

She was about to say so when Gianni forestalled her. "Never fear!" he told her gravely. "A good general is known by his attention to detail. Look!" With a conjuror's flourish he drew from the second parcel a dress, which whilst not so magnificent as the one which Isabella Orsini had worn, was still sufficiently handsome as to show that its wearer was richer than the common run. It was made of a deep blue velvet, with silver trimmings, sturdy enough for its owner to wear while travelling. A pair of elegant black leather shoes followed and a fine linen chemise to wear under it.

Angela gave a little gasp at the sight. She had almost forgotten that such beautiful things existed.

"I had no idea of what you really looked like, my lady," he told her suavely, "but I knew that such a lovely thing would not only suit you, but please any woman with a claim to beauty. When Beppo returns you must do as he has done, and transform yourself into someone, who, if she is not quite the lady of Novera, is sufficiently wealthy as to wear this dress with pride. And after that I shall turn myself into your husband, a rich merchant. And after *that*, our little party will split up. Beppo will return alone to…his home, and you and I will travel on together, looking quite unlike Gianni of the roads and his doxy.''

''But how shall we pretend to be rich, and be able to hire servants to accompany us, seeing that all the money we have is that which we have gained from your peddling and our singing and dancing on the way?''

Gianni's smile was a naughty and a knowing one. He placed his finger by his nose in a vulgar gesture which again reminded Angela of sinful servants at Novera. ''Now there, Angela, I have to confess that I have not told you the entire truth about our financial standing. The less you knew, the less you could give away. I had no knowledge of how discreet you could be, so I thought it best to err on the side of caution. But here,'' he took from its hiding place in the cart a leather pouch with a drawstring, opened it, and began to pour gold ducats from it into his hand, ''here, as you may plainly see, we have more than enough to enable us to pass as wealthy merchants.''

Angela turned crimson and then pale. Was there no end to his deceits? ''We have been scrimping and saving and eating poor food this last ten days, and all the time we were carrying a fortune with us…'' she exclaimed. She thought of how she had sung until she was tired, in the belief that all they had was what they earned. ''Oh…! You have done nothing but lie to me since we first met.''

''Dear girl,'' said Gianni gently. ''Had you known the truth, you would not have been as convincing a poor peasant as you appeared to be. We could not be both pedlars and rich as well. And this store was a reserve, to be called on only if needed. Now it is needed, and we shall still have to be careful, until we reach Burani, though not as careful as we have been. Ah, Beppo, you look uncommonly respectable, so respectable that I hardly know you."

And that was true enough. Angela stared at the burly bourgeois who had just emerged from a thicket and who had replaced the scruffy and disreputable looking peasant who had been riding Hey, You. She could not believe that he was the same man and so she told him. "And you cannot ride Hey, You looking like that! It would not be proper."

"No, indeed," agreed Gianni. "We also need to dress the cart up, and say that we are riding in it because recently you have been too frail to go on horseback. Beppo can hide in the back until we are safely inside Burani. There he will leave us, buy himself a horse, hire a servant and return home by another route from the one which we shall be taking.

"Who will think that the merchant Ottone Rinieri and his wife Emilia are Gianni of the roads and his doxy, Angela? Now be off with you, my child, assume your new clothes and be quick about it for I am eager to wash myself and wear some clean linen for a change."

Oh, he was intolerable, calling her child and sweeting, and ordering her about as though she were truly some wench he had picked from the hedge rows, instead of the lady of Novera whom he was manipulating for his own ends. What had happened to the kind man who had comforted her earlier in the day? Then commonsense told her as she washed herself in the little pool, dried herself on the towel which Gianni had given her, and put on her new dress, that he was doing the thinking and planning for them all. More than that, he had rescued her, and was still rescuing her from Gentile's dreadful clutches—to say nothing of those of Guido Orsini.

Angela had forgotten how handsome he really was until she saw him clean again and in his beautiful clothing. Like Beppo—who was now Messer Ettore Manfredi—and herself, he was quite transformed. All in all, they formed a handsome trio, very different from the ragged pedlar and his company.

"I shall forget who I am supposed to be," she announced as she paraded round the cart which Gianni and Beppo were beautifying, trying to get used to being a lady in exquisite clothing again. "After all, this is the third name I shall have answered to in less than a month, and not one of them is Montefiore, which I had expected to be addressed as by now!"

And then she said, a little anxiously, "What are we going to do with Hey, You? We are not going to abandon the poor creature, I hope."

"Oh, we shall sell him and put the money towards buying us a pack horse. I am afraid that we shall have to sell Nello as well, faithful though he has been, and buy a good horse to pull the cart, for I fear that you must be a delicate ailing creature, Emilia. Do you think that you can assume a die-away manner and be petulantly demanding of your put-upon husband?"

Angela thought poorly of this as a proposition, and grumbled at him. "I suppose it would be all the same if I said that I preferred to be a haughty creature like the lady Isabella, I should still have to do your bidding. Are you sure that this pantomime is really necessary?" And then she brightened a little. "Although I must say that I prefer wearing handsome and clean clothes after the dirty rags I have been crossing Verdato in. I thought that we should have been safely out of it by now."

"Burani is the last large town in Verdato, and we shall soon be across the border, but even then we shall not be quite safe. Gentile makes little of borders. Now get into the cart, Signora Emilia, and prepare to be demanding—that should surely please you."

But his voice was kind again and he was only teasing her, not cruelly mocking her. In his manner to her he had almost reverted to the man he had been in the night. So it was in amity and in some state, despite the poorness of their horse, and the ambling mule, happily free of his burden, that they drove towards Burani, Beppo hidden in the back of the cart.

What Marina, Angela and now Emilia did not know was what Beppo had said privately to Gianni before he had been hidden in the cart. "You will be kind to her, will you not? She is a brave lass, not at all what we had expected."

"Now what do you take me for, Marco? Of course I shall be kind to her. I have always been kind to her, have I not? But I have also to get her safely away, and to do that I need to have her obey me unquestioningly.''

Beppo knew that his lord was being wilful, he also knew that he could speak to him freely without restraint. ''I know that you have expectations of others which they do not always live up to, and that she is desperate to prove that she is not overcome by what has happened to her. I think that it might be a good idea to tell her the truth, and that you might regret it if you do not.''

Gianni took refuge in ambiguity, a favourite trick of his when challenged. ''The truth, Marco, Beppo, Ettore? Do you know what the truth is?''

Beppo's answer was sturdy. ''Yes, I do, but I sometimes fear that you do not. There is such a thing as being too clever. You would do well to remember that. Be kind as well as clever, and the Lord God will reward you.''

Gianni's answer was a shrug. ''I bid you farewell and good luck on your journey home. God grant that it may not be long before we meet again.'' He embraced his friend and suddenly grave, held him at arms length, looking deep into his eyes. ''Trust me, Marco, my faithful friend. I have never let you, or any man or woman down yet, and I do not intend to start now.''

''But you have never been in these circumstances before, nor with such a lady as that of Novera. She has proved to be true gold, never forget that. *Addio*, and God be with you, too.''

It was all the farewell which they could have. For once the merchant Ottone Rinieri and his wife Emilia had passed the guards at Burani's gates and had brought their cart to a halt before Burani's best inn, Beppo, now Ettore Manfredi, slipped silently and unobtrusively away, leaving them to their fate.

Burani was bigger than either Verdato or Ostuna, and richer. Had Emilia the ordering of it she would have chosen it for her headquarters, and not Verdato as Gentile had done, and so she told Ottone.

"My thoughts, too. But he conquered Verdato first, and Burani later, and by then he had made Verdato his capital. But it cannot hold a candle to Burani. Its cathedral is a gem, and its merchants are richer than those of Verdato—but then, they do not have Gentile perpetually on their back."

That was true enough, and once again Ottone had demonstrated his knowledge and grasp of the ways of the great world where fortunes and decisions were made. He must, Emilia thought, have been a successful *condottiero* if his military skill had matched his political and economic understanding. She wondered why she had not heard of him before, for she was sure that the name of Niccolo da Stresa had never been mentioned by her uncle.

Oh, but, she reproached herself, why did she assume that that was his real name? He seemed to shed identities and change names more often than he changed his clothes, and now he had her doing it, too. They drove down Burani's main street to a great square. Just off the square was the street where the goldsmiths and bankers had their headquarters, and it was thither that they were bound. To replenish their exchequer, Ottone said.

He stopped the cart to ask to be directed to the offices of the goldsmith, Giuseppe Farfalla, which were, they found, housed in a noble building. Once inside they were conducted to an airy room, where Ottone produced a note of hand from the Medici bank in Florence which had the goldsmith who was, as was common in smaller towns, also a banker, bowing and smirking at him. And where had Ottone got the note of hand from? Not honestly, Emilia was sure.

When told that they had planned to stay at an inn, the goldsmith flung an arm around Ottone's gilded shoulders and insisted that they lodge with him.

"But for one night only," Ottone insisted. "We must be on our way. My wife is delicate—you understand?" He placed his finger by his nose again, and winked.

Oh, the devil! He means that I am with child! Whatever next! But all that the bursting Emilia could do was what Marina and Angela had done, obey him by lowering her eyes, simpering, and waving the fan which Ottone had taken from one of the pedlar's packs in the cart and given to her.

"I understand." Giuseppe winked back, adding, "Lady, it will be my pleasure and my wife's to see that the food which we give you will not distress a delicate stomach."

Slops! They were going to feed her on slops, and here she had been congratulating herself that she might be about to eat a decent meal again. No hope of that with Ottone's fertile brain spreading lies in all directions.

"Now why did you tell him that?" she exclaimed crossly when they were in the elegantly appointed bedroom which Giuseppe had given to them. "Now I shall have nothing to eat but thin gruel, milk, and…slops. Why could I not have had a damaged ankle and a limp—like the one which you have lost—then they would have forced food on me to assist my recovery!"

"Dearest wife," said Ottone smoothly, bending down to kiss her. "Think how useful and disarming a breeding woman is. Besides, you were plainly not breeding at Guido's tower, or Ostuna or the village, and a rich merchant with a sickly wife, and several servants bears little resemblance to Gianni of the roads and his tattered train."

"Why does everything you say sound so right and proper and—clever—whilst everything I say sounds the contrary." Then, brightening a little, Emilia added, "I suppose it is because I am not so lost in deceit and trickery as you are, Messer Ottone. Tell me, what are you truly like? Is there someone real hidden beneath your many disguises? Or do you change as the wind changes, so that no-one ever knows who exactly you are?"

She had nonplussed him at last. He turned his back on her to stride to the window to stand staring out of it at the goldsmith's garden, as tidy and orderly as he was.

He swung round again to face her, and if she had distressed him, there was no sign of it on his face.

On the contrary, it was as smooth as a calm sea and about as readable. But she thought that somehow she had touched a nerve in him, though he would never confess to it.

"Alas," he told her, his voice as sweetly reasonable as he could make it. "My knowledge of the world is so much greater than yours that you must respect it. Later, when we know each other a little better and are not living in constant danger of death, or worse, then we may debate matters more fully, but for the present I must ask you to do as I bid without question. Safer so."

"As Master Ottone wishes." Emilia swept him a great curtsey, bowing her head to lift it to find him gazing at her with smiling approval.

"Trickery and deceit," he said softly. "Why, I must commend you as an apt pupil. You are already Ottone's consort to the very life, and Marina and Angela are long gone and forgotten. Shall I reproach you for the ease with which you change yourself—or admire you?"

Yes, he had an answer for everything. And, as usual, he was right. In the short time since she had met him, and had begun to live a life of danger on the roads, she had begun to change, and now she did not know who she was—other than that in a little while she must be in the goldsmith's parlour pretending to be two months pregnant, the merchant's ailing wife!

She looked around the bedroom, dominated as it was by a great carved and gilded bed. Its dimensions were noble but, alas, she would have to share it with him. There was a day bed before the window, but she suspected dismally that she would not be able to persuade him to sleep on it—and she was right.

"Oh, no," he told her. "We are a loving husband and wife. But be reasonable, sweeting, the bed is large and we may put the bolster between us."

"But I am not your wife," Emilia wailed, "nor your sweeting either, and if you will not sleep on the day bed, then I shall."

To no avail. He took her by the arm, and pulled her to him to hold her tight against him, blue eyes bright and glittering. "And would you not wish to pretend that we are truly husband and wife—for one night only? No-one need ever know."

Oh, he was the most cunning and tempting devil from Messer Dante's deepest hell, the vile Inferno itself! To lie in the cradle of his arms, to feel the strength of his shapely body, to be tempted by the very scent of him—clean Ottone, as handsome as the devil himself—was torture for a poor girl who wished to remain virtuous. How easy it would be to turn in his arms to offer him her lips—and everything that was hers. Oh, Mary Mother help me, for I not only love him, but I desire him, and I never knew before that love and lust are so intermingled. My knees are so weak so that he may yet take me, even without my willing it.

But that was a lie. She must not, could not yield to him. For was she not the virtuous lady of Novera who was promised to the lord Leonardo di Montefiore in marriage? It was her duty to marry that lord, and she could not go to him from the bed of a handsome fly-by-night mercenary soldier—who was offering her nothing but that bed.

Before propinquity and opportunity could do their dreadful work on her so that she would lie beneath him without willing it, but only because her will was as weak as her body, Emilia tore herself away from him, and retreated to the far wall of the bedchamber, trembling violently.

She put up a hand before her as though to conjure him away. "No! No!" she exclaimed. "I will not be your doxy, clean or dirty. I am the lady of Novera and I must do my duty and marry the lord Leonardo. Tempt me not."

Ottone never moved. He stood impassive before her, except for those speaking eyes. At last he said, "But you feel nothing for him, Emilia. Confess, you do feel for me what you ought to feel for him, for I could tell as you lay trembling in my arms just now that what I wanted, you wanted, too."

"And if I did?" she spat at him. "Honour forbids. Duty forbids. By all the Bordonis, living or dead, who kept their honour intact then I, too, must keep mine intact. *Amor vincit omnia*, the poets say: love conquers all, but that is not true: for it cannot conquer my honour or my duty." And shuddering from the very strength needed to refuse him, she turned away from him.

She did not see the strange look which crossed Ottone's face as she uttered her proud declaration. Nor did she see him close his eyes and clench his fists.

"Enough," he said at last, to her back. "I will sleep on the day bed if that is what you wish."

"I do not wish it." Her voice was as melancholy as a dying wind. "I would wish quite otherwise, but my wishes do not count against what I owe not only to Leonardo di Montefiore, but to what the Lord God demands of me."

She heard him leave the room and then, once his footsteps had died away, Emilia threw herself on the bed and began to cry for what could never be.

In the end they stayed in Burani for two nights. To rest and recover, and to allay any suspicions which their eagerness to be gone immediately might create. Ailing she might be, but under the pretence of wishing for the Lord God's blessing, Messer Ottone's wife Emilia visited the cathedral which, like Burani itself, was smaller than Florence's Duomo, though larger than Gentile's church in Verdato which pretended to be a cathedral.

Alas, she could not go to confession, for she dare not tell the priest the truth of her situation. But she could stand anonymously among the other men and women and pray to Almighty God to get her safe home again—only she was becoming a little confused as to where home was.

Novera and Montefiore both seemed so far away. The place which she knew, and the place which she did not know, both lacked the same thing. And, monstrously, that would be the presence of the man who had come to loom so large in her life that it seemed as though she had always known him. Could it be that home was where he was, and nowhere else? Could she bear to be alone with him, now that he knew she loved him?

And how and why had she come to fall in love with a man of deceits, who was carrying her to God knows where, and of whom she knew nothing, except that she loved him?

Emilia would have liked to stay longer in Burani and, perhaps one day when her flight was safely over, it was possible that she might visit it again, and admire its elegancies with a lighter heart. A river ran through it and villas and summerhouses had been built on its banks: it seemed like a miniature of Florence itself, possessing all of that city's civilised grace.

Their host was a man of parts with a small library of beautiful books: it was a pleasure for Emilia to renew her acquaintance with Messer Dante on the afternoon when the goldsmith took Ottone to the stables where he sold Nello and Hey, You and bought a more powerful horse to pull their cart.

He also hired two large men, Pasquale and Roberto Albini, the sons of a saddler who was a neighbour of the goldsmith. They did a good business by hiring themselves as guards and escorts to travellers out of Burani and into the neighbouring duchy of Montefiore. Occasionally they travelled as far as Milan, to the north of Montefiore's capital, and then hired themselves out again to escort another train back to Burani.

"Little chance that they will betray us, as wandering ex-soldiers offering themselves for hire might do,'' confided Ottone to Emilia before they made their farewells to the goldsmith and set off on the road which led into Montefiore, and to relative safety. They would not be completely safe until they were near to the city from which the duchy took its name. Whether he intended to visit the city, or where they were ultimately bound for, Emilia did not know. They were moving into lands of which she knew little, far from the familiar names of the territory around Novera.

Travelling as the merchant Rinieri and his small company was very unlike travelling as Gianni and his wife. Astonishingly, although she enjoyed the good food and the relative comfort of the inns and farmhouses where they stayed, Emilia found herself missing the friendly and easy life of the road. She would have thought when Ottone had first captured her that she would have been only too glad to live in relative comfort again, and without ever-present danger dogging their footsteps, but no. She missed Nello and Hey, You and even the silent Beppo, and the rabbit he cooked for them. Their escorts were friendly enough, but in a distant way. Inn landlords bowed and scraped to them, offered them their best fare, but the fun of country living, as well as its hardships had disappeared.

She said as much to Ottone, who had given her a slightly twisted smile: he had been a little distant with her ever since the scene in the bedchamber, and she was sorry for it, for she also missed his affectionate teasing.

''You would not have liked it in winter,'' he told

her, "but for a time, especially in the summer, it has its attractions. And I believe that you enjoyed shedding the responsibilities you carried in your old life." He was always circumspect in what he said to her in case their escorts overheard anything incriminating, and he taught Emilia to be the same.

No doubt he was right about their old life, and why she had enjoyed travelling the roads as poor Angela so much.

"And do not think that we are safe yet," he told her. "I hope that we are, but there are other dangers on our journey besides those which Gentile might create for us. I doubt that anyone will make the connection between us and a poor pedlar, but we must be careful still."

The habit of years ingrained in Ottone made caution a second nature with him, and he was right to be careful. They were three days out of Burani and travelling steadily away from Verdato when Gentile and Braccio degli Uberti paid Guido Orsini a visit.

Guido was someone of whom Gentile made use, and the reverse was true. Furious that Marina Bordoni and her mysterious captor had vanished into thin air, Gentile was still quartering Verdato and its borders when he decided that Guido might have something to tell him.

They sat at table together after a private feast where little had been drunk. Both men wanted their wits about them when dealing with the other. Gentile had Braccio with him. He had demoted Cecco after his failure to trace Marina, and had turned him away. Cecco's fall was Braccio's opportunity and he was determined to make the most of it. His leading sergeant sat at table, too, but so far had had little to say. That was not in his duties. He was there to listen and to learn.

Guido had no adviser with him but the lady Isabella. Woman she might be, but she was as shrewd and as wild as a mountain cat and saw possibilities hidden from Guido's duller sight. If Gentile was surprised by her presence he did not say so, which was fortunate. They had been talking for some little time, or rather Gentile had, of the steps which he had taken to find Marina.

"And all to no avail," he finally grumbled. "It is as though they all vanished into thin air when once they were out of Verdato."

Isabella had been staring at the sergeant, a comely man, who reminded her a little of Gianni of the roads, although he was cleaner.

"This wench of yours, this lady of Novera. What was her seeming?"

Bad enough that the woman should sit in their councils, but even worse that she should question him. Nevertheless to keep Guido quiet, he answered her.

"A blonde woman, tall. Haughty in manner: a very pillar of virtue. Thinks too much of herself. Once seen, hard to forget."

"A beauty?"

"Aye, very much so."

"And the man who captured her. Of what like was he?"

"Were you not heeding us, lady?" Gentile was

pleased to have the opportunity to rebuke her. "You heard us say that we never saw his face. That he wore an old fashioned helm with a nasal."

Isabella's smile was as poisonously sweet as she was. "Aye, I heard you, lord of Verdato. But what else of him? Tall, short, broad shouldered, good long legs, bandy legs, a pot belly? Lithe in his actions, or clumsy? Or were you all so stricken that you saw naught of him?"

For a moment there was silence. Gentile had seen little of Marina's captor, being held by him in such a way that all he saw was the roof of the church until he was thrown headlong before the church's altar. Braccio had been away with a troop putting down a village which was slow in paying its taxes. Only the sergeant, who had previously been Cecco's, had enjoyed a good view of the man, and into the silence he said so.

"Tall, lady, well shaped, good shoulders, long, powerful legs and thighs, and lithe, like a wild cat. No belly, and malignant."

His reward was a dazzling smile from the lady which had him uncomfortable for reasons which he would not have liked to confess to his superiors. "So, your sergeant is observant, Gentile. Now, has it not occurred to you that the reason why you could not discover the lady's abductor and his troop was because there was no troop, once Verdato had been left behind?"

"No troop!" exclaimed the three from Verdato. "But his troop was seen, a goodly one with seasoned soldiery."

"Aye, but your man is cunning. Witness how he brought off his coup. Suppose he disposed of his troop, and disguised himself and the lady, what then? He has you running around Italy's roads and forests looking for quite the wrong thing."

Guido began to laugh. "I should make you my battle tactician, wife. You are as cunning as the devil himself. Why not, eh? You had not considered that, Gentile?"

Gentile began to look downcast. Braccio said nothing. His moment of embarrassment was yet to come.

"This is all very fine, lady, but where does it lead us?"

"This." Isabella joined her husband in his laughter. "A tall blonde woman, and a large and well built man with the cheek and conceit of the devil, as lithe as a wildcat. Where met we with such lately, husband?"

"Why, where, lady?" Guido was staring at her. Cleverness was all very well, but Isabella was too often reckless with her suppositions—on the other hand, she was also frequently right in them.

"Where but here? The pedlar you brought in. Tall and well built, and lithe as a wild cat. Remember the tumbling act he and his man performed? He sang for us, too."

"But he had a limp. Had your man a limp?" And Guido addressed the sergeant who shook his head.

"No limp, on my life."

"Neither had the pedlar, as I have reason to know," stated Isabella triumphantly. "It was a pretence, a deceit. And the blonde woman with him, for whom my husband had a fancy. He thought her a beauty beneath the dirt.'' She thought a moment. ''Wait, he had the remains of scar on his face. Someone had struck him with a whip recently. Had your man such?''

There was a dreadful silence.

Braccio's sergeant said faintly, ''By the Lord God, the pedlar at Ostuna, three days out of Verdato. Remember, Lord Braccio, the one you struck in the face after he had said that he had seen naught on the roads. If he were the man who took the lady and she travelled with him in his cart, they would reach Ostuna at about that time if they had started from Verdato and tarried at the village of Perrone... The lady is right—and that is why they disappeared. They didn't...''

''They turned into the pedlar, his doxy and attendant,'' almost sang Isabella. ''Body of God, he was a man to remember, not much like a pedlar if you looked closely at him. And he sang a good song.''

Gentile was incandescent with rage. ''If I catch him he'll sing such a song as would fetch the devils out of hell! And you had him in your hands, and the woman too, and you let them go!'' He was rounding on Braccio whose face was as white as the cloth on the table before them. ''God's teeth, have I but exchanged one fool for another?''

''Lord, how was I to know? And are we sure that this was the same man who took the lady...?''

''You have but one chance to save your skin, dolt, and that is to go after them, and bring them here. I'll warrant the lord Guido and I will make such mince-meat of him that no part of him will be left to defile the ground between earth and sky if he is the fellow who took my bride from me.''

Now he rounded on Guido. ''And why did *you* let them go? Seeing that you had a fancy for the wench yourself. But if your lady is right, she was no wench—only in seeming—although I find it hard to believe that such a haughty piece could pretend to be a peasant's trull!''

Isabella, delighted to prove once more what fools men were, put her oar in again. ''Oh, she did a merry dance before us all, your virtuous and haughty lady, and she and the pedlar were lovers if all the looks they cast on one another could be believed.''

Guido, ignoring her spite, snarled back at Gentile. ''No need to reproach me. The lady Isabella sent him away to keep the wench from me, though I have half a mind that she had the pedlar to herself before he left.'' He began to laugh helplessly, for the true joke was on Gentile, not on him.

''We were all fools together, were we not? The richest heiress loose in Italy, and my dear Isabella told her that she was a dirty doxy and she never turned a hair!'' He began to weep with laughter. ''Why, I could almost congratulate her for her impudence, and the man, too, if I didn't wish to rack him until the trickery oozed out of him with his life.''

But Gentile wanted to hear no more. He was bellowing for Braccio and the sergeant to saddle up, and take the road into Montefiore to catch the bastard who had made such a laughing stock of them all.

Chapter Ten

At much the same time that Guido and Gentile were conferring, Ugo Bordoni and his entourage arrived in the city of Montefiore. Even age and infirmity could not prevent Ugo from journeying there to discover what might be done to recover his missing niece. She had disappeared so completely that it was almost as though some magician had taken her, and was hiding her somewhere far from the haunts of men. All Italy was slowly learning that Marina Bordoni had been snatched away at the very moment when her forced marriage to Gentile da Cortona was about to take place, and gossip and speculation were rife.

Ugo had travelled at great speed from Novera, haste post haste, as the phrase had it, and had brought with him a large troop of his most trusted men-at-arms. It was his belief that together he and the Duke should be able to track down whoever it was who had stolen the heiress of Novera away.

Duke Theodore di Montefiore met him at the very

doorway of his palace in order to demonstrate to the utmost his consideration and respect for his visitor, once his companion in arms. He was in his late fifties, had been handsome in youth, and was still a man at whom people looked twice. His dark hair was now silver, but the power and nobility of his countenance made his age seem of little consequence.

"My poor old friend," he murmured, embracing Ugo. "I understand why you have come, but at your age, was it wise? I have this very morning sent another large troop on its way to Verdato to scour the countryside for your niece. They have my most express orders to stop and question all travellers, even those who show no resemblance to your niece and her captor."

"My duty, it is my duty," returned Ugo heavily. "I was wrong to palter when Gentile first took her, and I have paid for it. I should have sent an army after her to compel him to return her, but I could not believe that he would force her into marriage. And then, when he did, that another should snatch her away…"

"True, I had thought such adventures at an end." Duke Theodore was leading him into his palace, a superb building in the new classical style, filled with treasures gathered from all over Italy. Montefiore was on a par with Florence and Milan so far as power and wealth were concerned, and in marrying Marina to the Duke's son, Ugo knew that he was assuring not only her future, but that of Novera's. Like many rulers of Italy's smaller states he was coming to understand that power, in future, was going to lie with the larger ones. If a larger state was going to annex Novera, then better that it should be a benevolent one such as the Montefiores ruled, rather than a greedy one like Florence or Milan.

Later, after he had been taken to his apartments and had rested for a little time, Ugo and Duke Theodore sat down to dinner in a room distinguished by its civilised nature. It was as far removed from the crudities of Verdato and Guido Orsini's eyrie as the mind could conceive. The food was as splendid as the dishes on which it was served. There were no manchets of bread on which to put the food at the Duke's table, but plates of gold and silver, and forks were there for all. Fingers were for barbarians.

To Ugo's surprise, neither the Duke's son, Leonardo, nor his own wife, Caterina, were present at their meal. The Duke explained that his wife was an invalid who kept to her room. Her one wish in life, he said, was to see her son happily married. As for Leonardo, whom Ugo had hoped to meet, the Duke apologised for his absence, too, and his answer pleased Ugo. "Yes, I am sorry that my son is not here to greet you," he explained, "but on hearing the news of her abduction he took a troop with him into Verdato to try to find and rescue his bride."

"Good! It is what I should have expected of him from all you had said in his favour in Florence." Ugo drank his wine with a little more heart. "With your two troops as well as my own men quartering the countryside and questioning all travellers, we should have no difficulty in tracking down the monster who has snatched my poor niece away. Between us all, finding her should not be over difficult.''

For the first time since the dreadful news of Marina's capture by Gentile had been brought to him, Ugo began to feel hope.

The Duke, however, was not so sanguine. ''True,'' he said gently, ''but we must not forget that Gentile will be seeking her, as well as any other rogue *condottiero* who might see an advantage in capturing her. We must hope that Fortune smiles on us for a change, and not on them. Drink to it, my old friend. The red wine will put heart into you.''

Quite unaware that they were now being sought by no less than five small armies, all intent on capturing them, Ottone and Emilia were making their way across country. They were travelling at a faster pace than when they had been pedlars, and in far greater state and comfort.

But not in greater happiness.

Ever since their encounter in the bedroom of the goldsmith Giuseppe Farfalla, they had been constrained with one another. For the first time Emilia, the lesser experienced of the two, knew what Messer Giovanni Boccaccio had meant in his *Decameron* when he had spoken of lovers burning for one another. Oh, yes, she burned for Ottone, no doubt of that at all. She hardly dared to touch him, and yet touch they must, for they must not make their two bodyguards suspicious.

But torture it was for both of them to bill and coo at one another, to touch, to embrace discreetly, to pretend that they were ailing wife and loving husband. Because she was ailing, their guards were not suspicious when Messer Ottone and his wife lay apart—it was no more than was to be expected of a husband whose wife might lose their first child if they were not careful.

So, at night they burned separately. They slept apart from one another on blankets on the hard earth on those nights when they had not been fortunate enough to find an inn or a farmhouse with spare beds on their route towards safety.

"A farmhouse is better than an inn," Ottone explained to Emilia, "for few inns are as clean and comfortable as the two we lodged in earlier, and farmer's wives are houseproud."

Once Emilia would have stared haughtily at him and, remembering that in the first inn they had lodged at they had slept in the stables, she would have replied tartly that he had a peculiar notion of cleanliness and comfort. But her experiences had changed her, and she had become aware of the straitened conditions in which most of the children of the Lord God lived.

For the very poor whom she saw in the fields and the villages, in their ragged clothes, lived in huts and hovels of wattle and daub, and ate the hard crust of poverty. Even in her life as a pedlar's wife she had never descended into such depths as those lived in whom she daily passed.

They were sitting at dusk before a fire, and, as always, not far from water when he told her this. The life of the forest was all around them. In her wanderings Emilia had discovered that the birdsong of the night was different from that of the day.

"Where are you taking me?" she asked him abruptly. "And how far away are we from your destination?" She purposely did not say *our* destination.

Ottone lay back lazily, his hands behind his head. "You will find out soon enough, sweeting," he told her.

Sweeting again! He had not called her that since the fatal night in Burani. And if she were not mistaken the look on his face resembled the one he had worn that night, not the cold one of the few days since they had left Burani. Here, in the half-dark, almost alone, for their two watchdogs were seated at some little distance and could not overhear what they were saying, the old intimacy of the days when they had been pedlar and supposed wife, had returned.

The dim light softened his face, made him seem younger. She could imagine what he had looked like when he was a boy. Where had he been? What had he been doing when she had been a young maiden learning to be the lady of Novera? Ah, sweet Jesus, how handsome he was, and how much she now understood what Messer Boccaccio had been writing of in that book which Lucia had not wanted her to read, but of which her uncle had said roughly, earlier that year, "Let be, it is time that she grew up. Let Messer Boccaccio educate her a little."

But it was not Boccaccio who had educated her but Niccolo da Stresa, also Gianni and Ottone, who was looking at her with such sweet desire in his beautiful eyes, and with such a softening of his usually hard mouth that the lady Marina, also Angela and Emilia, felt her very joints loosen at the sight.

To distract her wandering and sinful mind, she asked him, as impersonally as she could, "You know everything about my life, Messer Ottone, for it was an open book, but I know nothing of yours. Of your goodness, tell me a little of it, for I have a desire to know something of the man who has carried me off."

"Now what, dear wife, would you like to know? That I was a wild boy, naughty as boys usually are? That my father despaired a little of me at one time, since I was so unlike my elder brother, who was a very paladin of all the virtues—which I never was, though I suppose that I do not need to tell you that."

"No, that is true," agreed Emilia. "And this brother of yours. What name had he? And where does he now reside?" For she thought to be a little cunning and have him betray himself and his origins a little as he talked so carelessly to her.

Ottone fell silent for a moment, and his face darkened. "He resides, I hope, in Messer Dante's Paradise, having passed through Purgatory. He is dead, wife, he died in a pointless skirmish. Being good, he lacked the knowledge to understand the brute cunning of those who are evil and so died of his virtues, which some might say—although not I—was better than living because of his vices."

He fell silent again, looking into the fire which was now burning brightly.

"And you, what do you say?" ventured Emilia at last.

"That good or bad I miss my brother, and wish that I had seen more of him, but we went our different ways. He to University at Pavia, and I to Paris."

"Paris!" Emilia was entranced. "You went to Paris!" She spoke with all the delighted enthusiasm of someone who, until her fateful journey to Montefiore, had never left Novera. "Of what like is Paris?"

He laughed, one of his mocking laughs, showing his splendid white teeth. "Paris? Large—and dirty."

"Oh," exclaimed Emilia. "You mock me. You know perfectly well what I meant, and it did not deserve that answer."

"No, but what I said is true. For the rest, it was the perfect place for a footloose boy who wanted not only to study at the feet of great teachers, but also to learn what life was about."

"And what is life about?" Emilia's smile as she said this was a little sly.

"Love and war, lady. Birth and death, what else?"

He was telling her nothing about himself, and yet in another sense he was telling her everything.

"And you speak French?"

He shifted a little so that he could see her the better. See the firelight on her face as the night grew darker. "Of course, and German a little."

"As well as Latin and a little Greek?"

"And a little Greek," he agreed smiling, "for who has more than a little, except the great pedants? And I am not a pedant."

"Indeed you are not. And speaking so, you serve both Venus and Mars?"

This delighted him. "Yes. The goddess of love and the god of war. Well said."

"And you have been a soldier? Marco called you captain once."

Questioning him was like being a dentist, the one who had visited Novera and had slowly, so slowly, pulled teeth. Except that he did not shout and scream like the dentist's victims.

"Yes, I have been a soldier." He was silent again. Oh, he knew what she was doing, and was evading her every question! He had all the arts, and was devious, too.

Emilia listened entranced. "Tell me a little of your life as a soldier, and how you came to be one, for your education was more like that of a scholar than a warrior."

He was silent for a moment, and then said, "Oh, my brother died in an ambush set by a man whom he thought his friend, and my father told me that the life of a scholar or of a clerk, or even a merchant was not now for me. I had been educated as a page in the house of a nobleman before I went to Paris, and I was skilled in all the knightly accomplishments. I sometimes think that Paolo, my brother, should have been the younger son, for he was more fit than I for a life indoors among books and papers—although I never fought against my father's orders that that should be my life.

"So when Paolo died my life changed completely. I became a soldier, not a clerk." He fell silent again, and Emilia realised that although he had told her everything, yet he had also told her nothing. He had given her no hint of his true name or family—for she was sure that it was not da Stresa, nor of where he had lived, or of the noble house in which he had been a page.

She knew that it was a commonplace for boys of good birth to spend some of their adolescence in the household of another nobleman, rather than with their own family, for only so, it was thought, would they be properly disciplined. There had been at least two in Ugo's household at Novera, and she had played with them when she was younger, but when she had reached the age of fourteen she had been forbidden their company.

And so she told Ottone. He laughed softly. "Your uncle did not want to expose you to temptation." He sat up suddenly, and asked her, "What would he say if he knew that you had been daily exposed to temptation and had so far resisted it? Would he believe you—or me?"

Emilia was honest. "I don't know. Sometimes…" she began and stopped, fell silent.

"Sometimes?" he echoed. "What were you about to say, Emilia? Why did you stop?"

She could not answer him, for a true answer would be that she was not sure that she ought to resist the call of passion—which might never come again. Instead she asked him again about his past as a soldier, and seeing that she would not reply to his question, he told her a little of it. No, not the horrors, but some of the commonplaces of comradeship and the problems of knowing what decisions to make when the lives of your men hung upon your every word.

She nodded gravely at this, but again, although he had revealed to her much of the man that he was, she was still in the dark about the essentials of his past. Perhaps, she thought sadly, she might never know them. Perhaps he would disappear from her life as swiftly and suddenly as he had arrived in it. She shuddered at the thought and to hide the shudder she turned the conversation again.

"You said that you studied at Paris. Was it at Paris that you learned how to deceive and to answer so that you gave nothing away?"

"No, I learned that from life. I was determined not to be deprived of it, like my poor brother, because I thought that men and women were naturally good."

Emilia shuddered. "But does not that make you unable to enjoy life as the Lord God intended it should be enjoyed? To be so suspicious? To be without trust?"

"No, not entirely without trust, for one has to trust someone. It is up to us to choose carefully those whom we trust, not assume blindly that all are trustworthy."

"And do you trust me?"

This came out heartrendingly. So heartrendingly that Ottone levered himself up and moved to where Emilia sat, hugging her knees, her eyes on him wide and questioning. He had forgotten that although she was innocent, she was also clever and intuitive.

"Implicitly," he murmured and took her in his

arms. He loved her for her intellect as well as her calm beauty and the courage which she had consistently shown in adversity. And also for the shrewdness with which she had questioned him, which had almost caused him to drop his guard.

She turned in his arms as lightly and easily as though she had done it a thousand times before, to offer him her lips. He trusted her, so she would trust him, and at that very moment, as they truly tasted one another for the first time on their travels, a nightingale began to sing.

They were lost. The liquid music which poured into the heavens, the touch and feel of another soul, the twin to their own, held them captive. If it was Emilia's first taste of true passion, then it was Ottone's first taste of true love. He had known many women, and made love to some of them, but he had never before felt what he was now feeling for the woman to whom he was beginning to initiate into the delights of love.

He was a boy again. The boy of whom he had spoken, who had lost the admired elder brother and was in a great city, alone but free, experiencing everything for the first time. Love and hate and learning. Her lips were sweet because he was the first man to whom she had freely offered them, and as blind passion began to hold him in its thrall, the cold something which had ruled him since his brother's death, cried warningly, "No, you are not to betray her by making her your doxy in truth as well as in pretence. She is innocent, and innocence is too easily betrayed."

He had spoken of trust, and he must not betray hers.

So he pulled away from her.

In Burani it was she who had ended their love-making, but here, in the dusk in the forest, it was he who called a halt, and she, her face lit with passion, who stared reproachfully at him.

"Duty," he said slowly, the word hurting him even as he spoke it. "You spoke of your duty, and because of it, you drew away from me in Burani. I would not have you go against your duty, nor would I betray you, after you spoke so touchingly of trust."

"It was not I who spoke of trust," she told him, "but you."

"Well, then, lady," and there was nothing mocking about him now, "if the word I used was trust, and the word you used was duty, then those are the words which must rule us, if we are to be true to ourselves."

"And love, Messer Ottone? What of that word?"

"Oh, lady, you denied it at Burani, as I deny it now. It is the splendour of the night and the bird which is singing to us so sweetly, which have together led us astray—as Messer Boccaccio once wrote."

But Emilia had not read that story. It was not in the manuscript of the *Decameron* which she had read, being one which the scribe who had copied it out had considered to be too improper to be repeated. But she remembered what Ottone, when he had been Gianni, had told her of the other meaning of the nightingale's song, and her face flamed at the memory.

Had she been so wanton as to forget what the end of their loving would have been? Had she forgotten that she was the lady of Novera, seduced by his answers to her questions which had revealed the boy he had been, a boy whom she wished to love—and be loved by?

"I forgot everything in your arms," she muttered miserably and turned away from him. "It was I who should have said no, not you. How weak I am, not to remember that I am promised to the lord Leonardo. I so nearly gave you what should be his alone."

He made no answer to that, for one of their bodyguard was coming over to them, to discuss the night's arrangements for sleep and for safety. So far they had met few on the road by day, and none at night, but as they neared Montefiore that might change.

Ottone felt Emilia shudder and mistook its meaning. He was all solicitude. "You are cold, wife? Shall I order the men to build us a larger fire—or shall I fetch you a shawl from the cart?"

He used the word wife so often that Emilia thought that he must like the sound—or the thought of it—which had her smiling sadly.

She shook her head. "No, I am not cold, but I am rather tired. Even so, before I retire I should like to walk a little."

"Not on your own," he replied, and rose swiftly.

"If you will permit I will walk with you for I, too, feel cramped after a day spent driving the cart."

She could believe that, so she allowed him to take her arm, and they walked a little way into the forest. It was not yet dark. They were in the half-light between night and day when objects were strangely clear, before they disappeared from sight altogether. They had only walked a little distance when the trees ended and they were on the edge of a cliff which looked down a great valley.

In the far distance, blue against the growing grey of night was a settlement, with its few evening lights already shining and twinkling. Ottone said, "If I were to take you to Montefiore, Emilia, it is there, beyond the town which you see before you, which is Morcote, the name of the lordship which Leonardo di Montefiore owns."

Montefiore, which if he so willed would be her journey's end. Did she wish her journey to end? Once, at the beginning, she would have welcomed it but now, all had changed. Could she marry Leonardo di Montefiore when her heart was given to another? For now she not only desired Ottone, but she had come to be his friend, someone to whom she could talk, as she was someone with whom he could talk. So strange it was that after all their amorous encounters they could be so impersonal, that he could speak to her of music and books, pick up his lute and sing to her as though they had never been in one another's arms…

It came to Emilia that in one thing they were alike. They were both strong-willed. Was Leonardo strong-willed? Would he speak to her of books and music, laugh over Messer Boccaccio's stories?

When he came to her in their marriage bed, would the nightingale sing?

The thought that it might not was unbearable. Especially since she knew that in the arms of the man beside her the nightingale *would* sing, and sing sweetly... Duty was only a word, and here beside her was life and love, and duty and Leonardo seemed far away.

It was not Leonardo who had saved her from Gentile, it was Ottone. Why should she not reward him? Was it not her duty to reward him? Passion rose in her, and as the night grew darker and the stars began to appear as they wandered back to their small camp, Emilia was wondering whether she was not being a fool to hold him off. If she but said the word... what then?

Because if she did not give him that word soon she never would, for were they not almost at journey's end? If nothing went wrong, that was. To tame her errant thoughts she said as much to Ottone. "Think you that we are safe?"

In between wishing Emilia in his arms and in his bed, Ottone had been thinking the same thing.

"I hope so. But experience teaches me to be wary. Until we reach our destination we cannot account ourselves safe. All our enemies are cunning, else they would not be alive and successful. I will only say that we are but a few days from deliverance."

She had expected that he would say as much, so said nothing herself. As on every night, they parted to lie down at no great distance from one another, but for their own different reasons, neither of them slept easily.

In the morning Emilia wondered how she would be able to look Ottone in the eye again after she had betrayed her feelings towards him so plainly but, strangely, she found that far from being embarrassed, some barrier between them which had existed since Burani had fallen. From that evening on they were easy with one another again, and the days passed happily and uneventfully by. So uneventfully that even Ottone began to believe that they might reach their journey's end without further trouble.

Such thoughts always tempt the Gods who watch over the affairs of men, for they mean that men consider themselves the masters of their own destiny. So, as fate, or the Gods, would have it, even as they neared Montefiore, Emilia's beauty brought them trouble again.

It was late afternoon. They were ambling along, Pasquale ahead of them, Roberto covering their rear, when a small party of young men on horseback, falcons on their wrists, galloped along the rough road towards them. Their leader put up a hand and bade them stop. His eyes roved keenly over their little party, and came to rest on Emilia as she sat silent by Ottone.

He was young, only a little older than Emilia, but carried himself with the arrogance of someone who has given orders all his life, and who expects them to be obeyed immediately.

"Why, who are you?" he asked. "And whither are you bound? It is Naldo da Bisticci who asks you, the lord of this valley." He waved a careless arm around him, so that his hooded falcon fluttered angrily at the movement.

"Lord, I am Ottone Rinieri, a merchant of Florence bound for Montefiore, where I have business." Ottone's tone was not as servile as it had been when he had been Gianni, but he was careful to speak after such a fashion that he did not offend the haughty boy before him.

"Oh, indeed! And the woman beside you? Your lady, is she? And why do you travel in a cart more suited to a peasant than a merchant of note?"

"My wife ails a little, lord, and this is an easier mode of travel for her." Ottone's tone was still decently humble.

"Indeed! She does not look as though she ails, merchant. Quite the opposite, in fact. But that being so, where do you intend to rest this night? For you are in territory where neither farmhouse nor inn is available."

"Why, on the earth, lord. It is summer, and the weather is kind."

"But not tonight, merchant," riposted Naldo, who was now frankly appraising Emilia so that she shivered before him. "My castle is nearby, and you may lodge there in comfort—as long as it may please you."

"That is most gracious of you, lord," replied Ottone, keeping his voice and his temper as level as he could. He had only one desire, and that was to strike the boy before him for the insolence with which he was stripping Emilia with his eyes. "But I may not stay for more than one night, if it please you. I am already late for my appointment in Montefiore, and would wish to hasten on my way."

"Oh, I would not have you reject my hospitality, merchant, and I would require you to remain for at least two nights. We lack entertainment and knowledge of the great world outside our valley, and would have you supply that lack. Is not that so?" And he turned in his saddle to address his men who loudly chorused a willing answer.

"You see, merchant, we are all agreed. Two nights, and you shall drink my best wine, and sleep in a bed more comfortable than that the earth supplies—or even an inn or a farmhouse. Come, follow me, you, your beautiful wife, and your twin guardians."

There was no help for it. Emilia whispered to Ottone, once they were on their way to Naldo's castle, travelling behind him, out of his earshot, "I do not like this, Ottone. Indeed, I greatly dislike the way in which Ser Naldo looks at me."

"Neither do I," Ottone whispered back. "Were I Niccolo da Stresa again with a troop at my back, I would make sure that he would sing me quite another song. As it is, we must do as he says. I do not wish you less beautiful, Emilia, but were you not so, then you would not present such a temptation to every chance-met rogue between Verdato and Montefiore, and we should be the safer for it."

After a time Emilia began to think that she had

misjudged Naldo. His castle might not be as large or as imposing as that of Guido's, but it was more comfortable, and he not only made them welcome, but he placed good food and even better wine before them, and made no further attempt to distress Emilia by his bold looks. He was no fool, and asked Ottone some shrewd questions, and fortunate it was that he knew enough about the ways of merchants to give knowledgeable answers.

He possessed no wife, and the few women present, as they dined in his great hall before a huge fireplace, were the respectable wives of his courtiers and followers, and so all was decorous. He told them that his father had died when he was a boy, and an uncle, now also dead, had brought him up. Since his uncle's death he had been his own master.

The merchant, Ottone Rinieri, like his supposed wife, began to think that he might have misjudged the young lord before him, who was so busy ladling his charm over them both. He was not ill-looking, and only his arrogance prevented him from seeming to be as fair and pleasant a young man as either of them had ever met. Naldo rose when Ottone asked him if they might retire, explaining that his wife must be feeling weary after their long journey, and needed to rest, and, giving his grave consent, he watched them leave the room.

"We might, I hope, escape from here without harm." Ottone was seated on the great bed in their room, watching Emilia who was brushing her long hair. "But I do not like it that both Roberto and Pasquale have been lodged so far away from us. On the other hand, there is little enough that they could do to help us if things went wrong. Three men could not do much against Naldo's household.''

''We may be wronging him.'' Emilia sat on the bed beside Ottone as naturally as though she had shared a room with him all her life. ''He does not seem to be another Guido—and,'' slyly, ''he does not seem to possess a lady Isabella to pursue you!''

''To some extent,'' Ottone told her slowly, avoiding her eyes, ''all men in positions of power are likely to be Guidos. That is, they may use their position to gain the women they want! Oh, not invariably, but the temptation is there—which is why men guard their wives, their daughters and their mistresses so carefully.''

Emilia thought about what he had said, then conceded ruefully that there was truth in it, and told him so.

''And,'' pursued Ottone, continuing Emilia's education, ''there are women who will offer themselves to men of power.''

''Or even to a pedlar—if they catch their fancy,'' interrupted Emilia, a trifle pertly.

''True—and we have to hope that neither of us will become Naldo's victims.''

He had hardly finished speaking when there was a knock on the door, and before either of them could so much as answer it, the door opened, to reveal Naldo's major-domo, a middle aged man. Two large soldiers stood at his back.

The major-domo advanced into the bedroom, bowed low to them both and straightened up to announce, "The lord Reynaldo da Bisticci would have a private word with the merchant's lady this night. I am here to escort her to his room."

Ottone rose. He stood quite still and tense in the middle of the room as Emilia's hand flew to her mouth and her face turned as white as the snow which crowned the Appenines.

"And if *I* said that I do not wish my wife to have private words with the lord Reynaldo da Bisticci in his room at night—what then?"

The major-domo bowed low in what could only be understood as mockery.

"Why, Ser Ottone Rinieri, I have brought two of the lord's guard with me to persuade you to agree to what the lord wishes and I have several more down the corridor to assist them although I do not think that they will be needed. You are not armed, I see." And now the major-domo's mockery was plain.

Emilia said, standing up and walking to Ottone's side to take his hand, "And if I said that I do not wish to go to the lord's room, what then?"

"Then I shall give orders to the soldiers to carry you there." He bowed low again. "But I would prefer not to have to order them to do so."

Hysteria rose and bubbled in Emilia's throat. She had escaped both Gentile and Guido, only to fall prey to a spoiled boy who had taken a fancy to the merchant's wife—and this time, there was no-one to save her.

Ottone threw off Emilia's hand, and strode forward. "No!" burst from him. "You shall not take her, for you know as well as I what the lord wishes to do with her.''

''Merchant,'' said the major-domo, no whit abashed. ''I have the lord's word that if you will go quietly on this matter, he will give you payment to the extent that the lady pleases him, so you see that you will not lose by this transaction. But if you try to oppose him by attacking us, then I fear that you will not simply lose the use of your wife for one night, but your life as well.''

Face livid, his hands fists, Ottone began to speak again. ''I would be a cur to let her go to him without trying to prevent it—'' And he continued to advance on the major-domo so that the two soldiers moved into the room to come between them.

''No!'' It was Emilia who spoke, and in tones of command such as she had never used even when she had been the lady of Novera.

''No, husband. You shall not needlessly give your life for me. For there is no way that we can successfully defy the lord, and your death would not save me from dishonour. Indeed, it would dishonour me further, and that I will not have.'' She turned towards the major-domo. ''I shall go to your lord since I have no alternative, but not willingly, and he will have so little joy from me, that he shall pay my husband nothing. No, Ottone,'' she told him proudly, as he tried to stand between her and the soldiers. ''You are not to stop me. I will not have you die for me, not after all that you have already done. And,'' she added meaningfully, ''what you would once have done for me, I will do for you.''

Now Ottone turned away from the soldiers to take her in his arms, to look into her eyes, to say hoarsely, "You do not know what you are asking of yourself. It is not the same, and you know it."

The major-domo interrupted them to announce in a bored voice, "Come, cease this. The lord awaits the lady and will grow impatient if you haggle thus. It is not the end of the world if you share your lady with another."

For one dreadful moment Emilia thought that this insult might have Ottone throwing himself at the soldiers to die defending her. She clung to him, and almost shouted, "No," before releasing him as she felt him falter. "I will go with you, sir, and may you ask the Lord God's pardon for your part in this, for I cannot pardon you, or the man whom you serve." She was through the door, taking one last look at Ottone who had sunk down onto the bed, his hands over his eyes, before the major-domo closed the bedroom door behind her—and locked it.

Chapter Eleven

Braccio, Gentile and Guido were plotting together. Guido had allied himself to the lord of Verdato, after a good talking to from Isabella. She had ordered him to keep a close eye on Gentile whilst they were on the pedlar's trail for she did not trust him. Her last brisk words to him before he left her to join them had been, "Never forget, that if the man who took the lady of Novera from Gentile is the pedlar, and clever enough to deceive us all, he might change himself again, like the shape-changers who deceived the ancient Greek heroes."

Guido, being unlettered, knew little of what she was talking about, but he obeyed her all the same, and kept a keen eye on his fellows in villainy. He, Gentile and Braccio and their combined troops travelled swiftly along the road and learned from those they questioned that, yes, a pedlar had passed this way, and it was to be guessed that he was making for Burani. But once they had gone through Burani and were on the road north east again, all traces of the pedlar had disappeared. None they questioned in inn or farmhouse, had seen him, his doxy or his servant.

Like the man who had captured the lady of Novera he had gone from the face of the earth.

Guido remembered what Isabella had told him of the pedlar's cunning, but before he could speak of it to his unlikely allies, Braccio's sergeant rode up, pulled off his helm, saluted and said with as much deference as he could summon up, ''Your pardon, lords, but would it not be wise to return at once to Burani? For since there can be little doubt that he reached Burani, then Burani he must have left. And since no-one has seen the pedlar *after* he left Burani, isn't it likely that he has altered his appearance again? Certes, if he could change himself and the lady once, he could do so again, The citizens there may know more than they think. They would bear questioning.''

So they all trailed back to Burani, their tails between their legs, Guido, Gentile and Braccio all thinking up different and dreadful punishments for the devious swine who had them dancing to his tune.

More to the point, they searched the town, asking whether any strangers had been seen, and if so, of what kind they had been, and whither they were bound.

It was the sergeant, who was compelled to watch his inefficient superiors fail in their search for lack of imagination, who visited the stables and the saddlers. On his visit to the last saddler on his list he struck gold.

"Strangers, ser sergeant? We see few such in Burani. Nor have three resembling those you have described visited me. Now, had you asked about two strangers, then I might have been able to help you."

"Two strangers, then? Of what like were they?"

"The man was a merchant, rich, splendidly dressed, no pedlar he. His wife was young, blonde and as beautiful as an angel. Ailing, he said, expecting their first blessing. He bought several horses and hired my two sons to escort him to the north. He was passing rich, had letters from the Medici, they said, and was lodged with the goldsmith Farfalla. His name, I remember, was Rinieri, Ottone Rinieri."

Lodged with the goldsmith—and rich. It didn't sound very likely that he was the missing pedlar—and where was his fellow, who had accompanied him all the way from Verdato?

Nevertheless. "You are sure there was no other man with them?"

"Quite sure, your honour." The saddler thought a moment, then added as an afterthought, "He sold Alberto of the stables a mule."

"A mule!" The lady Isabella had said that the pedlar's man had ridden a mule. The goldsmith and Alberto of the stables would bear visiting.

But after he had talked to Farfalla and Alberto and told Gentile and Braccio of what he had learned from them, it was only to have them mock him. But Guido, who arrived late to their meeting—he had been scouring the taverns and was already a little merry—said roughly, "What better change of disguise to deceive us all than from ragged pedlar to merchant, travelling in state? And a blonde beauty with him. Was the lady of Novera a blonde beauty, Ser Gentile? The pedlar's woman was blonde, and pretty beneath the dirt.''

"Blonde and beautiful—beautiful as an angel. Perhaps Braccio's sergeant has smoked him out. The goldsmith is the man to visit.''

"No," said Farfalla brusquely, when they questioned him closely. "He could not possibly have been a pedlar. I have no doubt that my man was a merchant. He had letters of marque from the Medici Bank in the name of Rinieri—and he had the seal which sat beside theirs on the letters.''

Afterwards, sitting round a table in Burani's best inn, they had a conference. They argued and squabbled noisily about whether chasing a wealthy merchant of such credentials was a piece of arrant folly when they ought to be looking for a poor pedlar.

Guido rose at last. He had drunk well, and intended to eat well before he left Burani.

"You," he told Gentile and Braccio, "may do as you please, but I shall ask Braccio's sergeant to accompany me north after the merchant. I am sure that he has the right of it. My bones tell me so. I have a mind to capture the lady and offer her for ransom myself."

"It's the drink telling you so," returned Gentile, but all the same, after hurried words with Braccio, he announced roughly that if Guido was determined on a wild goose chase, then he would accompany him. "For that is all we have to go on, and it is little enough. And if it prove that the lady is with this so-called merchant, then I do not want him killed when we take them. By the living God, I want him for my sport before I despatch him at the last!''

And so it was agreed. They would pursue the merchant who already had several days start on them, and hope to catch him before he reached Montefiore.

All unknowing that their enemies were in hot pursuit, and caring little had she known, for a greater danger stared her in the face, Emilia was hurried along the castle's narrow corridors to Naldo's bedroom.

Unreality walked with her. It could not be true that she was hastening towards the bed where she would be robbed of her virginity—she must be asleep back in Novera and this was all a nightmare. But no, this was all too dreadfully true and thinking so, she bitterly regretted that she had not offered her maidenhead to Ottone, for were she to lose it before she reached Montefiore then better with him than with some chance-met careless boy.

Naldo was eagerly awaiting her arrival and started up from a great carved chair to greet her when the soldiers and his major-domo escorted her into his room. The room was something of a surprise. Although what she had seen of the castle had been comfortable enough, it was nothing like the sumptuousness of Novera, but here all was luxury with a carpet and hangings brought from the East, with a large wooden bed, fantastically carved and painted. Its coverlet, embroidered in rich red and gold, showed the sun in splendour.

He wore a houppelande to match the coverlet, but was plainly naked beneath it, which almost brought on the shivers, but Emilia had told herself to be brave, not to show her fear and disgust of what was about to happen to her.

There was a fire in the hearth and thick candles in sconces. Once he had dismissed the major-domo and the soldiers, Naldo motioned to her to sit on a long settle, and then sat himself down again in his great chair, and chin in hand surveyed her as though he were looking at some beautiful thing brought in for his delectation. He was drinking in every aspect of her from the crown of her golden head to the tips of the elegant shoes which Ottone had bought for her in Burani before they left.

"You are beautiful, merchant's wife," he said at last. "A very princess. I like beautiful things."

Emilia tried to keep her voice steady. "You do not break beautiful things, I hope. So why break me?"

"To lie with me would break you?" His voice was offended.

"To lie with anyone other than my husband would break me."

"So virtuous, lady?" He leaned forward to inspect her the more closely, and broke into a knowing smile. "You know what they say? A slice off a cut loaf is never missed."

He rose to advance on her. His houppelande had fallen open and she could see the curling red hairs on his chest. He was smiling at her, ready now to take his pleasure. Emilia closed her eyes. I am not a cut loaf, she wanted to shriek at him. I am virgin, no one's wife, who is meant to be Leonardo di Monte-fiore's bride, but who would rather bed with Niccolo da Stresa, or whatever he is calling himself at the time! Not with you! Never with you!

But she said nothing.

His strong and urgent hands were around her waist now. If she opened her eyes she would look into his. Not Ottone's eyes. Never his. For if she became this selfish boy's trull she would offer herself to the Holy Mother afterwards and never hold a man in her arms again.

Emilia shivered.

He felt the shiver. "Open your eyes, lady," he whispered. "I do not wish to hurt you, only to give you pleasure."

"No," she told him, and though her voice was low he could hear the iron in it. "No, you may do as you will with me, but I shall not open my eyes whilst you are at your work."

He shook her and said roughly, "You must look at me. I would have you give yourself willingly, for I would rather not force you, that is never my way. But if you continue to refuse me, then force you I will."

Emilia opened her eyes and traded stare for stare with him; became again the lady of Novera. She gave him a distant icy smile. "Then force me," she told him proudly, "for I will never willingly surrender to you. You may break my body, but not my will," and she closed her eyes again.

She felt him shake against her. Naldo had never

been denied before, and told her so. "I will not be treated thus." He put her from him a little. "I may not be as large and splendid as your husband, for all that I am lord and he is merchant, but I am not ill-looking. Why fight me, lady? Why should not the nightingale sing for us? Why struggle against what will happen? Who is to know or care what delights we share tonight? A night of pleasure—and then, on your way."

"That is not my way, never my way." The pun was unintentional, but Naldo caught it. Why, she was a treasure, such looks, such spirit, and such wit when she was trembling before him like an animal caught in a snare—but she would not show her fear. Not she!

He drew in his breath, and seized her again by the waist. Then his hands roved her body, and what he would do next was his choice—never hers—she must endure it. And so they stood for a moment. He muttered, "Oh, lady, so soft, so fair. I would have you willing, but have you I will. Two can play at word games." He was kissing her, and now she was truly in the snare. Only the Lord God could help her, or His Mother, and she prayed silently to them, giving a great sob as her prayer ended, and he was leading her to his bed…to break her there…

But even as they reached it the door opened, and a child's voice said reproachfully, "Oh, Papa, you did not come to see me today, so I have come to you."

Naldo's eyes opened wide. He stepped back again, his seeking hands falling to his side.

"Sofia! What do you here? Where is your nurse?"

"I had not your nightly blessing, so I could not sleep. Give me your blessing."

The child walked further into the room until she stood in the light of the candle by the bed, her large eyes on her father and Emilia, who had been twined together and were now apart. Thus Emilia, opening her eyes, saw her for the first time. The voice, sexless because of its youth, was that of a girl child of some five years of age, a charming cherub clutching a rag doll to her breast.

Sofia looked up at them. "You have a pretty lady with you, Papa. Perhaps she could mend Lisetta for me. She has a poorly eye." She held the doll out to Emilia.

From being in the harem they were now in the nursery. High drama had declined into farce. Naldo's expression was one of mixed shame and pride. Shame at being interrupted in what was rape by his child, and pride in the child herself.

He muttered, "Sofia, you should not be here. I have told you before not to enter Papa's room without knocking." But there was no anger in his voice.

"You do not knock when you enter my room," she reproached him, adding, "If I had known that you had a pretty lady with you, I would have come before. Is the pretty lady to be my new mama now that my old one is in heaven?"

Emilia, avoiding Naldo's gaze, had taken the offered doll. The stitching of one of its eyes had worked loose and it hung down. She fell on her knees before the child, and said softly, "If you will find

me a needle and thread, I will mend your doll for
you, Sofia.''

"There is no need for that," interposed Naldo
roughly. "Her nurse may do it for her in the morning."

"There is every need," Emilia told him, looking
at him over the little girl's head. "What is broken
must be mended as soon as possible, or life would
become a chaos of shards and patches, without meaning."

She was speaking of more than the doll and the
man before her knew it. His arousal had vanished.
He could hardly look at the woman whom he had
been about to ravish. His little daughter's arrival had
changed everything, as though the Gods had thrown
another dice, and a new game had begun. Sofia had
made him man, not monster, had restored to him the
humanity which he had been trying to deny by behaving like a brute beast.

Emilia rose, holding the doll. Sofia, clutching at
her skirt, began to pull her to the door. Emilia said,
before she left the room, with Naldo making no effort
to detain her, "She is yours? Her mother is dead?
You must have been very young when you were married."

"I was sixteen, and so was she," he told her
roughly. "She died having Sofia. She was my only
love. I want no other wife."

"So you take merchants' wives instead." This was
said tonelessly, factually, and so he answered her.

"Not now. Mend Sofia's doll and get you to your
man." He turned his back on her, and Emilia did as

she was bid. He was not wicked, only weak, and the child's presence had shamed him, so the Lord God willing, he was not beyond salvation.

If Ottone had ever doubted that he was beginning to love Emilia as he had never loved a woman before, the feelings of anguish which overwhelmed him as he waited for her to return from Naldo da Bisticci's bed, finally revealed the depth of his love to him.

He lay down and tried to compose himself, for he was fearful that he would lose all self-control and begin to hammer on the locked door demanding her to be returned to him unharmed.

Which would be stupid and would merely serve to increase her shame and his. But lying there, he was doomed to endure the torments of his lively imagination. Writhing, he tried to banish the picture of Naldo and Emilia entwined—or else he saw her fiercely resisting her fate, and being compelled to suffer it...

No, the damned in Messer Dante's Hell had never endured such misery, and even as his fists clenched and his body tensed and he promised himself that when he reverted to his proper self he would bring a troop to the castle and hang Naldo from its highest battlement, he heard footsteps outside and voices. It was Emilia returning, and the night not yet a quarter over.

Unbelievably, Ottone experienced anger. Had she been so willing that he had joyed in her so rapidly and was sending her back with the payment which he had promised? Was she no more than any other trull who would lie with anyone if profit came from it? Oh, he was shamed to think such things, but even as the door opened, he started up to face her fiercely as she entered...

And she came in with such a holy calm written on her face, so coolly lovely, so untouched... How dare she look so untouched who had brought shame on them—for now Ottone was so beside himself that he almost believed that he was truly a merchant and this was truly his wife who had betrayed her marriage vows so lightly that she showed no ill effects from the rape she had suffered. He, *he* had been in Hell—and where had she been?

"So soon," he said bitterly. "So soon. I had thought that you would have pleasured the night away between you." He turned his face to the wall, for he loved her, and her shame was his.

Emilia was bewildered. She would have thought that he would be both pleased and relieved to see her back with him so early, and unharmed. But his words and his actions showed her that he thought that the worst had happened.

"Oh, no, Ottone," she told him earnestly, walking over to him to touch him on the shoulder and when he turned his ravaged face to her, to stroke it lovingly. "Oh, no. He never touched me. The Lord God sent me a miracle and I was spared," she whispered as low as she could. "I am maiden yet."

He stared at her, then said faintly, "You speak true?"

"Indeed, husband," for she thought it best to continue to dissemble, for who knew whether or no they were being spied on. "His little daughter burst in upon us even as he began his wicked work, and he was shamed by her presence and let me go, for he is not truly evil, only young and selfish."

Ottone bethought him of his own wicked thoughts of a moment ago, and said humbly, "As I am older and selfish. But, yes, the Lord God was with you. Oh, comfort me, Emilia, for I was so wracked by jealousy and shame that I thrust it all on you. I have been in Hell, forgetting what you might be suffering." Then he added anxiously, "You are sure that he has not hurt you?"

All unknowing of the mental hell through which Ottone had just passed, his self-reproach puzzled Emilia. To try to calm him, she held out her hands to him, and said, "I am unmarked, and I have spent my time away from you repairing his daughter's doll."

"I think that you had better try to repair me! Oh, Emilia." Now she had Ottone's arms around her, who had so recently nearly suffered at the hands of another man, and remembering that she held him away.

"He says that we may leave in the morning, but he will not bid us farewell. He does not want to see you, I think."

"I do not want to see him," returned Ottone savagely. "For although in the end he spared you, you must have suffered before he did. I am like to attack him if I see him again."

"Indeed." Now it was as though all the fear she

had suffered, and the strain of the long day fell upon Emilia at once. "Oh, Ottone, I feel so strange." The room darkened about her, and she fell into his arms, half-fainting with delayed shock.

"Battle weary. You are battle weary," said Ottone briskly, and he lifted her up to lie her on the bed. "And I am being careless of you, for one thing is certain. A woman who has so nearly been ravished by a man is likely to want to avoid all men for a space. Rest, my darling, and let sleep cure you."

Sleep she did, and Ottone sat all night in the chair by the bed, and watched over her. She was his first love, and would be his only love, that he knew—and that he must get her safe to Montefiore.

"I had not thought that he would truly let us go so easily."

It was Ottone speaking. They were sitting in the shade of a large tree having just eaten, the mountains above them and the road below. Neither of them had said anything to their two escorts of what had passed the previous night, but it was plain from the way in which Roberto and Pasquale looked at them that they had heard tell of the merchant's wife visiting the lord's bedroom and of her early return.

"I, too, was fearful, but it was as I said. He was weak not wicked." Emilia paused, began to speak again, but paused again. It was, Ottone knew, a habit of hers when she had something important to say to him.

"What is it, wife?" he asked her gently.

She looked at him, eyes almost blind.

"Nothing, no, that is not true. It is everything. You remember that we discussed whether one ever ought to do an ill thing that good might come?" She paused again. Ottone nodded, wondering what was coming.

"You said that it was easy to discuss such problems in the study, but that outside it was much harder when one was faced with a decision and no time to make it. I see now what you meant, and I also see how much I wronged you over Isabella." She fell silent, but, again, he did not answer her, for he could see that she was thinking, and that in some measure her thoughts were painful.

At last she looked frankly at him before she spoke, as though she had been another man, disputing with him in a discussion among students. "You see, I was prepared last night to save us by lying with Naldo—which was committing a sin to gain a good—when a priest would have said that I ought to have suffered both our deaths first. And what is more, and is a reproach to me, I understand now why you agreed to pleasure Isabella to save me, and that I was both wrong and cruel to hate you for doing so, and to be unkind to you."

"Oh, no!" He rose from where he was sitting and came swiftly over to her to take her hand and stroke it. "It was but natural for you to think and behave as you did, for when I thought of you with Naldo I behaved and thought exactly as you did when you resented me and Isabella! We are but poor weak creatures, Emilia, and the Lord God often asks too much of us. We must always pray that we bend and never break, and forgive one another, even as we wish to be forgiven.''

He had never in his life thought to make such a speech—and to a woman, too. But last night had proved to him how much he loved her and he did not want her to suffer by reproaching herself for the sin of being human.

''We are,'' he said, at last, ''what we are, with all our imperfections on us. If we love one another it is because we recognise that they exist, even as the Lord God loves us—despite our imperfections.''

Emilia acknowledged this with a grave nod of the head, and her hand tightened around his. Thus, barely touching, but together in silent communion they sat a while. She wished that this moment could last forever, but such a wish was futile for presently they would be on their way, and all too soon they would be in the busy corrupt world of men again. Alone here, among the mountains, fearsome and dangerous though they were, as all men and women knew, she was finding a peace which she had never known before.

Yes, all too soon after their rest, Ottone was saying that they must press on. They passed a farmhouse early in the afternoon and their escorts suggested that they spend the night there—which would mean that they would not reach Montefiore for another two days, so Ottone said them nay. Something was whispering in his ear that their luck was running out, had almost run out at Naldo's tower, and he had lived as long as he had done by not ignoring such whispers. The sooner they reached Montefiore city the better.

Emilia had decided that she never wanted to reach the city. For there she would have to say goodbye to Ottone, and she had no wish to do so. Satan was whispering dreadful things in her ear:

Item: that she should tell Ottone that she loved him.

Item: that because of this she would go with him wherever he wished to take her, as Ruth had followed Naomi in the Bible.

Item: that the lady of Novera should disappear, so that Leonardo di Montefiore might take another bride, and the lady become the wife, or the doxy, of the *condottiero*, Niccolo da Stresa.

The devil's voice grew louder with each passing mile, and that of the good angel, her conscience, grew softer. That told her that what she was contemplating was a sin, that her duty waited for her at Montefiore city. The lady of Novera had pledged herself long ago to carry out God's will, and the will of her uncle, and never to follow her own sinful desires.

Oh, how easy it had been for her to be good and true when she had no sinful desires!

But now she had them, and they all centred around the person of the man seated beside her in the cart whom she had come to love, not only because she desired his body, but because she also desired the mind and the companionship which he had given her, and which no-one had ever given her before.

He had taught her how to live, to fulfil herself, to endure without complaint, who had never endured before.

She was going to lose him, and her life would become a desert without him.

I would rather live with him as Angela, the pedlar's wife, than be the greatest lady between Milan and Florence, was her final thought, and the voice inside her was so strong that she was sure that he must hear it.

But he could not, and slowly the miles slipped behind them.

Behind them Gentile and his company followed in their tracks. They traced the merchant and his wife along the road to Montefiore and it became plain to them all that the man who had snatched her away from Gentile—if he were disguised as the merchant—was taking her to Montefiore whence she had originally been bound. Doubtless to claim the reward for rescuing her.

And because the cart slowed the merchant and his supposed wife down, with luck they would catch them up before they left Verdato. And if they did cross the border into Montefiore, why then, they would follow them and hope to capture them before they had travelled far into territory where Gentile's troops ought not to follow.

When they were only a day behind, although they were not to know that, like Ottone and Emilia, they came across Naldo and his men out on another day's hawking.

He stopped them, shouting, "The road to Montefiore grows busy these days."

"Why so?" queried Gentile pleasantly, for he

thought that he might be able to use the young man before him.

"Why, because you are the second party I shall have entertained this last few days—for night falls, and I crave company and you doubtless crave beds if you are travelling the road, Lord Gentile." He had recognised the badges on Gentile's pennons and on the jerkins of his men. Guido's he did not recognise.

"True," agreed Gentile, "but this first party of yours. Was it a merchant and his wife, together with two escorts?"

"You have the right of it, Lord Gentile. You know him?"

"I would know him," and Gentile's smile was wolfish. "I will tell you more later—when we have supped. You do intend to feed us, I trust."

Now this was not a request but a command from Naldo's liege lord, and as such was readily agreed to. Later when they had eaten and drunk, Gentile heard the story of the merchant and his wife, suitably edited.

"You say she was beautiful?" Guido asked, putting his oar in. He had no intention of letting Gentile do all the talking.

Naldo, flown with wine and the pleasure of being with such great men, exclaimed loudly, "Beautiful as an angel, beyond compare."

"And blonde?"

"As an angel, yes. The merchant is to be envied. They were most loving."

"Were they, indeed," snorted Gentile. "Yes, he is to be envied." Inside he was seething. So, the villain who had snatched his bride away had laid his foul hands on her and made her his doxy. No-one would envy him when Gentile and his torturers had done with him!

Fortunate it was for Naldo that he did not tell of his own designs on the virtue of the merchant's wife, but he was not proud of what he had tried to do, nor how it had ended. He said nothing, and sent Gentile on his way the following morning, blessing the Lord God that such a numerous troop was not billeted on him for more than a night, or the Lord God would soon see him bankrupted, like the Peruzzi who had been ruined by the late King Edward of England reneging on his debts.

They rode down the track which Ottone had followed, sure now that the merchant was their prey, and that he would soon be meat for the rack and the gallows.

Chapter Twelve

It was Ottone and Emilia's last evening together. They had crossed into Montefiore and driven by Morcote which stood a little off the road and which Ottone had pointed out to her in the distance the night before they had reached Naldo's castle. It had been another eventless day. Contrary to their earlier experiences they might have been the only people in the world travelling along the road. They had said little to one another until they had reached the spot where they intended to rest for the night, and were sitting before a fire in the cool of the evening.

Something seemed to be troubling Ottone. From the very moment in which they had crossed into Montefiore, driving the cart through a small stream, he had retreated into himself. Twice he had begun to speak, and then had stopped. Emilia decided to speak herself, to try to provoke him, to lighten his mood.

"And now we have reached Montefiore, will you hand me over to the Duke? Or shall we go on—to wherever you decide to take me?"

She said nothing of her own longing that he would not hand her over, but would instead simply continue on their journey until they reached Switzerland, or crossed into France, where they might disappear, never to be known to Italy again. The thought both excited and frightened her.

He said nothing. Which might mean anything.

Why would he not answer her? He was wearing a rapt expression now, as though he were looking into a far distance.

''Ottone?'' Her voice was a query.

''Wife?''

For some reason this angered her. They were alone. There were no spectators for them to deceive. As usual, their two escorts were seated at some distance from them. So there was no need for him to pretend that she was his wife. She had told him so once before. Perhaps he called her wife because he proposed to make her so, by a forced marriage such as Gentile had embarked on.

Except that he did not need to force her. Did he know that? A thought struck her, sent by Satan, no doubt. If he did marry her by force, then no one could reproach her for not marrying Leonardo! Oh, yes, this was the devil talking, was it not? For she loved Ottone and wanted him most desperately, but perversely and impossibly she wanted him with her honour intact. But the Lord God, or her conscience, told her that she could not have it both ways. Oh, if only Leonardo di Montefiore were not waiting for her at her journey's end, expecting his bride to be a virgin, untouched! But even if he weren't, she would never be allowed to marry a nobody of a landless *condottiero*.

Oh, it was all too much for her, and she gave a great sigh, so that Ottone, alarmed, swung his head around and forgetting all pretence for once called her by her true name, exclaiming, ''Marina! What is it? What troubles you? You are not truly ailing?'' For during the last few days they had made some decorous jokes about her supposed pregnancy.

''No, I am not ill. It is only that I wish...that I wish...that this journey could go on forever, you and I together roving the roads, and that honour and duty do not demand that I should return to being Novera's lady and the bride of Montefiore. I have been so happy on the road with you.''

There it was, out at last in plain language. She might not have used the exact words, but she had told him that she loved him and wished to be with him. And she had done it without sighs and dropped eyes and false modesty.

Ottone moved towards her. Emilia's words had affected him more than he could say. No woman had ever told him before so sweetly and simply how much he meant to her.

''Oh, my dearest heart,'' he murmured gently into her ear as he put an arm around her shoulders. ''That would be to wish to live in one of Messer Boccaccio's fairy tales. You would soon discover if you were to live it for very long that the life of the roads is hard and cruel. It is summer now, and living in the open is easy. It is playing at life—but think of the cruelties of winter. And besides, you are only enjoying yourself so much because before, in your old life, you were so restricted that the freedom which you are experiencing now is pleasing to you. But you were meant and trained for more than this. And even if it were possible that we could disappear from the life which we lived before I snatched you from Gentile's side, and forget the duties which we owe to ourselves and to others, how long should we remain happy knowing that we have betrayed everything which we have been taught to respect?"

Emilia stared blindly into the growing dark. She knew that everything which Ottone had just said to her was no less than the truth. More, he had told her something else—that in his own life he, too, had duties. She wondered what they were. Another thing also puzzled her, and she must question him about that before their inevitable parting. From everything he had said and was now saying, he was going to return her to her future husband, and to the life which she had almost forgotten how to live in the few weeks of freedom which she had spent with him.

And she had never known how much she had been in chains.

So she asked him her question, for she was sure that he would give her a true answer, whereas when she was princess again she could never be sure that what was said to her was simply what would please her, and not the truth.

"Why did you treat me so harshly when we first met?"

She felt him stiffen, but the kind and loving arm remained around her shoulder. "Why, I knew you

only by reputation. That you were as beautiful as an
angel, but also that you were proud and haughty;
were cold and cruel in dismissing those who came
to you as suitors. I treated you as the selfish creature
that I thought you were, God forgive me. For I soon
came to see that all that icy hauteur was put on to
protect you, that beneath it was a shy, vulnerable
woman. And once you were tried and tested when
you were compelled to become Angela, the pedlar's
wife, I found that not only were you brave and true,
but that you put honour and duty first—even when
you were treating with poor peasants. A woman who
did as I bid her—not always, I admit, with the best
of grace—but then how gracious would *I* have been,
had I had to undergo what you did? Beppo told me
not to hurt you before he left, and God forgive me,
I know that I often have.''

''You have made me love you,'' Emilia told him
simply. ''Is that to hurt me?''

His arm tightened around her, but he made no
move to make love to her, only his voice was loving,
if a little sad. ''I don't know yet.''

Something was troubling him. In the close proximity in which they had been living, she had come
to know him in all his moods, as well as to love him
in all of them. Like herself, he could be proud,
haughty, brave, aye and cruel, as well as kind, com-
passionate, loving and tender—for were not God and
the devil mixed in all men? Father Anselmo had said
that belief might dub him heretic, but his experience
of life had taught him that it was true.

Also like all men, he could be fearful, and he could

be distressed, but being the man he was, he rarely made his fear or his distress overt.

The look which she turned on Ottone as she thought this was so tender and loving that it quite undid him.

He gave a kind of groan and pulled her to him, to place his lips on hers, his hands behind her head so that she was cradled there, returning the kiss he gave her with such passion that he was further lost to everything but the willing and loving woman in his arms.

His mouth still on hers, his tongue saluting hers, he dropped his hands so that one of them cupped her firm right breast, and the other slid down her back so that she was tightly pressed against him as though he were trying to make her one with him, even before they were truly united.

Emilia, who was Marina, who was Angela, was in a delirium of joy and pleasure such as she had never experienced before, and which she could never have believed it possible that she could experience. All her fear of men, of making love, had vanished as she returned the love of the one man who had pierced through the chilly armour which she had always worn to find the tender heart which beat beneath it. Broken words of love, caressing hands in which neither was the leader, but in which both met as equals were all that could be heard in the glade of the forest which had, by the end of their journey, seen the birth of their love.

For if Ottone had needed to strip Emilia of her defensive armour, she had, albeit unknowingly, stripped him of the armour of cynicism which he had worn since he was a boy. The nightingale had begun its song for them, and they were hearing it, not with their bodily ears, but with their inmost spirit, the spirit which told them both that here, at last, was their one true love.

And so, inevitably, as he bore her to the ground, they were both about to celebrate the liberation which they had together discovered after the fashion of which the poets sang, and of which Messer Boccaccio had written. They had forgotten both honour and duty, for these were but words, and they were beyond words. All that remained to them was to seal their love in bodily and spiritual union, for great love demands both, since without the spirit being involved, love is mere lust.

They were saved, if that were the correct word to use of the end to their loving, almost immediately before consummation of it by the busy world, whose demands would not let them rest.

Roberto came crashing through the trees towards them, shouting, "Messer Ottone, where are you? There is a mountain cat prowling about, and you and your lady should not stray far from the camp."

He stopped shouting on seeing them, but their moment out of time was over. Ottone sighed, pulled his arm away, and helped Emilia to stand. They were both panting in the aftermath of frustrated desire, staring at one another, their faces soft, their eyes glowing, mouths swollen and parted. Ottone muttered, "Oh, lady, forgive me for what I so nearly did. I should not have touched you, even lightly in friendship, for to do so is to start the flames of desire burning, and I must not take you, here in the forest, like a brute beast.''

"No," whispered Emilia. "I must take the blame as well. I forgot that I was promised to the lord Leonardo, and that my duty is to him." She saw Ottone's face change as she spoke, and asked urgently, "What is it, my love, which troubles you so?"

His answer was to take her gently by the shoulders again, and turn her worried face towards him. "Look at me, my darling, there is something which I should have told you before—" But he got no further for Roberto was calling again.

"Messer Ottone, for your lady's sake, do not delay."

There was no helping it. Ottone sighed again, and muttered, "That must wait for a better time. There's no use in posting sentries if we ignore what they tell us. Let us find this cat and despatch it. Would that all our problems could be so easily solved!"

But they never found the cat, and Ottone never finished the sentence he had begun. Emilia could not help wondering what was so urgent with him that it troubled him so, but which he was having difficulty in telling her.

She was still puzzling over this problem when kind sleep took her.

But it was long before Ottone slept, and when he did so his dreams were troubled.

It was a brilliant morning. The sun shone on them all. On the troops of Noverans and Montefiorans; on

Gentile, Guido and Braccio; on Niccolo and Marina pretending to be Ottone and Emilia.

Emilia awoke early. The camp was asleep. Pasquale, who was supposed to be playing sentry, had succumbed to temptation and was sitting propped up against a tree trunk, snoring heavily. Ottone was asleep too, and for a moment Emilia studied the face which after today she might never see again. He needed to shave, his beard was dark on the strong lines of his chin and jaw, but far from detracting from his beauty, it seeemed to enhance it. Emilia yearned over him before making her way into the trees. The humble necessities of living over, she walked towards the sound of falling water, to discover a large cascade dropping into a boiling pool.

It was a place where the nymphs and satyrs of legend might sport, and she had the odd notion that if she only stood still and quiet enough, they would emerge from the shadows to enjoy themselves before her.

Her delightful solitude was broken by the sound of someone walking towards her. It was Ottone. He came to stand beside her, and to say in a hushed voice, ''The Gods might disport themselves here, lady. Had we but time, we might imitate them and bathe in the pure waters below us.''

The mere idea was exciting. To stand naked before him, man and woman, Adam and Eve, Mars and Venus... But he had the right of it, they must away, and taking one last regretful look at this vision from Arcady, they turned away, hand in hand, Adam and Eve driven out of Paradise.

After that, to up camp was an anticlimax. They were setting off earlier than usual and Montefiore loomed ever nearer. They would not see it properly until the road bent sharply to the right some miles away.

Pasquale, now unashamedly awake, informed them, "It is a fair sight, Messer Ottone, if you have never seen it before. Not Florence nor Milan, but a jewel of a city with a good Duke, they say, who does not oppress his people."

Well, that was something, thought Emilia dismally, for she must think of herself as Emilia until this masquerade was over. Perhaps Leonardo was like his father, and would also be good. Oh, she did hope so, for otherwise life would not be bearable.

Ottone, after their early morning walk, was strangely silent. The odd humour which she had sensed in him yesterday was still on him, and when they stopped in the heat of the day to eat among the trees, and rest until it cooled, it was with him still.

His mood matched her own. For each yard they travelled brought them nearer and nearer to parting. Silently they ate, and silently they set off again. Since they had left Naldo's castle they had encountered few on the road, nor had they seen or heard anything of Gentile's soldiery. Perhaps he had given up searching for her, was reconciled to her loss.

She said so to Ottone. His answer was sceptical. "Pray God you are right. I shall not count us safe until we are inside Montefiore's walls. To be taken now would be the unkindest blow which the Lord God could deal us, so near we are to sanctuary."

They had been travelling for about an hour after their siesta, when they passed the bend in the road where Montefiore came into view. Shortly afterwards, the road began to run downhill into a valley where a river shone in the sunlight. Because of the steepness of the gradient the speed of the cart was slowed to a walking pace, which caused Ottone to fret further at the delay it was imposing on them. The nearer they grew to their destination, the more the shortness of his temper increased. They had almost reached the bottom of the slope where the road began to rise again—which would delay them even further—when they heard a great noise behind them. Pasquale, who had been riding well to the rear of the cart, rode up to report that a large party of armed men on horseback was approaching them at speed.

"Best pull over to the side of the road, and allow them passage," he urged, but he was too late, the troop was almost upon them. Ottone and Emilia saw, with sinking hearts, that the banners it was carrying were those of Gentile da Cortona and Guido Orsini. No chance that they would pass them by once they realised that the lost lady of Novera was riding in the cart!

And so Emilia thought. Eyes wild, she clutched at Ottone's arm. "May the Lord God be with us," she breathed, "for no-one else can save us."

Ottone said nothing, pleased only that now that the dread moment was on them, Emilia had not taken refuge in hysterics. He released her arm gently and swung the cart round to face the oncoming troops. To Pasquale and Roberto he shouted, "Ride, both of

you, ride. This quarrel is none of yours—save your-
selves if salvation be possible.''

Neither of them stayed to argue with him, but at
his bidding put spurs to horse and were away, climb-
ing the hill, perchance to reach safety. One of them,
Pasquale, stopped as they neared the summit to look
back, to see that the leading horsemen of the troop
had slowed their company to a trot, and had ridden
forward to speak to the two in the cart, keeping the
rest of their company at a little distance. The sight
had him urging his horse on again, for it was plain
by their behaviour, as well as Ottone's, that the new-
comers meant no good to the merchant Rinieri, or
any with him.

Once he had swung the cart round, Ottone had
leaned into it to pull out his huge broadsword which
had been hidden by a blanket, and a long slim dagger
with a beautifully ornate sheath. Placing the dagger
on the seat beside Emilia, he said urgently, before
leaping out of the cart to face his enemies, ''Hold
the horse for me, wife, and pray to St Michael and
all his angels that Gentile will see reason. He will
not attack us for fear that you are hurt in the ensuing
mélèe, and of all things he will not want that. I will
try to parley with him.''

Now, Ottone said this merely to give Emilia hope,
and not because he believed a word of it—other than
that a brute attack was unlikely for the reason he had
given—and for another reason which he had not told
Emilia. He was under no illusions as to what would
happen to him once he was captured. He was sure
that they wished to capture, rather than kill him, so

that he might provide sport for them in the torture chamber.

By now Gentile and Guido had ridden forward, ahead of their men, leaving Braccio in charge of them. A small group of men-at-arms dismounted and followed them, to stand quiet and steady until they were needed to lead the merchant away.

The expression on Gentile's face was exultant as he looked down at Ottone, who was now leaning on his broadsword, facing them as calmly as though he were going into battle with an army at his back, instead of standing before his enemies cornered and defenceless.

"So!" Gentile exclaimed. "We meet at last, soldier, pedlar, merchant, who treated me as though I were filth to be flung into the dirt, and took my bride from me. A pretty dance you have led us, lady," he added, looking over to where Emilia sat, the reins in her hands. "Shall I still call you lady now that you have graced this villain's bed?"

To answer him in kind, or at all, would be but to play his game. Emilia stared at him proudly.

"What silent, ser, and silent, your leman, too?" He was enjoying himself, no doubt of it, even though their refusal to return his insults irked him.

He swung his head towards Ottone again. "See how merciful I may be, ser kidnapper. For I am minded to tell you that if you surrender yourself and the lady of Novera to me humbly, I shall spare your miserable life, though little you deserve it. There, there is my noble offer, accept it, and live, where others might have cut you down on the spot."

Guido chose at this moment to stifle a guffaw. Gentile had spent the last few days detailing what he would do to the villain who had taken the lady Marina from him, and he, and the whole world, knew how worthless Gentile da Cortona's word was.

For a moment Emilia was taken in by him, was minded to shout to Ottone to surrender them both forthwith. Then her commonsense, and what she had learned of the world on her travels, took over, and she was fearful of one thing, and one thing only. That Ottone *would* surrender, and that Gentile would then break his word. But there was one way of testing the fell man before her, and before Ottone could check her she was speaking.

"Noble Lord Gentile, if you be so minded, then let me surrender, but only after you have allowed Messer Ottone to take horse and ride safely to Montefiore city in the wake of our escorts. Then, and only then, shall I know that you mean what you say."

Gentile's smile was ugly and he gave Emilia the answer which Ottone, staring long drawn out death in the face, expected.

"Why, lady, was he so potent a bed-mate that you wish to save him further trouble? No, you must accept my word. He will return with us to Verdato, and after several days...entertainment...he shall leave my castle."

Emilia shook her head, and would have answered him, but that Ottone forestalled her. Still leaning on his sword, and knowing now that Emilia understood what Gentile's plan was, he was plain in his speech. "He palters with us, lady. He does not wish to kill me immediately, for he intends me to suffer a slow death by torture for thwarting him and causing him trouble. Is not that so, Gentile? I shall be carried out of your castle at the end of your entertainment, a helpless, mindless cripple, to die in the ditch there.''

Gentile applauded him, clapping mailed hands together.

''Oh, brave. And how shall you stop me then?''

Ottone walked forward, the broadsword hefted in his hands. ''With this, for if I have to die I shall die in a manner of my own choosing, as a man, and not as a drooling thing, begging for mercy.'' And now he lifted the broadsword and continued his walk towards Gentile and the men-at-arms behind him.

Inside Emilia something shrieked in anguish. He was going to die here, in front of her, and she could not say him nay for the very reason he had given. And if he died, either here before her, or later, in agony, then she might as well die too, for she had no wish to live without him to become Gentile's thing. And she knew what she had to do, and by the living God she would do it!

''Wait,'' she cried as loudly as she could, seeing that Gentile was giving the signal to his men-at-arms to cut his losses and strike Ottone down. ''Wait! I have a message for you, Lord Gentile.''

The heads of all of them, Gentile, Guido, Ottone, and Gentile's men-at-arms all turned towards her. So engrossed were they that the distant sound of other men approaching on horseback behind the brow of the hill, whence Pasquale and Roberto had fled, went unnoticed. Only Braccio's sergeant, always alert, rode forward to check what the untoward noise was.

Emilia took no note of him, or of anyone. She was entranced. Unseen by them all whilst Ottone and Gentile had been parlaying, she had picked up Ottone's long dagger and drawn it from its sheath, in order to hold Gentile and his men at bay for a little when they came to take her. But this was not now her intent.

Instead she stood up, held the point of the dagger to her bosom and shouted, with all the power and strength that she, as the lady of Novera, could call on.

"It is this, Lord Gentile. If you kill Ottone, then I shall kill myself, for I shall have nothing to live for and will rather risk purgatory and hell than continue to live without him! Choose, Lord Gentile, choose whether I live or die!"

For a moment, time stood still. Stasis reigned—to be followed by confusion. Ottone, turning to her, lowered his broadsword, crying desperately, "No, Emilia, no!"

Gentile, stunned by this untoward turn, bellowed at his men-at-arms who had begun to advance on Ottone. "Stop, in the name of God, stop! The bitch means it." Emilia wore an expression of such dedication that he could not doubt that she meant what she said.

Guido Orsini, delighted by the stalemate which the pedlar's supposed wife had created, and the discomfort which it was causing Gentile, shouted, "No bitch, Gentile, but a gallant lady. If you do not want her, then you may have Isabella in exchange. Her nagging would keep even you in order!''

His words were lost in the din. And what Gentile might have said or done, or Ottone, or even Emilia herself, became irrelevant, because Braccio's sergeant, who had mounted the hill to gaze towards the north-east from whence the sound of horsemen came, was riding towards them in a mad gallop, shouting.

So urgent was he that Gentile, for the moment forgetting Ottone and Emilia, rode towards him in anger.

''What the devil is it, man, that you should disrupt our counsels so rudely?''

The sergeant skidded to a stop. ''Noble lord, it is right that you should know at once that a great host, many times larger than ours and sporting the banners of Montefiore is advancing on us at speed—and we in their territory, unasked and unpermitted.''

Even Gentile could not ignore this warning. He swore an oath so ugly that Emilia blenched at it, before she shouted, the dagger still held at her bosom, ''Let us go free, Gentile, for you cannot wish to fight a pitched battle against superior forces.''

''No!'' Gentile raised his voice to shout. ''Cut him down, and the bitch may die as well, if I may not have her.''

Emilia's wail of agony was unnecessary, for even as Gentile spoke, Guido Orsini, his face white, and in no mind to die a needless death, had drawn his sword, and lifting it, shouted to the men-at-arms who were once more advancing on Ottone. ''Cut the mer-

chant down, and I shall cut the lord Gentile down!''
The unlikely allies had become enemies again.

Gentile glared at Guido, and shouted, his voice
now hoarse between baffled rage and fury at being
baulked of his victims, ''Do as he says. I shall deal
with him later. Let the merchant live.''

It was as well that he had given such an order, for
now the forces of Montefiore were pouring down the
hill, banners flying, led by a young captain who was
a cousin of Leonardo di Montefiore, and whose reputation as a *condottiere* was as great as Leonardo's.
After him streamed his captains, and over twice as
many lances as Guido and Gentile commanded together. There would be no battle, for Gentile's position was too unequal. Neither did Montefiore wish
a battle, for to fight against Verdato would weaken
them both in their attempts to keep themselves free
from being conquered by Milan or Florence.

There was to be no sacrifice. Emilia lowered her
dagger as Gentile surrendered to the inevitable. The
after-effects of her courage and of her dreadful decision to die with Ottone were upon her. Her legs
were shaking and she felt sick and ill. She hardly
dared to look at Ottone, who had lowered his broadsword and was himself a trifle dazed by the speed of
recent events.

She saw Panfilo di Montefiore dismount and walk
towards him and Gentile, and begin to speak to them.
Unsteady though she was, when Panfilo looked towards her, she felt it to be her duty as the lady of
Novera to go to him to welcome him and to thank
him for his timely arrival, but her legs would not

permit her to do any such thing. She had enough sense left to see that Gentile was trying to make the best of things, for there was still the matter of his kidnapping her, and the slaying of her escort when he did so, as well as trying to marry her, to be taken into consideration.

All in all, although she ought, as the lady of Novera, to be wondering what dispositions and decisions were being made as they spoke together, she was too shaken to care greatly for anything other than that Ottone was safe—and might go on his way. Whilst she, she would have to go to Montefiore to do her duty. This knowledge only added to Emilia's distress. She might as well have thrust the dagger into her bosom.

Why did Ottone not come over to her? Perhaps it was because she was princess again, he but the lowly man who had rescued her, and their difference in rank divided them. And why should he, who had so narrowly escaped slaughter, seem so anxious when he ought to be looking happy? She was not destined to wonder for long. Panfilo, having finished his business with Gentile, Guido and Braccio—who began to argue furiously among themselves when he left them—walked over to her, Ottone a little behind him.

Panfilo bowed low to her, and took the hand which had held the dagger to her bosom, to say gravely, "Oh, lady Marina, it seems that I arrived but in the nick of time, and it is well that I did. A pity it were that my cousin, having almost got you safely home, should fall prey to Gentile at the last moment."

Emilia saw Ottone close his eyes in pain, and answered Panfilo dazedly, "Your cousin?"

Panfilo smiled, and when he did so she saw his likeness to Ottone. "Why, who but my cousin, Leonardo, who has brought you safe to Montefiore."

Ottone was Leonardo di Montefiore! No, it could not be, and Emilia, to whom so much had happened in the last month, overwhelmed not only by that, but by the knowledge that the man with whom she had fallen so desperately in love, was also the man whom she had so often said that she did not wish to marry, felt her failing senses leave her. Her last sight was of Ottone, his face ghastly, reaching out to catch her as she fell.

Chapter Thirteen

The window of Marina's bedroom opened on to a covered, open-sided corridor, much like a cloister, which ran round a quadrangle in the centre of Duke Theodore di Montefiore's splendid palace. The quadrangle was filled with a large green lawn surrounded by beds of flowers. In its centre was a lemon tree.

Inside the bedroom everything, as elsewhere in the palace, was of the most splendid. There were carpets on the floor and a fresco on the wall opposite to Marina's bed, showing the Gods disporting themselves on Olympus. Jove, a thunderbolt in his hand, had his wife Hera by his side, and in the background, Venus, the goddess of love, and Mars, the god of war, were making sheep's eyes at one another. Cupid, the little god of love, having transfixed their hearts with one of his arrows, was flying overhead, and laughing at their torments.

Worse than that, he had, down on earth, transfixed the heart of Marina Bordoni with one of his arrows and made her love someone whom she was now sure did not love her, and she could not forgive boy Cupid for that. She could hardly bear to look at the fresco, for Niccolo, Gianni, Ottone, who was really Leonardo di Montefiore, and who had lied to her so repeatedly, might have sat as a model for Mars, he was so like him in appearance.

On the wall beside her bed hung an oval Venetian mirror, set in an ornate gold frame. At her bed's end stood a painted *cassone*, a chest for holding clothes, which was so lovely that Emilia had never seen its like. She had thought that her home at Novera was sumptuous, but it could not hold a candle to Montefiore's glories.

Not that she had seen many of them, since she had not left her bedroom after she had been carried into it, semi-conscious. She had no memory of the last stage of her journey to Montefiore city, did not know that Ottone, his face white, had picked her up and carried her to the cart, to be driven straight to the palace.

But Lucia, her waiting woman, had hardly drawn breath since Marina had recovered consciousness, as she reported to her mistress the wonders of the state, of which, if she married Leonardo, she would one day be Duchess. She had travelled with Ugo as part of his train to be ready to serve Marina when she was rescued and brought to Montefiore.

"And the lord Leonardo, so handsome, so brave! And to think that he rescued you from that wicked man, and brought you safe home into Montefiore itself! Why, it is like something that the old troubadours made songs of, and one will surely be made of your adventure!''

Whilst she chattered on, Lucia was not idle. She was busy fetching clothing out of the *cassone* and holding up a series of magnificent dresses for Marina's inspection. She, who had once been Angela, and then Emilia, had turned herself into Marina again the very moment that she had learned of Leonardo's lies, and she intended never to be anyone else. Angela and Emilia were dead and gone, particularly Angela, who had so enjoyed being the wife of Gianni of the roads, the unconsidered pedlar.

''Come, lady, tell me which of these you would prefer to wear when you meet the lord Leonardo after noon has passed. His lady mother, they say, chose them especially for her son's bride. Seeing that you had no clothing with you, other than the one worn gown which you had on when you were rescued, she sent them for you to wear. It is most gracious of her to take such trouble for you.''

''None of them—or any of them. You choose. I really don't care which.'' Marina was still sunk listlessly back against the pillows. Her hair had grown again whilst she was playing at being Emilia, and was streaming, a golden glory, down her back. Lucia had spent the best part of the last three days since Marina's arrival in Montefiore lamenting over the state she was in, and washing and brushing her gilded mane until it was as lustrous as it had been before she left Novera.

Lucia dropped the dress she was holding and put

her hands on her hips to scold Marina as she had used to do when she had been a naughty little girl.

"I am sure that I don't know what has come over you since the lord Leonardo carried you in. You won't consent to see him, or the lord Ugo, or the Duke. You are scarcely civil to me, your faithful servant. Are you still ill, since you mope so? The physician said that you were recovered, and that being so, lady, you should not give way to foolish whimwhams and grievings. I would have thought that you would be offering thanks to the Lord God that you no longer needed to travel the roads dressed as a beggar!"

How to say, I wish that I *were* travelling the roads, a beggar, with Gianni by my side.

Instead Marina sprang out of bed, and tired of moping, as Lucia called it, exclaimed fiercely, "Go to, Lucia! I will not listen to your reproaches. If you cannot speak to your lady after a proper fashion, then I shall have you sent back to Novera and ask my uncle, or the Duke Theodore, to find me a new woman. Give me any of the dresses from the chest, never mind which, tire me, and do not say another word. And why I choose to receive, or not receive, the lord Leonardo is my business, and no-one else's."

Lucia's hands dropped from her hips. Her mouth dropped open. Never, in all her years with her lady, had she been spoken to so firmly. Marina had been so sweet-natured that, privately, Lucia had sometimes feared for her, since husbands frequently took advantage of a woman's gentleness. Whatever had happened to her since that monster had kidnapped her to change her so? There was a fire about her which had never been there before. It would be wise not to cross her. But it would be easy to respect her.

So she was unaccustomedly silent as she helped Marina out of her nightrail and into the most beautiful gown of all of those which the Duchess had sent to her. It was of blue and silver, the colour which suited her blonde beauty the most, and for Marina's hair there was a matching rouleau of blue and white silk flowers to match, as well as a fan which consisted of blue and silver feathers at the end of a black and silver rod. Attired thus, the lady Marina looked a proper princess most fit for the heir to Montefiore to marry. Lucia was already a little in love with the handsome Leonardo

"Yes, lady. As you wish, lady," she muttered submissively, below her breath, every few moments. She was so unaccustomedly submissive that Marina inwardly reproached herself for being so harsh with her. But to have Leonardo, his father, his mother, and his palace constantly held up to her to be admired was almost too much.

May the wretch burn in hell for having made her love him, when all he had done was rescue the woman who was to be his bride in order to marry her purely as a duty. Of course, he did not love her, for had he done so he would have told her the truth about himself the moment that she had betrayed to him the love she felt for him.

How he must have laughed at her! Particularly when she had spoken to him so frankly about Leonardo di Montefiore, telling him that she thought of her marriage to him as a hateful duty. Marina writhed at the memory of how naïve she had been.

Of course, she owed him a debt of gratitude for having rescued her—well, almost rescued her. It had needed Panfilo and the Montefiorean army to do *that*. Now this was hardly fair to Leonardo, when she remembered the dangers which he had run on her behalf, once he had decided to disguise himself and rescue her without using an army.

She could only wonder why he had chosen to do so. There was perhaps some good reason why he had, and one day he might choose to tell her why. But, in the meantime, there was the distasteful business of meeting him again, knowing how much she had betrayed of herself, and how little he had betrayed of himself.

Such deceit!

For there were a thousand occasions upon which he could have enlightened her—and he had chosen not do so.

And she thought of the times when she had almost given herself to him, and thanks be to the Lord God that she had not surrendered to the demands of her body. Had she done so, he must have dubbed her no better than a wanton, seeing that she was promised to another…

Oh, if only Lucia would leave her alone for a moment! But the lady of Novera was never left alone. Oh, if only she were, then she could cry for her lost love, and perhaps purge herself of it. And how could she go to confession? How could she say, Oh, father, forgive me, for I wished to lie with a man I could not marry, which was a great sin. And then I found out that he was the man I was to marry, and now I do not know what to think, for I feel so betrayed.

And then, But I love him so, still. Which was the worst thing of all, and she must never let him know. He must think that her love had dropped stone dead at the moment that she had discovered who he was, and so they would go to their marriage as equals in despite, if in nothing else.

So it was that when Marina entered the great hall of Duke Theodore's palace, she appeared so coldly beautiful that she took away the breath of all those present: the Duke, Ugo, Leonardo and Panfilo, as well as the assembled courtiers and servants. Lucia had already told her that the Duchess kept to her own quarters so Marina was not surprised by her absence. What did surprise her was that Gentile da Cortona and Guido Orsini were present.

She tried not to look at Leonardo, as the major-domo—who had escorted her in with such courtly grace, quite unlike the manner in which Naldo da Bisticci's man had behaved—presented her to the company. He insisted on calling her "The most noble lady of Novera, the Princess Marina Bordoni." Which magnificence made her feel less like the late Angela of the roads than ever.

And now it was her turn to curtsey to the Duke, who put out a shapely hand to lift her. He was sombre in black and silver, and when she looked at him, she could see how like Leonardo was to his father.

"Welcome at last, my soon-to-be daughter," he

greeted her, in his courtly fashion. "Although he needs no introduction to you, it pleases me to present him to you in proper form. I give you my beloved son, Leonardo di Montefiore, who not only desired to marry you, but made certain that he did so by rescuing you from those who sought to prevent your nuptials."

After which splendid speech, he first took her hand and then Leonardo's and joined them together, exactly as the priest would do when they were married. Perforce, Marina was compelled to look at *him*, and he was even more beautiful than she could have imagined him to be, tricked out in scarlet and gold. She had always wondered what Gianni/Ottone would look like if he were dressed like Leonardo, and now she was finding out.

The splendours of the merchant Ottone were as nothing to those of a prince of the house of Montefiore. He had bathed, his hair had been washed and cut and clung round his shapely head in a mass of dark waves, enhancing the deep blue of his eyes. He was newly shaven, too, the line of his jaw, stronger than ever, not blurred with an incipient beard.

His clothes were magnificent in their simplicity, but the chain around his neck was of gold set with rubies and pearls, and the belt around his waist was gold, too, and set with more of the same gems. His long legs showed to advantage in hose which clung to them like a second skin, one leg being scarlet and the other gold. The scarlet one had a garter around it, just below the knee, inlaid with more pearls and rubies.

There was nothing about him to remind her of Gianni of the roads, and Marina had never felt so desolate, so lost.

His face bore the impersonal imprint of his station. He was a living icon, meet to be worshipped by a kneeling populace, or ready to lead an army into battle once he had donned helmet and breast plate. In her desolation, Marina forgot that she bore the same stamp of pride and authority; that she was also sharing in a ritual designed to set them apart from those whom they were to rule.

But beneath the clothes they were as human as their subjects—as Marina had found on her long journey to safety with him.

"Lady Marina," he murmured, and lifted her hand to his lips to kiss it. "I am pleased to be able to welcome you to Montefiore at last."

"As I am pleased to be here," she answered him, but the words were a lie, and he knew it, for her voice was as cold as a mountain stream, and as impersonal as that of a judge passing sentence. The light in Leonardo's eyes which had been there from the moment in which she had walked in, died at the sound. He had been ready to smile at her, to hold her hand tenderly, to remind her that, despite all that they had endured during their time together, they had come to love one another. That she had been willing to die for and with him.

Alas! She had turned into the princess of whom he had been told. Who froze men with a look and who had made it plain that although she might marry, it was her body which she was offering to her husband, never her soul. She was quite other than the brave companion whom he had come to know on their travels—and whom he had partly created.

The devil of it was that he knew why—and that he would have to woo her all over again. This time he was not sure that he could win her, for she felt herself betrayed.

Leonardo could not but admire the way in which Marina played the part of a great princess, who had been carefully trained to obey all the precepts in those manuals written to ensure that young women were modest in all things, and would consequently arrive chaste and untouched at their marriage ceremony.

Everything which she did was perfect. She smiled as she sat beside him at the great banquet put on to celebrate her safe arrival and her coming marriage to him. She spoke to his father after a manner which suggested her admiration for him, as well as her deference to his superior station. She was perfect with Ugo, and with Panfilo, too.

She had even been perfect when Gentile and Guido had been dealt with, showing no unseemly emotion.

"Daughter," the Duke had said, turning to her immediately after her arrival and after he had insisted that she sit by him on his right, with Leonardo on his left. "It is only meet and proper that you are present when justice is done to those who ravished you away, and would have forced you into an unwanted marriage."

Marina had bowed her agreement, as did Ugo, who

was seated on a chair of state a little to the right of the Duke's party.

"Indeed, lord Duke," she replied, her voice calm, "I will defer to your judgment, as I am sure that my uncle will do—whatever that judgment may be."

The Duke rose. His voice as stern as he could make it, he announced what he had decided.

"If all men had their deserts," he announced, "then I should consign you, Gentile da Cortona, and you Guido Orsini, who bears a name which is not yours, to the dungeons, the torturers and finally the headsman, for what you attempted with Montefiore's bride. Furthermore, you compounded your offence by invading my territory and seeking to murder my son—no matter that you did not know that he was my son." He said this last as both men opened their mouths to remonstrate with him.

"Murder is murder," he continued, "whoever the victim is, and my son was but seeking to recover that which was stolen from Montefiore and Novera." He paused, to allow Gentile and Guido to stare at him ashen-faced, before going on to say with great deliberation, "Nevertheless, bearing in mind the threat which all three of our states, Montefiore, Novera, and Verdato, faces from our powerful neighbours, to begin a war between us which might give them the opportunity to intervene and take us all up, would be worse than foolish.

"That being so, I shall spare you to return to your own states, after you have ordered your citizenry to raise and pay a ransom which I shall name, and after you have gone on to your knees before me to swear fealty to me in the cathedral at Montefiore, before the High altar there. To break that oath would be to risk excommunication by the Holy Father himself.

"Furthermore, you Gentile, having no son or heir of your own, will swear to me that the state of Verdato will revert to Montefiore on your death. You understand, both of you, that if you refuse these terms, the rack and the executioner's block await you. This is the mercy that I offer you."

Gentile began to protest. The Duke raised a hand to silence him, and said, his voice like stone, "Many would have executed you the moment you were brought here, after your troops had surrendered to mine. You should be grateful that I am sparing you, even if am doing so only as a matter of statesmanlike policy which benefits all of us, not only myself. Although, as is proper, I am the greatest gainer in this.

"Decide quickly what your answer will be. I will not palter with you long."

Guido jumped foward to kneel before, not the Duke, but Marina.

"Forgive me, lady, for what I tried to do to you. Praise God, I failed. I will be your servant, lord Duke, and accept the generous terms which you offer, as will my overlord, the lord Gentile, once he has come to terms with your magnanimity." He kissed the toe of Marina's slipper, disregarding the shudder of distaste which she had given when she saw him kneeling so near to her.

And so it was decided. Gentile, when push came to shove, had no mind to die an ignominious death when a way out was offered to him. He and Guido

were led away to quarters, which, if not as sumptuous as those which housed the Duke and his family,
were rather better than the damp dungeons which
might have been their due!

Marina's only display of emotion had been to
shiver when Gentile, having knelt to the Duke, gave
her and Leonardo a baleful stare before the man-at-
arms took him by the shoulder to urge him on his
way so that the ducal party might process to their
banquet. After that she was impassivity itself, her
cold smile never reaching her eyes.

If the Duke and Ugo noticed how withdrawn she
was, neither of them said anything. To Ugo, indeed,
Marina was as she had always been, and as he had
described her to the Duke, so he was not surprised
by her manner. Only Leonardo tried to revive the
lively and loving woman who had sat beside him in
the forest, had eaten the rabbit which Beppo had
cooked them, had offered up her flowers to God at
Ostuna, and shared in the simple pleasures and sor-
rows of its citizens.

A great silver platter of beautifully cooked food
was placed before them, to be served by the pages
who ran everywhere to do their masters' bidding.

"This is a little different from our fare in the forest, is it not, lady?" he whispered to her, to have her
offer him her shoulder and say coldly.

"Indeed, ser Leonardo, very different," with no
warmth in her tone.

The only time her perfect control faltered was
when he caught her looking around the table, and at

the men-at-arms who lined the walls, there for their
protection.

"What is it, lady?" he asked her. "What do you
seek?"

She turned her beautiful face towards him, but to
Leonardo she was not as beautiful as she had been
as dirty Angela, because Angela had been warm and
human, and this woman was as cold as ice. "I but
wondered whether Beppo, I mean Marco, was present tonight, and if not, where he was."

This gave Leonardo hope. He replied eagerly,
"Why, lady, he is at present on an errand for my
father at the court of Milan, given him when he
reached here after he left us."

"I had hoped to see him," was all she said to that.

The beautiful food was dust and ashes in her
mouth, as it was in Leonardo's. He wished most passionately that he might speak to her alone, but that
privilege was denied to him. For the moment they
were on public display, surrounded by the many
friends and relatives of the Montefiore family, as well
as the most rich merchants in the duchy, who were
responsible for its ever-increasing wealth.

Tomorrow! Yes, he would see her alone tomorrow, when all those around them were about their
own business, and try to repair the breach which her
discovery of his deception of her had created.

But tomorrow was no better. He had asked if he
might wait upon her in the morning, and she had
inclined her head and answered coolly, "Of course,
my lord of Montefiore." But when he arrived in her

living chamber next to her bedroom, she had her waiting woman with her, who looked at him with great greedy eyes, and was certain to listen avidly to every word he said to her mistress.

Marina looked lovelier than ever. She was in a cream silk gown decorated with scarlet carnations, and the scarlet was repeated in the velvet of the sash which bound her tiny waist. She was wearing one of the new headdresses which had come from France, a tall conical cap from which a veil of the finest gauze depended.

He was dismally aware that his own splendour matched hers, and he wondered if she was as miserable behind it as he was behind his. If so, nothing showed: she was as great a dissembler as he was.

"You look well, lady," he told her, to such banalities was he reduced.

Marina inclined her head as graciously as she could. She could hardly bear to look on him. Today he was favouring a suit of black and silver similar to the one which his father had worn the evening before, and its sombre glory suited him even more than the scarlet and gold he had worn for the banquet.

He wanted to take her in his arms, to kiss her, to remind her of the times when they had laughed and talked together, had confessed their love not only in words, but in exchanges of glances, sighs and secret understandings.

But not only was the waiting woman there, presently Marina summoned a page who brought in wine and little cakes and pastries, and set them out on a small inlaid table which had come from Constantinople. There were goblets of silver, and a tall jug. The page hovered about them, awaiting further orders.

A plague on them all! He would have none of this! As Marina put out a hand to offer him the plate of pastries after the page had poured him wine from the jug, Leonardo seized her slender wrist, and exclaimed urgently, "Lady! I would speak with you privately. No offence to those who serve you, but I bid you send them away. We are affianced now, and may most properly be left alone."

He saw her tremble, saw her lip quiver and the colour mount in her face, but she could not gainsay him because he had the right of it. It would be most unnatural of her to refuse such a reasonable wish on the part of an eager future husband.

Marina waved Lucia and the page away. What could he have to say to her? And did he know that every time she looked at him her heart melted within her, and all that she wanted was to be in his arms again! Oh, how weak she was, to love him still. He who was simply taking part in a dynastic marriage, made for political gain. She would not wait for him to speak, she would attack first.

"What have you to say to me, Lord Leonardo, that may not wait until our marriage vows are made?"

"This," he said roughly, and putting out his hands, seized her shoulders roughly, and pulled her to her feet with such power that she felt the brute strength of him for the first time since he had freed her from Gentile's clutches. "Why are you treating me so coldly, so cruelly, now that we are at my fa-

ther's court? This is not how you were wont to behave when you were Emilia and I was Ottone.
Whence comes this change? Why have you transformed yourself into a cold princess again? Is this
the woman who wished to die by my side and so
threatened Gentile?''

''Why, ser Leonardo!'' she told him, trying to preserve her lovely calm even as she trembled at his
touch, and wished to lean forward to kiss the mouth
which was so near to her own. ''You know as well
as I why I have done so. This is the woman whom
you are contracted to marry, the lady of Novera. The
woman whom you deceived from the moment you
seized her at the altar, to the moment when the forces
of Montefiore arrived and compelled you to acknowledge your trickery. Think you that I could ever trust
a word which such a one as you have proved to be
said? I was Angela who loved Gianni, Emilia who
loved Ottone. But they were phantoms. You lied to
me. Compelled me to love a man who did not exist.
Humiliated me, because you even made me want to
cancel all the vows of chastity which I had taken.
Made me fearful that I might betray the man to
whom I was promised—who was you! And never
once did you so much as hint to me the truth of
yourself.

''I will marry you because the reasons of state
which made my uncle and your father agree to this
match are all-compelling—and for no other reason.''

''No!'' he exclaimed hoarsely, holding her still
against him. ''I regret that I never told you who I
was when once I began to love you, as I have never

loved another woman. But I—rightly as I now see—
was fearful of how you would behave when once you
knew the truth of me. Your safety was always my
concern, the more so as the days passed and our mutual passion grew. Do not shake your head. Remember your behaviour at Burani, and later, in the woods,
as we drew near to Montefiore.''

His grip on her had slackened for a moment, and
Marina pulled herself free, to retreat to the far end
of the room, to stare at him with tear-filled eyes.

''Oh, do not remind me of my shame. Leave me
only with the memory that, for whatever reason, you
saved me from Gentile, and for that also I will marry
you. But do not pretend that you loved me. If you
had, you would have told me the truth, and not
waited for me to discover it from another's lips.''

He was across the room, to throw himself on his
knees before her. ''Nay, no pretence, Marina. I love
you more than I would have once thought possible.
It breaks my heart to see you reject me, even though
I understand why you do.''

She made him no answer, but turned her head
away, and put out a hand as though to ward him off.

''Nay, my heart, my life,'' he cried, ''do but listen
to me. It is true that before I met you, marriage to
you was but a duty which I did not particularly want.
But once we were on the road together, and I came
to know the true lady of Novera, not the one of legend and rumour, I came to love you. There were
good reasons why I dared not tell you who I was. It
was best that you did not know so that you could not
by accident betray my true identity if we were

caught—giving Gentile and later, Guido, a hostage to bargain with. Better that they thought me naught but a lowly mercenary—which I once was, before my brother died.

"And later, when I could have told you, we were so happy together that I was fearful to spoil what we had come to share—and, if you would but listen to me, could share again." He picked up the skirt of her gown to hide his face in, before looking up at her to say with passion, "What oath can I swear to prove that what I am saying to you is true? Tell me, and I will swear it. Do but remember that you loved Ottone so dearly that you were ready to die with him. I am that Ottone, Marina. I and none other."

Oh, if she could but believe him. If only she could recapture what she had felt when she had faced Gentile and Guido with the dagger in her hand. She had been ready to sacrifice her life, as she had been ready to escape being the Noveran princess, to be lost, never to be found again, in order to live with the man whom she had come to love.

She, who never cried, was weeping. Weeping for the past, for the woman who had travelled the roads and found love, but now dare not trust that love. So many of her kind married for convenience, as an act of state, that she could not believe that he was telling her the truth. On the road everything had seemed simple, but now nothing was simple.

Something of her torment, her anguish, touched the man kneeling before her.

"Trust me," he said, abandoning justification,

abandoning explanation. "Angela trusted Gianni, Emilia trusted Ottone."

"But we are neither," she whispered through her tears. "I will marry you, Leonardo—but you must be patient with me." Her sobs renewed as she remembered the camaraderie of the road, the laughter, and the loving—and the fear, which had served only to bind them together, as high state and comfort never could.

Leonardo slowly rose. He recognised exhaustion when he saw it, and for the moment he must be content. The tears which his dear love was shedding told him that she was human still, not cold goddess.

Be patient, she had said, and so he would be.

He took her hand, so cold, so icy cold, and kissed it.

"Farewell," he said. "Patience shall be my mistress—if you will allow mercy to be yours."

Chapter Fourteen

"So, we surrender completely and you go home, not only empty-handed, but heavily in debt to Montefiore. A fine end to our expedition! And all done without exchanging so much as a blow. That is not how I thought Gentile da Cortona ordered matters. So much for reputations!"

Gentile was confronting an angry Braccio after telling him of the Duke's decision.

"Be reasonable, man," Gentile said wearily. "This pains me even more than it does you—you merely go to serve another master if you are discontent with me. But I, I have to pay the ransom, and sign my lands away. No!" He held up his hand as Braccio began to speak. "I had hoped to wed the lady before Montefiore and Novera's forces arrived to stop me. Once wedded there was nothing Ugo Bordoni or any other man could have done. But once I was in Montefiore and my gambler's throw had failed, and I was confronted by a host better armed and twice as large as mine, it would have been throwing all our lives away to have offered battle. This way I at least live to fight another day.''

"And Leo di Montefiore lives not only to mock us, but to make us the laughing-stock of all Italy. Snatching the lady away at the altar, humiliating us all, disguising himself and her, and achieving refuge just as his cousin's army arrived to save him: it is a song fit for a troubadour to sing—and bring us further mock.''

Gentile's smile was nasty. ''Well, you may thank your own lack of judgment, Braccio, for losing us this throw. After all, you had him and the lady in your hands at Ostuna, and let them go. I owe you no thanks, and another lord would not have given you your pay before turning you off, after you had caused him such grief.''

Braccio made no answer to that: there was none to make. His hatred of Leonardo was a living thing which gnawed at his vitals. He had spent more than one happy hour plotting what he would do to him once they had captured him and taken him back to Verdato's dungeons. All to no avail.

He looked at the moth-eaten old man who stood before him whining about his losses. And who now took the opportunity to jeer at him further. ''I hear your sergeant, the only one with any brains in your troop, has asked Panfilo di Montefiore to hire him to serve in his band, having no mind to serve further such a one as you. Do as he does, and as I am doing. Cut your losses. Forget this and resolve to be a little more careful in future as to whom you allow to escape from your clutches.''

Yes, every cruel word was like a white hot sword twisting in Braccio's guts. Oh, he could not have his revenge on Gentile—no point in that—but he was suddenly resolved that before he left Montefiore Messer Leonardo should pay for all his deceits.

He said nothing further. Best let the old fool before him think that he had swallowed all the insults which he had put upon him. What he had decided to do must be done secretly if it were to succeed—and if it did, why, then, Messer Leonardo might not think himself so clever after all!

The preparations for the wedding went ahead with speed. Now that the lady of Novera was safe, and her future husband with her, the Duke felt that it was imperative that nothing should stand in the way of the alliance which would benefit both states so signally. The splendour of the celebrations would show to all the world the power and the might which Montefiore would command when Leonardo inherited Novera.

This did not mean that he saw Marina merely as a pawn in a diplomatic game. He was pleased by both her beauty and the cool control which she had displayed from the first moment in which she had walked into his presence. His son was acquiring a wife who would do him and Montefiore justice, and so he told his wife, singing her praises so much that the Duchess decided to delay no longer in meeting her son's bride.

She had been ill again with a complaint which no doctor could identify, beyond the belief that the humours of her body were not in agreement, and there was little that they could do to help her—except dose her with strong medicine which made her feel worse.

Marina was seated in her room, trying to read when the Duchess's woman arrived to tell her that her mistress wished to see her on the instant—if that were agreeable to her.

It was not agreeable to Marina. It was not long after Leonardo had left her and she was still inwardly shaking from her encounter with him. Could she believe him? The words ran through her head again and again, preventing her from reading the book which she had taken up.

Nevertheless her strong sense of duty had her agreeing to visit the Duchess Caterina at once. She was pleased that she had done so when the waiting-woman told her hesitantly, "I must inform you, Madonna, that the Duchess is very weak, and finds it difficult to talk overmuch. If I am to be honest with you, I must also tell you that she lives only to know that Leonardo is married."

So Marina was not surprised when she entered the pretty room, where flowers blossomed in every corner, and which overlooked the park at the back of the palace, to find the Duchess reclining on a daybed in the loggia which adjoined the room. She was swathed in shawls, although the day was warm. She possessed the remains of great beauty, but there was a transparent look about her, which told of suffering, long endured. Her voice was still strong, however, when she welcomed her future daughter-in-law.

"Come, let me see you, child! Yes, you are as

lovely as Theodore and Leonardo said you were. Sorry I am that I have been too ill to welcome you to Montefiore before. Sit beside me, and we will talk of what women love—of men and gardens and books and the children that we have borne—and will bear.''

Marina needed no second invitation. Wine was brought in, and cakes and sweets, and as the Duchess had said, they talked of women's things. But, slowly and discreetly, the Duchess questioned her about her recent adventures with Leonardo and Marina answered her as honestly as she could.

She looked beyond the Duchess to the bright scene in the park outside. A serving maid was running along the path, a young man chasing her, and their distant laughter floated into the quiet room. How to speak truthfully, how to say, I wish I were that girl, and Leonardo the boy who pursues her?

She said at last, the Duchess watching her keenly as she hesitated, ''It was like one of Messer Boccaccio's tales, where a lady of high degree is disguised and performs tasks and duties which she has never dreamed of—and finds herself to be quite another person.''

''I see,'' but what the Duchess saw was not immediately plain. She continued, ''And Leonardo? Was he kind? I have always found him kind, although some, I know, find him severe.''

So she could be truthful. ''Yes, he was severe with me, a little, at first. Which was a good thing I now see, for I had to do so much that was foreign to me, and it was important that I did not give him away.''

Could she be completely truthful? Perhaps she

could. "The only thing which I do not understand is why he came himself to rescue me. It was such a dangerous thing to do. I quite see why the Duke and my uncle did not want to send an army after me, and provoke a war with Verdato, but there must have been others who could have been sent to save me."

"His father told me," the Duchess said slowly, "that Leonardo asked to go because he knew that he could trust himself to care for you properly, and see you safe into Montefiore. You understand me, I am sure."

She knew from Marina's expression and manner that there was something wrong, but what it was, she was not quite sure. Perhaps nothing more than the reaction of a young and innocent woman to the dangers which she had passed, and to the realities of the life of the helpless among whom she had briefly lived.

"My son is a good man, and will try to see you happy. He did not wish to be his father's heir, for he liked a roving life. He also loved his elder brother dearly, and was greatly distressed by his death."

Marina nodded her head gravely. "I know. He told me so, once, when we were talking. I did not know then that he was speaking of the heir to a duchy, nor that he was Leonardo, the man I was to marry." There was pain in her voice when she spoke, and the Duchess's intuition told her what the trouble was.

"And when did he tell you, child?"

"He never told me. His cousin Panfilo did at the very moment when he rescued us from Gentile. Oh, lady," she burst out. "Why did he not tell me? I...I said so much to him that was wrong. That I was marrying out of duty only…things I would not have said had I known who he was.''

Here, then, was the meat of it. The Duchess took Marina's hand which lay lax in her lap. "Do you love my son, Marina?''

Oh, to say it at last! "Yes, yes, I do, but does he love me? Why not tell me the truth?''

"If it will help you, I will tell you the truth I know. From the way in which he speaks of you, I think that my son loves you, and that he did not tell you who he was in order to protect you both. He is a man of honour, and I do not say that simply because he is my son, but because all Montefiore, and those for whom he worked when he was a roving *condottiero*, know it to be so.''

Marina kissed the Duchess's frail hand. "If I could but believe that…''

"Believe it…have pity on him…and now, drink your wine and we will talk of other things. I may not go to your wedding, the doctors will not allow me such excitement, but afterwards you shall tell me of it.''

Could she believe the Duchess? She would try to. Leonardo had asked her for mercy and the Duchess had told her to show pity.

They were both attributes of which the Lord God approved, and she took the memory of her meeting with Leonardo's mother to bed with her that night. Could she, as the Duchess had told her, trust him?

She fell into an uneasy sleep, and somewhere towards the dawn she began to dream. She was lost in

a forest at night. But she was not alone. Her hand
was in someone else's. A man's hand. Large and
strong and warm. He was urging her along, almost
running her through the trees. What man was this?
Why was he being so urgent with her? There had
been other men with them once, but they had been
sent away some days ago. How did she know that?
Did she know the man whose hand she held, or more
accurately, whose hand grasped hers? More importantly, did she trust him?

She stopped suddenly, so suddenly that he stopped,
too, and spoke to her.

For some reason she could not see his face, but
she could hear his voice.

"Do you trust me, Marina?" he asked her urgently.

"With my life," she told him. "With my life."

Even as she said the last words everything swirled
away into the dark: the moon, the forest and the man,
and she was awake again, remembering everything
which had happened to her since the morning when
her uncle had sent for her, to end forever the peaceful
life which she had been living as Novera's lady...

Marina sat up in her bed in Montefiore city. What
a strange dream! She might have thought that all she
was doing was remembering the past—but although
many strange and exciting things had happened to
her on her long journey with Leonardo, what had
happened in her dream was not one of them. Nevertheless the dream was trying to tell her something
and that something was that she could trust Leonardo. Her deepest self was telling her so. Many be-

lieved that dreams told true, and perhaps this dream had been sent as a sign.

If it were a sign, then she must speak to him alone, and soon. Perhaps then she might discover whether the dream—and the Duchess—did speak true.

But privacy was hard to find in the world in which Leonardo and Marina lived. Gianni and Angela had found it easy to be private, but they were simple people, not great persons of state surrounded by courtiers with many duties imposed on them. That afternoon Leonardo went hawking with some of the envoys from Florence, Milan, Mantua, and other great cities, who had arrived for the wedding. There were meetings to be attended where business was done. Merchants came to the palace, not only to buy and sell, but to consult the Duke and his counsellors. Scribes ran importantly about. Marina had thought Novera a busy state, but it was as nothing to Montefiore.

It was not until late on the following afternoon after yet another banquet that Marina was able to speak to Leonardo at all. He had been cool towards her as they sat together, as cool as she had been to him, and she supposed that she deserved it. Looking at his imperious profile, for the first time she felt a little afraid of him—which made her wish more than ever that she was simple Angela again.

She touched him on his sleeve as the meal drew near to its end. He was looking particularly handsome in a short tunic whose colour was a deep burnt sienna. His long legs were clad in hose striped in sienna and gold. For once he was armed; the dagger

with which she had threatened to take her life was
at his waist. His tunic was decorated with narrow
bands of some golden fur. Each day seemed to take
him further and further away from the man who had
been Gianni. Was this grave creature the pedlar who
had laughed and sung in the square, who had joked
with the peasants who came to buy the wares he
carried in his cart?

"I would speak with you, alone," she whispered.

His eyes shone a deeper blue at her words. It was
the first time since she had discovered who he was
that she had started a dialogue with him. Before she
had responded only to what he said to her.

"I will come to your room—but only if you send
your dragon away as soon as you return there. Is she
the know-all nurse with whom you belaboured me
on the road?"

For the first time since she had arrived at Duke
Theodore's court Marina gave a genuine laugh. Her
uncle smiled at the sound, and Leonardo's eyes grew
bluer still.

"I am pleased to hear you happy," he told her,
and lifted his goblet of wine to her in salutation, so
that, perforce, she was compelled to imitate him. Before she could stop him he leaned forward as she
lifted her own to drink from it, looking deep into her
eyes.

"Bravo," someone shouted, to celebrate the first
time that the affianced pair had shown any emotion
before others. Blushing, Marina ducked her head, for
Leonardo to chuck her beneath the chin, as he would
have done Angela.

"Courage," he told her. "There will be more than that to endure when we are wedded, and then bedded, so that all may know that we are truly man and wife."

Which made her wish more than ever that they were back in the forest again.

Something of this showed on her face, so that Leonardo, emboldened by her changed manner to him, whispered in her ear, "At least we do not have to seal the marriage in public as our ancestors did—we are spared that." And when her face flamed scarlet at the very thought, he added, "Until later, then."

It was very much later because Panfilo, flown with wine, shouted, "Let the coming bridegroom sing and play for us. Have the servants bring you your lute, Leo—and does your lady sing? Is her voice as beautiful as her face?"

"Go to," began the Duke, but then, as several of the younger men hammered on the table in support of Panfilo, "Oh, very well, but one song only, mind."

"But only if my bride will consent to sing with me. And it shall be *The Blackbird's Song* or nothing."

It was almost like being on the road again. To Ugo's surprise his shy niece, who had always avoided such exhibitions, rose to stand beside Leonardo when his lute had been handed to him and he had tuned it, betraying none of the embarrassment which he had expected. Nor was she overset when her pure voice soared into the Duke's newly painted ceiling, showing the Nine Muses celebrating on Mount Olympus.

The company cheered when the song ended, and Leonardo, compounding his naughtiness, asked Marina in a voice which none but she could hear, "Now shall we entertain them with *The Englishman and the Venetian Tart?*" bringing back memories of their evening with Isabella and Guido.

But he was only teasing her, they were let off after singing their one song, and more than one of the half-cut diners envied the heir of Montefiore his pretty bride.

"Not so cold, eh?" being the universal agreement of them all, "nor so haughty," for her coolness towards Leonardo had not escaped notice.

But Marina was not cool as she waited for him in her room. She had done as he bade her, and had sent Lucia away. She had taken off her grand clothing and wore instead a linen chemise with a *gamurra*, a simple wool tunic, over it. She had no idea of what she would say to him, nor had she even made up her mind as to whether she believed what he and his mother had both told her: that he loved her.

At his knock on the door she jumped fearfully before she walked over to let him in. Like her he had left off his garments of state and was wearing a simple brown woollen tunic over plain hose. When he saw her he pulled off his hat, a large one made of black felt, with a narrow brim and the top of it puffed out like a huge plum pudding.

He smiled when he saw her looking at it. "The latest thing from Paris, they tell me. I thought that we might walk in the park—the evening is warm and the air is full of the scents of flowers. I see that you have sent the dragon away.''

Unspoken was his thought that out in the open again, among the trees and shrubs, they might imagine that they were on the road, and the constraints of living as prince and princess might disappear.

Marina nodded, and took the hand he held out to her, after she had picked up her straw hat from a shelf by her bed. Leonardo put on his hat again, and they set off together, without courtiers, pages, waiting women, footmen, or men-at-arms to follow them and bow them on their way.

A sleepy man-at-arms, his falchion at the ready, watched them incuriously. It was not for him to question what the great ones of his world might do. Outside it was as pleasant as Leonardo had told her it would be. He said nothing to her as they walked along, only led her into the park towards a great pool of water where fish swam, gold and silver in the moonlight.

There was a stone bench in front of the pool, and he bowed her on to it, to sit beside her himself. Beyond the pool, dim in the half dark, was a statue of Apollo, ready to loose an arrow from his outsize bow. The bow which only a god from Olympus could carry. They removed their hats in homage to the God, and the warm night.

''What is it, Marina? What is it that you wish to say to me?''

His voice was gentle. He was neither Gianni nor Leonardo, but someone whom she did not know.

The world swam before her eyes. Apollo first faded, and then re-appeared. Amazingly, tears were not far away.

At last she said, "I saw your mother today."

"I am glad of that," he replied. "She is not long for this world, as you must have seen, and she is a woman worth knowing."

"Yes," said Marina, stricken by the desolation in his voice. "She explained a little why you acted as you did." She went on, "Perhaps I was thoughtless to reproach you for deceiving me."

His answer was an unexpected one. "No, you were right. I was a coward. After Burani, once I thought that we were safe away, and almost home— although I was wrong there—I should have told you. Several times I began to do so, but I could not go on. The last time was on the night before Gentile caught up with us. But I could not bear to think of you turning away from me. How strange, that in battle I never need to remind myself to be brave, but there on the road with you, I needed that reminder, and there was no-one to give it to me. Can you forgive me?"

Of course she could forgive him. He was speaking like the man whom she had come to love on the road. She could forgive that man anything.

"There is nothing to forgive," she said huskily. "It is only that I do not know myself now that I am once more the lady of Novera. Oh, how I wish that we could be Gianni and Angela again, and ride the roads forever. That I had never learned who you are.

Everything was so simple then. Is that stupid of me?''

''No, not stupid. But that is not our life. This is our life. We have duties and responsibilities that we may not shed. I never wanted them. I was happy to be Niccolo da Stresa, which was the name I took when I became a soldier, because I did not wish to feel that I owed any advancement I might gain simply because I was a son of Montefiore. But once I inherited my brother's life, that simple life was lost to me.

''I must be honest with you. I did not wish to marry you, for the same reasons that you told me when you were Angela and Emilia, that you did not wish to marry me. A marriage out of duty to a woman I had never met was distasteful to me. Those beneath us might marry out of love, or friendship, but that was to be denied to me, as it was to you. And then...''

He fell silent, and in the end Marina murmured hesitantly, ''And then?''

''And then...'' His smile was brilliant. ''But you know the rest, my lady. We shared danger, and those who do so frequently find that a bond grows between them, which those who have only known a life of ease and safety cannot experience. And that bond blossomed into love: a mutual love, I thought. Was it love, Marina?'' He looked deep into her eyes as he spoke. ''Was it a mutual love or was I deceived? Did the first difference which came between us destroy that love? For if it did, it was not love, but love's counterfeit. Tell me that it was love, Marina.

For if it be so, then the life of duty to which we are both pledged will be the easier to endure in the knowledge that another loves us and will share our burdens.''

So speaking, he took her in his arms, for he saw by the brilliance of her look, the very quiver of her mouth that she was willing to be his, that the love which they had found in danger and hardship, was not to be lost to them in easy prosperity. No words were needed, for those who love deeply share a common self which goes beyond the normal bounds of living, as though they also share a soul, even though they may only briefly be one body.

Marina had come home again. What she had temporarily lost had been found.

''You asked me for mercy, and your mother asked me for pity,'' she whispered into his chest, ''and I grant you both of them, on condition that you show them to me for having doubted you—which was ungrateful of me after you had risked your life to save me from Gentile's clutches.''

''Granted,'' he murmured, savouring the scent of her, the feel of her soft and warm against him, the only woman he had ever loved, or would love. Beautiful she might be, but he loved her for more than that, for the courage she had shown on more than one occasion, and for her compassion, freely granted.

Suddenly passion, long repressed, seized them both in its grip! One moment they were quiet and gentle in one another's arms, and in the next they were lovers who wanted nothing but the one true end of loving. Leonardo gave a groan as his mouth found

Marina's to discover that what he wanted, she wanted also. To be one, not two, was their only desire. There, alone beneath the moon in the beautiful garden, they had found their Eden.

Such sweet sensation! Such bodily joy! In the few short passages of love which she had shared with him before they reached Montefiore Marina had not experienced such unbounded pleasure. For a moment she thought that she was like to faint, as his hands and body taught her what true love can mean.

The nightingale had begun its song in earnest. But it was not to finish it that night. At the last moment, when consummation was upon them, the reality of what they were doing struck them both at once. The duty to which they had bound themselves called to them—and was heard.

Leonardo lifted his head from Marina's breast, and stared blankly into her blank eyes, to hear her say faintly, "Our vows, Leonardo, our vows. Those we are to make in the cathedral. I am meant to come to you before all men a virgin, or else the ceremony will be a mock. We must not begin with a lie."

To lift himself from her arms was an agony. It was he, this time, not she, who had begun their meeting with lofty talk of duty, and here he was, ravishing his love before the priest had said the proper words over them, before her uncle had handed her into his keeping. He was shaming himself before God and man if he could not wait the few hours left to them before he might lawfully lie with her.

Nevertheless Leonardo was shuddering with love denied when he said to Marina as, with shaking hands, she tied the strings of the chemise which he had loosened to find her breasts, "Forgive me. I was a brute beast to set upon you here in the open, before the priest had said the words which bind us as man and wife."

Marina put her hands over his mouth. "Do not say so. For you did nothing which I did not wish you to do. The shame, if there be any, is mine as well as yours." She looked at him, and saw the marks of passion on his face. Knowing how ravaged she felt, she said, "Let us walk a little in the park before we return to the palace, lest our faces betray us to any we meet. Whatever else, we must contain ourselves publicly before the world."

"Oh, wise child," he muttered, and taking her hand, he added, "There is something I must show you. It is but a short walk away, through the trees, and the moon will only add to its beauty. Come."

Hand in hand they walked, as though they were the first man and woman, alone in Eden. A bird was singing, but it was not Boccaccio's nightingale. That they must wait for. At the end of an alley they came into an open space, and there Marina saw what Leonardo had promised her.

Before them, silver in the moonlight, water cascaded down a gently sloping hillside in a giant fall to end in a basin even larger than the one before which they had been sitting. Seated by the edge of the pool was a marble statue of Narcissus, frozen as he stared into the troubled waters to find his beautiful face. Around the pool stood a circle of marble statues, each statue showing a satyr balanced on a pedestal, with a nymph leaning against the pedestal. Each satyr caressed his nymph after a different fashion, and their faces were like the faces which Leonardo and Marina had worn when they were making love.

"See," whispered Leonardo. "This place is dedicated to all lovers, and on the night we marry, I shall bring you here, to love you in the open, as Gianni would have loved Angela. This I promise you."

"Oh," breathed Marina. It was all that she could say.

They stood there for some time, watching the changing patterns of the water, until, as the night grew colder, Leo whispered, "We must be away before someone misses us."

Hand in hand again they walked back towards the world of duty—and the world of danger. Leonardo felt as though he were walking on air after having walked in mud ever since he had arrived home. They were entering the long alley beyond the pool where they had earlier sat, and were in the dark again. To the left there were lights coming from a small building which housed the pages of the court and their lieutenants. Before them, in the distance, were the lights of the palace, their future home.

Leonardo, anticipating their future life together, looked with affection at the sweet face of his true love, sure now that she would be not only a loving helpmeet but a brave one. Her character had been forged like strong steel in the troubles she had faced since Gentile had reft her away from safety, and from all the comforts of a life which had known only roses, never thorns.

Well, she had survived that nobly, and had captured his heart into the bargain, and when he uttered his wedding vows before the priest, it would be in a very different temper from the one which he had thought to bring to the altar. Oh, he was doubly blessed—as his mother had told him, after she had seen and spoken to Marina.

Even as he thought this, there were rapid footsteps behind him, and before he could turn to see who was coming he was seized around the neck from behind by strong and strangling hands. He had been caught, unwarned, around the throat, exactly as he had caught Gentile, and was consequently as helpless as Gentile had been.

Blinded, his consciousness already affected by his inability to breathe properly, he was only able to croak something unintelligible at Marina, in an effort to warn her.

He felt himself dragged backwards, losing her hand which had lain so trustingly in his. She gave a sudden cry even as Leonardo's hand left hers, and he felt the prick of a dagger at his throat. She saw how he had been trapped, and heard the man who had trapped him shout savagely, "Make a noise, lady, or run for help, and I shall cut your paramour's throat on the instant. I would prefer him to die slowly for the trouble he has caused me, but if needs be, I shall finish him off quickly—and then take my fill of you!"

Impossible to tell who it was who was speaking,

whether it be Gentile, Guido, or Braccio, and what mattered who it was, if he intended but to kill Leonardo, quickly or slowly. Under the strong hands which pinioned him and cut off his ability to breath, Leonardo felt his consciousness ebbing quickly, and cruel it was that just as he and Marina had reached haven, he should be snatched from her and from life. Desperate, he tried one last throw, brought up his right foot to stamp it down as hard as he could on his assailant's, either right or left, he did not know, nor did it matter which.

Dimly, as in the distance, he heard Marina's sobbing cry, even as the man holding him loosened his death-grip round his throat, under the impact of a blow which might not have been severe, but had been enough to surprise his assailant. This allowed Leonardo to swivel around, gasping for breath, sucking in air, and try to catch at the hand which held the dagger, ready to deal him a death blow.

By St Michael and all the archangels he would not go meekly to his death, but would die fighting, if die he must!

Leonardo's hand—his strength renewed a little with each breath, air had never tasted so sweet—grasped his attacker's wrist, even as the dagger sought to find his spine, to deal him a killing blow. He was at a disadvantage, having left off his own dagger which he had earlier worn as an ornament. Fool! Fool! I should have expected this, humiliated men will always take their revenge. What price my cunning now—that I, unarmed, fight an armed man, in the dark, and I am already weakened.

Their struggle had turned into a wrestling match, and the man who was now opposite to him was testing the wrist which held his. Slowly, slowly, he drove the dagger point forward towards Leonardo's ribs, there, where the heart beat, and was on the point of success when Leonardo, his strength still returning, caught him behind the knee with his foot, using a wrestling trick which the acrobatic Marco had taught him. This had the effect of causing the dagger to fall away as his attacker lost his balance, but before Leonardo could disengage himself, his opponent caught him round the waist so that they fell to the ground together.

At some point during the last few hectic moments they were both aware of Marina shouting, and of her shouts growing more distant. She was running for succour, having doubtless decided that to try to help him might hinder him. God grant that she found it in time!

His attacker swore, and came at him again, hissing in his direction, "Prepare yourself for death. The bitch cannot save you. You shall be a dead man when she returns."

He made no answer. He needed all his breath, all his wits, to save himself, to try to snatch the dagger away and use it on the man who would have used it on him. Once, the dagger caught him on the arm, tearing a great rip on his sleeve, as well as a shallow wound on the arm itself. The struggle grew more savage. For a moment he was on top, and then his attacker was above him, trying to manoeuvre in order to give him the *coup de grâce*.

He lifted his hand with the dagger in it, for Leonardo to catch his wrist again, and begin to twist it. His enemy's riposte was to try another wrestling trick, which had Leonardo letting go of the wrist, but succeeding in pulling the other man away so that he was unable to use the dagger as he wished. As was common in such struggles, both men were becoming exhausted—something which those who had not engaged in a fight to the death never realised until they were in one. Luck, more than strength or skill, might decide who survived. But luck is usually on the side of the better armed—and that was not Leonardo.

His wound had begun to bleed where the dagger had nicked it, making his left hand sticky—which made grasping anything difficult. His opponent gave one last thrust, pushing Leonardo on to his back in such a position as made it difficult for him to move—and prepared to finish him off...

When the murderer's attention was diverted from Marina as Leonardo began to struggle with him in earnest, once he was no longer held prisoner, she realised that there was little that she could do to assist the man she loved. To try to help Leonardo might make matters worse, given her inexperience. Instead, she picked up her skirts and began to run towards the pages' lodgings, shouting at the top of her voice—it was that which the struggling men had heard.

No one answered her. Light there might be, but the pages had not returned from their revels in the city to which they had repaired as soon as their duties at the banquet were over. Gasping and sobbing, almost falling, looking back once to see the two men still struggling, Marina made instead for the palace along the pathway which she had so recently taken, beyond the pool where she and Leonardo had been reconciled.

To see a man running towards her. It was Marco whom she had thought at Milan! He had a long sword in his hand and was dressed in half-armour. "God aid me," she gasped. "Leonardo, unarmed, is fighting for his life. We were ambushed in the park."

"Fools," snarled Marco. "Fools not to have you both guarded until after the wedding." He broke into a run with Marina staggering along behind him, out of breath, fearful, but determined to stay with Leonardo to the end.

Which was, she saw, as she stumbled into the clearing, almost imminent. Hampered by his lack of a weapon and the earlier damage to his throat which made breathing painful, Leonardo was losing the unequal battle. Marco said afterwards that it was a miracle that he had survived for so long—a tribute to his basic strength. The pair of them were on the ground, rolling over and over, until the murderer, with Leonardo pinned beneath him, raised his dagger to strike the fatal blow, precisely at the moment when Marco came upon them…

Without the slightest hesitation, or word of warning, Marco thrust his long sword into the back of Leonardo's would-be murderer, who tried to raise himself, then fell forward across Leonardo. Leonardo, expecting death at any moment, did not at first understand exactly what had happened, and could scarce credit that, at the last gasp of all, he had been saved.

He looked up, to see Marco throw his sword from him, after looking around to see whether any others waited to attack them. But all was silent, so he knelt by Leonardo who was trying to rise. Still wordless, Marco rolled the dead man over, to show his white face to the moon. It was Braccio degli Uberti, whom all men thought had left Montefiore after Gentile's failed coup to find new employment.

No, he had not forgotten the vow he had made to himself to teach Leonardo a lasting lesson. He had hidden himself away, waited for a suitable opportunity, had scaled the wall of the park, and prayed for his victim to appear. It was afterwards discovered that this was the third night on which he had looked for revenge on the man who had made fools of them all, and had almost found it.

Marina also knelt by Leonardo who was now sitting up, feeling his damaged throat. She threw her arms around him. "The Lord God be praised that Marco was here to save you. Ah, God, Leo, I thought that I had lost you, even as I thought all danger past," she cried. "Tell me that you are not hurt!"

Leonardo returned her embrace, then looked over her head at his faithful friend, and said hoarsely, "My thanks to you, Marco, for saving me when I thought all was lost. No, I am not seriously hurt, my love. Only a small scratch and some bad bruises. Speaking will be painful for a time. My pride is the most damaged, that I should so nearly fall a victim to the oldest stratagem of all!''

''A small scratch!'' exclaimed Marina, examining the blood on his hand, and trying not to look at the dead Braccio.

Marco shook his head, and said soberly, as he and Marina helped Leonardo to rise, ''Thank your lady, Leo, for running for salvation instead of fainting and wringing her hands. She behaved as Angela would have done, not some pampered princess. But what possessed you both to walk in the open, unguarded, when such creatures as this foul the earth?'' He stirred Braccio's body with his foot. ''Fortunate it was that I came early back from my mission, to ask for you and learn that you were in the park with your lady! I came a-running on the instant, without waiting for help, to find your lady doing the same thing!''

Leonardo's smile was wry. ''Why, I think that we thought that we were Gianni and Angela, and that my father's park was safer than the forests between Verdato and Montefiore! But you have the right of it.''

He looked at Marina's white face. She was clinging to him as though she never wished to let him go, lest danger strike again. All the doubts as to their future happiness had disappeared from both their minds—peril shared had revealed to them the strength of their love. Leonardo bent his head to kiss her warm cheek which was pressed against his breast. ''And thank you, lady, for keeping a steady head. Now you may be Angela again for a short time and help me back to the palace. I thought that you might have forgotten what you had learned on our travels, but I see that I was wrong.''

Marco listened to them approvingly, and nodded when Marina replied, still shuddering a little, ''I shall never forget Angela, but I will also remember that first of all, I am Marina, now the lady of Novera, who is to be the lady of Montefiore.''

''Who has helped to save Montefiore's future lord. Something, Leo, which you must never forget,'' Marco added.

Nor did he. A week later they were married amid all the pomp and circumstance which Montefiore could provide, and when they had been publicly bedded after being lighted to their room with music and with torches, Leonardo took Marina to the circle of satyrs in the park, which Marco had arranged to be guarded, so that none might try Braccio's trick again.

There, on a carpet of silk, brought from Constantinople's fall, Leonardo and Marina heard the nightingale sing, and she learned at last that when one loves truly it matters not whether a man be lord or peasant.

And the nightingale sang for them for the rest of their lives together, and for their children also when their time came.

* * * * *

Queens of Romance

WIN

a romantic break for two
worth over £500!

To celebrate the special Mills & Boon® centenary
Queens of Romance collection, we are offering
you the chance to win a very special break for two
to Paris – worth over £500!

To enter, visit
www.millsandboon.co.uk
and answer this simple question:

What are the names of the two founders
of Mills & Boon?

Note: The answer to the above question can be found on
www.millsandboon.co.uk

Entries must be received by 31st January 2009

Good luck!

The Regency
LORDS & LADIES
COLLECTION

More Glittering Regency Love Affairs

Volume 17 – 4th January 2008
One Night with a Rake by Louise Allen
The Dutiful Rake by Elizabeth Rolls

Volume 18 – 1st February 2008
A Matter of Honour by Anne Herries
The Chivalrous Rake by Elizabeth Rolls

Volume 19 – 7th March 2008
Tavern Wench by Anne Ashley
The Incomparable Countess by Mary Nichols

Volume 20 – 4th April 2008
Prudence by Elizabeth Bailey
Lady Lavinia's Match by Mary Nichols

Volume 21 – 2nd May 2008
The Rebellious Bride by Francesca Shaw
The Duke's Mistress by Ann Elizabeth Cree

Volume 22 – 6th June 2008
Carnival of Love by Helen Dickson
The Viscount's Bride by Ann Elizabeth Cree

Volume 23 – 4th July 2008
One Night of Scandal & *The Rake's Mistress*
by Nicola Cornick

M&B